NEW YORK REVIEW BOOKS
CLASSICS

THE DEAD GIRLS' CLASS TRIP

ANNA SEGHERS (née Netty Reiling; 1900–1983) was born in Mainz, Germany, into an upper-middle-class Jewish family. She was a sickly and introverted child by her own account, but became an intellectually curious student, eventually earning a doctorate in art history at the University of Heidelberg in 1924; her first story, written under the name Antje Seghers, was published in the same year. In 1925 she married a Hungarian immigrant economist and began her writing career in earnest. By 1929 Seghers had joined the Communist Party, given birth to her first child, and received the Kleist Prize for her first novel, *The Revolt of the Fishermen*. Having settled in France in 1933, she was forced to flee again after the 1940 Nazi invasion. With the aid of Varian Fry, Seghers, her husband, and their two children sailed from Marseille to Mexico on a ship that included among its passengers Victor Serge, André Breton, and Claude Lévi-Strauss. After the war she moved to East Berlin, where she became an emblematic figure of East German letters, actively championing the work of younger writers from her position as president of the Writers' Association and publishing at a steady pace. Among Seghers's internationally regarded works are *The Seventh Cross* (1942) and *Transit* (1944), both available as NYRB Classics.

MARGOT BETTAUER DEMBO (1928–2019) was the translator of works by Judith Hermann, Robert Gernhardt, Joachim Fest, Ödön von Horváth, and Feridun Zaimoglu, among others. She was awarded the Goethe-Institut/Berlin Translator's

Prize in 1994 and the Helen and Kurt Wolff Translator's Prize in 2003. Dembo also worked as a translator for two feature documentary films: *The Restless Conscience*, which was nominated for an Academy Award, and *The Burning Wall*. For NYRB Classics she translated *Transit* and *The Seventh Cross* by Anna Seghers and *Grand Hotel* by Vicki Baum.

INGO SCHULZE was born in Dresden, Germany, in 1962, and studied classics at the University of Jena. In 1998 he won the Berlin Literature Prize for his novel *Simple Stories*; that same year, *The New Yorker* listed him among the six best young European novelists. His most recent novels include *Adam and Evelyn*, *Oranges and Angels*, *Peter Holtz*, and *The Righteous Murderers*.

THE DEAD GIRLS' CLASS TRIP

Selected Stories

ANNA SEGHERS

Translated from the German by
MARGOT BETTAUER DEMBO

Introduction by
INGO SCHULZE

NEW YORK REVIEW BOOKS

New York

THIS IS A NEW YORK REVIEW BOOK
PUBLISHED BY THE NEW YORK REVIEW OF BOOKS
435 Hudson Street, New York, NY 10014
www.nyrb.com

The translation of this work was supported by a grant from the Goethe-Institut.

Originally published in the German language in the following volumes:
Anna Seghers, *Erzählungen*, 1924–1932. Edited by Peter Beicken.
Aufbau Verlag GmbH & Co. KG, Berlin, 2014
Anna Seghers, *Erzählungen*, 1933–1947. Edited by Silvia Schlenstedt.
Aufbau Verlag GmbH & Co. KG, Berlin, 2011
Anna Seghers, *Erzählungen*, 1958–1966. Edited by Ute Brandes.
Aufbau Verlag GmbH & Co. KG, Berlin, 2007
First published as a New York Review Books Classic in 2021.

Library of Congress Cataloging-in-Publication Data
Names: Seghers, Anna, 1900–1983, author. | Dembo, Margot Bettauer,
 translator, editor.
Title: The dead girls' class trip: selected stories / by Anna Seghers; translated
 from the German and edited by Margot Bettauer Dembo.
Description: New York: New York Review Books, [2021] | Series: New York
 Review Books Classics
Identifiers: LCCN 2020043349 (print) | LCCN 2020043350 (ebook) |
 ISBN 9781681375359 (paperback) | ISBN 9781681375366 (ebook)
Subjects: LCGFT: Short stories.
Classification: LCC PT2635.A27 A2 2021 (print) | LCC PT2635.A27 (ebook) |
 DDC 833/.912—dc23
LC record available at https://lccn.loc.gov/2020043349
LC ebook record available at https://lccn.loc.gov/2020043350

ISBN 978-1-68137-535-9
Available as an electronic book; ISBN 978-1-68137-536-6

Printed in the United States of America on acid-free paper.
10 9 8 7 6 5 4 3 2 1

CONTENTS

INTRODUCTION

BEFORE our German teacher started class, she would ask us to straighten the framed black-and-white photograph of Anna Seghers: "We wouldn't want her to fall down!" Clearly it hadn't bothered anyone that her picture was crooked—maybe we didn't even notice anymore. "Anna means quite a lot to me," the teacher added, words that surprised me so much, I still remember them today. It was unusual, to say the least, to call a writer by her first name. Not even my mother did that. Now a teacher, of all people, was committing this act of disrespect—and toward Anna Seghers, the president (or, by that time, president emeritus) of the Writers' Association of the German Democratic Republic. How could anyone have such an intimate relationship with such a famous woman?

Even though it was required reading, I had enjoyed her novel *Das siebte Kreuz* (*The Seventh Cross*). At the same time, it didn't feel very relevant to me, being set in a long-ago time whose horrors and torments were past and would never return—that seemed quite clear. One lasting thing the book gave me was the expression "emergency reserves" for all the things a person considers necessary to maintain their humanity. Later, shortly before finishing school, I read her story "Das wirkliche Blau" (*The Real Blue*)—I don't remember how I came across it—with an enthusiasm that almost embarrassed me. And at the university, we discussed *Transit* in a seminar. From then on, Seghers was part of my canon.

I don't know whether Seghers's photograph is still hanging in my former school. It's possible, but it's equally possible that it has been removed, that she really has "fallen down"—after all, for a long time they covered up the mural featuring Karl Marx's eleventh thesis on Feuerbach: "Philosophers have only interpreted the world in various ways; the point however is to change it."

Seghers is one of those rare twentieth-century German writers who had a need and a use for the short-story form throughout the entire span of her career. The genre enabled her to react relatively quickly to shifting situations. The stories in this collection span a period of just over thirty years—covering the Weimar Republic after the onset of inflation, the Great Depression, the Nazis' seizure of power, Seghers's escape to France, the Spanish Civil War, World War II, and her emigration to Mexico, and extending on into the postwar period, the Cold War, the emergence of two German states, and the Twentieth Congress of the Communist Party of the Soviet Union in 1956, which exposed the crimes of Stalinism. There is no other writer working in the German language over that long span of time whose stories and novellas have such stylistic diversity and such a wide range of approaches and aims. Seghers wanted to describe the world in order to change it. In this sense, each specific time finds its embodiment in one of her stories.

On November 19, 1900, Anna Seghers was born as Netty Reiling to a Jewish family in Mainz. She remained an only child. Her father ran a successful art and antique gallery with his brother, and also worked as the custodian of the Mainz Cathedral treasure. At the age of twenty, she began studying art history, sinology, and history at Heidelberg, earning her degree with a paper on "Jews and Judaism in Rembrandt's Work." In it, she took a stance against the "Rembrandt German" Julius Langbehn, whose book *Rembrandt as Educator*, from 1890, co-opted the painter in the name of nationalist and anti-Semitic attitudes. For Netty Reiling, Rembrandt painted Jewish faces "the way he painted a dark courtyard or a barren, nondescript landscape whose wealth of expression no one was able to see before him, and which we recognize only when we behold it in the painting."

That same year, her story "The Dead on the Island of Djal" was published in *Frankfurter Zeitung* under the pseudonym Antje Seghers. She had taken the name from Hercules Seghers, a contemporary of Rembrandt. As Christa Wolf said, "She knew the fate of that gifted man who perished before reaching fifty, misunderstood in his time, impoverished, outcast." A year later she married László Radványi, a Hungarian exile the same age as she who had come to Germany after the collapse of the Hungarian Soviet Republic. In 1926 their son, Pierre, was born, followed in 1928 by their daughter, Ruth.

This collection opens with the story "Jans Is Going to Die," from 1925, which Pierre Radványi found among notes dating back before Seghers's escape from Germany and published in 2000 with the collaboration of Christiane Zehl Romero, the author of the definitive Seghers biography. We do not know why the twenty-five-year-old Seghers made no attempt to publish her story at the time. She had no cause to fault its formal and dramatic force, precise descriptions, and vivid characters. "No one knows whether Jans fell down that day because he was dizzy or whether he got dizzy only after he had fallen." The story begins with dizziness and ends with death. The question is how does it happen, what does this death mean? Although the story unfolds with the progression of Jans's illness, what moves us most is not the character of the boy—except in the finale—but rather his mother and father. All that still keeps the two of them together is their love of Jans, which each one experiences in his or her own way. The certainty of his death, a threat that grows more and more terrible the more Jans seems to recover, calls everything into question. At the same time, it is their shared suffering that reunites them. The reader is brought close to Jans only at the end, when he undergoes the test of his courage. As in all good stories, the final sentence begs a rereading of the entire story, shedding as it does new light on what has been told. The father, who returns repeatedly to Jans's grave years later, keeping his suffering alive, is able to turn his pain into happiness: "From the center of his squeezed-dry, old gray heart there would arise, red and glowing, a burning joy, a mighty sense of pride, a wild feeling of triumph at having found his old despair again."

With this, her first substantial work, Seghers had already departed from the world of her origins. She had not yet arrived in a new one, however. Though Jans's father is a workman, his working-class identity remains little more than a label. What is missing here becomes clear when reading "The Zieglers," about Marie Ziegler, who supports her parents, her sister Anna, and her two unnamed brothers by working as a seamstress. This story draws its vitality from its historical and socioeconomic precision; here there is no blank space around the characters. The economic calamity of the 1920s, the "wolf's law" of capitalism, suffocates the lives of Marie and her family. Not only are they forced to give up the father's workshop in the courtyard, they have to rent out a room in their apartment. The eldest son vents his frustration, and not just at the dinner table. The father tries to uphold the facade of his former status while making his rounds to ask for work; Anna acquires an admirer from a family once on equal footing, now far better off than they ("The crease on his crossed trouser leg made a firm line through the empty, darkened room"); the despairing mother suffers a miscarriage; the shy youngest son is promised things that never come—all the characters are limned in unadorned language with a few confident strokes. Seghers illuminates the emotional and mental consequences that ensue when people fall down the social ladder and see their life snatched away from them, even as they resist with all their strength. Shame, self-doubt, and illness rob them of their speech.

Meanwhile Marie withdraws further and further into her shell. She keeps encountering the "girl with the red cap," who seems almost a critical self-portrait of the author:

"Well now, Marie." She walked along for a few steps beside her and waited. But that wasn't enough time for the words that were nailed inside her and buried. The girl would have had to have time enough to crisscross the entire town a hundred times with Marie. But she had to hurry on....Now the distance between them was like a crowbar that slowly moved the one away from the other.

The greatest act of rebellion Marie manages—the cry that ends the story, uttered with all her remaining strength—proves futile.

When Seghers published this story in the 1931 collection *Auf dem Weg zur amerikanischen Botschaft* (On the Way to the American Embassy)—her second book publication, coming three years after the novel *Der Aufstand der Fischer von St. Barbara* (The Revolt of the Fishermen of Santa Barbara)—she prefaced the four stories with a "self-indictment" that has something grotesque about it, not only in retrospect. The author criticizes the title story, while describing "The Zieglers" as one of the two more successful works. But she has her doubts even about that: "When you write, you must write so that the opportunity can be sensed behind the despair, and the escape behind the downfall." Her self-indictment concludes with the hope that her next works will succeed in this aim.

In 1928, Seghers had joined the Communist Party of Germany (KPD) and the Association of Proletarian-Revolutionary Writers. This may strike us today as a voluntary submission to aesthetic and philosophical constraints, and ones quite contrary to the spirit of emancipating the "wretched of this earth," but for her the political demands seemed justified. In light of the past decade's hardships, she did not want to persist in a noncommittal stance; rather than merely depict things as they are, she wanted to show the way to a more just world.

The Nazis' seizure of power at the beginning of 1933 upended the life of the Seghers/Radványi family. Seghers fled via Switzerland to France, where she met up with her family. They lived in Bellevue, near Paris, until Hitler's Wehrmacht invaded in 1940. As though it were not enough to cope with everyday life in a foreign country, raising two children while constantly plagued by financial worries and her vulnerable immigration status, Seghers plunged into a flurry of activity, both as a writer and as an editor and organizer. Together with Wieland Herzfelde and Oskar Maria Graf she founded the monthly magazine *Neue Deutsche Blätter* and spoke at major writers' conferences in Paris and Madrid. In exile she published the novels

Der Kopflohn (A Price on His Head, 1933), *Der Weg durch den Februar* (The Way Through February, 1935), *Die Rettung* (The Rescue, 1937), *Das siebte Kreuz* (*The Seventh Cross*, finished in the fall of 1939 and first published in 1942), and *Transit* (published in Mexico in 1944). Most of the stories in this collection, from "The Lord's Prayer" onward—except for the last two, "The Ship of the Argonauts" and "The Guide"—were written in exile, either in France after 1933 or in Mexico, before Seghers's departure in January 1947.

In exile, Seghers was reunited with former political opponents from within the anti-fascist movement. The Nazis' seizure of power had demonstrated, yet again, the catastrophic consequences of the split in the workers' movement, chiefly between the Social Democrats (SPD) and the KPD, in which the KPD party line had played a part. Now, rather than struggling to give the KPD the upper hand within the left, the crucial objective was to battle Hitler.

In the stories "The Lord's Prayer" and "The Square," heroic or silent resistance plays out against the background of the new rulers' brutality. The prisoners who are supposed to recite the Lord's Prayer sing "The Internationale" instead. Seghers seeks to commemorate those whose rebellion could be no more than a gesture, a self-assertion at the price of self-sacrifice. The title of "The Square" refers to the spot on the wall of a redecorated apartment where a picture of the communist Ernst Thälmann once hung—the only remaining trace of the murdered father of the family. "Meeting Again" and "Shelter"—set during the Spanish Civil War and at the start of the German occupation of France, respectively—are likewise sketches from within the resistance, offering assurance of a community of struggle or tidings of a quiet act of heroism. The French mother who "adopts" the son of a detained German émigré, thus saving him from being returned to Nazi Germany, symbolically preserves the possibility of a different, future Germany, while restoring dignity to the victims and meaning to their lives.

"A Man Becomes a Nazi," written in 1942 and 1943 in Mexico, explores the ultimate question: How does a person become a torturer and murderer? Within a tightly controlled narrative frame, the story

ventures out into unstable terrain. Fritz Mueller's life unrolls in front
of a Red Army tribunal: "He was charged with shootings, hangings,
and a series of acts of cruelty committed against women and children..." This German, the fourth son of a soldier and unemployed
metalworker, is born into a continuum of war and hardship. It is
impossible to say what plays the greatest role in making him a Nazi—
his circumstances, his education, his predispositions? Many of Seghers's
early stories, especially "The Zieglers," are attempts to explain how a
person might lose their humanity. But there is no law of necessity to
determine how or why—not even in literature; perhaps this is in fact
a cause for hope.

In 1943, Seghers suffered severe head injuries in a hit-and-run car
accident in Mexico City. After spending several days in a coma and
suffering a partial loss of memory, she recovered fairly quickly. The
publication of *The Seventh Cross* in the States and the film version
with Spencer Tracy released a year later made her world-famous. The
worst of her financial worries were over. At the same time, however,
she learned that her mother and other family members had been
deported from their homes to a ghetto near Lublin, Poland. This
news no doubt inspired her to begin exploring her own childhood
and youth, asking yet again what makes people turn out the way they
do. The question gains a particular urgency in "The Dead Girls' Class
Trip" because Seghers poses it to the world she herself came from.
The narrator, an émigré living in Mexico, is vacationing in the mountains. On a hike she stumbles across a decaying rancho where she sees
a swing—and suddenly seems to hear her name being called: "'Netty!'
Not since my school days had anyone called me by that name." What
follows is the dreamlike vision of a long-ago class trip with her two
best friends, Leni and Marianne. Netty seeks the affection of the two
girls, who are virtual embodiments of the antagonisms to come. Leni,
independent even as a girl, will remain strong, refusing to betray her
husband despite beatings by the Gestapo, while Marianne, a passive
mirror image of her husband, a high-ranking Nazi official, and proud
of his position, will end up denouncing her former friend: "Leni and
her husband had been justly arrested because they had transgressed

against Hitler." Leni dies in a concentration camp; her daughter is put in a Nazi reform school; Marianne dies in the rubble of her parents' home. The constant shifts between the present and a past that seems equally real and immediate—at which the narrator herself keeps expressing astonishment—produce a back and forth between on the one hand an extreme feeling of closeness to the girls and on the other hand horror and detachment or admiration of the adults they will later become. And the question as to why one could become a fellow traveler and perpetrator, while the other helped the oppressed and fought against injustice, becomes increasingly pressing.

It emerges that, by writing the story, Seghers is carrying out an assignment given by the teacher shortly before the group's return home:

> No one ever reminded us of this trip we took together while there was still time. . . . No one ever mentioned that our group of girls, leaning now against one another while sailing upstream in the slanting afternoon light, first and foremost belonged to and were part of this homeland.

The interweaving of the different time frames keeps stirring the hope that things could have happened differently, that nothing had to turn out the way it did. The pain at the root of the story becomes especially tangible at the end: even in the narrator's imagination, it is impossible for her to return to her mother's arms. In no other work does Seghers draw such clear connections to her own life. And in its subject matter and structure, the story displays a new openness and freedom, as though pain had demolished all the restrictions imposed on Seghers by herself and others. This kind of storytelling originates in rebellion against death and paralysis, from which it wrests the possibility of a different present and a new beginning.

Between the end of the war and Seghers's return to Germany, she wrote "The End" and "The Innocent Ones." "The Innocent Ones" reads like a fable, as the culpability for the crimes of Fascism is passed on up the ladder until even Hitler claims to be innocent—replicating how the war criminals at Nuremberg denied all responsibility. "The

End" is a story haunted once again by the question of evil, of why some people commit atrocities. This time, however, it is told chiefly from the perspective of a former concentration camp guard. He has just returned home when he is forced to flee again, having been recognized by a former camp inmate. In both stories, the protagonists pass judgment on themselves, albeit in very different ways. The guard Zillich continually exposes himself through his behavior, his desires, yearnings, and memories. He has trouble coping with the fact that he can no longer give orders and shoot people as he pleases.

"Mail to the Promised Land," which Seghers wrote at roughly the same time, is the story of the only Jewish family that was able to flee in the "final decade of the previous century, when almost the entire Jewish population of the little Polish town of L. was killed by Cossacks in a pogrom." Here the tone Seghers strikes suggests that the events are narrating themselves. A nearly forgotten relative invites the family to Paris, where they are able to live in equality and safety despite their background. The son, now a famous eye doctor, writes regularly to his father, who has emigrated to Palestine; finally, terminally ill, the son prepares a packet of letters to be mailed later one by one. In this way, his father goes on receiving letters in the Promised Land even after the Wehrmacht has marched into Paris. Seghers, who was not perceived as a Jew either publicly or privately, is telling an almost allegorical tale of European Jewry in the first half of the twentieth century, soberly, without exaggeration but with unparalleled urgency. The writer's words, his letters, are what keep up hope and courage even after his death.

"The Best Tales of Woynok, the Thief" is one of a number of stories in which Seghers uses the power of fairy tales and myth to illuminate the present, even as she explicitly insists that fairy tales are fairy tales and refuses to draw analogies. She begins "Woynok" with a much-cited epigraph whose subversiveness is difficult to appreciate today: "And don't you, for instance, have dreams, wild ones and gentle ones, when you're sleeping between two difficult days? And do you perhaps know why, sometimes, an old fairy tale, a little song, or even just the rhythm of a song can enter our hearts effortlessly, while we have been pounding our fists bloody on them?" Today's readers, at any rate, know that literature works differently than fists. But apparently Seghers needs to say it outright in order to open the door to a different kind of prose, in order to write as though liberated from all precepts imposed by herself and others. "Woynok" is a self-assured piece of impudence. The title evokes a series of adventures: Doesn't it lead you to expect a good robber stealing from the rich to give to the poor? But what we hear of his deeds is little more than background noise, the burning and pillaging of monasteries and villages. And Gruschek's band of thieves is not much different. At the same time, Gruschek himself presents a contrasting mindset: "In the course of his long life he had learned to weigh a man's words by the sheer weight of their sincerity. How else could he have kept his band of forty thieves together without any treachery or discord ever damaging its reputation?" These words, appearing in the journal *Das Wort* in Moscow in 1938, must have sent a strong message against the treachery and discord of Stalin's rule at a time when fear of political purges was running deep.

Even after several readings, the story continually reveals new depths. As soon as sympathy stirs for the independent Woynok or the collectively minded Gruschek, it dissolves again in the very next paragraph. Just as one thief has no scruples about immolating the whole band, the other does not hesitate to sacrifice the weaker members and replace them with stronger members. In the end, Woynok falls into a trap and is clubbed to death by peasants. But if you think that's the end of him, you're mistaken. These characters have a life of their own. And depending on how you choose to look at it, they have everything or nothing to do with reality.

By contrast, "Tales of Artemis" presents an alternative: the epiphanies of everyday life. No one in the story seems able to say what this ineffable happiness consists of and whether it is even bearable. Does it come from the goddess Artemis's existence, from one's closeness to her? The story is a comforting one, showing how belief in the extraordinary can become what *The Seventh Cross* calls the "emergency reserves."

"The Three Trees" is a literary gem, bringing together three legends under one title. Myth enables us to measure our own experience against the experience of humanity, as Seghers's colleague Franz Fühmann put it. "He was not afraid to lead his people into a battle that he knew was a lost cause. He was not afraid to die with them in that battle. But he did not die. His people were killed and along with his people, the sublime voice from which he was accustomed to receive instructions. That was when he began to be afraid," Seghers writes in the second legend, "The Tree of Isaiah." Because he has lost his people, he has also lost the voice that led him on his path. The tale is indirectly about the tribulations of exile, as is the third legend, in which Odysseus returns home and the gods turn away. Almost prophetically, Seghers anticipates the mistrust the émigrés would face on their return—and how difficult it is to rebuild trust even after proving one's honesty.

"The Ship of the Argonauts," Seghers's retelling of the great saga about Jason and his quest to find the Golden Fleece, was written in Berlin in 1947, the year when she received the Georg Büchner Prize, the most important literary award for German-language writers. In Seghers's story, Jason is a man everyone seems to know, someone who attracts people and transforms them. He captures the fleece, fleeing along with Medea, surviving the wreck of the *Argo*, and reaching his homeland—only to meet his death in a sacred grove where the prow of the *Argo* hangs from a tree. In a storm, the remains of the shipwreck fall on Jason as he lies stretched out under the tree, fulfilling the prophecy of his demise in the most improbable way imaginable. For a writer who had just returned to her homeland, the story is not exactly optimistic. But Jason also demonstrates an unusual, almost existentialist type of self-affirmation. Precisely because he has accepted the prophecy of his defeat from the outset, he lives a liberated life. To the extent possible for someone who is not a god, he has emancipated himself from external circumstance.

About two-thirds of Seghers's substantial short-story oeuvre was written after her return from Mexico. She wrote "The Guide" in 1957 in East Berlin, where she had been for ten years, soon after the Twentieth Congress of the Communist Party of the Soviet Union and the show trial of Walter Janka, a comrade from Mexican exile who had become the head of her publishing house, Aufbau Verlag. Seghers had met several times with Party Secretary Walter Ulbricht to plead Janka's case; in public, however, she was silent. It was a time of lost illusions and lost hopes. She cast about for ways in which individuals could remain true to themselves and their convictions—especially when betrayed by their own side. In her story "Der gerechte Richter" (The Just Judge), written in the same period as "The Guide," a young investigating judge in an unspecified eastern bloc country refuses to find a defendant guilty. For this, he himself is arrested and imprisoned in a labor camp. This story did not appear until the spring of 1990, thirty-three years after it was written, seven years after Seghers's death, and shortly before the end of the GDR. Her fears may have been partly to blame. During the trials against Jewish communists who had spent the war in Western exile—especially the 1952 trial of Rudolf Slánský in Prague—the defendants under interrogation had been asked about her. Paul Merker, a high-ranking KPD functionary who also went into exile in Mexico, had been arrested. Seghers's husband was questioned as a witness numerous times and testified against Merker. But the reason it went unpublished cannot have been fear alone, or she would not have written the story in the first place. Probably most of the blame was due to Cold War–era Communist Party discipline. She didn't want to play into the hands of the "enemy" whom she located chiefly in Bonn, as embodied in Hans Globke, a former architect of the Holocaust who was now the right-hand man of the West German chancellor Konrad Adenauer. Paradoxically, when reading her story "The Just Judge," you realize that this disastrous party loyalty is precisely what distorted her own mission past recognition.

With "The Guide," published in 1965 in the collection *Die Kraft der Schwachen* (The Power of the Weak), Seghers returns to the time of the Abyssinian War (1935–1941), the final major colonial war that the Fascist Kingdom of Italy waged against Abyssinia with extreme brutality, including the use of poison gas. "It had all been in vain," the story begins. "And their final resistance with knives and teeth—

in vain." The voice that is speaking belongs to the vanquished. Hope has been destroyed as well: "If there is not going to be any future, then the past will all have been in vain." But soon the story abandons this voice to follow three Italian geologists looking for "gold and many other metals." A boy as beautiful as an angel, who actually has to fend off the advances of one of the geologists, shows them a bag of gold sand and convinces them to follow him rather than continue on their route as planned. The journey deeper and deeper into the jagged mountain landscape is vividly described. The faces of the apostles have been carved into the rock, among them Saint Paul and Saint Peter. By this point, the three geologists have clearly become an inverse version of the three Magi. Instead of bearing gifts, they are after loot, and the "child" is not their savior. The story draws its effect from the contrast between the boy's amiability and grace and the unexplained matter-of-factness with which he leads the three men to their death and sacrifices himself. Neither he nor the narrator needs to explain his actions. We already know why he behaves this way: in order to redeem himself and his people from the futility with which the story begins, in order to imagine a future again and thus to rescue the past as well. Much in this story points ahead to Seghers's subsequent work, especially to her unsurpassed *Karibische Geschichten* (Caribbean Stories), which are more relevant today than ever before. Ideally this selection will inspire readers not only to explore Seghers's protean oeuvre further and turn it to good use but to increase their awareness of the power of the weak.

—Ingo Schulze
Translated by Isabel Fargo Cole

JANS IS GOING TO DIE

NO ONE knows whether Jans fell down that day because he was dizzy or whether he got dizzy only after he had fallen. He stumbled, fell down, and jumped right back up again. He touched his head, but his finger didn't come away bloody. And so he walked onto the bridge, where he was in the habit of going every afternoon. A couple of boys straddled the railing, and Jans climbed up to join them. But it wasn't nearly as terrific today to be sitting on the bridge railing as it usually was. He continued to sit there only because he couldn't think of any reason why it wasn't so great anymore. But today the bridge and the water and the riverbanks were all coated with a fine dusting of boredom.

A few boys climbed carefully down off the dangerous side of the railing, then along between the timbers under the bridge, and back up again on the other side. In the middle of the day, when the sun shone through the cracks between the planks, you could see a mirror image of the bridge in the brown water under the bridge span, as well as indistinct glints of the young boys who had drowned the previous summer while playing this game still climbing nimbly around between its piers. Despite what had happened, they had not given up their game. Whoever was fortunate enough to climb up again had little dark dots of vanquished fear in his eyes to bring back to his companions, and an adventurous radiance in his sweaty face that was only to be found down there. But today Jans had no desire for radiance; rather, he felt homesick, an agonizing homesickness that was choking him. This was odd, for the house in which he lived was only ten minutes away, looming glum and multistoried above the river at the end of the street. Jans could identify his kitchen window by the geranium pots.

Jans scrambled back down and ambled home. The front door was so heavy and the stairs so steep. A summery, rotten smell came from the courtyard where the garbage pails stood. Jans could taste it on his tongue. He went up the stairs more quickly, and suddenly he was dizzy again and the steps swam before his eyes. The door handle he had to use, yellower than the others on the floor, glimmered so unpleasantly that he couldn't decide whether or not to press down on it. At last he did and found himself standing on his doorsill. He was seven years old, wearing short red pants; his shoes were worn down at the heels, his bare legs with circular bruises and scrapes on the knees.

Everything about him was a golden brown, ripened by the summer, his skin, his shiny round eyes, the hair that fell down from a cowlick in dense, tousled bunches. His mother, who was standing at the stove stirring in a pot, turned around when she saw him, surprised that he should be coming home so early in the evening.

Jans's parents were still young. They had married early and were the same age. But while Martin Jansen with his shaved chin and blue workman's smock still resembled a good-natured, gangly youth, Marie had become a sturdy young wife. What was she thinking back then when she took this Martin who suddenly turned up in that stifling living room so painfully overcrowded with parents and sisters and brothers, offering a little gentleness and cheerfulness? And for whose sake it was worth ironing her white Sunday dress and who sometimes bought her a bunch of violets from the kiosk at the bridgehead? Did she think, back then, that the new room she couldn't wait to move into would consist of more than a ceiling, four walls, and a floor? Didn't she have even an inkling that his little bit of gaiety, boosted by all sorts of anticipatory joy, would soon wear off, and that she'd have the same experience with his few displays of affection as with the sound of his footsteps, which she used to listen for impatiently in earlier days, but which she was now used to hearing come up the stairs a couple of times every day around the same time?

And Marie wasn't stupid; she was quick enough to understand everything instantly. Pretty soon she was having a flirtation with a handsome young fellow one floor down. But before her husband's objections could have any effect, the other man had already started a love affair with another young woman in the neighborhood, and soon the two of them had no qualms at all about being caught in an embrace in the public hallway by Marie as she passed them with her market basket. At first it had cut her to the quick, but eventually it didn't matter to her anymore. She saw him for what he was, good-natured, affectionate, and indifferent, just like her husband; the one was like the other, neither better nor worse. She would have preferred it if Jansen had become furious and grumpy, if he had flipped out so that she could be afraid and disgusted; instead he just sat there peacefully with his long legs, smiling, a little embarrassed most of the time. He didn't feel any changes were necessary, didn't understand Marie's bitterness. He would have gone on calmly whistling his little tune, buying her little bunches of violets. Naturally, the way things stood now, he would have preferred it if Marie, for her part too, were somewhat faded and skinnier. Then he would have left her behind the kitchen window with all her bitterness and gone his own way. But how could he do this with Marie sitting up there, young, fragrant, and healthy?

The last weeks before the child was born were the worst of all. The summer had been hot and the work hard on her heavy body. Jansen was totally unsettled by this strange Marie with the changed voice and bleary face. Marie was almost relieved when he began to go his own way and started drinking, and she at last had a tangible reason for her contempt.

And then the child arrived. It lay there and screamed. Actually, it was just one more body in the cramped room. And if the walls had kept moving ever closer together and finally enclosed her in a coffin, Marie wouldn't have cared. It was all over—her big expectation and her thousands of little wishes. She had something to love, everything had been attained! Not only when she freed her breast for the child but also when, just for herself, she loosened her braids or picked the wilted leaves off the potted geraniums she'd kept only for the first weeks of her marriage and then gotten rid of again, she did it all with the constant vague smile of those who love. When her husband stepped into the room, she would be startled and pull a towel over her breast and the child, or pull the curtain around the cradle.

Had she glanced even once at her husband, she would never have recognized him. His even-tempered, calm face had recently become pale and gaunt, almost haggard, the way it is with people who worry, and in his eyes there was the flickering sheen of a dreamer. He had as little understanding now of Marie's calmness as he'd had previously of her bitterness. This man who could now understand the bitterness, the anger, the expectations of the world, who could, in fact, top them all—for him nothing was over. For him, hopeful expectation in its glittering dress now moved into this bare, cramped room that smelled of soup and laundry. And even when his glance just casually grazed the child, his heart filled with complex, absurd plans, with shining, adventurous wishes. If one of the child's little feet with its clenched toes peeked out from under the blanket, he was overcome by a desire for tenderness that could have competed with a hundred Maries in her most wistful moments. But he kept it all to himself. Only once Marie had left the room would he take his index finger and dab a little dent in the child's soft flesh. Or he would place a toy among his pillows in the evening, which Marie, when she found it the next morning, would gaze at with jealousy and mistrust.

Jans grew. He ate, slept, and played. Sitting between his parents at the table eating his soup, he didn't notice how they sometimes reached across the table for the bread just so they could touch his hair or his bare arm. Later, when he left to go to school in the mornings at the same time his father was going to the factory, he was glad once their ways parted and he could run off while his father stopped to look after him, feeling a twinge at each parting.

In spite of all that, Jansen was untalkative, and Marie was by no means resourceful. How else could she have shown her love for her child other than with a skimped-for calf leather schoolbag and a gold-wrapped crayon or the remarkably eye-catching red of Jans's new pants? And Jans grew stronger day by day and more tanned. But there were other strong, tanned boys among his companions who rode astride the bridge railing with him. He had no sign branded on his forehead; he was in no way like something or someone to whom wild expectations and desperate hopes were attached.

After Jans came home that afternoon he straddled a chair and put his face on its back. A gnat, a shiny little dot, settled on his hand, but he was too lazy to shoo it away. It crept along and when it silently wandered up his sleeve, he was suddenly afraid and cried out, "Mother!"

His mother was just putting plates on the table and about to say something to the boy when she heard Jansen's steps on the stairs, and so she quickly ladled out the soup. Jans listened, too, as his father walked along the hallway, and he became alert and cheerful. Something new had to happen now; at last, this hot, bleak day that for some reason was so completely different from all other days he had so far experienced, would come to an end.

Martin Jansen entered the room with his always slightly self conscious "Good evening" and hung up his cap. They all sat down silently at the table. Jans was about to start eating as hungrily and happily as always, but then, after he had taken two or three spoonfuls, he couldn't stand the smell rising from the soup a moment longer and rested his spoon against the plate. Distractedly he looked across the table and out the window, the corners of his mouth abjectly turned down. At that moment Jansen looked at his boy for the first time that evening. Seeing his face with the half-open, forlorn mouth and the dull unfocused eyes made his heart contract with shock, and an unspeakable fear took hold of his soul.

How often Jans had come home bloodied and covered in scratches or coughing and soaking wet! Yet Jansen hadn't paid any attention to that! He had always been so unshakably confident. It was just as likely for the world to burst asunder as that something would happen to Jans. Why give in to foolish worries?

And now the earth had burst. This was no longer Jans's round face, the spot to which Jansen's future was anchored, the focus of his dreams; this was a strange, unfamiliar face that deflected all his hopes.

How was it possible that Marie hadn't noticed, that she could just stand there at this terrible moment breaking a roll into her soup?

"Go ahead and eat," she said, and Martin ground the bread between his teeth while his heart beat in time saying, "God in heaven, help! God in heaven, help!"

"I can't eat," Jans suddenly said in a surprised, piteous tone of voice. Now his mother took notice too. But her heart certainly didn't stop in shock. She just put her arm around Jans's shoulders and smiling gently, her chin resting on his hair, urged him to finish eating. When the little picture on the bottom of Jans's plate became visible under a thin film of soup, she stacked all three plates together and carried them away while Jans followed her, but Jansen remained sitting at the table, his head in his hands. But since he usually did that, no one paid any attention to him.

All at once Jans began to cry. There seemed to be no reason; he sobbed and buried his face in Marie's skirt. Jansen raised his head and started drumming his fingers on the table. The jerky sobbing made Jans's face twitch, and after each sob a soft whimpering rippled through his body. Marie, casting a contemptuous glance at Jansen sitting there drumming on the tabletop with his fingertips, enfolded the child in her skirt, and rocked back and forth with him until he stopped crying. Jans would have liked to go on crying, it felt so good to cry away all the boredom of this dreary failure of a day, but his head began to hurt, which did not offset the pleasure he got from crying. And now his mother put him down on his bed with her strong, capable arms, and taking off his shoes and socks, shirt and pants, wrapped him in his blanket. It was the best thing he'd experienced in a long time. "He's already asleep!" he heard his mother say.

My mother is stupid, he thought.

When Marie started clattering with the dishes, it seemed to Jans as if someone were scratching a scar with their fingernails. Finally she was done. She came over to his bed again, but Jans shut his eyes tight to keep from being disturbed. Barely a moment after she turned her back, he opened his eyes wide. It wasn't easy; they were stuck shut, and it required some effort to tear them open. It got dark. Jans was amazed. All the things seemed to be swelling, stretching. They could no longer bear to be standing there in their firm, clear outlines; they didn't want to keep on being pots and chairs and shelves and hooks; they extended over their edges and pretended they had living faces and limbs. His mother had thought up a new sound: She was now rustling. He peered over at her. She was just slipping out of her clothes; she was shining white; unsuspecting, she let everything emerge that she kept hidden during the day and that he slept through on ordinary nights. She had deceived her boy; in reality she looked strange and horrible, like some mythical creature. She didn't in the slightest resemble a real human being. She didn't look at all the way a mother should look. On top of that, she now stretched out her arms and began to sway and dance, and the big bed swayed and moved around with her and the chairs and the shoes on the floor and the hat on the wall and Jans's little bed, no matter how much he tried to resist. The stupid room swayed back and forth, back and forth without stopping as if someone had given it a kick. It was unbearable. Then Jans saw his father, only a shadow in the darkness, but a solid shadow, the only shadow in the room that night which had not given itself over to swaying. No, Jans's father was not a dancer, not an adventurer; he was Martin Jansen, a slow, stodgy man, still sitting there in the same spot where misfortune had caught him off guard, his head in his hands, staring straight ahead. He was no different at night from the way he was during the day; he was Jans's father, and Jans became calm, and his fear would almost have left him, if he didn't still have this rotten, stale taste on his tongue.

It came from the garbage cans in the courtyard; suddenly Jans was again standing downstairs in the entrance hall; he had to go upstairs, but the stairway was so immeasurably steep that it was impossible to climb. His tongue cleaved to the roof of his mouth; it was an oppressively hot afternoon, and it was also empty and silent. There was a very strange silence in the stairwell, a silence in which his heart raced with terror. Suddenly there was a shrill whistle, and a moment later a shriveled dwarf, a disgusting little old man, came whizzing down the stairway banister quick as a flash, tumbling over Jans's feet, touching his bare leg, and shooting out into the open.

Jans opened his eyes wide. His arms and legs were rigid with terror. It was nighttime, but even though it was dark in the room, there was still a whirring and swaying, especially by a narrow strip of light that was cast on the wall by the solitary lamp in the courtyard. Jans was thirsty. His father was sitting across from him at the table, but he sat there so big and solemn that it was out of the question for Jans to call out to him just because of a little thirstiness. Was Jansen sitting there because it was good to keep a vigil when there was a sick person in the room, or didn't he know that night had fallen?

A short while ago he had ventured a look over at the boy's bed, but he had immediately put his hands up to his face again, forcing his foolish mind to imagine the unimaginable and his poor heart to keep on beating without hope. But he found it impossible to think of sleeping and eating in this room, of walking along the street and standing at his job in the factory without the expectation, without the joyful anticipation of those seven years. He moved his chair. But no, without hope, it made no sense to go to sleep, no sense to keep watch, so he continued to sit.

What is my father doing? Why is he doing that? Jans wondered. Does he do this every night? And he wondered what his father was doing with his hands, wringing them until the knuckles cracked, and what the strange sounds were that came out of his mouth.

Gradually the strip of light from the courtyard lamp faded, and his father's cap, the stovepipe, the chairs, and some of the other things came back into view, like foam bubbles in milky, white light. Jans realized that a new day was dawning. But he had no desire for another day; his eyelids were sticky, he felt ashamed in the light.

The sparrows in the ivy of the courtyard started to chirp. Jans felt even more ashamed. He glanced over at his father, the only one who had endured the night with him. But just at that moment his father stretched his pale arms out over the table in the early morning light, his poor face slid involuntarily down onto the tabletop between his arms, and he fell asleep. And Jans felt disappointed, thinking that his father had let him down after all in this final hour. Then his bed again began to rock back and forth, but more evenly and gently this time, and he stopped thinking. This was the first time in all his life that Jans had ever been awake the entire night long.

At half past six the alarm clock rattled; Marie habitually placed it on a saucer so it would make more noise, for she slept deeply and soundly. Marie yawned and stretched; she enjoyed waking up in her fresh, rested, sleep-warmed body. But then she stopped abruptly in mid-yawn, jumped up, and ran over to Jans's bed. She bent down and tried to pull him out, for he had burrowed himself into a hollow place in his bed like a suffering little animal. But when she touched his rigid, burning body, from which the head was dangling backward with unseeing eyes like a doll's head, she drew back, peering at him. She pressed his head to her bosom and again peered hard at him. And at that moment her eyes got those same little dots as back then when she had seen her flighty companion from the floor below with his current love in the hallway of the house.

But now she began to beg and plead and caress him, whereupon Jans blinked a little and gave her a dull, distrustful look from beneath his long, crusted eyelashes. Marie's arms dropped, and she looked around the room for help. She saw her husband, his upper body across the table as if the tabletop were a well into which he wanted to plunge. She grabbed him by the shoulders and shook him back and forth, quite wild with contempt. She continued to shake him even after Jansen had awoken with the usual embarrassed smile on his lips. "Jans is sick!" she yelled in his face. "You bastard! You scoundrel! Jans is sick!"

But Jansen merely nodded, and Marie threw herself on Jans's bed. Jansen just stood there, tall and gaunt, with his confused smile. This Martin Jansen had tightly bolted his heart, and he could harbor a great store of fear and torment therein without it all pouring out and troubling others.

Marie spun around. "Take your hat and get out!"

And Jansen obeyed; he took his cap and put it on, and he didn't cling to his child's bedposts. He would go to the factory; he staggered a bit; but it was still the safest way. He stopped on the threshold and turned around once more. "Someone out there is calling you, Marie."

Marie ran out of the room, and Jansen bounded over to the bed, pulled the child to him, and covered him with kisses from head to toe. The door slammed, and he quickly put him back down under the covers.

"No one called me," Marie said angrily. "Get a move on and get out of here!" He had hardly left before Marie started to cry, crying her heart out. Sometimes, when she begged the boy for something with dull, teary eyes, there really was some focus in the boy's bleak gaze, an expression of sorrow and distrust, as if he were suffering from a completely different, much more mysterious illness than the one whose name his mother was racking her brain for. He pulled away from her and tried to bury himself in a corner of his bed, occasionally raising an arm that had grown thin overnight, and pointing up in the air as if there was something much more urgent and strange to see up there than the nearby face of his mother, which was red from crying.

The morning started as usual. The sun burned down on the courtyard, and the neighbor women hung up their laundry. Marie felt like going over to the window and shouting down her misfortune, but then suddenly shook her head. It was a shame that Jans, her beautiful, bright child was sick; and it would be a disgrace to show strangers that her happiness was stained and cracked. Better to bear one's shame alone, and she took Jans's hot little hand in hers.

There was a knock on the door; Marie started. But it was only the doctor—where had Jansen found him?—a short man with a straggly beard and spots on his suit. He'd been running up and down the stairs of the suburb all this hot morning long. Marie watched him with mounting fear although he was doing nothing more than washing his hands and cleaning his glasses. He himself, after all, was just a harried, sweaty man. But when he palpated and listened to Jans, stroking him with his cool fingers, it seemed to Jans as if he were slowly being pulled out of a pool of deep, dark water, and from far away he saw two tiny bright dots—the round lenses of the doctor's glasses in which the sun was reflected. He felt indescribably well and wanted to laugh—the doctor's beard was tickling him—and so he giggled softly and dove back down into the water. When she heard the giggling, Marie turned quite pale. The doctor got up. "We'll have to wait and see," he said. "You should darken the windows and apply compresses. That is all one can do."

In the evening Jansen padded back into the dark room. He sat down at his usual place. The table had not been set, nothing had been cooked; he was dead tired and hungry. He put his head in his hands, and gradually the darkness, which had hidden him so well, became transparent. He recognized Marie crouching by Jans's bed. The alarm clock rattled; a door slammed shut in the hallway; someone ran down the stairs laughing; Marie got up to get some water. Meanwhile Jansen went over to Jans's bed. Marie came back, a pitcher in one hand, a lamp in the other, and with a nasty look she indicated he should go back to his place at the table. But Jansen just shrugged his shoulders disdainfully; he stayed where he was. He tried to get a look at Jans's face. At first his entire body shrank in horror, but he bit his lips and forced himself to look at the face, that little old shrunken face with the open mouth and open eyes that had flickered for seven years, crying and laughing, in anger and pleasure, and sometimes even with cruelty, but always with life and all the possibilities of a living being, and was now a mockery, the little dead face of an old man. The clock rattled, and Jansen, suddenly turned energetic and resourceful, went over, turned it off, and returned to his place at the table. But now the room was so quiet it became unbearable.

"Jans is going to die," Marie said softly to herself.

Jansen recoiled; he had known what she was saying was true yesterday already, had known it from the first moment on, but how could she be so shameless as to say it aloud? They looked at each other, and something like hate quivered in Jansen's face—as when two enemies are restrained in the same prison cell. Jansen clenched his fist. He might have struck out if Jans hadn't just then let out one of his strange breaths, rather like a long, thin whistle. Then it was quiet again.

Toward morning Jans's little stiff body flinched, and Jansen saw a large, glittering, strange, and almost ridiculous-looking foam bubble coming out of the mouth of his child, his onetime son. Jansen ran out of the room. He no longer believed what he had seen; it was a crazy dream; he didn't have to put up with that. He ran out of the house, crisscrossing through the streets, bumping up against things here and there. At a bakery the rolling shutters were just being raised; he dashed inside, bought a loaf of bread, and bit off the heel, right there in the store. By the next corner he had devoured it all. But once his stomach was full and his hunger assuaged, he stood still, and hot shame flooded his face because he had felt hungry and had eaten something on a morning like this.

At the factory he went about his work silently and quickly, but once he was outside on the street again, he swayed and staggered; he walked past the door to his house a couple of times, finally turning to walk in the opposite direction. He couldn't decide to go up into that terrible, dark room and accept such a reality. There was a pub at the corner, the same one he had gone to back then, when Marie had begun to turn mean and hard the first year of their marriage. He sat down and tried to imagine Jans's face the way it was before the illness and how it had still sparkled three days ago, but he couldn't remember it, no matter how hard he tried. He could hardly wait for them to set a glass in front of him; he believed that somehow it might help him achieve his hopes. He wouldn't be missed upstairs. As long as Jans was cramped up, time would stand still, and it would get a push only when he twitched.

Another day dawned, and it seemed to Marie as if Jansen had just now closed the door behind him. She took the pitcher and went for fresh water. Jans stirred under the blanket. Suddenly his bed was again being spun around; he drew up his legs, bit down on a corner of the pillow, and clutched the bedsheets to keep from falling out of the bed. But then the spinning slowed, the bed started to sway back and forth in calm, broad swings and finally stopped and stood still. Jans blinked; the curtains were closed, but little spots of sunlight lay scattered on his hand and on the floor and jumped in golden stars around his bed. And downstairs in the courtyard there was scurrying about and laughter, children—a girl's voice among them—clapping hands to their singsong ditty:

> Me and you,
> the miller's cow,
> the miller's donkey,
> and that's you.

Jans blinked even more; curious, he craned his neck and sat up. At that moment his mother entered the room. She hesitated and then, trembling all over, approached the bed. She asked him in a strange, shaky voice whether he wanted something to drink and put her hand on his hair. Jans nodded in his former, grumpy manner, the way he used to when people were affectionate toward him. Marie brought him a cup of milk—her face getting paler and paler—and Jans drank it all. After that he felt tired; the bed started to quiver once more, but when he heard his father's footsteps on the stairs, he sat up again.

Jansen dragged himself up by the stair railing, his legs heavy and tangled. He wasn't thinking anything, he was just afraid, afraid. Yet no matter how hard his heart pounded, he could no longer remember why. With each step he tried to overcome his growing cowardice, but to no avail.

His hand wobbled around the yellow door handle, and he pressed it down and up ten times until at last he wrenched the door open.

Jans was sitting in his little bed, his face red and impish. Jansen stared at him, the corners of his lips stretched into a confused smile, and then the smile turned into bitter weeping.

Marie quickly occupied herself in a corner with the dishes and didn't turn around until Jansen had stopped crying. But little Jans, his head falling back onto the pillow, placidly gazed at his father's face with curiosity and even a little distaste.

Late that evening Jansen went over to the window. He looked up at the high, hazy sky, then down into the courtyard where a white kitten was just then flitting from one corner to the other. He looked across at the walls of the neighboring houses that casually revealed their interiors to the common courtyard, their dirty, squalid kitchens and living rooms full of crying, laughing, sleeping, eating, and drunken people. And anyone who wanted to from over there could look into Jansen's room and see his damp, white face above the pots of geraniums. But what difference did it make, if day after day the same rotten smell came up from the garbage pails down there—his son was alive; what difference did it make, if over there a child cried in the evening the way only battered, defenseless children cry at dusk—his son was alive; what difference did it make if, across the way, two women were convulsed in mean, shameless laughter—his child was alive. The people over there, glumly chewing their last bites and throwing themselves, exhausted, onto their filthy beds, they didn't know yet that his child was still alive.

It was only three days ago that Jansen fell from his mountain and lay at the bottom with shattered limbs. But the peak was so enticing that even a little hint was enough for him to pick himself up, gather his shattered limbs, and start climbing again without the slightest hesitation.

The next day after work, Jansen took a detour to the city. He was able to persuade the people at a shop that was already being cleaned and tidied for Sunday to let him in. He had the week's pay with him, and he picked out the most complicated and versatile toys he could find. He carefully took the large lumpy package wrapped in tissue paper, and holding it in his extended arms, carried it home. He was excited as he came into the hallway and opened the door. The room was dark, and he was met by a sweetish, musty smell. A thin whimpering came from the bed in the corner, a long drawn-out *i-i-i-i-ih* that resembled a giggle. Jansen groped for the table and put down the package containing the toys.

The summer weather went on for two or three more superfluous, uncounted days, hot and oppressive as it had been when Jans was born. But now no one in the room cursed or scolded anymore. Jansen was a peaceful man. Granted, it wasn't long ago when in a bout of excessive joy or pain a couple of peculiar remarks might have slipped out. But now he tiptoed about peacefully. He'd long ago used up the few odd remarks he was granted. Had it been up to him, he wouldn't even have added the strands of white hair that looked so strange with his youthful face, and were forced on him during those uniform, uneventful summer days. And Marie, well, there she sat on Jans's bed, her eyes emptied by her nightly vigils. And once she did fall asleep and was awakened by Jans's high, sharp whimpering, she would groan like a prisoner sentenced to the punishment of insomnia. Sometimes a neighbor in the hallway or a fellow at work would ask, "Well, Jansen, is your Jans sick?"

"Yes, he's sick," Jansen would reply.

"He'll surely make it," the other would say.

"No," Jansen would say, "I don't think he'll make it."

When Jansen came home in the evening, a disquiet would well up in him after the emptiness of the day, a vague expectation that he might find that final thing on the other side of the door, and that they would at last be granted the chance to surrender to the most terrible, the ultimate, irrevocable pain. But the room was still dark and the sweetish smell was still there, and Jans lay with drawn up legs, open mouth, and round eyes, like an ancient shrunken dwarf, an evil little sorcerer making incomprehensible signs in the air with his wizened fingers and whistling weak, enigmatic, plaintive tones.

And Jansen sat down at the table and ate his supper and undressed and slept his sleep.

Then one night Marie roused him, "Get up, Martin, he's dying!"

Jansen jumped to his feet. At the sound of her cry, his head had suddenly become as bright as back then, when Jans unexpectedly had sat up among his pillows, smiling; and that stain within him that had been lying there, fallow and bleak, began to lash out and sting so badly that he cried out. Jansen grabbed the bed, and Marie did not deny him a place there. A thread of blood trickled out of Jans's mouth, running down his little shirt and blanket, but Jansen, with his flickering eyes, couldn't make out what was happening in the bed. He only burrowed his chin into the bedpost and pressed his knees into the wood as if at that moment the bed were the chief enemy to be tackled and won over. But the wood remained hard and patient, and Jansen was exhausted, and his hand, which had drummed against the bed until it was sore, stretched out and touched Jans's hair and stayed there. And Marie too wanted to have a bit of that hair that still felt warm and alive. Their fingertips touched; they looked at each other, and each stopped short at the odd aspect of the other. Their looks became more fixed and something new gleamed deep in their eyes. It wasn't love but something like love, which even wiser people couldn't have differentiated from love. They pressed closer; he stroked her poor, emaciated, betrayed arms, and his caresses that had begun as a woeful consolation turned into a mad, all-out thing.

The next day the stained sheets were taken off the bed, and Jans got a clean blanket, a clean sheet, and a clean little shirt. But even though he lay there, clean and solemn, he still twitched now and then, and in the evening he even hiccupped, spraying a few drops of blood on the fresh pillow. Then Marie put her head in Jansen's lap as if that were the sole gesture left to her, and his lap her sole eternal and un-failing place of refuge.

Jans had heard the humming, and he retained a soft hum in his ear. Yesterday in the evening, when blood had come out of his throat, he had suddenly felt free and light, and he wished then that it wouldn't ever stop. It had all felt as free and wonderful as being outside on the bridge railing above the rushing water; he gave a little push and soared into the air; he spread his arms and kicked himself off into the air. He flew over the table, but his parents who had always made such a fuss about him weren't at all surprised; his parents who had always followed him with eager, anxious looks didn't even look up at this marvelous moment, and the moment quickly came to an end, and he became heavy again and fell into his bed. He opened his mouth and said, "Thirsty," and his parents separated at once and took turns supporting his head while they poured milk down his throat. Neither of them had turned pale when he said the one word; neither had the strength to arm themselves with new hope. When Jans stirred, they hastily uncurled their entwined fingers and now it even happened sometimes during the day that they would sit there leaning their heads against each other.

So Jans was not going to die a sudden, quick death. He was to die slowly with the fading autumn. The doctor, who had come again, said so too, and he also said that it made no sense to keep him in bed in that dark corner all the time, that they could put him in an easy chair by the window. So Jans, along with all his pillows and his blanket, was packed into the easy chair to get his share of the sunshine that was already falling more moderately on the courtyard pavement.

Jans actually didn't care that much for the easy chair. In the dark corner he was safe; that was where he felt at home, not in the large, bright room of the grown-ups. As for the sunshine—it hurt his eyes, and the games of the children down in the courtyard didn't awaken the slightest envy or admiration in him. He was glad when his mother finally got around to moving him back to his bed at noon, even though he did nothing but lie on his back there and count the patterns in the wallpaper, the stupid faded stripes and garlands.

To be sure, as soon as he heard his father's footsteps on the stairs, his face, grown small and pale and wrinkled, took on color. He was waiting, yes. What was Jans waiting for? His father always went immediately over to him in his easy chair, stroked his hair, chucked him under the chin, things he had only done surreptitiously and shamefacedly before. But now Jans was waiting, and he didn't know for what. How could he have known? And his father turned away and put his head close to Marie's across the table on which she was spreading small white rags with a vague, loving smile, and he rooted around in them with his fingers, gently stirred by a fresh expectation that had put its first tracks there on the cracked table in front of him.

This time Marie didn't feel ashamed and weighed down by her heavy body, and Jansen had no reason to run to the bar on the corner. Seven years had passed; the eighth stood on the threshold, and they behaved exactly like people who had aged seven years. Back then, it had once seemed as if the four walls would enclose them and choke them, and during the seven years they'd had time to expand and to pull together again and once more to expand. And eventually they stopped moving, leaving a space not generous enough for a person to take big leaps into the air but still enough to be able to breathe. Through the winter they both worked patiently and quietly the way you work when there is a small joy in the offing; not some crazy bliss that you can't bear in the end anyway, just a simple joy suited to their space.

And Jans was still there. Before, he had filled the room with his bright sunshine, but now he was a pitiful little spark his mother could carry in one hand. Sometimes she looked up from her sewing and over to him with sad eyes that were now older and graver, and then she would fearfully cross her arms over her body where something of her own was still safely preserved. Once the faded plants had been removed from the sill, Jans liked sitting by the window even less than before. He would sit among his pillows, slumped and silent, with his lower lip protruding. Only once, when he saw some boys flying a kite down in the courtyard, did his pointy white nose quiver and his eyes glitter. But then, when the boys were invited to come up to the room where Jans was sitting in his armchair like a little old man, silent and serious, they crowded against one another in embarrassment and didn't know what to do or say.

Why didn't they let him stay in his bed? What did they gain by taking him over to the window? In his bed he merely had to close his eyes, and he would see the bridge and the river, blue and green, the clouds, the sun, and various other things. But here he constantly had to stare down into the gray, stuffy courtyard, and sometimes people from the other buildings looked over at him in a peculiar way. But he didn't complain. In fact, he said almost nothing at all. When he did say something, it confused, almost shocked his parents, so it was better not to say anything.

Something else happened, too. Namely, one afternoon, a few flakes came floating down, light and cheerful, out of the heavy, murky air, and right after that there were more flakes, heavy and full at first and then toward noon, glittering and drizzling. Jans pressed his face to the windowpane; from that moment on, he had ten thousand companions every day, these little dancers from somewhere, dancing in courtyards and on windowsills to a music that no one could hear. It was the kind of dance that made Jans breathless just from watching, and when he had to turn back into the room, his flickering eyes had trouble adjusting to the table, the lamp, and his parents, those heavy hulks.

Christmas Day came, and Marie let him lie in bed until evening. She put the Christmas tree into a ceramic pot and clipped on the candles. Jans could easily have crept out of bed by himself; several times recently, he had stood up all by himself when his mother wanted to shake out his pillow. But it was better this way.

The previous day, Marie, her head lowered, had asked her husband, "What are we going to give Jans?"

Jansen had remained silent for a long time, then suddenly he said, "I have something!" And he pulled a package out of his drawer. He unknotted the string and was about to unfold the paper, but when the white tissue paper made an unusual festive rustling just as it had back then in the store, he quickly folded the corners over each other and tied it up again. No, there wasn't much money left; there had been the rent and the wood to pay for and the Christmas present for Marie, but there was enough still to buy a little horse or a ball and a gingerbread man for Jans, and so he hurried off.

They were all sitting around the table that evening: Marie with the lean shoulders of a confirmation candidate in a black dress that fitted tightly over her body, Jansen wearing an unusual collar, and Jans among his pillows, quiet and tiny. The small candles on the ragged little tree flickered and twinkled. And they would sit there until the candles on the tree burned out, having been granted this interval, a little island in time. For, after all, they usually sat bent over their work from morning to night, and any happiness that they would otherwise have a go at in quiet secrecy, they could now in this interval smile about to their heart's content; or during this festive time they could cry unhindered about any pain that wasn't appropriate for ponderous, ordinary days. But there they sat, trying in vain to wrest something festive from their tired hearts. And all of them— Martin, daydreaming with drooping lips, and Marie, incessantly smoothing the fringes of her new shawl, and even Jans, who kept fingering his toy with his skinny, sick hands, until finally, tired and forlorn, he just let it lie there—wished that this interval would end and the bad, normal, everyday time would begin again and they would be released from their sad anxiety. But the tree with its candles continued to burn. It was on this earth in order to burn, and it took its time and burned until the tips of its branches were singed and drops of wax fell onto the tablecloth.

The deeper into winter—the snow was followed by gloomy, damp days with fog coming right up to the windowpanes—the more Jans shriveled. The sleeves of last winter's wool jacket hung loose around his wrists. Maybe Jans, who disappeared in his armchair like a little dot, could have filled the whole room with his chatter and scurrying around, if only someone would have clapped their hands and cried out, "Come on, Jans! Up with you!" But no one came through the door to the Jansens' room clapping their hands and shouting, "Get up." On the contrary, anyone who came in always looked at Jans sideways in a furtive, almost false and peculiar way like the people on the other side of the courtyard did, and Jans shrank even more into himself.

One day they took Jans's armchair with him in it, as if he were only some head on the chair, into the room of the next-door neighbor. He stayed there in that strange, overcrowded room for just under a week. And even though the neighbor's wife was cheerful, almost too cheerful, and her husband was a joker and the children wild, and all of them together were a family rich in laughter, arguments, and happenings—as long as Jans was with them, their cheerfulness was one tone quieter. As if, rather than a little boy, he were a mysterious, distinguished guest in whose presence it wasn't appropriate to talk and play normally. And so while he was there, their laughter and shouting stopped. They were all relieved when he was carried back home again.

The child was lying in the crib by the window. It was a girl; her name was Anna, and the room shrilled with her little voice and fluttered with her pieces of laundry. She was lying in the cradle that Jans had occupied eight years earlier; it was freshly painted and its curtains newly starched. The silk ribbons that had held back the curtains then were gone. But Jans couldn't have known that, and now the cradle stood in the sunniest spot by the window, and another spot, between the end of the bed and the door, had been picked for Jans's armchair. But Jans would rather give that up completely. If he couldn't have his old spot, then none at all. By now he was able to stand pretty well on his own two feet and could, if need be, sit upright on an ordinary chair without an armrest, even though his shoulders still strained a bit.

And he watched wide-eyed as his mother opened her dress and freed her breast for the child. Jans was well aware that her usually pale, calm face changed as she did this. Though now she only smiled the way you smile when putting on a piece of jewelry, whereas eight years earlier she had smiled as if she could reinsert her own heart, which for some senseless reason had been outside her body, back into her naked breast. But how could Jans have known this? He felt a pang whenever his mother opened her dress, and a second pang when she put the child to her breast. Then he would press himself against the wall or even go out into the hallway, where in the last few days he was often wont to sit on the topmost stairway landing. But when his father came home, he would follow him with his eyes as he stepped up to the cradle and lifted the curtain. Eight years earlier, Jansen's eyes, fixed on the same spot, had taken on a dark, fierce expression. Now his features turned good-natured and almost amused. Jans, though, stared at his father with sullen watchfulness.

And at mealtimes, too, now that he was again sitting between his parents, bent over his plate, he would steal quick sidelong glances at his father. And Jansen, too, would briefly gaze at his boy in the same strange way, only to quickly go back to poking around in his food whenever Jans turned his head expectantly toward him.

What was the matter with Jansen? Didn't he see his son's brief, mute, sidelong looks? Had he gotten older the way ordinary, simple men get older? A tired, flawed human being who'd had just enough in him for a little burst of light, not evil but weary and indifferent? Oh, no, Jansen wasn't that kind of man. He was no dreamer, not one to catch a burst of light. Oh God, if only there were more men like him. He hadn't forgotten it, his one hope, his one possession. How could he ever stop thinking of him? His little Jans, who had made him tremble and despair, and whom he had finally given up one night, and had long ago permitted to move to the cemetery outside the town—the terrible, final stone on the grave—and whom he loved with all the sacred strength with which you love that which is lost. And what was still with him here in this room, sitting next to him at this table, this he could only stroke with feeble hands, a trace of what he had lost that the next breath of wind would blow away? A thing that reminds you of something precious. And however much they tried to avoid it, it did happen that their glances would meet and then their eyes, which had only been waiting to slip out of their big and their small master, would lock firmly into each other, with the same sorrow and the same reproach.

Of course, with time their eyes had become accustomed to avoiding such awkward collisions. More and more frequently Jans would go out into the hall, wandering from one landing to another. And the street was beginning to beckon to him again with its trash, its noise, its puddles. He could see, with longing and fear, a section of it through the doorway. What use was it to wait and to keep waiting up here and to watch something so attentively when he already knew what it was like and what its outcome would be.

He knew, once and for all, that his father would first go over to the cradle, fold back the blanket, and take out little Anna. And of course, deep down Jansen, too, would rather not feel those eyes fixed on him from the corner, would rather hold the little one close without being watched. This time Marie wasn't jealous; she even nodded encouragement, settling the child into a comfortable position in his arms. With Jans watching, Jansen would have been embarrassed to puff out his cheeks, for instance, and make all sorts of funny sounds with his lips. And he certainly couldn't have closed his eyes and pressed his face to

Anna's little head for so long, feeling the calm, heartwarming tenderness that he longed for even when he was at work, and which he could find only and exclusively in this round, fluffy creature.

No, Jans no longer tried to catch his father's attention. On the contrary, he did everything to avoid it. One day he really did end up outside the house. Suddenly, there he was, the firm ground beneath him and the open air all around him. He now remembered everything that he had long ago forgotten, and the more he remembered it, the more ashamed he felt. He would have liked to hide in shame from this street, from the lantern post he had once clambered up, from the pile of sand heaped in the same old spot, the posters on the wooden fence, the crack in the pavement from which a thin thread of water welled up, spread, and flowed along the edge of the sidewalk. But all these things kept their fixed, clear outlines and were in no way thrown into confusion because of Jans's sudden appearance. And so Jans pulled himself together; he walked a bit farther, even though he was overcome by a miserable feeling of dizziness and desolation in this extravagantly wide, open world. He stumbled to the next corner; there, in the other street he saw a bunch of boys arguing about a ball, and he felt so ashamed that he stopped and stood leaning against the wall, rigid with embarrassment. The ball flew on, and the boys moved their game just to that corner. But they paid as little attention to Jans as if it were only yesterday that he had come down the last time, and they brushed by him, almost knocking him down and without stopping because of his being there. A small, barefoot, red-haired boy with the kind of blue eyes that some redheads have, came out of one of the houses. He was grubby and covered with scratches, a little devil who could crawl through any openings. Last year he'd been Jans's friend. The boy caught sight of Jans, looked him up and down, and his peaked, laughing face took on a note of embarrassment; he turned on his heel and shouted, "Jans with the red pants! With the red pants!"—it felt good to be pulled out of his embarrassment by all this shouting. A couple of the boys turned around, shouted too, made faces, and ran on. Jans stood there a while longer; then he turned around. He had shriveled up. He was really almost nothing more than this piece of red stuff that no one had noticed before when his legs were still firm and brown inside it. But the boys were right; the pants truly looked ridiculous now, these bright, showy things, and Jans stumbled home despondently. The street was slowly beginning to revolve around him and starting that gentle swaying that made Jans uneasy. But by now it was comfortingly familiar.

Yet he did return the next day, and the day after that, too. Already the houses were no longer quite so tall, and he felt less embarrassed. He went of his own accord close to where the boys were playing. Whenever he walked down the stairs and toward the hubbub on the corner, he dreamed the same thing. He dreamed that he grabbed the ball and, with a powerful, never before seen toss, threw it far beyond the goal. But then, when he finally succeeded in pushing his way into the knot of players and got hold of the ball, his hand twitched so much in this wild dream that he threw the ball much too hastily and it landed just a couple of steps in front of his feet; whereupon the other boys, all whistling derisively, pushed him against the wall. And so Jans sat down on the edge of the sidewalk and watched with lowered head. Let them whistle at him and make faces—it was much easier anyway to sit here and twiddle his thumbs and swallow his shame than to torture himself for the ball and then with a tremendous effort try to toss it in the air, all in vain. His mother came by once, saw him sitting off to the side, and her heart contracted and she bent down to hug him. But Jans drew back and looked at her not only with anger in his tiny, mean, old face but with distaste and hate. And Marie was startled; indeed, she was afraid. She also pointed him out one morning to the doctor who just happened to be walking down the same street, sweaty and in a hurry. And while Jans was racking his brain about where he had seen that scraggly beard and the eyes behind the eyeglasses before, the doctor suggested that they should try sending Jans back to school where perhaps he would bestir himself a little and perk up.

So Jans got a schoolbag, the straps of which bothered him, and he walked into the dusty schoolyard that was planted with just a couple of plane trees. The boys who were hanging out there at first greeted him with whispers and nudges. But they soon got used to him and forgot him in his corner where he was gnawing very slowly on his bread so that it would last for the entire break and he'd have something to do. For he didn't like the breaks. Even though he was in a class with much younger boys, he felt best when he was safe on his bench in the classroom. Deeply buried there, he'd smile to himself with dull eyes, and oddly enough his smile became more marked whenever the teacher called on him and he would stand there for a minute without saying a single word. When the bell rang, he was usually the last to slide reluctantly out of his bench and to loiter in the hallways and corners. Then he would sit down again, put his chin on his school desk, his mouth open a little showing the gaps between his teeth that had appeared a couple of days ago.

If anyone seriously believed that Jans would bestir himself and perk up in school, he would be mistaken. There was nothing more to be gotten out of Jans at this point, nothing at all. And when he arrived home, he would immediately, without looking around, rush over to the table, sit down, and, bent over his plate, eat his food in a new, alarmingly hurried and greedy way.

Sundays, when Marie and Jansen made their excursions along the river, taking turns carrying the child dressed in white, sighing a little with the heat but nevertheless with contented expressions, the way you carry a large bouquet of flowers, Jans was either not to be found or he hung back so far right at the outset, that soon they just left him at home. Sometimes it would occur to Marie later in the afternoon that they could visit someone to show off the little one. One day they went to see one of her sisters who lived with her husband on the other side of the river.

It happened that they were in the middle of a celebration. The living room was full of people. There was beer, singing, and cake, and those already sitting at the table squeezed together to make room for Marie and Martin. The child was passed from lap to lap, fondled and pinched; Marie's clear, brown eyes sparkled, and she constantly found reasons to laugh, throwing her head back and squeezing her eyes shut. Jansen, too, ate and drank and spoke with the people to his right and left, and at one point he stood up and went out for a while into the fresh air. He wasn't very good company and no one missed him, and he was already back half an hour later. He had merely walked across the bridge, through the empty Sunday street, feeling more and more uneasy the closer he got to his own house. As he opened the door his glance stopped involuntarily at the table where—the only disorderly point in the neat room—Jans's emptied cup stood with crumbs on the saucer. Oddly enough, on seeing this his heart contracted, yet not with that familiar, well-known pain that hit him like a knife from outside so that he could have pointed to the spot with a finger but rather with an unfamiliar sadness from inside, of which his heart wasn't the target but rather the source, and it came without much fuss, soft and silent, almost like a caress.

He looked around and caught sight of Jans, who was lying asleep on his bed all curled up, his knees drawn to his chin. He approached the bed on tiptoe, bent down, and stretched out his hand to stroke the boy's hair. But he immediately drew it back again, shrugged, turned away, and left the house.

After the door closed behind him, Jans jumped up like a spring, stared at the door, and in the very same second curled up again. He had heard the footsteps on the bottom step; he had heard them coming closer and become more and more real and probable; he had fled to his bed and didn't even have to hold his breath for he couldn't breathe anyway because what he had been waiting for was about to come true much too suddenly. It had come very close to him, and in the next moment it was completely there. But the moment passed; what had come so close moved away again, and the door had closed behind his father. And even though Jans was alone now and no one else was there who could have heard his sobs, he bit the corner of his pillow to keep from crying.

A couple of days later, when Jans came home from school, his parents had gone out into the hallway, and little Anna lay alone by the window in her cradle. Jans stood in the middle of the room, shrugged off his schoolbag, and listened. Then he stepped over to the cradle, pulled up a chair and knelt on it so that he could get a better look inside. He had never before been able to look at his little sister undisturbed. And looking at her now, he felt no heartache. He simply held back the curtain and looked at everything, her round head with the short blond shock of hair, the tiny fingernails. It was as if two little stars emerging from different directions of infinity and brushing against each other for one second in eternity were gazing at each other.

When he heard his parents' voices, he quickly pushed the chair back to the table and sat down. Marie ladled out the soup; for a while nothing was to be heard except the slurping and splattering of their spoons. After the meal, Marie sat on the bed, opened her dress, and Jansen handed her the child. Jans busied himself with his schoolbag, waiting for the moment when his mother had not yet freed her breast and his father was already far enough ahead of him that there was no danger of their colliding.

It was toward the end of summer, a windy day, alternating between sun and rain. Just as Jans was going out the front door, such a strong gust of wind blew into his ever-open mouth that he was jerked back coughing.

He was going to walk up the street, but the wind swiveled him around, and since he hadn't made a definite decision about where to go, he allowed himself to be blown down the street toward the river. Lots of paper, leaves, and God knows what else was flying the same way; a man ran shouting after his hat as if he were chasing a little dog; gates slammed shut, windows rattled, bricks clattered down off roofs and flowerpots off windowsills. Jans's little bare legs walked miraculously without effort; he spread his arms, laid his head back, and looked up into the air. The sky seemed lower than usual; shining white jagged clouds brushed the rooftops in their flight. The wind had probably landed on one of these clouds like an unfamiliar guest emerging from a magnificent ship, and hardly had it arrived when it caused the heavy, multistory houses, this deeply anchored, unmovable world that at other times would not be moved, neither with threats nor with prayers, to become impatient and gently inebriated.

There was white foam scattered on the surface of the river, and red spots were burning in Jans's face as he came up the stairs to the bridge. Boys were running back and forth on the bridge, or perched on the railings, spitting between the cracks, or trying to climb between the crossbeams. When Jans appeared, they all turned to look at him for a moment: "What's he doing here!"

Maybe the wind was to blame, but everything seemed easier today than it usually was; at any rate, Jans took a little run-up in order to swing himself onto the railing with the others. But he merely bumped against it with his knees and slipped back down. The boys began to laugh, and Jans turned around and, smiling, lowered his head. Even on the stair landing he could still hear those who had remained behind shouting and laughing.

All at once the smile left Jans's little face, and even the red spots disappeared. Something else appeared in his face that had never been there before. He quickly turned around and took a new run-up. What a run-up it was! There he hung now by his skinny arms over the water in his wide red pants, tiny and emaciated, but totally possessed by a fierce wildness. He could feel the crossbeam under his bare feet; he was quite beside himself; he forced his head between the bars and then his legs after it; he hung like a fly in a web of bars and beams above the foul brown water. He crept on, his heart whirring like a little wheel, the hum of it droning in his ears. But Jans didn't pay any attention to the little wheel. He had but one single thought: to climb along under the bridge and then up again on the other side for all to see. And the boys immediately understood. When all you could see from the railing were Jans's bare, bent toes, they'd run to the middle of the bridge and lain down flat on their bellies so that they could watch through the cracks.

Jans crept on. The water gurgled; he hesitated a moment; instantly his body felt so heavy that he thought his little arms would tear like thread. But above his head the boys scratched and scraped, and the sound made Jans furious. He bit the bars with his teeth and crept on; he had to climb up. He thought of nothing else; he forgot everything else. He forgot what lay behind him; he forgot the winter and the room and the window looking out into the courtyard. He forgot his sister in the cradle; he forgot his mother and her breast; he forgot his father and all the sorrow he had ever experienced. He had only the one thought: to climb through under the bridge to the other side. The boys, who had all run to the other railing, caught sight first of his arms, and then the part in his hair, and then his little, shiny white face above the railing. "Look, he's really made it!" the redhead yelled, jumping from one foot to the other and clapping his hands. "But he looks so pasty-faced!" another said. But Jans didn't hear that comment anymore. He had merely given the redhead, whose laughing eyes sent out little sparks, a short, hard look and then, as if he cared neither for the cheers of his friend nor for any other acclaim in this world, he went in the opposite direction to the stairs, his bare feet slapping down firmly. The small internal wheel kept whirring; he didn't care. Nor did he worry about what was beginning to worm its way up through his throat. When it made room for itself and began to flow out, Jans remembered that this had happened to him once before, and it was a good memory. He wanted to put his foot on the steps, but the steps were hopping. He made a misstep, tripped, and fell flat onto the landing. His forehead and arms were torn open, but he no longer felt that. Ever since the redhead had cried out "He's really made it!" as Jans was going over the bridge, he felt only what everyone feels having reached and achieved a distant goal. And even the last, pale memory of any pain had vanished from his heart. His little soul was too small a dwelling to house this large guest. But during those two minutes there was as much joy in it as it could hold.

A couple of workmen who were the first to ascend the steps on their way home, picked him up, wiped off his face, and one of them said, "But that's Jansen's boy!"

On the day of the funeral Jansen, wearing a quaint stiff collar, and Marie with a tear-stained face and wearing her black dress, were sitting in the middle of the room. There was nothing special visible in Jansen's face, no flicker of anything to be seen; he just looked ever more embarrassed every time someone shook his hand. Although he tried to take up as little space as possible, his legs seemed to twist and turn around the feet of all the guests. Occasionally Marie would hurriedly get up and busy herself at the cradle as if to show that there was something still left to her.

From that time on, every Sunday, instead of walking along the river, they would go to the cemetery, taking the main road. Marie would lead little, round Anna, who could already walk, in her stiff white dress, by the hand, and Jansen would follow a step behind them, his eyes fixed on the firm, bare legs of his child. He always stood to one side when Marie busied herself at the grave, and he looked quite relieved when they left again. Anna already had the bright brown eyes and quick graceful manner of her mother. And then, one Sunday they were kept from going to the cemetery by some incident; that Sunday was followed by others, and in the end, they were going there only on holidays.

Anna grew tall and beautiful. Sometimes she would tell her girl-friends, the way you tell people about strange things, about the brother she never knew. But many years later, when her daughter had long been out of the house and Marie had turned into a gaunt elderly woman with prominent cheekbones and stringy hair, it would some-times happen that Jansen would ask for an hour off work in order, so he said, to take care of an urgent matter. Then he would hurry across the bridge and through the suburb, along the main road to the cem-etery that, on such ordinary workdays, lay there, still and deserted. He didn't stay long. He would look around to see if there was another visitor or a gardener nearby; then he would bend down over the small grave and pass his hand up and down the narrow side of the stone a few times. Or he would absentmindedly twist a blade of grass around his finger and then pull his finger out again.

But when he walked along the hot dusty road back to the suburb, his head down and the strong sun on his neck, then from the center of his squeezed-dry, old gray heart there would arise, red and glowing, a burning joy, a mighty sense of pride, a wild feeling of triumph at having found his old despair again.

1925

THE ZIEGLERS

ON AN AUTUMN afternoon that muffled the lights of the little town rather than coaxing them out, Marie was standing outside a door that had just been slammed shut behind her in the stairwell of a house on Betzelsgasse, holding the money she had collected for some knitted goods she had delivered. She closed her hand on the money and went down a flight of steps. It was almost dark. The brass spheres on the banister glinted. On her way up, the red and blue panes of glass in the stairway window had been glowing; now they were dim. She stepped closer to the window, counted her money, and put it in her pocket. Very slowly, she went down to the next landing; there she stopped again. She looked around her; the brass spheres were now small half-moons. She hesitated as if waiting for something. Her heart contracted with fear or perhaps grief. She lowered her head and waited. But nothing happened. Slowly and reluctantly her heart relaxed again. She didn't understand any of it; looking around in confusion, she squeezed her body close to the window. She pressed her face to the single clear pane of glass among the many colored ones. There was a courtyard between the adjoining houses with sacks piled against one wall, a lantern, and an unhitched wagon. A worker was waiting for his companion who was flailing his arms while trying to put on his jacket. She watched until he had both arms in the sleeves, then she walked out to the street.

The streetlamps were already lit. The tilled land was so close by that the air smelled of fall. The last shutters were clattering down in front of the shopwindows in the open square. She walked more quickly because she was cold. Two girls were walking ahead of her, laughing and swinging their arms. She recognized their red and dark blue hats from behind. Last year they had sat in front of her at school. It startled her and she slowed down. But the girls stopped and turned to look at her. "Oh, Marie!" The girls stood tall and beautiful on their long, white legs. "What are you doing these days?"

"I help out at home."

The girls looked at her; she compressed her lips. They already knew her dress, her necklace, her hair, the light eyebrows. Everything was just as it had been before Easter, only a little faded. They felt embarrassed and shook hands.

The hallway of her house smelled of burned fat. Suddenly she felt hungry, nothing else. She rang the doorbell, and with her index finger traced the letters on the nameplate worn shiny with use: Ziegler. Her sister, Anna, and the young man who was her fiancé were sitting on the sofa under the mirror in the living room. Anna was wearing a fresh white blouse and a tightly cinched belt. She was a pretty girl. Her companion was holding her hand, stroking it with his thumb; it made Anna's eyes shine. The crease on his crossed trouser leg made a firm line through the empty, darkened room. Marie slipped into the kitchen. Her little brother was doing his homework at the table. His round, pale face floated above the table like a small moon that cast sufficient light onto his notebook. Their mother was chopping up herring for a salad. She asked Marie, "Did they order any more?"

"The Friedlers, yes, and the Karstens, no." Marie looked fixedly at her mother's hands as they cut an egg into thin slices and pressed them in a pattern on the salad. Where her hunger had been, there was now something sticky and disgusting.

Marie and the mother crossed the room together. The young couple moved from the sofa over to the table and sat down across from the mother. The two children pressed themselves against the wall, quiet and flat, as if they wanted to save space. The father came into the room. He had been sitting in the bedroom by the rear window, looking down at the white, bare, rectangular courtyard. He had dozed off for a while. When he woke up, it was dark but nothing had changed. Except that there was now a thin, bright stripe under the door. It made him long for light, and he went into the other room.

He didn't sit down at the table but rather on the sofa, as if something were holding him back, too, keeping him from decreasing the space in the middle of the room. Young Gintler didn't want to let go of his girl's hand, but suddenly there were so many faces in the room and all so close to him. The children, as if they had guessed at his discomfort, pressed themselves deeper into the wall and the father into the sofa. Gintler thought, I might as well stay.

Marie walked quietly around the table, setting it. Even before you could see her hands, she had already pulled them away. Everyone jumped when the bell rang. It was the older brother. Now the room was full and close. The boy's long limbs wove themselves through the room. There was a track of muddy shoe soles on the floor. He leaned against the wall next to his siblings, took a hard look at the face of the boyfriend, and then stepped over to the table. There was now a damp spot on the wall where he had been leaning against it. They all looked at it. Young Gintler let go of his girl's hand. "I think I'd better be going home now."

After he had left, they sat down around the table to eat. They hesitated a moment before destroying the pattern of egg slices in the bowl. Then the mother helped herself. Under her calm eyes, everything felt steady and orderly, the food substantial. Only the older boy ate as if in isolation, hunched over. He looked at the empty plate with half-shut eyes, scraped it, and went on scraping, viciously, the way a dog scratches in the dirt. Finally the father said casually, as if it were nothing out of the ordinary, "Stop that scraping."

The older boy put his spoon down after once more going over his entire plate with it, laughing with bared, mean teeth.

In the morning Marie opened the workshop, which was situated on the ground level behind the courtyard. She raised the shutters and pulled the sack off the machine. With her foot she set the wheel in motion. The day started with a hissing that turned faint and thin like the endless chirping of a cricket. Her hands detached levers, tangling themselves in a furious series of moves. With a jerk, a piece of rust-red woven stuff began to come to life between the clips. There was already a fine layer of reddish woolen dust on the roller, on Marie's hands. Her hands were forgotten, as if they'd been cut off.

She could see the mailman coming across the courtyard and frowned. He put the mail on the table and watched her with a smile. With a severe look, Marie pushed him back out into the courtyard. Little bright hammers were pounding at her forehead. The sun cast a bit of light in through the courtyard window; the wool supplies on the shelves along the wall came to life in glowing, useless colors. Someone shuffled noisily across the courtyard; it was her father. He sat down in front of the desk in the middle of the shimmering cloud of sun motes and opened the mail.

The previous summer, six girls had worked in the workshop. Marie had replaced the sixth one at Easter. Her father tossed the mail back on the desk and squeezed his eyes shut. Then there was still Marie. And the remainder of the wool supplies on the shelves, glowing red and blue. He said, "Why didn't the Karstens order anything?"

Marie said, "People can't always be ordering things."

Her father said in a know-it-all tone of voice, as if he were arguing with the stubborn Karstens, "But people like them have to order something; we can't keep up with the others." Adding, "The girls all went to work for Matthews."

Marie said, "Maybe we will keep up."

Standing, her father reached into the shelves. He circled around Marie, stopped somewhere behind her, looking at her back, which immediately doubled up. He started again: "It's already turned quite cool here, and in the afternoon it gets completely dark. It would be much better for you to be upstairs in the apartment, much warmer. And it stays light longer. We could, for instance, set the machine up next to the bedroom window. Then we could rent this space. We can put the shelves upstairs too, and you, little sparrow, you don't take up any room at all."

He touched her hair. Marie recoiled; she hadn't realized he was so close behind her. Her father pulled back his hand, waiting. Marie said, "Yes, we could do that." Her father went back across the courtyard, no longer dragging his feet but with a lighter, younger step.

The bright little cloud of sun motes moved on from his empty chair and reached Marie, encircling her head and shoulders. She felt the warmth on her eyelids. Behind a window facing the courtyard she saw a couple of women with milk cans standing in the much too strong sunshine. They were laughing like crazy, shaking with laughter. Then it was completely still. Suddenly something within her contracted, just as it had last evening. There must be some misfortune or some sorrow very close by. She could already feel the sharp edge of something heavy, something hard. But she couldn't quite focus on it because she was too tired. All the tiredness came from a tiny dot between her eyes. Without it, she could have taken flight. Just then her mother called from the bedroom window, "Marie, lunch!"

Upstairs they were all kind to her. She felt relieved sitting between her brother and sister, held in a tight circle at the calm lunch table. Afterward, her mother folded the tablecloth but did not put it in a drawer; instead, as if she had something particular in mind, she suddenly took the bread out of the basket that Anna had been about to put away. Placing the bread on a chair, she sat down on the sofa. The children watched their mother from the doorway. She braced her arms on either side of her on the sofa and swayed back and forth with her upper body, moving her cheeks as if she were chewing on tears. Her little son approached her timidly and touched her knee. The mother grabbed him by the shoulders with both hands and shook him back and forth. She quickly let him go again, but the child was quaking inside his all askew shirt as if he were still being shaken. His mother looked at him; her gaze steadied and she drew him close again, and gently stroking him, she pulled his face toward her own. Now, surprised, she caught sight of the bread lying on the chair and picked it up. She stood very tall with her old, calm gaze, as if she were commanding all the things that had become disordered just now to return to their places.

The dust lay like bright fuzz on the walls of the workshop. But

Marie had barely begun when everything turned dead and gray. Red spots of sunlight lay on the wall. Marie clung to them, would have liked to pull them toward her, stuff them deep inside her where it was completely hollow and empty. She pulled the linen sack over the roller. The older boy walked across the courtyard, pressed his face against the window, and opened his mouth wide. It scared Marie, whereupon he opened it even wider. Suddenly he was gone. Marie stepped outside and looked fearfully around the empty, quiet courtyard. Then she saw his face above the courtyard wall.

The boy ran down the street toward the open square; panting, he stopped to think a moment. He looked all around him into the small, crooked alleys and up to the cloudy, scantily starred sky. Then he ran off again. The wind was driving a few leaves from some distant beech forest through the empty town. Some boys were clinging to the railing of the railroad bridge, staring down at the train platform, which was already lit up for the late train. They waited until the train arrived and then went off again into the windy, boundless night. If they hurried to the ramparts, they would be able to see the same train again, shooting across the bridge to the plain, leaving a bright trail on the water. They climbed up the street along the wall, then continued on toward the barracks. A couple of people were already hanging out between the back wall and the ramparts, because that's where the canteen windows were. And cheeky, scruffy, straw-colored Elise would be there, as well as the little humpbacked one, and you could already hear the soldiers laughing at her from afar. On the other side of the wire grating, where it was light, they could make out fat, white hands and massive, laughing heads. A heavy swathe of heat and the smell of sweat and soup surged through the grating like a substance being pressed through a sieve. Slices of coarse bread, sometimes a morsel of lard were quickly pushed through the space between the grating and the windowsill. Elise pushed her withered arm under the grating; the soldiers tugged on it to get more of her. Suddenly something happened inside the barracks; dishes clattered, and everyone ran to the back. The light went out, and the windows flew shut. With shining eyes, Elise pulled her red, scraped fist, full of crushed bread, back in toward herself.

It was now dark and cold between the rampart and the wall. They walked with the wind at their backs into the moat. There was brush growing in it, and from above it looked black and bottomless, like an abyss. The short, humpbacked girl crept part of the way down, but came back up again. Then Elise and another fellow crept down and stayed there. Then another one climbed down after them, and the first one crept back out and sat down, staring into the dark, swollen thicket. The boy would have liked to climb down now, too. And he would have liked to ask the one who had come back some questions, but he was acting so tense and strange that the boy didn't ask him anything, postponing everything for the next time.

Later, as he was going back to town through the quiet, unlit streets, the clock striking full midnight fell oppressively on his heart. He was frightened, too, because someone was waiting outside the house door. But then it turned out to be merely his sister and her fiancé. They let go of each other and stared at the boy's earth- and grease-smeared face. Anna let him in. She opened the living-room door and lay down on the sofa, and he went through the kitchen, which was clinking softly, and lay down in the small bedroom next to his little brother.

Marie pushed the table against the wall, climbed up on it, and took the wool down from the upper shelves. She carried the stuff through the courtyard so rapidly that the women with the milk cans couldn't even make out what she was carrying. Her father opened the door for her, surprised, as if he had forgotten their arrangement. He took the things from her and stroked her lowered head. He put everything on the bench on which Marie usually slept at the foot of the two big black beds. He looked around, undecided; then he began to explain how everything in the room was going to be changed. He stretched out his arm, and with his index finger he pointed to where the row of shelves would be from now on. Marie raised her head just a bit as if it were an effort for her to follow his explanation. Then her father stopped and quickly began to tear the photographs on the walls off their nails. As he was tearing down the first photo, the oppressive weight that had tormented his heart all year long fell away from him. He rattled around among the pictures with his now nimble hands. Marie came through the door and cleared off the wall shelf. Together, they dragged the washstand around the beds and pinned up the curtains. Marie pressed her lips together; her forehead glistened, but her father merely whistled and laughed whenever a piece of furniture bumped into the wall, tearing off a little piece of wallpaper. He just spit on his fingers and stuck it back on. Then, suddenly, he left to fetch some neighbors to help him carry the shelves and the machine upstairs. All around the courtyard, windows were opened to see what the rolling and shouting down below was about. Her father, who normally remained aloof and quiet, was making a tremendous lot of noise, yelling out orders, red-faced in the bright sunshine and clapping his hands.

After the men had left, he sat down on one of the beds, even though he hadn't helped with the carrying. He covered his face with his hands. Marie looked down at him; because he was a tall man, she had never seen his head from above. The skin was as white as wax; the bunches of hair were yellowed and seemed singed at the ends. Sighing, he stood up with his now old and heavy body. He looked around him, saw the shelves, the wool, and the machines, the whole room full, and he was appalled. His eyes fell on the pile of photographs lying on the night table; he shuffled through them. At that point Marie said, "They're coming back already."

The mother and Anna were returning home from the market. They stopped in surprise on seeing the living room, which they had cleaned before they left. Now it was dirty and untidy. The father stepped to the door and said calmly, "We've already done it all."

The mother looked around, wide-eyed, wordless, gripping the door handle tightly. Then she said, "You should have covered the beds first." Noticing a tear in the wallpaper, she ran her thumb over it. She looked at it all one more time, more seriously, but nothing righted itself, everything remained as it was, red and blue and yellow, and tossed all over the place. She turned and went into the other room.

Marie started putting things in order at one end. Her father asked, "Marie?" but forgot what he wanted to say and just looked at her. Looked at her the way you look at someone before whom you're not at all ashamed; there was such fear in his eyes.

The sisters swept out the workshop. Now that it was empty, it was a large, airy room. Anna kept talking about young Gintler. Marie wished she'd stop talking. The days were firmly circumscribed; maybe there was a little crack somewhere through which one might slip, if one had something to show. Anna showed her lovely face and was allowed through.

Upstairs, the table was set and their mother had put the little bunch of violets young Gintler had brought on it. All of them sitting around the table were tired and ate slowly. Only the boy pointed at the violets and laughed because something was different, showing his mean, young teeth.

Downstairs were the gray, dead windows of the workshop—already forgotten. Red trash was falling onto the windowsill and onto Marie's arms from the sky, which had moved closer. Their father had gone into town to talk to Matthews about the November delivery. The little one was studying at the kitchen table. Young Gintler was already sitting next to Anna on the sofa again, holding her hand and wishing it were her breast, her young body. White clouds of curtains floated in the evening room. The floor and tabletop still gleamed in the evening twilight, and furniture and vases seemed to be swimming on the shiny surfaces.

Suddenly, as if they had all been hiding in various nooks and crannies, restraining themselves with great effort, they came in through all the doors. The father came from the stairway, Marie out of the bedroom, the mother with the little one from the kitchen. They invited Gintler to stay for supper, but he said he had to go home.

The father couldn't sleep, fretting about the answer Old Matthews, of all people, had given him. He, Ziegler, had had to say please and thank you to old man Matthews. They had gone to school and started a business at the same time, had married and raised children at the same time. Then this evening had come when they stood facing each other, and he, not Matthews, had been given the bitter pill to swallow. On the way home he passed Gintler's father. They had greeted each other, but Gintler's father had scowled at him, holding it against him that his son was seeing Ziegler's young and beautiful daughter. With a feeble, discourteous greeting Gintler's father had reminded Ziegler of his obligation to send this only son back to his father from the crumbling Ziegler living room. On Ziegler's way home that evening, all the older men of the town had been standing along his usual route home; they let him pass through their midst, gazing coldly and astonished at his gray head.

He hadn't done anything wrong; some succeeded and some didn't. Elliser was even worse off than he was; there was nothing at all left of his business. Elliser usually went for a drink at ten o'clock. He'd once met him without a vest and his shirt awry. He himself owned a black Sunday suit, two everyday suits, and one old, worn-out suit. Now, in the early-morning dawn, he calculated when it was that he had bought the old worn-out one and how long it had lasted. Later that morning he told Marie what had happened with Matthews. Marie said nothing. After that it didn't seem so bad to him anymore.

On Saturday Marie got dressed, put the things in her basket, and was about to go into town. There was a pail of water standing next to the door; the rug had been folded back, and her mother was on her hands and knees, scrubbing. It was unusual to see her mother scrubbing, down on the floor, like a broad, low-slung animal with gray and black bunches of hair. She looked up at Marie from down there with dark, sad, shiny eyes like those of stray animals on the street. Marie was puzzled; usually Anna did the floors. Even after closing the door behind her, she could still hear her mother scrubbing and scrubbing as if there were something hidden under the floor.

It was already dark outside. It was cold on the open square, biting cold. Marie went first to Matthews's workshop. She dropped most of the things off there. A couple of guys were waiting outside by the back door, stepping from one foot to the other. Marie crossed over to the other side; sounds of conversation, footsteps, and laughter were coming through the gateway. The faces, the young guys, and the laughter: all of it was far away like things in a dream, unintelligible, set against a dark wall.

She had to deliver knitwear with replaced sleeves or inserted back parts to four or five families. At one stop, a man took the things from her in the doorway; at another they led her into their living room. It was hot and smelled of coffee; a clock ticked. A boy wearing glasses looked up from a photo album. Someone spoke to her pleasantly, offering her a chair. She stepped up close to the table, but did not sit down. For one moment she belonged in the bright circle of light cast by the lamp. It turned bright within her, her wishes, her sorrow, her fear. The woman said she had nothing for her to take along this time but would next week.

At another place someone took a bowl from the buffet and offered her a zwieback. She blushed, took it, and quickly bit off an end; startled, she held it in her hand. Then, as fast as possible she ran down the stairs and, looking about her, gobbled it up.

In the stairwell back at home it seemed deserted. She rang the bell and waited uneasily. It was quiet behind her apartment door, as if everything had come to a standstill. She rang again, and her little brother opened the door, trembling all over, up to his hair and out to his fingertips. The door to the bright living room stood ajar. Her mother was still on the floor at her feet, but no longer crouching: she was lying flat and heavy on the floor. She turned her head, said, "Marie." There was blood flowing from between her legs. It came out from under her skirt and onto the scrubbed floor, slowly increasing. Her mother lay there like a sack that someone had simply turned upside down, so that its contents, which you didn't want to see, spilled out. Marie put her hands under her mother's shoulders and became as hard as steel; her mother took hold of her and slowly pulled herself up. Marie brought her over to the bed. She took the cleaning rag out of the pail, wiped up everything, and put the rug back in place. Now the others came home and learned that the mother was sick. A woman who had also come into the apartment locked herself into the bedroom with the mother. A strange smell came through the crack in the doorway that made them all wince in dread. They sat around the table with lowered heads. By and by, their fears subsided; they got sleepy. They were too embarrassed to ask one another what to do about supper. They longed for it to be like every other evening, to have supper and go to sleep.

Suddenly the woman came out of the bedroom, looking bright, fresh, and satisfied, because everything was all right. On the other side of the open door, their mother lay on the bed, her face red and her eyes hard and shiny. They all turned to look at her face; the room turned a bit on its axis so that everything could be directed to this point. The mother saw her family through the open door. A swarm of thoughts hummed in her head. Supper, her little boy, the weekly market, the bloody clothes. But a new thought, stronger and more insistent than all those other tiny, stinging thoughts, emerged from deep within her: Let it go. She turned her face to the dark side. Then those in the living room stopped looking at the door and soon each went his or her own way.

Walking along, his steps cockily slapping the pavement, the boy didn't stop on the bridge but immediately ran toward the embankments. He was the first one there. Grabbing the grate of the canteen with both fists, he rattled it angrily. In the dark, they wouldn't be able to make out much more of him than a strip of shiny teeth. They held a chunk of bread as hard as iron out to him. He just took it between his teeth and, frowning, chewed on it. Eventually, the others came along and pushed him aside because by now he was heavy and full. They climbed up the embankments. The little humpbacked one wasn't there, but Elise and two tall, stout girls, Emil's sisters, were there. Then, it was like all the other evenings. Elise climbed far down into the brush, hiding, and meowed like a kitten about to drown. Even though they all knew that it was Elise, they nevertheless moved closer together in fear. One of the fat girls who never talked sat down next to the boy and kept opening and closing her knees like a pair of scissors. Then the boy got fed up, and he rolled down the slope into the ditch. But nothing much came of it because suddenly there was a lot of noise from above. A guard shone his lantern along the embankment and grabbed someone. The two tall girls, who had spoken so little all evening one might have thought they were deaf and dumb, began suddenly to swear incredibly fast and strangely.

At the end of the week the mother got up and started working again. She brushed a pair of shoes, made soup, dusted in a corner, and then sat down again. Anna went on working alone. The baskets with torn socks and dirty laundry were beginning to overflow. The mother looked at them strangely, listlessly, and turned her head away. Nothing special happened; everything remained as it was. The little boy's trousers got more worn, a button on a sweater dangled and would perhaps get lost. But that was no reason for her to set her weak, tingling legs on the floor and raise her heavy body up onto them.

But then one afternoon she *did* put the washtub on the stove. She soaped everything and was almost finished when Anna came home from the market. She pressed her lips together and wrung out the pieces of laundry. When everything was hanging white on the clothesline, she sat down in front of it and gazed at it. Her face was angry and tired. All the items on the clothesline were grumbling at her out of round holes. They had defeated her, forcing her to scrub them white until her thumbs were sore and her body weak.

The father now slept on the sofa in the living room where Anna used to sleep. One evening, when Anna was sitting on the sofa next to young Gintler, she caught sight of a felt slipper under the table. She was startled and let go of Gintler's hand; she bent down for the slipper and quickly threw it through the bedroom door where all the other things were.

The father put the slippers on over his socks, but then immediately changed his mind and put on his boots. He only mumbled when they asked him, "Where to now?" Where was he supposed to go with his poor, heavy, stout body that had once been big and strong enough for children and grandchildren to pull themselves up on it, but now was nothing but an unwieldy thing that occupied a lot of space, and into which one had to stuff a lot of food and which required a lot of sewing and ironing and darning. Yet he was still the father. He alone knew what was what. The others sighed and crumbled and knew as little today as they had yesterday. He alone, the father, bore the real grief within himself. Without the father, there would have been no terrible grief in the whole family. He had never before walked away just to be outside, out of the house. He now walked down the street. Once the door was behind you, things would go on, today a bit, and tomorrow a bit. He thought of death. There on the dark, open square his sad heart overflowed. He walked on. Only a few people were clattering around in the empty town, like dice you shake in a cup. Before his eyes a drunken man came out of a pub along with a door full of yelling and racket. The man tottered down the street a ways, but then stiffened quickly in the cold air. They recognized each other. The man, Elliser, began to talk. It would have been better for Ziegler to have crossed to the other side of the street, but the drunken man's shining eyes were the only bright thing in the entire city. He'd had bitter wine and was now going elsewhere because he didn't want to go home this goddamn night without some conviviality. He blamed two or three of the town's citizens for having destroyed his life, for having misappropriated his property. He mocked and cursed them. He was ready to throw a rock through their windows where they were sitting in light and safety, while he was going to ruin. Ziegler followed him reluctantly step by step. He thought in desperation, What does he want from me? Who does he think I am? Doesn't he know who I am? Does he even know I'm Ziegler? "People like us," he'd said. Is it something about me? Is there something wrong with my coat or my shoes?

The tavern sign appeared above the bend in the street. Elliser grew quiet. He forgot his companion, walked on ahead and quickly opened the tavern door. Ziegler was startled, finding himself alone now and hurried after him just as fast. The tavern was a decent place. Ziegler knew the proprietor who shook his hand. The tables had white tablecloths. He heard someone call his name. Old man Matthews himself and a few others were sitting at the large table under the mirror. They greeted Ziegler and made room for him. Ziegler calmed down and listened to their stories, laughing and telling some of his own. He searched for his face in the steamed-up mirror over the table. He found it among the other faces above the white tablecloth. It resembled the other faces so much that it was strange even to his own eyes. He thought then that everything would turn out all right and things would improve.

Marie tossed and turned on her bench at the foot of the large oak beds. People and furniture filled the room with a heavy darkness. The little lights behind the curtained windows in the courtyard had gone off one by one. The leaden room had sunk ever deeper into the night. Marie trembled in fear. Nobody would be able to find her here. Maybe someone was looking for her, ceaselessly, day and night in all the streets and squares of the city, but she was not to be found anywhere. Not even God could see her on her bench in the bedroom inside this black darkness. She touched her skin, her breasts, her belly. Her body had not melted and was still with her; it wasn't deserting her. She slept for a little while. Suddenly she saw that her mother and sister were sitting up with their chins resting on the bedposts, watching her attentively but uncaringly. She started up in fright, and hitting her head on the wood of the bed frame, woke up. A door opened next door; for a minute there was a bright crack of light. The night went on. Far, far away a steam whistle screeched. Perhaps a train was going across the bridge. It occurred to her that she could get up and leave. But her limbs felt heavy with exhaustion. All night long she had thought of the darkness as heavy and oppressive, but now she realized that the darkness was light and soft; she was the one who was as heavy as lead.

The next day—everything was nearby and visible, and nothing

had been hidden except for the ordinary things, the courtyard, the windows, and the sky, gray and cold—Marie was sitting on the windowsill, hemming colorful strips of trimming. From time to time she stretched her neck to look down. A metalworker had moved into their former workshop. He was a greasy, funny little man who made quite a clatter with his metal rods and tubs.

Backs, fronts, sleeves, and pieces of trimming were strewn on the beds, on the bench, everywhere. The red, crackling warmth from a little iron stove made all the tossed-about things look colorful and gay.

A door slammed shut outside, and then another. Her father was speaking rapidly, excitedly; then a chair fell over and her father was shouting. Marie put her things down and ripped open the door. Her father's hand had hit the chair back instead of the boy, who had quickly dived under the table. Now his smudged, sallow face was peeking out from between the table legs. He opened his mouth, snapped his teeth shut on a corner of the tablecloth, and proceeded to chew on it. His father wailed, "That Emil, whom they took to the police that night, he told them everybody's name. And now the boy has to leave his school and go off to the Holztor School."

The boy wasn't thinking about his father anymore; he was looking at his sisters' legs—the one sister's thin and rough and the other's round and silky. His father yelled at him, "Come out of there at once."

Anna said, "Don't be foolish; come on out."

The boy kept chewing on his tablecloth corner; the cloth slid off, and the little vase with the violets rolled around on the carpet. Grumbling, Anna picked everything up.

Marie came through the door; the face under the table was yellow and angry, it looked strange and wild; she was afraid of his teeth; she had always been afraid of this brother; softly she said, "Come on."

The boy turned his head in her direction. What did she want? His father and mother were boring, and his little brother was boring and pasty-faced; Anna was boring and stupid, but Marie was the worst of all, the grayest. He felt like attacking her spindly, thin legs with his teeth, and those hands of hers that were always busy with something. He wanted to bite the heart out of her and make her hop around screaming. Marie walked over to the table, stepping very gingerly out of fear; she bent down—after all, you could feel sorry for someone who was so totally wild and yellow. "Come on!" she said again. The boy lowered his head; her legs were so pitiful; he crawled out, jumped up on both feet, and ran out of the room.

He was glad that it was going to be the Holztor School. It was down by the river, ten minutes from the railway bridge, and almost all the students going to that school were boys from the streets along the river, young water devils who knew their way around the rafts and jetties. Passing steamships made the classrooms restive with their whistling. A few boys drowned every summer, and every winter a couple of them would break through the ice. Then a guy like him would come along, who'd collect a couple of fellows in the evenings and lead them out onto the ramparts where it was hard to believe that the strange, white thing down there—that this was their own river.

It had been cold, and he was freezing. He thought of the living room. In the evenings the door to the bedroom was kept open, and heavy, good heat came through. That bad place was the only place where it was warm and neat; all the rest of the world under the wide sky was cold and windy. They pressed up against the ramparts. But even with six or eight of them squeezing together in a bunch, they were still something quite tiny.

The canteen windows had been closed. The boy jumped angrily with both feet up onto the windowsill, took hold of the grate and pounded on it. Then, grabbing the edge of the roof, he'd pulled himself up; he had a whole cluster of boys sticking to him. He knew the exact spot where the bread was stacked; he could smell its coarse, grainy fragrance. They'd never have been caught if they hadn't already been sitting up on the roof. And so they were taken to the police station, still chewing, with fists, pockets, and nostrils full of bread.

He'd been sent home first. His father intercepted him at the apartment door, grabbed him by the neck, pushed him down on the floor, and started hitting him. It was dark on the landing; the doors to the kitchen, living room, and stairway were locked. Now and then his father missed. He had something warm, alive between his fists in that dark hallway without an exit. The boy was hard and firm; one could feel what one was hitting. He had brought bitter shame upon him, and that was something he could bash. Not a thin-as-air, invisible kind of shame. As he struck the boy harder and faster, his misery, fresh and relieved, dropped from his heart. Then suddenly it was over. The boy braced himself on his arms and raised his head. His father, exhausted and stooping, stepped through the living-room door and carefully closed it. The boy got up and shook himself. In the living room, his father threw himself down on the sofa and pulled up his legs. He remembered with a start that he was still wearing his boots and was about to get up again to take them off. But his arms hurt, and his back was tired. He was overcome and, stretching out, purposely trod against the cushions with his heavy, dirty boots.

Christmas intervened. Thin, wet snowflakes fell, already turning to rain in the afternoon. The living room was heated; everything had been thoroughly cleaned; the curtains hung at the windows like white clouds. The porcelain bowl on the buffet was filled with cookies. For even without butter and eggs, they'd been able to make the dough and shape it into lambs and stars. The little one chewed on his small pile of cookies, noticing only that they tasted of cinnamon and anise. His small face was round and shiny white like the glass balls hanging on the tree. Finally, his belly was filled with sweets, his eyes with colors, light, and silver; he had everything.

It was as if a bell had been upended over the little town, wearying foreheads with its clappers. There was a respite, a pause in time, an island. Father and mother were sitting on the island with everything they had: their children, their Christmas tree, and their furniture. They all wished that time would move on; after all, what could they do during this respite; it would be better if this gray, terrible time were to keep flowing along.

On Christmas Day they went for a walk together. The father already had the letter in his pocket that said the boy was going to be picked up early in January. But the boy was walking with them too, ahead of his parents. Many other families were out walking to the right and left of them under the bare, wet plane trees. They met Matthews with his wife and two daughters. They greeted one another. Old Matthews remembered that someone had told him the Zieglers weren't doing well. He looked at them, checking their faces, shoes, and clothes. But he discovered no tear, no spot. Ziegler thought, Yes, take a good look at us, we're just like you. Take a long, thorough look; you won't find anything different.

He saw Matthews again early in the new year. They were standing across from each other; Matthews's desk was between them. Each had gotten up in surprise. Matthews was surprised because Ziegler was certainly the only man in the city who hadn't heard that his business had been sold. The company had taken over everything, house, office, and workshop. There would be no more deliveries.

Ziegler twisted the piece of paper on which he had intended to write an order and put it in his pocket. He shrugged. His face had come apart in amazement as if the thin thread that was holding it together had torn. Matthews took a closer look; indeed, Ziegler's collar had been turned, his vest was worn. Ziegler looked over at the desk where papers and samples seemed to be curling and twisting, living piles of orders.

Ziegler stared at a bright, round thing on the desk. He shouldn't have come in this suit. He should have rearranged his suits and worn the good one. Matthews suddenly sat down and nodded to him. But Ziegler just wouldn't leave. The bright, round thing on the desk turned into a letter scale. He was thinking he would have rearranged the suits anyway. Then he pushed his chair back and walked resolutely out.

Some impulse drove him straight back to town, to the open square; there the impulse waned; it wasn't even strong enough to get him home. One small street led to another. It was odd to be dawdling in the middle of a bright morning. Then he found himself buffeted in a jumble with a lot of men and women, some well-dressed, others not; they all knew one another slightly. So he evidently had not been walking around at random. He had landed here at the Heumarkt as if it were the lowest point in the town with all the streets flowing down to it like streams. He looked out across the crowd. Far away, above all the heads and caps, hung a sign illuminated from inside for the sake of his weak eyes that said: UNEMPLOYED. No one in the world, not even Old Matthews himself, could force him to line up here on the open Heumarkt, among this horde of blue and gray jackets. They were shameless and noisy. Hanging around, shifting from one foot to the other, waiting in their places in line, as if it meant nothing to hang out here, both before and afterward. A person would have to be really inured to shame if he could bear to stand in line for his money like this under the open sky.

He walked down to the river. It was cold but calm and sunny. There were mountains and clouds on the other side. He had never been by the river at this time of day. Some people who had nothing else to do were hanging out near the guardrails. Some were in rags. They had nothing to look forward to. They allowed their time to flow away in small, golden whorls of water. They had given up their own ventures because everything was now being done by big ships that whistled, blew smoke, and hauled wood, and destroyed and chased away the clouds that gathered. Ziegler stepped up to the railing. He wished for nothing but to stay here for hours and hours, day after day. And what if someone came by. Who would recognize him from the back? Someone touched his arm, said, "There comes a new Dutch-man." Ziegler turned to look at the other man's face; it was red and fat, with tiny little eyes. He tore himself away. He walked home.

At home they looked at him because he was late. But he didn't tell them anything. After eating, he followed Marie into the bedroom to talk with her. Suddenly he liked the idea that she slaved away, unaware that Matthews was no longer taking any deliveries. He wanted to tell her, yet restrained himself. He looked at Marie; her face was damp, and her arms seemed to have gotten disproportionately long in the last few weeks. Her eyelids twitched. He said nothing to her the next day either. Nor the day after that. He allowed her to work the week through; then he stroked her hair and told her that it was all for nothing.

Anna had wanted to meet Gintler somewhere else. But then she did meet him in a small pastry-shop café. The marble tabletops gleamed; the place was empty at this hour. But the room was so warm and pleasant and smelled so deliciously of coffee and cake that it would probably soon be full. Young Gintler pulled Anna into a room in the back. He moved over to be close to her, touching her face with his. Anna smiled in that strange room, squinting in a sudden access of contentment at the big mirror in front of which a buffet had been set up with untouched, growing mountains of cakes and *Mohrenköpfe.** Young Gintler spoke softly and stroked her hand. She started when they brought the dishes, pulling her hand back. Gintler took her hand from the back of the chair. She lowered her head, distracted by the smell coming from the cups and plates. He put his arm around her shoulders; she looked down at her cup on top of which floated a swirled ball of whipped cream. There also was a swirl of snow-white cream on the apple cake they had brought. She forgot everything else, took a spoonful, and licked it off. Young Gintler stroked her shoulder, her breast. She thought that she shouldn't be stuffing herself but rather should eat very slowly, spoonful by spoonful. She wondered whether all the white reflected in the mirror back there was white whipped cream. Perhaps Gintler would order some more. She looked at him quickly. His face was red; he was looking at something with shining eyes, held it, caressed it—but it was her. She suddenly felt tired. She put her head on his arm, feeling a soft, cozy sadness.

Back home the mother had set the large tub on two benches in the kitchen. She was getting a hot bath ready for the boy. Today was the day he would be picked up. He hadn't seemed to care very much at first, but yesterday he had begun to feel anxious. They all acted as if it were nothing special, didn't discuss it with him or with one

* Chocolate-covered, whipped-cream-filled pastry puffs.

another; maybe if you didn't make anything of it, it would turn out to be nothing. His mother had put his things in order and packed them. She had added sandwiches to make the trip feel like an ordinary one. He got into the tub. His mother wanted to be the one to wash him. She began to soap his hard, yellow body, his hair, his neck. He pressed his elbows to his ribs and lowered his chin. He felt the soapy foam on his limbs, on his big ears. His anxiety turned into a great fear pounding inside his wet, soapy body. He was afraid of his mother's soft, slippery hands that were moving stupidly and blindly around on his rough, skinny, ugly body. It was his, this body that had rolled down sloping banks, climbed up on walls, hidden in ditches, dived into the deep river water. She handed him a stiff, unfamiliar towel. He rubbed himself hard all over to rub away his shame. Then the doorbell rang. The father opened the door. His fear also had become unbearable. The man sent by the city to pick up his boy would have been walking through the streets in the middle of the day in a uniform, or maybe wearing an armband, and up his stairway.

Actually there were two ordinary men wearing dark clothes on the doorstep. He led them into the living room. Since the boy was ready, they didn't sit down on the proffered chairs. The boy took a step toward his father to push through that wall; then it would all be over anyhow. They shook hands; his father turned to the window; his mother started to cry silently; one of the men took the boy's package, then they led him down the stairs.

At that point the boy tore himself free, took a leap, and jumped through the side door into the courtyard; the men ran after him. The boy wanted to climb the wall, but slid down and ran instead into the workshop. The little metalworker grabbed him by the neck. But he broke free and started to scream. Windows opened all around the courtyard. Upstairs, his father and mother looked at each other; they heard his screams. Their eyes darkened and leapt despairingly into each other's black eye sockets. Then there was a continuous screaming, as if he'd been burned and bitten. Never again would such terrible screams come out of this courtyard. Anna, who was just coming up the stairs, gripped the banister, white-faced. She knew who that was, screaming with all his might. With outspread arms, he was screaming away her wedding, her filmy, soft wedding dress.

The boy whirled around, ducked down somewhere by the cellar door among the potato sacks. The men searched, returned to the stairway, and looked out into the street. Marie, up at the bedroom window, had seen what was happening. She saw her brother among the potato sacks, and she came down the stairs and stood in the middle of the courtyard. The boy jumped out and threw himself against the courtyard door. The men pushed from within, but he pressed against it with his chest, forehead, and arms, with both feet stomping on the pavement behind him. There was a knock on the door; then Marie jumped over and pressed against the door next to him; but the door moved; the courtyard beneath their feet seemed gradually to slip away; they fell on top of each other. One man grabbed the boy by the arm and took him away; the other picked up the package from the step and followed.

The father and mother came down the street looking so somber and determined that no one turned around. The red zigzags of the screams were by now scarred over in the courtyard. The lunch table was set. Above the circle of plates was a circle of faces just as clean and white. The mother ladled out something with chunks floating in it. She was surprised because they didn't all get up right after eating it but were waiting expectantly. She looked around sternly; maybe there really was something else coming. But then she got up and collected all the cutlery on her plate to show them that this wasn't just the soup course but it was all there was.

The father put on his best suit and went into town. He had a few schemes; he would make a few inquiries. This time Old Matthews was away on a trip. At another place they gave him some advice. By then the barren winter day was coming to an end. The lights went on in the offices. Work wasn't too pressing. His complaints and worries mingled with the worries of others into a winter evening's warm chattiness. They were already eating supper by the time he arrived back home.

Again plates had been placed around the little bunch of flowers. Gintler had been there. The smoke of his cigarette flavored the soup left over from lunch. There was a scraping sound. They all frowned and looked up. Then it occurred to them that the seat where the scraping usually occurred was empty and that it was each of them scraping their plates.

Marie walked through town. Wherever she stopped at the thresholds of living rooms she would say, "We accept all knitwear, runs, worn-out elbows, new hats, and jackets." Behind her lowered eyelids, the people and the living rooms appeared almost familiar to her. There were now apples on the brown sideboard. The woman, who had always been kind, offered her apples just as she had offered her zwieback a few weeks ago. Except that, in the meantime, Marie's hands had become heavy; zwieback was still all right; the apples, much too wonderfully yellow shiny ones, weren't anymore. The woman wondered about Marie's jacket. It was totally worn, even though the girl was so clever in repairing knitwear. On Betzelsgasse, as she was going up the stairs, the fading windows in the stairwell still showed little red and green sparks in the cracks. The boy with the eyeglasses was sitting in that living room with the same album whose pages, it seemed, he had not turned since the last time she was there. The tall, dark woman was not her mother; the boy with the eyeglasses was not her brother; she had to get away from the light of this lamp because it wasn't her lamp. That she should belong within these four walls and with these same people . . . It was just as it had been at Easter time at school: Now that you've been seated in your assigned seats, you can calm down.

But the streets, on the other hand, were again unfamiliar. She was a little afraid of any kind of darkness. This winter she walked around the town on one evening or another. How could one ever get used to the darkness? Her heart was pounding, blinding her eyes with its wings. Her shirt was sticking to her. Behind her someone called out, "Marie!" She refused to pay attention to the voice and walked faster. Then someone behind her called out three times, very loud, "Marie, Marie, Marie!"

She had met the girl last fall around the same time and at that same place. The girl had changed during the winter. She had grown tall and strong. Her firm, young breasts, which weren't yet important to her, moved with her strong, breathless gestures. Her face was red and white. She was quite beautiful, and would have been even without all that, because of her sparkling eyes. Marie had liked the girl at school. Now she looked at the girl in utter delight, her golden hair and the little red hat. The girl said, "I'd like to say something, Marie. Would you like to come to our house? There are always a lot of us, please come to see us sometime."

Marie said, "I always have so much to do."

The girl said, "Everyone has a lot to do. Do come see us sometime."

Marie said, "Yes, maybe, sometime."

The girl looked at Marie; her eyes sparkled with a hard, alert brightness. The girl let go of her hand, slowly, slowly. A terrible, unfamiliar, powerful force was drawing Marie away from where she was standing, away from the girl, the way one sinks down into a swamp: As yet their hands were still holding on, their fingertips, their eyes, but the force was so much stronger than the girl was. It drew Marie down the street to the open square. Then for one instant it let go; Marie quickly turned around, but the street was empty again. Then she went home of her own accord.

Back home everyone had pieces of knitwear in their hands. The father was an expert at measuring patches. It was warm and bright in the room; there was chatter, it was almost cheerful. They were already finished, and Anna was sliding around on the floor, picking up lint and scraps. Just then young Gintler rang the doorbell. Anna jumped to her feet, brushed her hair, put on something bright, sprayed stuff from a bottle, and changed her face and voice. Father and mother looked at each other, smiling. Gintler always came here directly from his municipal job in the afternoon. A positive message streamed from his new, ironed clothes through the entire apartment. He was loyal; Anna's young white body pleased him; he had eyes for nothing else. The living room had slowly unfolded around his beautiful fiancée. Its husk had torn and fallen off. Its innards had been revealed. But young Gintler had looked at the room only once, on his first visit. His eyes thought that it was still the same. They didn't check the pillows, which had been turned; nor the wallpaper, which had been pasted back on. With both arms he held Anna and kissed her bosom.

The father put on his good clothes; he was going into town to see Matthews, who had come back from his trip in the meantime. At Matthews's place he wiped his face with a handkerchief. His eyes searched among the white papers for the shiny letter scale, a familiar spot. In the bright light coming into the room, the striped wall, the armchair, the desk, all had the bleak, cold appearance by which spring announces itself on pieces of furniture. Old Matthews noticed Ziegler's suit, his good shirt, his watch chain. Perhaps it would have been better if he had worn his worst clothes, for Matthews said, "I can't help myself, and I certainly can't help you, even with the best of intentions."

Then, on the way home it was as it had been the first time. The streets themselves passed him from one to the next. Except this time it was still light instead of dark. He felt very much like going down to the river. A whole string of idlers was snoozing on the railings. Soft, bright light had thawed the distance—large clouds were moving away over the mountains. Everything was much too far and too bright. It wasn't the riverbank he wished for; it was a hole. He pressed close to the walls of the houses he passed. There was one door that yielded to his touch. He went inside. He started to drink. A group of boatmen had moved their tables together. They called something out to him and laughed, for he was dressed in black. He hardly ever drank. Now he thought he could force everything to spin and become blotchy. But everything stayed clear and orderly, one thing on top of the other. So he went home. His family had already gone to bed. He sat down in the dark on the sofa and retched. He was pumped full of sadness like some heavy fluid that threatened to rupture his insides.

The following day he took his little boy by the hand and went down to the river with him. He had thought this up with the idea of doing something nice for the child, for the river was really bright and beautiful.

The little one walked silently beside him. What a good, patient child he was. For Easter he had been promised a new school, but it didn't work out. He had been promised books, an atlas, shoes, jackets, but nothing had ever come of it. He forgot all the promises; he never asked. Even his legs remained soft and thin, as if they didn't want to offend his tight velvet pants. The father liked walking hand in hand with the little one. He intended to take him along the river, then make a wide arc through the town. He wanted to meet people; he wanted to be seen with his little son, dressed in black, calm and kind. He put his arm around the child and explained to him about the steamships, the villages, and the mountains. However, the boy didn't look up into the air, only at his father's face. But the father didn't want his face watched by two eyes the way dogs watch over a house. He asked the boy to wait. He went inside and sat down. He held on to the tabletop; he waited. Time condensed and ran down the walls in pearls. It made him feel wretched, and he moaned. Two hands simply took hold of him under his armpits.

Then it was hard and cold. The little one tugged at him until he got up. Instantly it was all over. The boy was pasty-faced from all the waiting; he himself was dirtied and grubby. The boy was too small to hide him, so he went around him quickly. They didn't go through the town, but went back home taking the same way they had come.

As Anna was beating the red duvet with her young, carefree hands, it burst open and a swarm of feathers escaped. She stopped beating the duvet and sewed it up. It had gotten warm. The much too early sunshine smelled of sand and lye. The beds and cabinets had been moved from their places, and now dents and cracks, unfamiliar ones, turned up in the middle of one's own room. Colorful items that had disappeared and been given up on in times gone by, so different from nowadays, were suddenly lying there, covered by a dense fluff of dust. Anna tossed the duvet onto the bench and called out, "You can't use it to cover yourselves anymore."

From the adjacent room, her mother called into the pail, "With what else, then." Anna stepped to the window; she felt dizzy from the light; she smiled, looking forward to the coming Sundays: a white dress, old warm foliage, and beech woods. She said, "You can cover yourselves with coats; you don't need any quilts now after all."

Her mother said, "Come here, come here." Anna climbed over the broom with her skirts pulled up. "You can't beat the pillows, Anna, they'll tear."

"Oh, let them be, Mother. I'll crochet stars for you, very thin, pointy ones; you just need to brush them."

"I can't hang up these curtains, Anna; they're so brittle and worn."

"Let them be, Mother. We won't hang them up this time."

"But the carpet will fade, Anna, and everything else too."

"Oh, you know what? Let's put the table with the Austrian linden plant in front of the window."

The little one came home and then the father. The mother sat down on a chair, letting her legs dangle, and said, "It's so hot, and I feel so weak in my belly."

The father touched her rough, gray hair, recoiled, and stepped away from her. He looked around his disarrayed living room in confusion, then went into the bedroom where things were just as bad. He looked down into the courtyard; it was quiet and cool. And he felt like going down there. In the courtyard there wasn't enough sunlight to fill it all the way to the ground. He looked around carefully as if trying to find something that had fallen down from upstairs. He turned his head to look in all directions, just to show the curious people at the windows why he was standing there in the empty courtyard.

Suddenly he stamped wildly on the pavement; everything turned bright inside him, and all the misery streamed out of his heart in bold, glowing colors. The colors flooded the courtyard, causing it to blaze and glow in a strange, despairing brightness. Then, exhausted, it abated. The bold, flaming, divine colors faded all around him, and the courtyard was gray and cool once more.

There was an elderly woman on the fourth floor who, in former times, would frequently have coffee with the mother. Various little happy coincidences, like the fact that she lived alone, meant that there was never a lack of raisin stollen and sausages in her pantry. Mrs. Ziegler shut the door much too quickly behind her. Even so, the woman with half-closed eyes would sometimes catch sight of worn-down shoes, a frayed handkerchief, or a dirty milk pitcher. The woman ran into the young Ziegler boy on the street. His little pasty face, the scrawny neck made her feel sorry for him. She loved children. She invited the boy to come into her apartment. He stopped in the doorway totally amazed by the singing of a bird. A glittering cage was swinging gently amid a forest of leafy plants. She busily set the breakfast table for herself and the child. She put cake on the table, yellow and red cheese, and butter and ham. The boy put his ten clean fingers on the table in front of him. She urged him to help himself; the cake on his plate consisted of more raisins than dough. But the plate was strange. And the cake was an indivisible part of this strange plate. He dug around with his spoon; and as punishment he began to feel his throat constricting, and the bite of cake wouldn't go down. He looked at the woman, moving his lips, and got up. His eyes filled with tears. The woman was annoyed about the crumbled cake. She suddenly felt annoyed with the people from the floor below, who had completely forgotten that she was still there, ready to talk on the landing, to help, and to give advice at any time. She wanted so much to wedge her foot into the fearfully closed door. She wrapped cake and cold cuts in paper and gave it to the child to take home with him. The boy went downstairs and put everything on the table in the living room. Stunned, the family watched things tumble out of the paper package that had burst open. They were about to scold the child, but he began to cry. Then they talked softly among themselves and agreed to send the Austrian linden plant upstairs on Sunday.

The father never drank again. He went out less and less often. Soon he would go out only on Sundays when the rest of the family went out. Then he would put on his good black suit, amazingly intact in the bright sunlight, like the summer coat of an animal. He was very much afraid that his good gray workday suit would wear out like the brown one had; then he would have to start wearing this black Sunday suit. He got used to sitting quietly on the sofa. Then it seemed to him that the small, worn places only he knew about were slowly healing. The soft gray material became ever more a part of his own flesh. He began to look at it the way one would look at one's own sickened skin and discovered that the fabric was woven not only of black and gray yarn but also had a yellow thread secretly running through it, which always was the first to tear.

He longed very much for the town. He thought of the rusty railing by the riverbank where there was always a motley, scruffy string of people. They dipped their gaze into the flowing water. They let the sun and rain totally destroy their greasy jackets. He thought of Elliser, who measured time from one pub to the next. The man didn't mind, when he was heavy with drink, slipping off his chair and under the table or into puddles. He thought of the Heumarkt. He remembered the day he had turned away from the sight, stricken to the core. He was no longer afraid. It was none of his business. They crowded together, like children tearing at the holes in their shirts and making them even bigger. He had to sit here by himself and wait.

His abdomen, which didn't know what he was thinking, swelled as he sat there, stretching the fabric and tearing it and threatening, in its own way, to break through all precautions. He wished it were winter so that he could put his coat on over his gray suit and leave. He didn't know what would happen next summer. Then he got sick.

For a long time he thought that the heavy, painful lump was simply a part of his insides. One evening as he was getting undressed, he suppressed a scream. His wife felt inside his open shirt with her bare hand. The next day they went to see the doctor. In the waiting room, they looked around anxiously. The men and women waiting there were carelessly turning the pages of worn old magazines, tugging on tassels, and trying to engage one another in conversation. Gradually they all became calmer and were rather kind to one another. But whenever one of them went in to see the doctor and, after a while, came out again, his face would have a dazed look as if he had not only brought his troubles back out with him but had had more added to them inside. He no longer recognized the people he had been waiting with just moments before. They had become strangers to him.

The Zieglers came out, the way they had come out of the house the first time when their boy had been picked up: very heavy and dark.

Back home, Anna was crying because Gintler had canceled their date. He had brought the movie tickets but had to leave again with his parents. Anna gave one ticket to Marie, and the sisters went together.

Anna cried softly in the dark movie theater. Completely at a loss, she watched aimlessly teeming streets, surging seas, lost ships, and fleeing people, all of it blurred by tears.

Marie held on to both armrests. Why hadn't Gintler come? Then she wouldn't have had to go along with her sister into this cramped, hot darkness. A few years ago she used to come here occasionally; she didn't know much about it. She turned her head away from the strange, white light, looked down the tight rows of faces, all silvery, rigid, and eager. She turned back again and felt her forehead white and cold. Something flickered before her eyes that resembled a sky, mountains, and trees. People came on horses. She wished she could understand it all exactly. She had never dreamed that there could be such deep abysses. And yet at the same time her heart insisted that they should be even deeper, and that these wonderful riders who pursued one another over bridges and tombs should not catch up to each other. They mustn't ever catch up to each other. She didn't know why. She longed to understand everything thoroughly. Yet not only the horses but the mountains and trees also ran away from her gaze. Sometimes they took pity on her and waited; then, in the twilight of a simple room, people would show their big white faces for a moment. They would show her in an intimate way their unhappiness or their joy. The horses too were calm, tied to a fence. A sun that made her heart feel light shone above dense grass, above a solitary white house. But she missed the moment when it all changed. There was weeping about a misfortune that she hadn't seen coming. The mountains had disappeared; a rider rode into a street; it was already night. She didn't need to torment herself anymore. For slowly, out of a dark doorway, slowly enough so that she could follow it, stepped a young woman holding a lamp; she set the lamp down on the stairs and embraced the new arrival.

The lights came on. The people began to get up. Anna had stopped crying; her face was not as beautiful as it usually was, but was swollen and morose. She paid no attention to Marie. It was late evening; they walked quickly one behind the other. Marie lowered her head. From time to time, she would look briefly to the right or the left. She finally understood many things and had gotten used to things. What was she supposed to do now on this unfamiliar street that led to the open square?

The father was sitting up straight. Their food congealed into rotten, tasteless lumps inside their mouths, because they knew that under the table his belly was hard and sore from the disease. The father did not complain. He pressed his abdomen under the table with both his hands and looked around him sternly.

One evening, Marie came into the room with a basketful of knit-wear; he asked her whose orders they were. Then Marie had to spread everything out for him. He stroked her hands, her hair. Perhaps at that moment he was not in pain and wanted to be kind to her. He spoke gently to her, her hand in his, tapping her knuckles with his thumb. She said yes and no and looked hard at his face. Something relentless had, with all its power, squeezed the last drop of hope from the evening room; the furniture, vases, and crocheted stars were lying around, wasted and shriveled, like dried-up peelings. The father, intimidated by Marie's cold, despairing look, stopped talking. He laid his hand on her head. Then suddenly he started, frowned, and stared straight ahead. He forgot to take back his hand. It lay on Marie's head, pressing down, as heavy as lead. She didn't dare take his hand and put it back on his knee. She waited. She picked some cotton fuzz off the cushion. She thought that maybe he had died and that the hand lying on her head was the hand of a dead man. But then he sighed slightly. He took his hand back of his own volition as if it had merely been lying on the table, and having forgotten Marie, he turned to the wall. Marie put the things back into the basket and carried it to the bedroom.

Two or three weeks before he died, he felt like going outside. It took a long time to get ready, and he winced as he was buttoning up. But he absolutely had to go to town, and he dressed in his good clothes. Wiping off the sweat, he walked laboriously down the sunny street. He could feel the good black cloth on his sick body. He ran into Old Matthews on the way. Ziegler's face froze as if he had expected this encounter and had prepared himself for it. They greeted each other. On seeing Ziegler, Old Matthews regretted having been annoyed by him when he had come to his office a year earlier. A terrible disease could strike anyone. It had not been able to change his suit, his collar, or his watch chain. The old man's greeting was generous and respectful. Ziegler returned the greeting slowly. His face changed; he savored the greeting with lowered eyes. A bit of joy stirred in his heart, and he returned home less forlorn than when he had left.

He was dead now, but his photograph hung in the living room above the sofa on which the little one usually slept because they had rented the small bedroom to the metalworker. Now at last his rejuvenated face was immersed for all time in a calm self-assurance, and his smooth new suit would never wear out. The woman from the fourth floor came to pay a condolence visit. She could now go into the middle of the living room and draw laments from their poorly guarded hearts. Mrs. Ziegler did not cry, but her face and the faces of all the children and everything in the room were blurry and dulled by mourning. The woman couldn't see things as clearly as she had thought she could. Evidently everything was still nearly the same as it had been. All in all, the same things were still standing in the same spots as they had been on her last visit. A mirror still flashed between the windows, something golden glittered on a wall shelf. Mrs. Ziegler looked worn out, but a valuable brooch was fastened to her black dress. All through the week, lots of faces of neighbors, business friends, and school friends had been turning up; it was as if an unknown hand had forced them to take a detour through this living room.

At the end of the week, the landlord came just as they were all sitting down for dinner. He wanted to talk about the apartment, which he would rather rent to the metalworker than to the Zieglers, who paid the rent badly and irregularly. They offered him a chair. The mother and her children sat at the set table. It seemed as if a glass bell jar had been inverted over these dark, sad people sitting there upright and slowly eating something mushy from their blue-rimmed plates. The man changed from being a landlord into a mourner. He decided to postpone what he was going to say for another day, said a few words, and left.

Then they all went back to work. Marie took her basket and made the deliveries. It was only afternoon, but the pavement and the slate roofs were wet from the rain; the sun was but a fading, yellow stain. Marie hesitated inside the front door, then walked on with lowered head. This had always been a bad route to take. Now after a lengthy break, the stone and masonry walls turned toward her in open, cold enmity. In the square, the rain fell on her hair, on her shoulders. Her hip hurt from carrying the basket even though it wasn't all that heavy. She could probably never get rid of it, the stockings and jackets would probably crawl right back in, and the basket would jump onto her hip again. She walked up the street. Brass moons blinked in a dark stairwell; today for the first time she touched one with her free hand. Someone had stirred up the red and blue colors in the big window so that they flashed and glowed. The stairs were so soft and beautiful that they lifted her up, step by step. But at the top Marie was not able to cross the threshold. In the half-light she wasn't even able recognize the face that belonged to the hands that were taking the goods from her in the doorway and counting out the money.

But then at the next house she was allowed to go inside as far as the table. The boy with the glasses stared at her in her black dress. Without the album his face was quite naked. In the next living room, the woman who had always been kind to her put something sweet into her basket. Outside, the streetlamps were lit now, and she could see the raindrops skipping on the puddles. She was ill and tired. The empty, wet streets twisted and stretched, tying themselves into knots around her feet. Then she heard footsteps behind her, soft, happy ones. The girl with the red cap said to her over her shoulder, "Well now, Marie." She walked along for a few steps beside her and waited. But that wasn't enough time for the words that were nailed inside her and buried. The girl would have had to have time enough to crisscross the entire town a hundred times with Marie. But she had to hurry on. Marie simply watched her narrow, erect back. Now the distance between them was like a crowbar that slowly moved the one away from the other.

Back home, Anna and young Gintler were sitting together on the sofa in the dark living room. As Marie entered quietly, their legs came down to the floor in alarm.

One morning the older boy came up the stairs, tall, strange, and lean, wearing a brown leather jacket. He had been sent from the school in the strange city to serve an apprenticeship. From time to time, he had mailed them a postcard and then, eventually, nothing. The mother had just gone down into the courtyard. Surprised to find the door ajar, he went in. His glance fell on the photograph above the sofa. He sat down at the table and looked up at it, puzzled and relieved, for he realized that, if his picture was hanging there in that spot, then his father, of whom he had been so afraid, must be dead. He took the cap off his head and shrugged. He got up, took a couple of steps. The air in the room was heavy and thick; it took away his breath, and he mentally subtracted one of the three days he had planned to stay. He began to look around. What kind of room was this? As he gazed around at it, the walls became warped; scraps of wallpaper had been torn off and pasted back on, no longer covering the triangles of mortar. The rug was frayed; cushions had burst and been sewn back up with big stitches. The heavy sofa resembled a large, half-eviscerated animal with its guts spilling out. There were just a few firm spots that still anchored the living room, a photograph, a mirror, a small golden vase. He had only to step down hard and everything would fall apart and he would be out in the open. He longed for wide streets and broad squares where people were pushing and shouting; actually he longed to get away.

Marie came out of the bedroom. Her arms dropped; her face turned dark gray. She lowered her eyelids, perhaps the eyes behind them were now glowing and bright. How could something so gray, so pale, even be a girl. Gradually they all came home. He couldn't understand why he had come. His mother hadn't been able to hold herself together either. Her body had slipped down here and her bosom there, and the corners of her mouth as well. His little brother was wearing long pants and his face was pale and gentle. A tired hand had placed itself on the smooth brown hair of the child to make sure that he would not grow any taller. Anna was beautiful and red.

They sat down around the table. He turned the blue-rimmed plate in his hard, broad hands. His mother said, "Well, tell us how things are going with you."

He said, "The way things do, Mother. Sometimes this way, sometimes that way; better than a hobnail." His mother dished out something. He hadn't been hungry, but now he was suddenly famished.

His mother said, "You came quite unexpectedly."

He said, "Yes, I had some work near here, and so I thought that I could make it home."

They ate. He scraped his plate. He thought of other towns, of his companions, of his work, of parades, gatherings, flags, clubs, hunger, and of squares dark with people. He shouldn't have come. It wasn't even a good thing that his father wasn't there anymore. He felt sorry for them all. He couldn't help them; he felt very much ashamed.

He gave the little one some money and said, "Run along and get a loaf of caraway bread and beer and half a pound of mettwurst and half a pound of chopped meat."

At that point the gathering suddenly got louder and more cheerful; a state of excitement and suspense reigned until the little one came back. There was soon a regular disarray on the set table. Scraps of paper and beer foam flew about. They flicked sausage skins at each other with their forks. The mother said, "I haven't laughed like this in a long time."

Toward evening Anna went downstairs. When she came back up, she was holding violets. She said, "I told Gintler not to come up this evening."

She prepared a bed on the sofa for her brother. He looked at her, putting her in a row with all the other girls he had looked at. Her bosom was firm and round; her skin was smooth and soft. He said, "Gintler still comes to see you?"

Anna said, "Yes."

And he said, "You're pretty much the eternal fiancée."

She turned quickly to look at him. His face was lean and impudent, but his eyes were clear. Suddenly, now that he was here after all, she felt like talking and talking into his bright, open eyes. "Sometimes we go out to eat. Sometimes on Sundays we go for an outing. And often we go with others. At first I didn't want all that, but he said, 'We can't always be sitting looking at each other like people in a train compartment. We have to go out and be among other people now and then and have fun.'"

He said, "Well, yes, Anna."

Then she put her arms across the table, laid her head on them, and moaned aloud, "Oh, oh, oh."

He was about to say something else, but decided not to. She straightened up again and passed her hands over her face. All at once she seemed transformed, quite cheerful. She whistled to herself and turned to wink at her brother as she shook out the blanket. But he was tired; he'd had enough and was glad when she left. Then he lay there alone in the thick, heavy darkness. He'd had to see them all once again. Now he didn't need to come back anymore. Now he could go away forever wherever he wanted, to be hungry and work and live and die and never, ever come back. He had to pull himself together until this one night was over and then another day and another night and half a day.

In the morning he was hanging around his mother in the kitchen.

A piece of sky was stuck in the kitchen window, along with roofs and the courtyard wall, like an old greasy picture postcard. The sour smell of an endlessly cooking dish had not dissipated from the day before and was already steaming anew in the little kettle. There was mold on the walls, but his mother polished a glass with her apron, breathed on it and turned it in the light. He wished he could catch a bit of that former look of hers that used to make him cower. Then he remembered how he had sat in the bathtub set up on two chairs. He didn't hold that against her anymore because she had shrunk and he felt sorry for her. Later he pulled small boxes out of the automat for the little one. He gave Anna money for silk stockings. He stood behind Marie and watched her as she did the mending. She bent her back and kept thinking that he wanted to speak to her. Her heart contracted, hoping that he would remember how they had pushed together against the courtyard door, just the two of them. But he had forgotten that a long time ago; other things had happened to him since then. When they were sitting at the table, he looked at them one by one with gentle, resigned pity. But he never looked at her, and if, by accident, his eyes fell on her, then they were hard with scorn. She didn't know why he looked at her that way. She lowered her eyes, pressed her chin to her chest, and shrank into herself in shame. For it seemed to her that he was right.

From time to time, he sent the little one down for more beer and sausage. He told them some things he had heard and made the mother laugh. But with such diversions the day moved forward only slowly, stretching out thin and endless like rubber. In the afternoon time passed even more slowly and seemed to stand quite still. While the others laughed and talked, he was afraid that it would not keep going and he would remain trapped in this sleepy living-room hour. After supper the darkness turned sour, as if stagnant. He soon got up again and went downstairs. He hurried along the streets slapping the pavement with loud, audacious steps. He was looking for a street on the other side of the Heumarkt. He found a girl so thin that he felt stung and itchy. She said, "It's easy to see that you're not from around here."

He was pleased and said, "You're on the wrong track there. I'm from here, but I haven't been back for a long time, and tomorrow I'm leaving for good." He looked around and saw that all the colors that had been glaring and gay before were now becoming dim and running together because another day was dawning. He was very glad.

He went back to the house early and went to bed. During the morning he found all sorts of things to do. He hammered in a few nails, glued back the wallpaper. He left them all the money he had with him and promised to send more once he got a job.

When he left that afternoon, Marie went to town, too. She walked alongside him. In the old days he sometimes thought about his little brother and also about Anna. But he'd always forgotten Marie. And he forgot her now, too, on this route, every moment, from one step to another. He was surprised that she was still walking alongside him. He felt like saying something that would startle and frighten her, something nasty, saying it to her, directly, not mincing words. He said, "If things go on this way, you won't last much longer. You don't have a lot of resources." Marie pressed her elbows close to her body. He went on, "The sort of work you're doing, you won't be doing that much longer. Just look at you!" Marie said nothing. He continued, "It won't go on much longer. You'll be dead soon."

Marie said softly, "Yes."

They came to the train station. From the bridge, Marie had sometimes looked down at the tracks, firm lines on the ground. She hadn't thought any more about it. Now she thought you passed through this building to get to the tracks in order to ride off. Once he had his ticket, her brother became quite cheerful. They went out on the platform. Her hair fluttered. She quickly looked to the right and the left and then down at the ground. Something moved out of her and away along the tracks and disappeared. Her brother stepped from one foot to the other. She pressed her lips tightly together. Something in her throat begged her brother to take her along and not to leave her behind. After all, he was the sort of brother who did everything you asked of him. Then the train pulled in. Her brother turned around, saw her again, still standing next to him, took her hand and let it go, and jumped on. She lifted up her basket and watched the train leave.

The rails blurred a little, jerked chaotically into strange, tangled lines, then straightened out again, solid and fixed.

Anna and her mother started cleaning in preparation for Easter. Her mother poked around here and there but had to sit down every few moments. That evening she said, "It's already so hot, and I feel so weak in my belly, and you have to do everything by yourself. We'll do the rest of it toward Pentecost."

On Sunday Anna brought them a huge Easter egg that Gintler had given her. Other friends had given her a lot of smaller eggs. Her little brother quickly nibbled two, three of the eggs. The sweetness made the inside of his mouth pucker. Then he lost interest and just licked at it sadly. In the afternoon, they all went down along the river. The mother thought of the father. He could have been walking beside her. As always she led his children up and down among the plane trees. They met many other people. They also met Old Matthews with his wife and daughters. The bells chimed; their clappers swirled up clouds of golden summer dust around their foreheads. Mountains, clouds, and a river had been painted on a blue wall next to them.

After Easter, Marie's basket was light because people didn't need woolen things in the summer.

In the evening, just before the stores closed, the mother went quickly to get some wilted greens and a bag of mushy berries. It was cool in the store. The vegetable lady offered her a chair. A tall, stout woman from next door talked in a hoarse voice about the mishaps of the day. A young peasant thing sat on a basket and told about her betrothed. A young woman came in, panting, carrying a little child in her arms. She told about her husband who'd had an accident, about her mother-in-law with whom her child stayed during the day, and about her job. Their faces were red with vexation at their bad luck, and their voices turned hoarse when they told about the mishaps that had befallen them and were consuming them like the plague. The mother opened her mouth from time to time to say something about the illness of her dead husband. But the others talked louder and faster, and she would fall silent again. Yet probably none of them was as afraid as she was that the light would go on in the back room and the vegetable lady's husband would call out "Enough now." Then the shutters were closed. The women went reluctantly out into the street, grumbling softly. They went on talking outside the shop door, face-to-face, clustered together as if they, each one of them, were afraid to be snatched away from the group, each one having to go up her own stairway, each one into her own room.

The mother was the only one who immediately left the store and went home. She straightened up, tore herself away, and walked alone up the street. The women watched her, squinting.

Marie rang a second time, then finally she heard steps coming along the hallway and a voice said through a crack in the door, "They've gone away for the summer and will be back in the winter." Marie took up her basket and turned to go downstairs again. The enormously large stairwell was filled with a fine dust, like cobwebs, behind which glowed an unfathomable wilderness of colors. Marie stepped close to the banister made of polished brown oak and, holding on to it, looked up. With her eyes she followed the winding balustrade beset with bright little brass balls, up and up, until she got dizzy. No matter what was up there, she'd never get that far. Even climbing this first flight of stairs, from which her heart was still pounding, had been futile. She went down. The steps started swimming; the brass rods moved forward and back. She felt so dizzy that she had to sit on a step. Red, green, and blue fluttered from the window into her lap and onto the back of her neck. Until winter. She would never see this window again. She would never again set foot on a train platform. She would never again see pictures in the movies of a ravine, of a forest, or of a rider. She began to cry, but not having had much prac-tice in crying, her tears were hard and painful. So she got up again and walked down to the window on the next landing; supporting herself, she tried to look out through the one colorless pane that was set in among the colored ones. She hesitated, then pulled herself together to make one mighty wish: Would that on the other side of the windowpane there'd be something completely different, something totally unexpected. She put her face up to it. Down below, among the adjoining houses, was a courtyard in which a lamp just went on. An unhitched cart stood under it. One worker was waiting for his companion, who was flailing about to find the other arm of his jacket. Marie waited until he had put his jacket on, then she took her basket and went down to the street.

The metalworker had rented the bedroom leading to the small room for his brother-in-law from out of town, who was supposed to come and help out in the enlarged metalworking shop. The three women dragged the beds from one room to the other. The frayed, raw-red bedding billowed out into the living room. The massive beds now stood there, wide and clumsy, squashing the pictures, rugs, and small cupboards. The little boy pressed himself silently against the wall, but he bumped into the shelf, and the golden vase rolled off and under the sofa. He bent down, but hit something and started to cry. Nobody paid any attention to him because they were all upset, looking around this room in which the furniture had gotten the upper hand, turning voracious and aggressive like animals in a cage.

Hot, reddish-gold streams of sunlight came through the windows, were reflected in the polished wood surfaces, and ran along edges and picture frames. The women stopped and stood quite rigid for a few minutes. Suddenly the mother winced, something old within her had straightened up, and she quickly straightened her back and cast a steady look around her. Her eyes became darker and drier. Speaking calmly, she asked them to do this and that. She compressed her lips and tried once more to push the cupboard against the door and the sofa to the other wall and the beds under the window. She didn't stop until everything had found its place. Toward evening, a new living room had come into being in one corner of the room where they could sit around the table under the lamp. This was where the mother now set the table.

They frequently had to sweep up after the metalworker, who always ran quickly through their living room instead of going through the kitchen. And sometimes he would leave a pair of pliers or a box, as if he couldn't get used to where one room began and the other ended.

The boy became as still and flat as a fallen leaf.

Anna dressed herself behind the closet door and went quietly downstairs.

Marie often lay on the bench as if that way she used up less space than standing or walking. She put her hands around her drawn-up knees. She didn't know that darkness could sway too. She waited for night to fall. But the darkness, which itself was an immovable block, swayed, as if it also were being thrown back and forth in a sea of darkness.

There was shouting and a bit of music coming from the street. Laughter came from the stairway, sounding like bright glass splintering on the floor. Anna took her shoes off outside the door and came in. Marie got up. They didn't recognize each other in the dark. They stared at each other with wide-open eyes like two blind people. In the morning the mother said sadly, "What was all that, Anna?"

Anna said softly, "Well, I can't bring him up here anymore, after all."

Once a postcard came from the older boy, with a picture of a memorial. Anna took the postcard with her and showed it to Gintler. The mother put her arm around the little one and explained the postcard to him like a picture book.

Then Marie took the postcard and pulled it back and forth between her teeth. There had been a picture hanging in school on which an angel with large, black, feathered wings was leading a child. There were angels who found children in wild forests and deserted gorges and brought them back home. But angels who came at night and took children from their rooms, took them away from their families and led them along the thin, shiny rails to totally different places, to totally strange towns—angels like that didn't exist.

Nor was there any help.

There was nothing. There was nothing except this one single strength within herself, and this, too, by itself was useless. Marie bit into the postcard and spat out the scraps.

She tried to get up. She sat down at the table. She put her clasped hands into the bright circle of lamplight. Her little brother was etching thin, fine letters like embroidery into his notebook. She thought of the boy with the glasses; he would be looking at an album just now. There, they were passing a similar evening, also with a table and a lamp and a boy who wasn't her brother.

Anna said in alarm, "Oh, you're sick, Marie." She held her mirror out to her. Marie took a quick look at something that was strange, dark gray. She turned her head aside. She wanted to lie down again on her bench. But they took her by the shoulders and put her in one of the beds instead.

The mother and the boy put on their good clothes and went into town. The mother was looking straight ahead with a fixed expression as if she were clearing the way for herself and her child through this morning town, in between these people all moving back and forth, to the place where she was heading. Her face was redder than usual. She went to Matthews's house, asked for him, and was allowed to go in. They had to wait a little. The walls were light and faded, but a strong smell of summer came through the window from Matthews's garden. The boy raised his eyes and was startled to see white and blue piles of letters and papers on Matthews's desk. His gaze was caught by something glittering brightly. Just then Matthews came into the room. He extended his hand to the woman and stroked the boy's hair. The mother wanted to ask for advice for her son who was supposed to start an apprenticeship at Easter. Old Matthews tipped up the boy's chin and smiled a little. The boy looked at him gravely with his white, wet-with-fear face. Then Old Matthews said, "It's hard, but I'll see what I can do."

The boy looked straight ahead at the man's broad vest with the horn buttons climbing up it and a heavy watch chain crossing it. His mother was speaking quietly to Matthews, but Matthews said, "Yes, but you'll be coming again; it's still a long time till then." The boy stared at the desk; the brightly glittering thing in which the sun got caught might be a letter scale.

They walked back down the same street on which they had come. His mother was silent, twisting and turning around in her mind the few words Old Matthews had said. The little one stumbled. Two lads, snotty, scruffy fellows, who were riding on the shaft of a wagon, stopped rocking, pointed at him, and laughed.

The little one turned red with shame. The narrow street stretched out as if it were being rolled off a spindle. All the houses had windows from which looks dripped down on them. On an ordinary morning, he had to walk alone through town, dressed in long black pants, as a punishment for something. He stayed close to his mother and tried to get a look at her face. But his mother had turned Old Matthews's words back and forth so much that the inside of her head was all worn out. So she gave it up and let it go. At that moment her face was unsure, not something you could hold on to.

The little one was glad to be back home. He felt like tapping on everything, the chair backs, the doilies and antimacassars, his sister's hands. He brought Marie's plate to her bed and tapped her braid which was as hard as braided rope. Marie didn't know what she could do to please him; she said, "You eat it. I can't."

Then there was a great deal of noise all around because the metal-worker's betrothed had finally arrived, along with a whole bunch of her relatives. They didn't bother to take the detour through the kitchen and walked repeatedly diagonally through the room between the table and beds. The door burst open and a great deal of laughter came spluttering, choking, and exploding out of it. Once a girl with big violet earrings, who might have been the bride herself, stuck her head in and yelled, "Come join us, the more the merrier."

A phonograph was playing. Anna moved her feet under the table; bright dots hopped around on her face and disappeared again, leaving it bare and tired. The little one pressed his thumbs into his ears. But then they thought up something new in the adjacent room: Now there was stamping and clapping. The whole room vibrated and shook as if it were on wheels.

A week later Marie got up, packed the things into the basket, and carried it into town. The light was coming to an end in golden threads along the eaves of the houses. It smelled of autumn in the open square. Everyone had probably gone home already; it was as quiet as if time were broken.

Marie was freezing. She wondered if she had turned onto the wrong street. She had never before passed this recessed gateway from which came the sweet smell of wine. Never before had there been whistling above her head from one window to another. But then this certainly was the same old living room where the evening meal, a little late, was just being removed. The boy was drinking hot milk from a blue-rimmed cup, like the cups and plates back home, and took his glasses off because they were steaming up. The woman offered Marie a chair; she sat down quickly, overcome by weariness. The woman looked at her, a bit puzzled.

In the next room the woman brought out a bowl of apples. She coaxed Marie until she took one of the apples, which felt as smooth and cool as brass balls.

It was night outside. Her hair had fluttered on the train platform, too. The moon stood above the roofs as shiny and round as a balloon that had escaped from a child's hands. The open square gleamed at the end of the street. It expanded and pushed back the houses with their many little lights that, if you kept looking at them steadily, went out one by one. Only a few streetlamps still circled around like will-o'-the-wisps over a swamp. Marie leaned against a wall. But the wall pushed and pressed against her back, trying to shake her off and out into the open square. Marie dropped her basket and held on tight with both hands. The light basket rolled away from her feet.

Far away, on the other side of the open square, someone emerged from a street and walked along between the lamps. Marie recognized the girl with the red hat. She gathered all her strength and called out to her. She didn't hear her own shout, but it tore at her internally. She let go of the wall then, pressed both hands against her ribs and screamed.

The girl stopped short and stood there. She looked all around her, puzzled, for the square was empty. Then she shrugged and walked quickly on, because she couldn't see Marie, who was lying stretched out on the pavement.

1927–1928

THE LORD'S PRAYER

IT HAPPENED the first week of April, on a Thursday, I think. Our street had been closed off early in the morning and systematically searched. Then, toward evening, they loaded us into trucks, three of them, and took us away under strict guard. Gerber, Jussitzka, Adolf, and Franz—all from my cell—were in my truck, and also the Zieglers from the neighboring cell, I think. There were many people I knew on the other two trucks as well. We were driven to the SA barracks. The SA personnel were waiting outside the entrance, along with many people from the neighborhood who had gathered there. We were unloaded very slowly, one by one, while the people screamed and hurled threats at us. In the crowd I recognized Blaugräber who'd been our shoemaker for six years and the fat Engel woman, the grocer's wife. We passed through a veritable gauntlet of blows, kicks, spit, and punches.

We all spent the night in the courtyard behind the barracks; on the right side were the rear walls of the houses on Gerbergasse, on the left, the low wall of Victoria School. As yet there was only a little foliage on the trees, and no one was in the school garden because the Easter vacations had been extended.

Early the next morning, the SA troop leader came into the court-yard with at least a dozen others. He had a short subaltern always at his side, and whenever he yelled something, the short fat fellow stamped his foot and yelled the same thing. The troop leader bellowed "Line up!" and the short, fat one stamped his foot and bellowed "Line up!" Then most of our group was led back into the barracks while the smaller remnant remained in the courtyard. Barely a dozen.

I was among those left in the courtyard, along with Jussitzka, the cashier from the Freidenker,* and Adolf and Franz from our cell. I knew the others, too. We all knew one another. Our names were read off a list that must have been drawn up during the night from our official documents. So those of us in the courtyard were not there by chance. The SA troop leader shouted, "Line up in rows of four!" The short fat one stamped on the pavement and shouted, "Line up! Line up!"

We became a square composed of four rows of four each. Guards were posted at the four corners of the courtyard. The SA troop leader went to stand in the very center of the courtyard. He bellowed, "Hands up!" The short fat one also bellowed, "Hands up!" We swung our arms up, our shoulders were rusted stiff. As I was swinging my arms up, I felt Paul Gerber's hand, who was standing next to me. I felt his hand in the air.

The troop leader shouted, "No, fold your hands!" The short fat one shouted, "Fold your hands! Fold your hands!" The troop leader shouted, "First, you are going to learn how to pray!" The short one kept stamping on the pavement: "Learn how to pray! Learn how to pray!"

I cast a sidelong glance down my row. The bald guy at the end, whom I didn't know, his hands simply snapped together over his chest. Next to him was Jussitzka. His hands twitched and twitched again over his chest, up, down. Gerber, next to me, he simply spread out his thumbs. So then I also spread my thumbs out, but let my arms hang.

The short one shouted, "Follow the orders!" Then the guards posted at the corners walked along the rows and hit all unfolded hands; my hands turned into lumps of raw flesh. Blue and red, but that was nothing compared to Paul's hands. There was shouting behind us and shouting in front of us. The troop leader called out, "Our Father, who art in heaven—!" The short one called out, "Hallowed be thy name—!" He clattered with his heel and it sounded crazy because otherwise it was quiet, except for the shouting.

*Free Thinkers.

Behind me someone growled, "Hallowed be thy name," and two others also growled. I don't know who the rascals were; they weren't in my row. The troop leader called out, "Thy Kingdom come, Thy will be done!" The short one hacked around on the pavement: "On earth as it is in heaven!" Suddenly, from behind me, Alfred, the little fat cashier, is singing; I recognize his voice; he has cashed my dues some fifty times; so, little fat Alfred, he's really gripped so profoundly that he simply sings out: "Awake you damned / Arise you starvelings from your slumbers!" Suddenly there is a deathly silence, a silence like a bulwark surrounding the song. We pull ourselves together and move our jaws; we have so little saliva in our mouths that it's hard to sing. The stillness explodes. I hear a blow behind me and then another. They are aimed at Alfred's head and Alfred's shoulders. We can feel in our backs that they're dragging him away. The guards push us close together. They've drawn their pistols, the short one shouts again, "Fold your hands!" Gerber actually raises his clumps of flesh. My hands twitch. I can't help it. They're doing it against my will. My wretched hands. I look sideways at the bald man. His hands are folded so terribly hard, I mean, I can hear his knuckles crack. Jussitzka, he doesn't have such miserable hands; his hands obey him; they stay down. The short one keeps shouting: "In heaven and on earth!" Then there's a whistling. The bald one doubles up, of all of us there, it was his ear that was hit; he wants to hold on to his torn ear and at the same time keep his hands folded. So he doubles over praying without a break: ". . . and on earth, and on earth!"

The troop leader prays crazily as if they had already put a bowl on the table: "And give us this day our daily bread!" The little one shouts, "Give us this day, give us this day!" In the row in front of me they were actually crawling: "Give us today, give us today!" Behind me the guards kept beating someone; I don't know whom; they kept pushing us closer and closer together, hitting us on our hands. By now we formed a very small square. "Lead us not into temptation," the troop leader called out, "but deliver us from evil," the little one stomped around on the pavement. The guard reached over me and struck Jussitzka a blow on his chest where his hands were supposed to be.

Jussitzka fell against me. We all fell together in a jumble. They beat Jussitzka into another corner. In that corner Alfred actually started to sing again: "Awake!" But he got no further than "this earth!" They stepped on his mouth; that's how his face looked afterward. The troop leader prayed: "Forgive us our trespasses," and the short one rattled along, "As we forgive those who trespass against us!" In front of me—I think it must have been Paul—someone laughed aloud. You cannot possibly imagine what that sounded like. I saw the troop leader's arm flying; he hit him in the face, it was quite something; Paul fell backward on us. We became completely disarranged. "Amen! Amen!" called the troop leader and the short one also called out, "Amen! Amen!" Then they struck us and beat us until we were all lying on the pavement, and even then it wasn't enough for them. They kept kicking us. Little Alfred still sang out from time to time, but toward the end nothing came out of his mouth except blood. Maybe he thought that he could nonetheless be heard who knows how far away.

1933

THE SQUARE

AFTER her father's arrest, Marie was immediately sent off to live in the country.

Months later when the child, holding her mother's hand, stepped into the redecorated apartment, her eyes at once fell on the square. They had changed everything: The scratched and worn floorboards were freshly oiled; the armoire that had been smashed open and rummaged through back then was refurbished, and there were now porcelain dishes behind its shiny glass panes instead of books; where her father's bed had stood, there was now grandmother's bureau; and they had set the grandfather clock on the spot where her father had stood at the end.

The place had been turned into a cozy new apartment, but they hadn't been able to wipe away the square. They had ripped the picture off the wall and stuffed it into the stove, but they had forgotten the small dark square left on the faded wallpaper where Thälmann's picture used to hang.*

Looking at the spot, Marie instantly remembered the picture that had hung there. And she understood why everything had been changed. She realized that they wanted to fool her, to trick her. She looked around and seeing her mother's old, dyed dress, she knew that her father was dead; she also thought about how he had died. She realized that her mother was a coward and wanted to deceive her child and

*Ernst Thälmann was the leader of the Communist Party of Germany during much of the Weimar Republic. He was arrested by the Gestapo in 1933 and shot in Buchenwald in 1944.

that it would be useless to ask any questions. In order to hide her face, Marie bent down to smell the cake and went to stand next to the grandfather clock, and even though it tasted like sand, she swallowed more cake and more cake, just so she wouldn't have to talk.

Her mother was glad later on when Marie went to school regularly and adapted. She sang what she was supposed to sing. She embroidered and painted swastikas; at Christmas the two of them lit the candles on a little tree and for Easter they colored eggs. But no festivals and no parades, no music, and not her mother's face, nor any other human face, nothing on earth could have covered over the square that Marie saw before her every day. Had the dead man magically hung a glowing, colorful picture there, it would have been nothing compared to the square. The Lustgarten demonstration, the real May of last year, erupted out of the square into the deceptive stillness of the clean-scrubbed room. That day her father had handed her over to Albrecht, who at first had let her stand on his motorcycle, then on his shoulders. She sailed away with the flags above the heads of the crowd, she and another couple dozen children, all at the same height as the flags and the face of the speaker. His bald head shone in the sun. His fist shot from the wall at short, regular intervals, hurling the words out like stones.

Her father was dead, beaten to death, but Albrecht might still be safe and sound. Marie kept thinking that she had to meet him or find him. Sitting between the strange, indifferent faces of her mother and grandmother, she stared at the square above the neatly set table, and continued to stare at the square, the hole in the wall.

1934

THE BEST TALES OF WOYNOK, THE THIEF

And don't you, for instance, have dreams, wild ones and gentle ones, when you're sleeping between two difficult days? And do you perhaps know why, sometimes, an old fairy tale, a little song, or even just the rhythm of a song can enter our hearts effortlessly, while we have been pounding our fists bloody on them? Indeed, the song of a bird effortlessly reaches to the very core of our hearts and thereby also to the very roots of our actions.

ONE DAY the thief Gruschek, having spent the winter in the Bormosh Valley with his band of thieves, came upon the trail of Woynok, a young thief who always worked alone.

Gruschek's men had been telling stories about Woynok all winter long, even though none of them had ever seen him. Now Gruschek followed Woynok's tracks for half a day until he caught sight of him sitting in the sun on a rock at the second highest of the Prutka Falls. Woynok reached for his musket, but then he recognized Gruschek by all those signs by which one thief recognizes another. He climbed down from his rock and greeted Gruschek in the way you greet your elders. They sat on the ground facing each other and ate their bread together.

Gruschek looked closely at Woynok, who looked much younger than Gruschek had been led to expect from various reports. His eyes were as clear as if their blue transparency had never been clouded by the scum of even a single unfulfilled, unfulfillable dream. Gruschek could find nothing in those eyes except his own hairy old face and what was visible of the clouds and mountain peaks behind his shoulders.

Gruschek said, "I have forty thieves in my band. That's just the right number. Why do you always do your stealing and plundering alone?"

Woynok replied, "I want to be on my own when I steal, always. Once, in Doboroth, I joined up with a runaway soldier. The soldier had a girl. At first she chased after me; then she betrayed one of us to the other and both of us to a third. It cost me quite a bit just to get away with my life back then. No, and I don't want a girl anymore either. I want to be a solitary thief, always."

Gruschek looked at Woynok in surprise. In the course of his long life he had learned to weigh a man's words by the sheer weight of their sincerity. How else could he have kept his band of forty thieves together without any treachery or discord ever damaging its reputation? Woynok would stick to his words, not just today and tomorrow but always. Gruschek gave him another searching look. A lot of thoughts were flying through his head without a sound except for the cracking of his interlocked fingers. Woynok raised his head at the sound. Then his gaze immediately left Gruschek's face and moved to the brown tufts of oak forests in the deep mountain clefts.

Gruschek said, "If you ever need anything—food, clothes, a warm fire, or weapons—come to us. We'll be making our next winter camp in the lower Prutka between the larger and the smaller Wolf Canyons in the gap between the two Paritzka Cliffs."

They said goodbye. Woynok climbed back onto his rock, and Gruschek carefully clambered down the slope. Now it looked as if his small, knotty body had been bent not merely by age but so that it could more easily adjust to the curvatures of the mountain slopes.

Woynok forgot Gruschek as soon as he lost sight of him. He no longer thought of what Gruschek had said about his winter camp; he forgot it. He went up the Prutka Falls all the way to their origins in southeastern Prutka, where summer arrives first and most intensely. Here there were no cliffs; steep meadows touched the sky in one place and dense, almost black forests in another. Down below in the Paritzka

Valley you could see farmsteads, beehives, and two mills. At that moment, the air was so still that even high up there you could hear the whistling of the ferryman and the sounds of the mills, as well as the clanging of broken scythes and all the other metal stuff that the farmers hung in their fields to scare away wild animals.

What Woynok did that summer has been told and retold so often that it doesn't have to be repeated here: how he outsmarted the ferryman on the Paritzka River, how he snuck into the wedding of a wealthy farmer in Marjetze Upra posing as a wedding guest, and how he set fire to the Saint Ignaz Monastery...

Gradually this summer, too, cooled down. Woynok went back to the place he had come from. He could still hear the whetting of the scythes occasionally, but only when the wind was blowing from the Paritzka. When it blew from the Prutka, he heard only the rustling of the forest. After all those still, clear nights spent roaming the country, Woynok now rested, but without any desire for sleep. At first he burrowed himself up to his ears into the dry leaves that were piled at the edge of the forest, then into the leaves of the old forest itself. Soon rain began to fall, but the leaves were still warm and dry. Woynok—up to his ears in dry leaves—listened sleepily; then for a long time it was quiet again. He realized from the persistent dimness that it had begun to snow. Eventually sleep overwhelmed him.

He woke up when the tree limbs began to crack. This was no longer just an ordinary storm; it bent the tall old-forest trees apart as if they were clumps of bulrushes. This was a winter like none Woynok, young as he was, had ever experienced. There was no safety to be found, even in the deepest part of the forest. Like everything without roots, Woynok had to move on with the driving snow—even big trees were being uprooted this winter.

Woynok, constantly walking in circles, was driven toward the western Prutka, into the cliffs. His throat and ears were filling with snow, and the snow froze. He drew up his knees and made himself small and light, as if he might, like a leaf, be able to outlast the snowstorm. But wherever it tossed him, he crashed down hard. When he had a moment to catch his breath, he tore open his eyes and saw, just below him, a valley full of lights: the city of Doboroth. He was startled. But the storm grabbed him again; it had not even reached its full power yet. Woynok was now being driven back to the Paritzka and from the Paritzka back to the Prutka. On the evening of the third day, he could feel solid ground under his feet again. He was caught in a rock crevasse. Now he was faced with the choice of either flattening himself and rapidly freezing to death or continuing his flight and walking around in circles; he'd definitely had enough of the latter.

Suddenly the snow turned a reddish gold before his eyes as if in its descent it had brushed against an immense brightness, a light or a fire. Woynok knew that there was no such light in the Prutka, and that death conjured colors like this. Despite that, he crawled toward it. Then he saw a huge fire below him in the deep crevasse between the Paritzka Cliffs. It was where Gruschek had set up his winter camp, undisturbed by the driving snow and cold, in the very spot he had truthfully described to Woynok that spring.

Down in the camp they heard Woynok's voice immediately, weak though it was, perhaps because the storm was already letting up. Or perhaps Gruschek's bandits seriously expected that this man of whom they had been talking incessantly would at last materialize, or perhaps Gruschek had simply calculated the likely direction of the storm and Woynok's endurance, and had positioned men to keep watch for him, just in case... The thieves now crowded together and approached Woynok in amazement. Woynok climbed a little way down; then suddenly his strength gave out, and he sat in the snow. Gruschek at once climbed up and sat down facing him. Then he had his men carry Woynok to the camp and give him some hot *plishka* to drink. He made Woynok put on the good clothes he himself was wearing and had his men bring him some others. Then he ordered them to bring meat and the rest of the *plishka*. He had them put as much wood on the fire as they would normally have used in the course of several weeks. Woynok sat where they had put him, not moving. Behind his closed eyelids there was still the monotonous wildness of the driving snow. When he finally managed to open his eyes, the flames of the fire were higher than any he had ever seen before.

Gruschek, now that his orders had been carried out, was watching Woynok, who not only immediately closed his eyes again but covered his face with his hands. He mentally checked out his body for any damage it might have sustained. He moved his fingers and toes. Though he'd found nothing wrong so far, he continued to feel for any possible injury. When he finally opened his eyes again, Gruschek's face was almost a palm's width closer to his, blocking the glare from the campfire. Gruschek had his shaggy little dog clamped between his knees. It was getting restless because the bandits were beginning their celebrations. The continual mournful tones of an accordion drowned out all other camp noise. Suddenly Gruschek let the little dog hop down, put his hands on his hips, and started swaying back and forth with his upper body. The sight shocked Woynok, and he lowered his eyes in embarrassment. Gruschek let out a cry as if he had been stabbed, jumped up into the air, and then snapped back down onto his knees. The bandits yelled and applauded. Gruschek kept jumping up and down as if his age were a deception, his white hair a lie, and cheating were his chieftain's distinction. The bandits were beside themselves with joy because here was Gruschek performing this deception in their midst. The little dog was just as wild. It stared at its transformed master with teeth bared, fur standing on end. They were all bellowing loud enough to be heard in Doboroth, and the people there trembled and thought: They're that close! But the snowstorm and the wolves were their protectors.

I want to get out of here, Woynok thought in despair, but why leave now? After all, I haven't fallen into the hands of soldiers, I'm among thieves. I want to get away while I still have a chance. But why should I leave? After all, this isn't Doboroth; it's Gruschek's camp.

The thieves were shouting, tossing back their heads, and stomping on the ground. Suddenly Gruschek collapsed as if someone had cut through his springs. He looked even older now than he had before. The little dog pressed happily against his knee. The thieves eased off too. And was it the same wretched accordion that now soothed everything, putting to sleep all those it had stirred up? Soon it seemed to Woynok that he was the only one by the fire who was still awake. Here was his chance to steal away unnoticed.

Once there was a girl who lived with her mother in the black forest of Doboroth. Every night when the light went on, the wolf came right up under the window...

Why not listen to their songs? Woynok thought. After all, they're robber songs. Why not lie by their fire? After all, it's the fire of a band of thieves. Why not rejoice with them? After all, these are the joys of thieves.

The mother said to the girl, "Take the hunter—for he has a shotgun; take the merchant—for he has a box of apples, shoelaces, and pictures of saints; take the charcoal burner—for he has a hut. But you must never take the wolf."

When the year was out, who should be sitting outside the church door in Revesh? The girl. —And what did she have tied into her red-and-green-checked kerchief?

The priest said to the girl, "All kinds of children can be baptized, but wolf children cannot be baptized."

Then the girl wept and went back into the black forest of Doboroth.

The thieves laughed, but Woynok didn't feel like laughing. He wasn't sorry for the girls from the villages, he wouldn't mourn for them in the future, he didn't need them, and he wouldn't need them. But he did feel sorry for this girl. She was fair and pale, she moved with small steps and downcast eyes; she was tan and cheeky and had flapping braids. She was whatever you wanted her to be and yet she wasn't there at all—wasn't that something to be sad about?

Now the thieves really got going. The sound of their songs was as clear and pure as the sound of the organ of Saint Ignaz on that Pentecostal morning when Woynok mixed in among the churchgoers for

the first time, in order to scout out everything before he set the fire.
He had never coveted anything that one couldn't steal, either by force
or by guile, disguised as a pilgrim, or with a foot jammed in the door
and the help of a shotgun barrel. He had never known a sorrow that
one couldn't cut or burn out of one's flesh, or simply shake off like
lice. But now, for minutes at a time here, around the fire, there were
joys that could not be stolen and sorrows that could not be burned
away, for they didn't even exist. Woynok held himself erect to conceal
his unhappiness from Gruschek's steady gaze. How could Gruschek
know that the same campfire that made them all so happy—following
some hidden law concealed even from him—made Woynok sad?
Gruschek thought, and later too, that Woynok was doubled over
because he had finally been overwhelmed by sleep.

Then, unexpectedly, Woynok straightened up and said, "I'm going
to leave now."

Gruschek hid his disappointment. He presented Woynok with all
the fur and leather clothes he had loaned him on his arrival. He had
the men roast a few pieces of meat for him and gave him all sorts of
other things that could in some way prove useful. Woynok thanked
Gruschek and said goodbye. Just as on his arrival, the thieves crowded
together and gazed after him in astonishment as he distanced himself
from the camp and climbed out of the gorge and into the deadly soli-
tude of the Prutka, which had in the meantime turned silent and icy.

No sooner had Woynok left the crevasse between the Paritzka Cliffs
behind him, than he forgot what he had just experienced. He no
longer thought about Gruschek and his winter camp; he forgot him.

They say that after leaving Gruschek, he had followed the western
wall of the shorter Paritzka Cliff somewhat too long. They say that's
why this happened to him: The cliff walls all around him were suddenly studded with yellow eyes; it seems he had ended up in the
upper Wolf Canyon. Woynok knew about the wolves and that, unlike
bears and lynx, they couldn't swallow things whole, that they had to
tear everything to pieces first. That despite their terrible greed, they

can't devour anything immediately or in one piece. Woynok threw the various items he was wearing to them, one by one, all the good things made of fur and leather, item by item, and was thus able to keep them at bay while he made his way out of the canyon.

The winter was long and hard, but Woynok found the second half somewhat less difficult. He spent the time of snowmelt in the forest of Marjakoy; then he moved on to the upper Kirushka Falls. In the autumn and spring you can hear the thundering of the falls as far away as Revesh. The soft golden mist of their waters not only fills the entire Kirushka Valley but vaporizes into the summertime above the Prutka Mountains. Woynok followed along the ridge of the mountains, with the Kirushka Valley at his back. There were still some scattered settlements close enough for him to be able to hear the sound of timber being cut from time to time. But soon he could see nothing but forests below him, forests so dense and impenetrable that the crowns of the trees formed one single green plain on which the clouds cast their shadows. When the days were hazy, the forests melted into sky. Sometimes, when it was very clear, Woynok could see, between the sky and the timberline, a narrow jagged mountain ridge that he didn't recognize at all. That spring Woynok had not undertaken anything, in order to save his strength for something new: He was going to make his way through these impenetrable forests to this new mountain ridge where there would surely be monasteries, villages, bridges, and mills.

One night Woynok awoke in his treetop. He had no idea what could have awakened him. He crawled into another crotch formed by the tree limbs and went back to sleep, but he was immediately awakened again. Far below him something was scratching at the trunk of the tree and whimpering. Woynok wrapped his arms and legs more firmly around the tree limb. He knew of no animal in these forests that would whimper so piteously. And so he leaned down again. The tiny, bristly animal he saw was of no significance at all, if something so pathetic even existed. And yet even if it was just a dream, it was pitiful and irksome. Woynok went back to sleep; he dreamed Gruschek's little dog was running around the tree so quickly that its eyes created bright circles. Suddenly it made off and was gone. Now Woynok could get back to sleep properly. Then it was already back again, sliding on its belly and forefeet and growling. It attacked the tree, leaping at it. This made the thief laugh in his sleep. Woynok had barely become aware that its obsessive leaps weren't slackening but reaching higher each time when he felt the teeth of Gruschek's little dog nipping at his feet.

Now Woynok was fully awake; he climbed down. Gruschek's little dog had brought him a message tied to its collar: Gruschek was camped with his people on the other side of the forest of Marjakoy in one of the canyon-like secondary valleys of the Kirushka Valley. Soldiers from Marjakoy, Revesh, and Doboroth occupied the exit to the valley. So Gruschek and his band would be done for unless Woynok came to their aid, just as Woynok would have been done for that winter if Gruschek had not helped him.

Woynok chased the dog away with a handful of acorns. He climbed back up to the tree crotch where he'd been before. Why had Gruschek sent him this message? What use was it to him, Woynok, to learn that Gruschek was going to die? Gruschek had never interfered with him in any of his quite different undertakings, so Woynok now felt neither satisfaction nor relief. Gruschek was going to perish, just as he, Woynok, had often enough come close to perishing or might even do so tomorrow. It just seemed strange to him that Gruschek should take this opportunity to remind him of his stay in their winter camp. The wolves on the other side of the Paritzka Cliffs could have reminded him just as well that he had left their gorge in time.

Woynok hoped day would dawn soon, a day not too damp and not too misty, so that he would be able to see the jagged mountain ridge, still unknown to him, on the other side of the forests. On this day that was about to begin in just one minute, he wanted not only to leave behind the mountain slope but to push on a bit farther into the forests. But he already had an inkling that once it was daylight, he would be following Gruschek's little dog in the opposite direction, rather than proceeding with his own plan.

They say that Woynok freed Gruschek's band by tying a burning fuse to the little dog's tail. The soldiers, so they say, told the people in Revesh, Doboroth, and Marjakoy that a whole swarm of little fiery-tailed devils had come flying in to help the thieves. Later many stories and songs recounted all this at length and in great detail. What is more important to us, though, is the face-to-face conversation Gruschek had with Woynok the evening of that same day as they were sitting on the ground a little apart from the others.

Gruschek said, "There isn't another band of thieves in all the world like mine—and there's nothing they can't do." He broke off as if to indicate that it was now Woynok's turn to say something. But Woynok just sat there facing Gruschek, without moving. To Gruschek, Woynok's eyes still seemed clear and transparent. And again he saw nothing in them but his own face. So Gruschek continued, "Those soldiers will no doubt come back with reinforcements. I'm old. That's the problem. Wouldn't you like to lead the band in my place?"

Woynok said, "No."

Gruschek showed no disappointment. He ordered his men to treat Woynok as a guest. This time Woynok felt no need to hide his face. Perhaps because they had made only a moderate summer fire, perhaps because none of it surprised him anymore—he continued to sit there upright, not moving, subjected to Gruschek's constant observation. Nor did he lie down until Gruschek, groaning, stretched out next to him. For a while, the celebrating got louder, then it suddenly died down along with the fire, except for the *i-i-i* tones of the accordion and the smoldering embers that were always saved for the following evening. Woynok thought that Gruschek had been asleep for quite a while. Gruschek, however, didn't think this about Woynok. Gruschek understood people well enough to know that you don't always have to give gifts to get something in return. You don't need to kidnap the most beautiful daughter of the big farmer from Marjetze Upra; you don't need to have Gypsy girls come over from Doboroth; you don't even need to make any promises; and threats are quite superfluous, too. The plaintive notes of an accordion can give the heart a final push when everything else has already been done before. Suddenly Gruschek said, "Woynok, if I myself ask you to do it, would you at least lead us out of the Kirushka Valley?"

To hide his surprise at finding that Gruschek was still awake, Woynok waited a moment before answering. Then he said, "I'll lead you up above the Kirushka Falls toward Preth."

Even as Woynok was guiding Gruschek's band, he followed the old leader's instructions without any deviations and without obsequiousness. It was as if Gruschek's band were at last giving him the opportunity to actualize his own plans. On their way through the Kirushka, above the waterfalls, he and Gruschek's thieves raided a wealthy village where they were just celebrating Saint Stephen's Day. The thieves easily overwhelmed the drunken farmers. In the evening of the same day, they also attacked the Saint Stephen Monastery in the mountains just as the monks were ringing the bells in honor of their patron saint. They burned the monastery down to the rock on which it was built. That night, the monks moved to the other side of the mountain above Revesh, and even before the sun came up, they had founded there on top of the shrine a new Saint Stephen Monastery with the spearhead their abbot had salvaged.

The news that Woynok had joined Gruschek's band spread through all the villages from Preth to Doboroth. The eyes of the peasants' children turned glassy at night when they heard or thought they heard the thieves yelling at a burned-down farmstead someplace in the mountains.

Once the rainy season started, Woynok led the band deep into the western Kirushka forests. How the rain used to patter in the past when Woynok would curl up among the fallen leaves, the only human being alive in the forest between Revesh and Doboroth! But what sort of rainfall was this now, if the songs of a few thieves and old Gruschek's moans were enough to drown out its sound?

One evening Woynok caught sight of a few snowflakes in the air. They instantly became transparent and disintegrated. Woynok looked about him as if now all their faces would become transparent and disintegrate too. He came to Gruschek's face, which as always was turned toward him with an intense stare that was not diminished by any false trust. For the first time that evening, Gruschek saw that Woynok's eyes were no longer clear but, like all their eyes, were dulled by unfulfilled or unfulfillable desires. Gruschek would have liked to know what these desires were. At that moment, however, Woynok had only one worry. He was wondering what precautions Gruschek had taken so far to protect himself and his band from him, Woynok.

Once the winter was over—and it was over while Woynok was still intently waiting for it to begin—the band of thieves, at Gruschek's suggestion, which coincided with Woynok's wishes, moved back to the steep slope on the east side of the Kirushka. They set up camp at the place Woynok had chosen the previous year when Gruschek's little dog had found him. The camp clung to the outermost edge of the mountains like a bird's nest.

It was impossible for a human eye to gauge the breadth of these forests, which turned darker as the summer sky turned bluer. If the jagged outlines behind the forests were actually a new mountain ridge and not simply a strip of clouds, Woynok thought, then everything there must be completely different from what existed here. After night fell, once all the thieves were sleeping, he left the camp to carry out his old scheme at last. He climbed down the mountain face and tried to enter the forest proper. The smell and the darkness dulled his senses. Each of his movements seemed to be reproduced into infinity; it was as if the forest winced because of this splinter that had invaded it. Woynok climbed into a tree to check his position. He saw that he had barely put any distance between himself and the mountain slope. And the endless forest was still as infinite as the starry sky. But quite close by, just a hop and a skip away on the side of the cliff, there was the little glowing campfire.

Woynok did not venture any deeper into the forest that night but returned, instead, to Gruschek's camp. Gruschek was pleased that Woynok had them break camp the next day. The time had arrived to pursue their main ventures.

Woynok, meanwhile, had decided to destroy Gruschek's band the way you would demolish something you don't ever want to see again or think about even in your dreams.

He led the band on a zigzag route through the Kirushka and the Prutka, leaving behind scorched villages, plundered pilgrim groups, and charred farmsteads. Eventually Woynok led the band to the western Prutka, between the upper and lower Wolf Canyons, into the crevasse between the two Paritzka Cliffs—the same spot where they had camped the previous winter—to rest and sort through their booty. At this time of year, the crevasse was filled to a man's height with the warm dry leaves of the Paritzka oaks. The thieves curled up in them and slept. Woynok placed an explosive fuse in among the leaves, blocked the exit, and lit the fuse from outside the crevasse. Then he walked on and in a few hours had left the entire Prutka behind him. He thought no more of Gruschek and his band, simply put them out of his mind. He stretched out to sleep on a bluff on the other side of the Schwesternberg, from which the Kirushka Falls descend; the rainy season hadn't begun and the falls were merely a ripple and not yet thundering down in full force.

He was awakened by a whimpering. As he was about to brush off whatever was sniffing at him, he found he couldn't move his hand. Opening his eyes, he saw Gruschek's little dog. Gruschek himself was looking down at the shackled Woynok, laughing. He said, "You lived among us almost an entire year, Woynok, but you still don't understand what a band of thieves really is. You set fire to the Paritzka crevasse, but I ordered my thieves to climb out, one standing on the shoulders of the other. The lowest rungs of the ladder of course turned to coal, but in this way most of us, as you can see for yourself, managed to escape."

Gruschek then had his men carry the trussed-up Woynok alongside him back through the Prutka Mountains. While his little dog kept jumping around Woynok, whining and whimpering in a mix of plaintiveness and joy at being reunited, Gruschek continued to lecture his prisoner: "Of course the human ladder had to be built quickly. In spite of that, my old head remained clear; I figured out exactly which man I would choose to be the bottom rung, which one the middle, and which one would be the upper rung, and above all which of my men I would allow to climb up. My dear Woynok, as you know, stalwart young fellows from the Prutka and Kirushka villages have often found their way to our campfire. These fellows would beg me on their knees to let them learn the work of a thief with us. Reliable, strong fellows they were, a joy to look at. But a band can't have more than forty men—nor can it be allowed to dwindle to fewer than that. I often secretly regretted that I couldn't simply exchange one or another of my people who was worn out and expendable for one of these fellows. But I never said anything about it, of course; you should always give only clear instructions for what needs to be done—mere wishes and partially formed plans you should keep to yourself. In that, Woynok, you and I agree, of course. But then yesterday, when your explosive tore a gap in my band, I remembered those fresh, eager-for-action peasant boys, and I realized that I would be able to turn this loss in a direction where renewal had long been needed. So you see, Woynok, rather than doing us a disservice you did us a favor."

In the meantime, Gruschek and his men had reached the lower Wolf Canyon with their captive, the band having moved their camp there for the time being, for it was only after the first snowfall that the wolves occupy the canyon. Gruschek had his men untie Woynok. Then he drew a small cross on the ground and told Woynok to stand on it. Next he ordered the thieves to load their muskets and form a circle around Woynok.

The thieves hadn't thought much about Woynok the entire year he had spent in their midst. You could say they'd forgotten him. But now, after such a long time, there was again a distance between him and them—the distance between his chest and the muzzles of their muskets. He was once more the Woynok of earlier days who at most might approach their camp in the worst of winters, or whose trail one might occasionally come across or think one had. Would the thieves shoot on Gruschek's orders? But Gruschek didn't order them to shoot. Pushing his way inside the circle, he faced Woynok and said, "Go to hell, Woynok, but go! Don't ever entertain the notion, even in your wildest dreams, of crossing our path again. Don't ever let us catch sight of you again."

From the moment he awoke on Schwesternberg to find himself tied up, Woynok hadn't said a word. He said nothing now either. His eyes were clear and transparent. Silently, he left their circle, which immediately fell apart behind his back. In no time he had left Wolf Canyon. He no longer thought about Gruschek and his band; he forgot them. A couple of the thieves quickly ran over to the edge of the canyon, but all traces of Woynok were already covered by the unceasing and massive autumnal Prutka leaf drop.

From that day on, a new era began that no one could have predicted or thought possible. Such a thing would not have been possible before that time either, nor would it ever be possible again afterward. It lasted for a little more than a year. In the course of that year the world, mistakenly thought to be a small place, stretched to an infinite size; the Prutka expanded, and there was suddenly enough room for both Woynok and Gruschek. Was there anyone during that year who would have claimed one thief was superior to the other? If during that year, someone had actually given Woynok the preference, then it would not have been a judgment of Woynok but rather a reflection of the man who had expressed the judgment.

Never before had there been so much talk in the villages about Woynok and Gruschek; but after all that had happened, Gruschek forbade his own people to make mention of Woynok's name. And they understood that this was the least Gruschek could ask of them.

The band spent the next winter in a newly discovered rock crevasse behind the Schwesternberg. A charcoal burner told some lookouts

Gruschek had posted that Woynok had died not far from there, only a couple of hours away, and that it had happened just yesterday. He had suffered a miserable death. Hunters from Doboroth had come to the Prutka villages with some strange, newfangled traps. Woynok had stepped into one, and the trap had snapped shut on his foot. It wasn't until he had spent an entire night jammed into the trap and almost frozen to death that the peasants dared to come close and beat him to death with sticks. The lookouts who had been sent out and the rest of the thieves, once they heard, were dying to pass along the information. Finally, they couldn't hold back any longer and broke their silence, disobeying Gruschek's instructions about not mentioning Woynok's name. Gruschek could guess from their faces and their whispering what had happened. And then he did exactly what his thieves had hoped he would do. He sat down among them, and wringing his hands until the knuckles cracked, he lamented loudly and wept. They all wailed and cried with him in painful relief.

They sat around the freshly stoked campfire bewailing Woynok and all that they knew about him in a kind of joyful despair. They lamented his death, and the fact that such a fellow had ever existed. They wailed and moaned until they were all exhausted and fell asleep.

In the middle of the night the man assigned as lookout at the edge of the canyon called out that Woynok was coming. The fog seemed to be thickening over the face of the mountain. Woynok was approaching the camp extremely slowly. The thieves bent over the embers of their campfire. A hand that was about to toss another piece of wood on it froze in horror and a sudden chill, for a draft of icy air was coming off Woynok and streaming around the thieves' heads. Yet it seemed that Woynok himself, who was giving off this icy cold, did not feel it. He sat down on the ground beyond the circle of men around the fire. He resembled the former Woynok as much as a dead man can resemble a living one.

At that point Gruschek plucked up his courage; he greeted Woynok, and sitting down on the ground across from him, face-to-face, he addressed him: "Woynok, why aren't you keeping your promise? Why did you come back to us again?"

Woynok did not answer. The thieves were somewhat reassured when they heard Gruschek's voice; they admired their Gruschek and the way he was able to deal with all kinds of people, even with dead ones, and they felt safe. Gruschek went on, "Can't you keep your promises even now? What do you want from us here? We asked you for one small thing, but you won't even fulfill this one tiny request."

Woynok did not move.

Gruschek went on, "Even though you lived with us for only a very short time, and even though your time with us did not leave us with a good memory, we mourned you today as if you had spent your entire life inseparable from us. Woynok, listen to me. Woynok was beaten to death by the peasants on the other side of the Schwesternberg. There has never been a thief like him, and there never will be again. What is Gruschek compared to Woynok? Gruschek is old; if his hands falter tomorrow, then his band of thieves will scatter in all directions."

Gruschek put his arms on his hips and swayed with his upper body; his joints crunched.

Why have I come here? Woynok wondered. Why did I come all this dreadful distance through the mountains? I could long ago have been at rest; I could long ago have been covered with snow.

The thieves all swayed to and fro, sometimes bumping heads in the process. They felt scarcely any fear now; it was as if they understood how little a dead man can do to so many living ones. They forgot about their guest. But their laments were so generous and intense that you had to wonder how such a short life could have encompassed this much.

Woynok was much too weak to move any closer to the fire. And who was there who would have thought to drag him closer to it? The sooner the cold cracked his heart, the better, thought Woynok, the sooner his useless flesh, already ripped to the bone, would freeze. He raised his head slightly. For a moment, a life came into being above the fire, a young and seductive life, a regular thief's life, daring and happy. Woynok mourned this life that was ending so quickly with their tempestuous song and a fire burning too high, for they had thrown all the wood into it at once.

Gruschek was the first to stop talking; he had seen that their guest was gone.

The next morning the thieves discovered fresh tracks made during the night. Gruschek consoled them: He couldn't have gone far. Then, groaning, he got up; these days it was always hard for him to get up from his camp bed. It was as if the earth would like to hold on to him. But he knew what he owed his band of thieves. He set out with his best men. They soon found Woynok. He had burrowed headfirst into the snow. The men asked Gruschek, "Should we bury him at the camp?"

Gruschek said, "That would be going too far." So they simply laid Woynok out, faceup, and covered him with snow. It did not take long.

1938

MEETING AGAIN

YESTERDAY we ran into L. on the boulevard Saint-Michel. We had been walking behind him for several minutes without recognizing him, but were unsettled by the distinctive three-quarter rhythm of his limp. We had walked behind him once before. That was in the early summer of this year, in the countryside outside Madrid. Now he stopped before a shopwindow, and we recognized his face. On the left side of his forehead, just below the hairline, he had an incredible scar. He stood there, with this hole in his temple, in the middle of the colorful Parisian winter-evening throngs, like one risen from the dead, like the captain of a ship of the dead. Such people wear their own legend like a heraldic crest wherever they go. And whenever we see such people, their external appearance reminds us of this legend.

Severely wounded in one of the battles around Belchite and bleeding to death, surrounded by his friends, he had asked them not to take him straight to a doctor but to take him first to the commissar of his brigade. They gave in to his request, the way one gives in to the dying, even though it meant a half-hour detour. L. told the commissar, of whom he was very fond, that he had wanted to tell him once more that he loved the Party.

"Why do you say you loved it? You'll go on loving it." It was probably this detour that saved L.'s life.

Now, seeing us, he opened his mouth, the strong teeth. There were embraces, laughter, astonishment. "Have you ever heard of a thing like that going right through your head and you're still alive?" We heard this, like so many other things that year, for the first time.

We walked slowly up toward the Luxembourg Gardens. Any talk had fizzled out after the first joy of seeing each other again. We were all silent together about the same thing.

Back then, in early summer, the two of them were walking ahead of us, L. and his commissar, the same one to whom they had carried him, bleeding, at the time—over two hills, along a small river. A division at rest in a gully was practicing firing machine guns. In the shade of some bushes sat two groups composed of a mix of Spaniards and Poles; the focal point for each group was a book. They were learning the Spanish alphabet. A naked youth with scraggly wet hair, the youngest in the Polish Brigade, was lying under a tree. L. upbraided him as he passed because he was always swimming instead of joining the others in studying. The youth squinted after the commissar, who was probably smiling. The commissar was a tall, rawboned man with a long, angular face. He didn't turn to look at us, but we saw the glow of his face reflected on all the other faces wherever we passed, an intense, happy attentiveness.

Suddenly the commissar extended his arm, pointing at a little white corner of an envelope in one of the men's breast pockets. "Did she write at last?" The man he'd asked was as tall as the commissar, perhaps fifteen years younger. He unfolded his letter and pointed to a section that had obviously upset him considerably. L. left the two alone and came over to us. He said, "The one with the letter is a Silesian, a painter. In our group here, besides the Poles and Spaniards, there are Silesians and Jews and Ukrainians. That little Jew over there was a tailor in Lemberg and has six children. Over there, those are four miners from the Dombrowa Basin who joined up together. That one there is a Ukrainian farm boy who ran away from home; he had heard road workers talking about what was happening here. We're going to change over to giving commands in Spanish from now on. We were deployed wherever the fighting was most severe. Why is the brigade called Dombrowski? For the Pole, Dombrowski, who fought in the Commune for the workers of Paris."

We came to a group being instructed in the use of gas masks. The commissar was called away. Now the Silesian joined us too. L. went on: "Our commissar is the right man for the right men. I don't think he's ever left us, even for a minute."

The Silesian said, "Not for a minute."

L. said, "When things get tough, he knows how to get every last bit out of us. When you yourself don't think you have anything left in you, he always gets something more out of you. And he explains the most difficult thing in such a way that even the young boy over there can understand."

The Silesian said, "At night when you can't sleep and you toss and turn, you hear his voice, 'Well now, Stanek, what's bothering you?' Then Stanek talks a little about his wife or his girl, and after that, it's better again."

It occurred to me then how rarely it happens that two men are in total agreement about the reputation of a third.

Suddenly the Silesian began to speak rapidly. "Right at the start, when I joined up, I was wounded in the head. Not seriously, but I was so worried. About my eyes. I'm a painter. I'm really ashamed to admit it, but I didn't want to keep going, I was too afraid. So I go to him, to the commissar, I tell him that I would like to go home. I'm really ashamed about this, and I told him that suddenly I couldn't go on, and so forth, that I was a painter. Even back then he already liked me quite a bit. He listened to it all. Then he said, 'If you really feel like that, then go home. But wait a while. In my own case I found out just what it is, this being afraid. If you're afraid of something, whether it's death, or your eyesight, or something else, it always means that you're afraid in general. Afraid that the whole thing could come to a bad end. But if you are totally convinced that everything will turn out well, if you are, so to speak, certain of victory for the operation as a whole, then usually this partial fear disappears. A small fear that you definitely cannot overcome always means an overall fear.' So then I waited patiently some time longer. Whenever fear overwhelmed me, I said to myself, 'Come now, that's impossible, you can't be having any doubt that the whole thing won't end well. You certainly don't doubt that.'"

L., who was also hearing this story for the first time, said, "You don't think of your eyes anymore now?"

"No."

A farmer with a mule came walking through the evening countryside. Over the back of the mule hung a braided, four-sectioned saddlebag. L. said, "We often carried our wounded off the field in bags like that."

The commissar caught up with us. He still had the letter in his hand. We heard, ahead of us, a beautiful song coming from a group we could vaguely make out through some sparse bushes. When we reached them, they crowded together and sang three songs for us: a Ukrainian one, a Polish one, and a Spanish one. The man who sang most beautifully was the one who sang the first one by himself. He was a short Ukrainian with round blue eyes, and when he sang, he frowned and put his hand on his heart.

We mentioned none of this as we were going up the boulevard Saint-Michel. Then L. said, "Do you still remember the little Ukrainian who sang so beautifully? He was killed. The Silesian, too, the one who received the letter back then. Do you still remember? But our numbers are complete again. That boy who went swimming back then instead of learning Spanish isn't our youngest anymore. They brought us one who claimed he was seventeen, but I think he wasn't even sixteen yet. That boy had ridden from Poland through Europe and all the way to Paris as a stowaway between the wheels of a train. They found him unconscious at the Gare Saint-Lazare and put him into an institution. After a few days, when he had perked up somewhat, he ran away. He again rode between the wheels of a train as far as the Spanish border. He climbed over the mountains in the winter. Then suddenly, when he looked around on the other side of the border, he began to realize he was in the wrong Spain, in Franco's Spain. So he climbs back over the mountains again into France. Then he makes the trip a third time. This time they send him to us, to his family, to the Polish Brigade."

We asked, "And the commissar?"

"Always the same. When I was so seriously wounded, they said that I made my comrades take me to him. I still can't quite imagine that I won't be seeing this man so soon again. Yes, I cannot actually believe that I won't be seeing him again in a few minutes. If I really believed that I wouldn't be seeing all my people again tomorrow, I'd start crying on the spot. But even now I can't conceive of such a thing." He shakes his head. He still has the tonsure on the right side of the back of his head. He laughs. "Teruel was captured without me."

We said, "But not entirely without you. After all, you left much there."

He thought that over for a little while. Then he said joyfully, "For sure. Some part of me must have remained back there in the brigade. What a lot of things come together to form the spirit of a brigade. Certainly that clear, conspicuous posture. The determined fighting spirit, for sure. But also many details that you forget right away. Individual words that made rings like little stones do in the water." Suddenly he says, maybe out of an abrupt need not to have to talk any more, "Don't miss your train on my account. We met up again, that's the important thing. Ah, what a good feeling it gives you, meeting each other again."

We caught sight of him once more from the bus. He was making such slow progress that it seemed almost as if he were standing still in the middle of a very restless, colorful, somewhat gloomy crowd, whose focal point he was for us.

1938

TALES OF ARTEMIS

"ME? NO, never! Not even once!" the youngest one said. "I'd be willing to give my life for that!"

"There's nothing so remarkable about your feeling this way. All the things young people love to do and are ready to give up their lives for! Or half their lives, or the best part of their lives! Then afterward, once the wish has come true, they don't want to be taken at their word anymore. And the young are right. Isn't one deception worth another? But the remarkable thing about your wish, young fellow, is that even afterward, once your wish has been fulfilled, you would still think it had been worth it. Afterward you still think: Yes, that was worth it. Yes, that was something I was prepared to give up my life for. And you even feel like a miser because you don't have a second life to give."

All eyes sought out the face of the old hunter through the acrid, smoky air. A miracle that he was even speaking, and then to say what he had said. Usually you hear only about the things that excited people, never about what silenced them.

The youngest of the hunters now asked straight out, "Is it true that you really saw her once? People say you did."

They were all shocked. No one had ever dared to ask the old man about *that*. Was his question brave because it broke a silence on which a man who was never asked to answer the question might choke? Or was it merely foolish? The old hunter said nothing. He poked around in the fire—maybe he would fall silent again for several more decades.

The young hunter laid his head back and stared up into the air. If you looked up long enough, then the rising smoke made you dizzy.

You felt as if you yourself were drifting upward. The chimney seemed endless because it was so narrow and appeared to lead straight into the sky whenever a gust of wind pushed a plume of smoke off the roof. A vessel for heating water hung from a crossbar above the fire. It was perpetually swinging gently back and forth on its long chain. At short intervals, a forceful blast of wind would blow the rain against the eastern wall, and not only branches but tree limbs would bang against it and break off as if the forest were pushing the house away.

The dogs had their noses pressed against the men's knees and feet, except for the one dog who was lying with outstretched legs some distance from the fire. They were all calm; they were used to the wind. The youngest hunter's dog had his almost glowing nearly golden-yellow eyes fixed on his master's face as if, for the sake of this one human being, he had put aside his wolfishness.

The fire burned fretfully, giving off acrid smoke. The walls were almost black except for a bit of copper that gleamed on the door lock. The door itself looked as if it had come from a totally different house. Its artfully carved moldings were made of a type of wood that didn't grow in this forest. Because the smoke had only blackened the surfaces and not the grooves of the carving, a light, sketchy pattern had been created, quite different and softer than the carver could ever have intended. Had it been the innkeeper himself? Had the innkeeper, uncounted years ago, after a conflagration had destroyed the house that this door originally belonged to, dragged it into the forest on his shoulders, or had it been some other less fiery but no less drastic fateful event?

In any case, nowadays the innkeeper and his wife were churlish and gruff in their manner, wary but reliable, as if they were born for, predestined to preside over this forest pub that was frequented only by hunters and maybe, once or twice a year, a couple of strangers whom the hunters would take to the other side of the forest for a fee.

A second, narrow, almost invisible door led through the back wall out to the well, which also served as a watering place for all kinds of wild animals. A low-ceilinged little room, without a separate door, where the innkeepers slept, adjoined the main room, which was overarched by the chimney hood. The innkeeper's wife was sitting in that little room now, supervising the new servant girl. They'd had to get a girl from the next village because, unfortunately, the wife's wrists and ankles were swollen with gout. The innkeeper had walked for half a day to meet her yesterday.

The new girl wasn't talkative. And all you heard from the innkeeper's wife were sighs. Apparently, the girl gave her no reason either to scold or to praise her. The work she was doing could be done in the dark, once she had been trained while there was still some dim light. She was plucking horsehair to fill the wife's mattress.

Suddenly the old hunter said, "Yes, I saw her. Those who say I did aren't lying." He said it in the tone of one making a confession.

Ever since the young hunter had asked him, the old hunter had been struggling with himself. What it would mean to him to reveal his secret! The last remnant of his pride! You confess everything, and from one second to the next, your life becomes slight and impoverished. Under all the stubble, his face had probably turned ashen pale. He was silent, expecting a storm, but his companions were silent along with him. They had known his secret for a long time. After all, he was referred to as "the old hunter who's seen her."

A gust of air blew a handful of horsehair out of the little room; some of it fell into the fire, sizzled, and charred. The dogs became restless. The young hunter took a bunch of horsehair, twisted it in his fingers. He turned around for a moment. He couldn't see the girl; she was sitting in the dark. And so he turned his face back to the fire; he was breathing more quickly. Of all the girls he had ever imagined, the best one might be sitting there in the dark, finally close enough to touch.

Putting a fist on each of his knees, the old hunter began, "Well then, I'm going to tell you everything now. It was like this…" His four companions looked at him. The young one forgot about the girl in the room behind him. The one-eyed hunter squeezed his good eye shut. Even the handsome, brazen one sitting to the left of the old hunter, the one who always looked as if he were checking his reflection—and who actually always found the most unlikely mirrors everywhere: a shiny pot lid, the metal on his dog's collar, the blade of a knife—seemed to tear himself away from his reflection. When the old man hesitated again, the short, roguish one sitting to his right jabbed him with an elbow.

"It was an evening like today. We had left the village on a beautiful late-summer day. Fall had come suddenly, from one hour to the next. I remember still how the sky suddenly turned gray. At first it looked like an ordinary twilight, only a little too early. When we turned around, we could see the two valleys that met at a sharp angle lying below us, with all their farmsteads, villages, and beehives, in extraordinary clarity. As if we were being shown everything in detail one more time before it was to be curtained off from our eyes by a heavy downpour. You could even count the cattle grazing there. Everything seemed so close it was as if instead of having climbed for half a day, we had only climbed for half an hour."

"Yes," the little hunter next to him said, "that's how it was. I've never thought about it since. But now I remember. It was like that." Like all graying redheads, he looked as if he had started out with gray hair and then, later on, his gray hair had gotten rusty in spots.

The old hunter stared at him. "Ah, yes, you were there, too, back then." He had quite forgotten that this smart little hunter had witnessed it. All these years he had been convinced that he was the only one with this memory, that there had been no witnesses. "We had just reached the forest when it began to rain."

The little hunter nodded.

"We got a hut ready. There were eight of us, not counting the boy, of course. At first he kept running around with the hounds, which had instantly gotten used to him. I'll come back to the boy later. We immediately lit a fire. But it burned poorly because we didn't have any dry wood. We discussed the hunt. The rains had come too soon and too hard. We were put out by that. Eventually, we'd talked about everything. So we had a bit to eat.

"The boy who had come with us had been listening to everything, turning his dark, round eyes to look quickly at each man as he spoke. He was a bright, strong boy. He had badgered his father all year long for permission to go along with the hunters just once. Then the day before, his father had given in for the first time. While the boy with his shining, prominent eyes hung on my every word, I wondered what it was that fascinated him so, what it was that made him so happy, and just to tease him I asked, 'Isn't it boring for you to be here? Wouldn't you rather go home?'

"He shook his head. We had promised his father to take good care of him. Now, first of all, we gave him a lot to eat. Then this is what happened: We were all chewing slowly and had practically stopped talking. My glance fell on the boy again. He had been beaming with pleasure the whole day. But now he looked as if he were seeing something he had never imagined, not even in a dream. I still remember that it seemed a little odd, even to me. The boy was chewing, his cheeks bulging, and at the same time he was staring wide-eyed . . . I quickly turned around to see what he was staring at. And there she was, sitting behind me on a flat rock on the ground, her arms clasping her knees. She had probably been sitting there for a long time already . . ."

The little hunter said, "She was sitting diagonally behind you."

"Yes, she was sitting behind me. The way she looked . . . The way she looked would have assured her complete safety among us, even if she had been not a goddess but only an ordinary girl. A slender, delicate neck on straight shoulders; in her face, the calm of a perfect and unassailable peace of mind. No sorcery, no magic was required for her protection, no evil transformations. All the things they say about her are fairy tales thought up by people who can't ever have seen her. No human being would dream of even clasping her wrist. Such a human being doesn't exist. Anyway, she was sitting diagonally behind me. I thought that I could feel her breath.

"I didn't dare turn around a second time. She was sitting there, after all, as if she might jump up at any moment. The dogs hadn't barked on her arrival. They weren't sniffing; it was more as if they were sleepy. I was sitting there quite rigid. But I could tell from the boy's face that she was still there. I remember thinking: What a lucky fellow! All the things I had done throughout my life just to get to see her once. I often left the game I'd bagged behind in the forest. I frequently sacrificed the best pieces of meat to her, calling out her name. I crawled on my knees, I banged my head against trees, I ran till I was out of breath—and this scamp comes along with us and gets to see her his very first time. In the meantime, all the others had seen her too of course."

The little hunter said, "We weren't afraid at all. We even kept right on talking."

"It's just that she'd keep interrupting. She asked the boy, 'Do you like this?' He swallowed his last bite and said, 'Yes.' She asked, 'Is everything the way you hoped it would be?' Again he said, 'Yes.' Later, I could tell from his face that she had left. The day wasn't yet over when the disaster occurred. The disaster that was to change my entire life. It was the boy's own fault. Even though he had promised his father that he would be obedient and do what he was told, he kept doing stupid things. He didn't listen to our warnings anymore. The hunt, the nighttime forest, it all went to his head. He clambered around everywhere. We lost sight of him. He ended up in the hunting ground. It was my bullet that hit him.

"A stretcher was made from some tree limbs. The hunt was called off. A messenger was sent ahead. I was the last one to come down out of the forest, and already at the outskirts of the village, I could hear the father's unremitting cries. My blood froze, and my hair turned white on hearing his cries. I don't know how I made it through the door of his house. Probably with the help of the kicks and shoves of the neighbors on the street who had met me with curses. I dropped down before the father and offered him my sight, my right hand, my life. But when he saw me, he, the boy's father, stopped his lamentation. He raised me from the floor. He had food brought for us both. Calmly and in an ordinary tone of voice he said that what had happened was his child's destiny, and my shot had only been the means; that I wasn't much more significant in all this than the little feather that decorates an arrow rather than causes it to fly. And that I was greatly overestimating my importance with these self-recriminations and excessive demonstrations of despair.

"The people who had crowded into the doorway had fallen silent on hearing his words. Nor did they curse me later on, treating me with a kind of respect. Moreover, the father, as if it were up to him to console me, counted off on his fingers not what his child had lost but rather all the things he had been spared from experiencing. And he and I saw in each other's eyes all the unavoidable terrors of life."

The narrow side door was suddenly torn open. A gust of wind blew the smoke to the front of the room. A couple of horsehair bunches flew toward the fire. The dogs snapped at them. The innkeeper held the door open with his foot. The wind must have let up for a moment, and the smoke now slowly streamed off in thick plumes through the side door. The previous night, a couple of clattering boards had deprived the innkeeper of sleep, and he intended to nail them down before dark today. He called for his tools. The young hunter turned around, but he had missed the right moment. The servant girl had already gotten up. She was walking toward the door, around the sleeping dog, her face averted. The kerchief covering her hair was knotted under her chin; her dress was made of very coarse material that fell in heavy folds. The young hunter's gaze was fixed on her slender, naked heels as they came up out of her clumsy shoes at each step. She brought the innkeeper his tools; he closed the door. The girl went to the front of the room, her face perhaps intentionally turned away. She bent down and swept up the bunches of horsehair with both hands. Then she went back to her work.

The young hunter sat down at an angle to the center of the room. His dog sat up, bracing itself on its front legs in order to look at his face. At that point the old hunter took up his story where he had left off, and the young hunter quickly moved back to the place where he'd been sitting before so that he could watch the old man's lips. The dog settled down with his head between his front legs.

"No one said an angry word to me. Nor, for that matter, a friendly one either. People stopped talking whenever I joined a group. With time I stopped talking, too. After all, with whom could I have talked, and about what? I think some two or three years had passed, when almost by chance I returned to the place where all of us had been sitting back then. I could still remember where each one of us had sat. I had been sitting here. Diagonally behind me...You wouldn't have believed it. I didn't either. After it happened, I had stopped thinking about her. She had, so to speak, slipped from my memory just like any random girl. In a terrible way, my life had begun anew from the moment of the accident. Everything that had happened before didn't matter anymore. But now, suddenly, I remembered it all again. She herself had been sitting almost next to me on that flat rock—her arms encircling her drawn-up knees, her calm face looking straight ahead. She had been running through the woods. She had rested here for a while, then she went on running. That was all. How could it have been possible for me to forget so completely the most important thing in my life, no matter what the misfortune that caused me to forget?

"Back then, it had been an evening like today, windy, rainy. But this time when I came back to the place, it was midday. It was quiet; only the birds were chirping. Broken sunlight fell on the grass in golden flakes. Don't look at me like that. No, nothing unusual happened. She didn't come a second time. Oh, if only it were so simple. I wanted to put my face down on the rock, but I didn't. I sat in the same spot where I had been sitting back then, the first time. At that moment I felt a great joy about having seen her that one time. Most people never get to see her. I had seen her. Of course it wasn't the joy I had expected back then when I called after her, crawling around on my knees, going crazy whenever a branch snapped. The boy that evening, staring at her with his cheeks full, chewing, felt a different joy. But still, joy is joy. I asked myself whether it wouldn't have been better if I had never seen her. If she had run through the forests in a different direction. If we had left the boy down below in his village. For I understood that it wasn't for my sake that she had decided to rest by our fire. Suddenly, when it was so still all around me and also inside my head, I knew that I didn't want to change places with anyone for anything in the world." He poked around in the dirt in front of him. Then he gave a start: "But you were there too! That I could have completely forgotten that!"

The little hunter scratched his tousled, rust-flecked hair. He was a bit portly, stocky, of an uncertain age. He said, "Ah, but it wasn't the first time for me."

The old hunter spun around. "What?"

"That I saw her. It was the second time I saw her back then."

"Twice? Is that possible?"

The young hunter heard a slight sound at his back. He turned around. The servant girl had gotten up. The horsehair had all been plucked, the mattress filled and sewn up. Meanwhile, the innkeeper's wife had fallen asleep. The girl had probably been listening to them for quite a while. To the dismay of the young hunter, she walked quietly over to the fire. With each step that brought her closer, a painful suspicion arose in him—the time of mere dreams was over—he was almost glad that at least there was still that gray smoke in front of her face.

She didn't look at him. She looked at no one. Her short greeting was meant for all of them. Despite her clumsy shoes she stepped lightly and carefully in among the dogs, who paid no attention, neither growling nor sniffing at her. She leaned against the wall, her arms crossed behind her head.

The old hunter, his jaws trembling, exasperated by the interruption, and quite beside himself because of what he had just heard, gave his neighbor a hefty nudge. "Go on! What then?"

"What do you mean, 'Go on'?" The little hunter happily let his round eyes roll up and down the girl. "What of it? Well, all right.

"We were farmers, we were poor. Of course there were some who were even poorer. We had two cows, some pigs, poultry, and our fields. The village was down in the valley. We never went any higher than our fields on the slopes. We had to toil from morning till night. Of course there were holidays, too. Then there'd be dancing, music. There would be races and target shooting, maybe not as great as elsewhere. We certainly weren't as nimble; after all, we were peasants, but we were just as happy.

"Boys and girls from other villages came to our meadow, too. We didn't know all the faces by any means, and that lent a bit of wildness to such festive occasions. We offered all sorts of prizes, for we wanted to appear generous. But I rarely won; I am what I am, tough but not agile. A girl I didn't know came up to me and said I should run a race with her. She said, 'To the birch tree over there, okay?' It seemed odd to me that a girl should ask me. Maybe it was the custom in the other villages. You always look down on the customs of other villages, after all. And I thought that I'd surely be able to beat a girl. So we started running."

While he was talking, his eyes moved away from the girl's face and up toward the young hunter's face, a deadly serious face, the face of a man who had just begun to come to grips with his fate. The little hunter's round eyes sparkled with delight. He went on.

"She called to a child who happened to be nearby, a snotty-nosed kid, one of my fiancée's many siblings. I had a fiancée, you see; our families' fields adjoined; everything worked out. The child was supposed to count, one, two, three, and on three we would start running. I didn't notice anything special about the strange girl until she turned around to see whether I was following her—for she had immediately taken the lead—I, a farmer's son, saw that she was different from our girls. I don't mean to say that it occurred to me that she was beautiful. I just thought, 'What the devil, that woman can run.' I made a tremendous effort. She was already way beyond the birch tree. I was furious. I ran after her. I fell down, cursed, got up again, and ran. It was autumn. It was a field of stubble. She bent apart the hazelnut bushes that we used to mark the edges of the fields. I ran after her across the meadows, up a couple of hills. For a moment she stopped and I, totally out of breath, followed. She had torn off a switch and, laughing at me, ran into the forest. I heard branches snapping, and occasionally I caught a glimpse of her dress. And then I didn't see anything anymore. I listened, but I couldn't hear anything either. I wanted to call out to her, but I didn't even know her name. I thought, 'Well, so what.' I took a break to catch my breath. I stretched out on the grass. I already told you that folks like us, we never went into the forest. When would we, after all? It's there in front of your nose, but much the way the clouds are there in front of our noses. People like us had nothing to do with it. Now, as I was lying up there in the grass, it smelled so good; little birds were chirping; it was neither too bright nor too dark, and I thought that it really would be very good to live up there. I slept a little. I woke up late in the afternoon. 'Now they'll be looking for me down there,' I thought. I suddenly didn't feel at all like going back. My mother and my fiancée would ask me, 'Where were you? Where are you coming from?' I really detested their questions: 'Where, why, for what reason?' I wandered around a little. I came to the edge of the forest. But what I saw wasn't the right valley; it was a valley without a village, without fields, with incredibly lush grass. I wondered about that grass. I went back into the forest. It got dark. I was groping my way around. Then I heard something; there were voices, too. I walked toward them. And it was you, do you still remember? I sat down with you, do you remember that? How I enjoyed your bread, how good it tasted. You asked me whether I wanted to stay and join your group. That you just happened to be missing a fifth man. I said, 'I'd like that,' and I stayed."

The one-eyed hunter said, "So it had just occurred back then, when you first happened to find us and immediately agreed with our suggestions?" His one eye flashed. Whenever he was listening intently he closed his good eye, and then it seemed to the others as if he were looking out of the dark hole of his empty eye socket. He was a tall, strong, rawboned fellow, ragged and battered. Even though he was probably the same age as the old hunter, he looked as if he were only just past middle age, maybe because his life span was set to be longer.

They could hear the innkeeper hammering on the boards outside. The wind had let up a bit. The whole house trembled slightly but unceasingly as if the wind had thought of another way to move it from the spot.

The girl had changed her posture a little while she was listening. Her left arm now hung down. The young hunter could have accidentally touched her hand. He took hold of his dog's neck with his right hand; the animal trembled with happiness. The hunter even held his breath. A trifle would have been enough to chase away what he needed forever. Forever, that was not in doubt, whatever this forever might cost. Or maybe it was a gift. Just because she was so close, he couldn't, for the moment, see any more of her than the piece of skirt before his eyes, made of a coarse bluish material and carefully mended just at that particular spot. You didn't have to see her belt, which she had knotted, as was the custom among the girls of her village. A girl, without any doubt, but just as certainly, one who was very close to getting married. She herself didn't know it yet. But one knew, or thought one knew.

The girl didn't move. With one arm raised behind her head, her knee a bit forward, she waited for him to go on with the story. The young hunter was afraid that the silence might go on, that she might then return to her old spot. But he was also afraid to begin. He hadn't experienced any of the things the others were talking about. And he hadn't faced any of the misfortunes the others boasted of. He had no confessions to make, no secret to reveal. He began only because the girl was waiting; his tone of voice was dry, but timid.

"Back home there is a wall that encircles the entire town; it has towers. There is also a watchtower outside the town. A second wall runs from this watchtower to the town wall. The watchman can stroll along on top of this wall. He can see a lot while he is walking there. The countryside is pretty flat, sloping slightly downward on both sides of the wall. There is a river. People go fishing there. The women do their laundry there. The watchman of course has time to look closely at the women and girls. Sometimes he would call out a cheerful word to them. Those girls who hadn't already noticed the low wall with bushes growing on both sides, got quite a scare."

The young hunter was now talking passionately, as if he had forgotten the girl standing beside him—even though he was really telling the story on her account. "It's still the same today, by the way. The watchman in those days was a fairly young fellow. He wasn't married yet. Probably because every day he watched too many women doing their washing."

Just then, when he wasn't paying attention to her anymore, the girl turned her face and looked down at his hair. The dog was looking up at him with his cold, shiny, almost golden eyes.

"One windy, cold autumn day when all those who could had stayed home, there was one who had to come with her laundry basket. She must have had harsh masters. She was very young and skinny. She was afraid to dip her hands into the icy cold water. And yet she had a towering load of washing to do. I can't really tell you much about it, you know, because the watchman didn't see any of it. I'm just telling the story. This girl I was just talking about, she has nothing to do with the story itself. For she was only the girl whose place *she* was taking that day. You understand. *She* was just coming along the river. She parted one of the bushes and saw that the girl was afraid of the water. She saw the delicate girl trying three, four times to put her hands into the cold water. She called the girl over. Then she went down to the river and found a suitable rock. There she rubbed one piece of laundry after another. The little one could nibble on rose hips meanwhile."

The girl brushed the smoke away from her face with one hand. She was still looking down at the young hunter. The others saw, though he didn't, the soft shadows of her long eyelashes on her cheeks. But the young hunter, even though he was telling the story for her, was now seeing the other girl in his own story.

"One morning, the watchman was walking along the top of his wall when he saw her doing her washing. It was windy; the river was foamy. She was different from all the others he had ever seen doing laundry. He climbed down off his wall. He looked at the girl from close up as if he couldn't believe his eyes. But it didn't help. His eyes had not deceived him. And how she could wash! How quickly! How clean! And no complaints about the cold, about roughened hands. She straightened up after each piece of finished laundry. He saw her bosom, her shoulders, the long legs . . .

"Up to that moment he hadn't wanted a girl. This one he wanted on the spot. She must have thought his courtship on that first day was crazy. He consoled himself with that. He asked her every week, whenever she came. He felt that his persistence must in the end persuade her. She didn't laugh at him. Nor did she turn him down outright. She simply said she might still be too young to get married.

Too young, but the weeks were passing. In any event, her shoulders seemed to him at first glance to be getting sturdier, her bosom more ample. So he waited. Each time she came, he asked her. After all, it must be more alluring to be the wife of a watchman than to do the laundry of strangers. Each evening she turned down his courtship, not curtly or harshly but gently. And even though she turned him down each evening, still, with all her firmness, she always left him with a tiny bit of hope for the next evening.

"Eventually it wasn't his patience that was exhausted but his equanimity, I mean the outward equanimity that he had always maintained out of pride. One evening he told her that this time she had to follow him at once, had to leave the washing, right now, and not ever return to the town *or* return at best tomorrow, as his wife. On hearing this, she laughed for the first time, this girl who up to then had hardly even smiled. She said, 'Just take a look around you!'

"He did what she told him and looked around. Up to then, even when she wasn't there, he had seen only her face. Now he looked around. Autumn was long gone. And winter too, and probably spring as well. For the sequence of the seasons hadn't changed. The cuckoo-flowers were in bloom by the riverbank. And blackberry bushes were blooming along the wall. It would probably soon be autumn again. He was amazed. Then he looked toward the town. He had really been neglecting his professional watchman's duties recently. The town could have been attacked. He hadn't even noticed that the stonework had been repaired here, and there a new and higher wall had been built. One old tower was missing; two new ones had been built. A bridge had been put up across the river. He shook his head. Took a few steps onto a promontory along the riverbank to be able to see everything better. Then he looked down at the calm, clear water at his feet, a small, shiny lake between two rocks. He saw himself. His skin was wrinkled; his hair was white. He turned slowly toward her standing behind him. One could probably say that he looked at her for the second time. His first look had lasted long enough. She was as she had always been, beautiful and calm, if a bit too young, a bit too delicate to marry immediately. Then he recognized her. He fell down before her. But it was a falling down from which you don't get up again."

The hunter who was sitting next to the one-eyed hunter, the handsome, self-assured one—he was perhaps forty years old—asked with a smile, "Did he die from it?"

The young one said, "Of course."

"Still, he was old, you said. He would probably have died soon anyway."

The young hunter was about to answer him angrily. But the one-eyed hunter spoke first. He said calmly, "You can really say that about all people. Even those who throw themselves at the enemy with bared chests. You can say that they would have died at some point anyway."

"Yes, I could. Certainly."

With a start, the young hunter suddenly looked at the face of the girl. All this must have displeased her, for her face had turned red, then pale again; now mocking, then gentle. It alarmed him. Until he realized that it was only the reflection of the fire and the smoke drifting away that kept changing her face. Actually, it had remained expressionless.

The one-eyed hunter asked almost brusquely, "Naturally you never saw her?"

The handsome hunter gave a resounding laugh. "Of course not. Why should I have seen her? I don't ever want to see her. It's all madness. Exaggeration. Luckily there are beautiful girls in our country, girls you can look at without running the risk of being bewitched or involved in other troubles." He winked at the servant girl. He really was a handsome fellow, there was no denying it. He leaned back, stretched out one leg. The girl returned his gaze calmly without blushing. He could have spared himself all his winking, and the young one, his jealousy. Only a woman who didn't know what he was alluding to, or was fed up with such things, could look at that handsome face so coldly and calmly. But he, for all his boasting, couldn't tell the difference.

"If she ever did bewitch you," the one-eyed hunter said, "then she'd immediately have to magically create a brook or a lake so you could see your reflection."

"Oh, well, you were lucky in any case; her arrow flew into your eye."

"I lost my eye because of a very stupid accident. From a splash of lime. When I was still half a child. I've told that story often. But you hear only yourself talk. True, I saw her—but much later on. It has nothing to do with that."

His dog, the one who was lying somewhat to one side with his legs stretched out, suddenly began to whine in his sleep. A thin, almost singing tone that made the servant girl laugh out loud. But no one noticed because they were all busy calming down their own dogs who'd been driven to a frenzy by the whining. The one-eyed hunter woke his dog; it shook its shaggy fur and trotted over to him. Finally, the dogs had all been reassured and were lying again where they had been lying before, their mouths on the floor or on the feet of their masters. You could again hear the wind and then an intense, continual shower of spruce needles.

The one-eyed hunter continued, "Just when I was feeling so very sad because I couldn't go back up into the forest—I was afraid back then of losing my second eye as well through some accident, although now I'm not afraid of that anymore—my father sent me to live with a relative far away in the city. At first I was totally confused by all the noise. I walked around in the streets like a drunkard, bumping into everything, and finding that everything got in my way, and I, in turn, was getting in everyone else's way. But soon I not only got used to the noise and all the hubbub, but I began to feel at home there.

"My relative owned tanneries down by the river, and in the beginning he had me unload the bundles of hides. Next, I had to learn all the different types of tanning processes. Then he made me the supervisor of the unloaders and the tanners. He used to say that I could see more with my one eye than his sons could with both of theirs. When I heard of the death of my parents, I formed even closer ties with this relative. I was already an older man when he died, too. By then, I felt as at home in the city as if I had been born there. And as familiar with the tannery as if all my ancestors had been tanners before me. I never got married because I was totally wrapped up with the family my relative had commended to my care. I wondered in secret sometimes whether I should marry his widow, who was a bit too old for me, or his daughter, who was a little too young.

"Then everything changed because I was seized by homesickness. I had gone to a pub, and there were three men sitting there who were from the part of the country where I was born. One of them was wearing a jacket just like the jacket my father used to wear. I tried to suppress my longing; I thought it was mere childishness. In the end it turned out to be more powerful than I was, more powerful than everything. So, under some pretext or other, I left my relative's family after assigning the overall supervision to one of the sons who, I thought, was by now sufficiently capable.

"And so I began my journey, following the river. Finally, I came to the bend in the river behind which lay the village where my grandparents had lived. Back then it had still been at the edge of the forest, but the forest had been cut down—there wasn't even any timber stacked anywhere. The entire area was covered with wheat fields and grape vines and all sorts of fruit trees. The people had changed their way of life completely. They had turned from being hunters, lumberjacks, and charcoal burners to farmers and vintners. I didn't recognize anyone. Then, leaving the river, I climbed uphill and came to the ridge of the mountain range beyond the hills. Nothing had changed there; I still knew the individual peaks. I climbed over the mountain range on the other side of which was the valley where I was born. But I must have made a mistake. I couldn't find my village. I couldn't have missed the dense forest that used to stretch down to the floor of the valley. Yet there was no forest. I must have climbed down into the wrong valley. This valley was completely bare. On one of the mountain slopes you could still see the tree stumps left in the clearings, but on the other mountain slope and in all the neighboring valleys the trees had been cleared down to the roots. Only grass was now growing where they had not yet etched out pits, or rammed in poles, or diverted the water.

"There was an enormous amount of bustling activity in this strange valley into which I must have come by mistake. A cloud of sawdust hung over everything. The place was teeming with construction workers. The hustle and bustle extended all the way to the second bend of the river, and all along the river stood warehouses, completed ones, half-completed ones, and some that were just being started. There were a few that consisted of only four corner posts, and already they had unloaded boxes and barrels inside them.

"Totally confused by the jumble, I asked someone how I could get to my village. He called over some others, and they just laughed. No one even knew of the village. I asked about the valley. That's what they used to call the valley, they replied. Which valley? This one. I looked around me. Then I slowly walked on, hearing their laughter at my back. I climbed the slope with the tree stumps. And then, finally, I did recognize my valley by some of those indestructible features that are actually intrinsic to the land. After all, down there was the second bend in the river. And up there were the two mountain peaks I knew. And they hadn't been able to entirely remove the low, round hill at the other end of the valley.

"So I sat down on a tree stump and looked at the valley that stretched, broad and flat, to the plain toward the west, and to the low, rounded hill beyond the valley. Instead of my old impenetrable wilderness, everything was now teeming with people hauling and building, and lots of individual little activities that were all clear and comprehensible. My heart and my eyes were virtually feasting on disappointment. In spite of that, no matter how much there was to see—and after a while, I felt I had seen it all three, four times, in detail—I soon tired of these groups of people, the unfinished construction projects, and the half-paved roads. Whereas, one would never tire of gazing into a forest, which is always just one single forest.

"So now, I closed my eyes out of boredom. I was suddenly too tired to feel despondent. I'd come from far away, and now I was bored. I even longed to be back in distant parts, the way I had longed, while abroad, to come back here. In the big city, the houses and streets were at least finished, and the air was not full of sawdust; it didn't smell of mortar. People had lived there for ages; the maze of city streets, one might say, had a lot more to do with a wilderness than what I saw before me now. I felt the light of the setting sun on my eyelids. I could have been imagining that the deep, dark forest was now below me. But that isn't what I imagined. I was visualizing the city I had left, with its streets and markets.

"I don't know what finally made me open my eyes. I don't think anything had touched me. Maybe it just felt a bit cooler because of a shadow momentarily falling across my face. I opened my eyes, and she was standing before me. She was bareheaded; otherwise she was dressed just like the girls back home. She even wore a belt like the ones the girls back home used to wear before they got married. A little bit of white fuzz clung to her hair. I think I wanted to blow it away but didn't. She nodded to me briefly, said nothing.

"Suddenly it flashed through my mind that she wasn't just any girl from my hometown but one of the immortal gods, related to the highest of them. Her brother was a powerful god, perhaps even *the* most powerful. I threw myself down before her and showed her, not with words but with my demeanor, how ashamed I was that I hadn't immediately greeted her befittingly. I clasped her knees with both my arms and buried my face in her dress. I wept. I must really have wept a long time. For when I straightened up, I saw, to my shame, a damp spot on her dress where it was stretched tight by her extended knee. She said, 'Why are you crying?'

"At that my heart opened up, for its hour had come. I told her about everything that had happened to me. I told her about my entire youth up to the moment I had the bad luck to lose my eye. I told her about my life abroad. I didn't conceal a single detail; I didn't forget for a moment, of course, that this was a young woman before me. I told her how I had been overcome by homesickness—only occasionally at first, and then ever more frequently, until almost everything I smelled or touched reminded me in some roundabout way of my home: when they were unloading wood on the canal, when someone whistled somewhere in the night, or when I stepped through a pitch-dark gateway, or a woman's rough hair brushed my skin. I told her how in the end, my homesickness never left me, night and day, because in the end there was nothing that didn't remind me of home. I told her how I eventually pulled myself together and left it all behind. And then the disappointment that awaited me. I told her all that had happened to me up to the moment I opened my eyes.

"When I was done, I heaved a sigh of relief. Now she will console me, I thought; she will demonstrate the extent of her power; she will stand by me. My pain, after all, is her pain too. But when I looked at her, I was shocked. Her face was hard and severe. She frowned. She said, 'So that's how things stand with you. You were looking for your old forest, and it wasn't there anymore. And because of that you're crying. You wanted to find your wilderness again, your own, old forested wilderness, and instead you came upon a construction site. And because you didn't find your old forest there anymore, you call the woodcutters evildoers, and the masons, scoundrels, and the city builders, fools.'

"I said, 'Aren't you angry, too? Doesn't it drive you to despair, the things you see down here? Aren't you sad about what has become of your forests: sawdust for storage sheds, and hoops for barrels?'

"She said, 'Why should I be angry? With whom? You forget that my sister is the goddess of this city. That's her down there, sitting astride a hoisting crane; see, she's waving to me, laughing. I'm happy for her. I know that she likes nothing better than the hammering and squealing of winches and saws. It pleases her. But I don't object to it either. When I walk out of one forest and up over a mountain ridge or a great steppe to go to the next forest, and I have to close my eyes because of the unaccustomed brightness of the daylight, then I can already hear my sister whistling at the outer edge of the steppe or in one of the valleys. And I whistle back. I walk a bit toward the light. I stop and look around. I have to laugh. There she is again, the most intelligent and brightest of us sisters, trotting along humbly and silently behind some hefty fellow with an ax over his shoulder and a bundle of bread and a whetstone on his belt. She follows him into every barren wasteland he chooses to go to, right up to the edge of the forest. Then she squats on some moss nearby and watches with delight as he, the first in that wilderness, hauls back for his first blow with his ax. She is in love with the coarse fellow. In her eyes he is a founder of cities. But I walk on.

"'And now you want me to be sad. A clear-cut area is supposed to fill me with despair. Take a look and see what's in my hair.'

"She turned her face away from me. On top of her thick hair, over one ear there was still this little white fuzzy thing. It didn't occur to me that this was what she wanted me to see. It was a little white, feathered seed; a couple of them had got tangled in her hair. She shook her head vigorously. All the delicate seeds flew off. She said, 'One got stuck in your shoelaces. Too bad. One is going to get caught over there at the edge of the lime pit. And one between the floorboards of that large warehouse they're just building down there. They will be the new forest.'

"I felt a fleeting joy, but my heart was too weakened by disappointment to be able to hold on to it. I said, 'A new forest? But when?'

"At that she laughed. 'You, with your competitive games: Who'll be the first; we, with our games? Who'll be the last? When? When? Then, after thousands of you have lost your patience to wait for who knows what all. After all, you usually lose your patience first, then your faith, and then the thing itself.'

"I said, 'But one day when all the forests are gone . . .'

"She mimicked me, 'All the forests, all the forests. That's what you're afraid of, that's what you think when you lose your patience. Because losing one's patience means to be secretly afraid it might turn out badly, that you might lose it entirely.

"'You may as well assume the worst. Or whatever you think would be the worst. Go ahead and assume that all the forests are gone. That there are no more forests on earth. What difference can that possibly make to me? If somewhere, someday, there's some man who holds his head in his hands and wonders what that thing—a forest—might have been: Something an old man once talked about, that such a thing had existed in times gone by. And he rests his head in his hands and puts his fingers into his ears so that he can hear the forest rustling, this forest that he has imagined half wrong, half right . . . Then I brighten up; then my power is as unchanged as it was in the days when the entire earth was covered with a forested wilderness as yet untouched by any ax.'

"I closed my eyes so that I could think about all she had said. When I opened them again, she was gone. A singular bleakness had come over the clearing, over the entire mountain slope that was bare of trees anyway. It was if something more had been taken from each tree stump. I was no longer sad. I don't know why. Besides, the day was at an end. And I was cold."

He made a gesture with his hand to indicate the story was finished.

One man asked, "You never saw her again after that?"

"No. At first I went back to the city. I lived there for years, the way I had lived there before. Then, much later, through some coincidence, I got the chance to come up to this part of the country. I hadn't been actively looking for such an opportunity, of course, not even wishing for it, but when it came along, I took it."

The young hunter asked, "So when you were back in the forest, here with us, didn't you ever follow her, didn't you ever call on her?"

"No. It's a superstitious belief that you can reach the gods by calling on them. Actually, they come when you forget about them. It's when you don't even want to see them again that they're suddenly standing there before you."

"But now, don't you wish that she would come, that she would suddenly be standing before you the way she was back then?"

He thought it over briefly, then he said, "No. Actually not. It's all still very fresh. I don't need it anymore."

The young hunter was about to tell him that he didn't understand, when the innkeeper entered the room. He was soaking wet from the rain. He chided the maid: "What are you standing around for? Did you come here just to listen to stories?"

The young hunter jumped up. He was itching to hit the innkeeper. The girl looked right at the innkeeper's face. There was no change in her bearing; it was neither overly proud nor overly relaxed. The innkeeper asked her, "Are you finished with your work?"

She replied, "Yes."

The innkeeper looked the girl up and down. She watched his face without blinking an eye. Her own face had turned paler, probably only because it was turned away from the glow of the fire. The young hunter thought the girl didn't need to put up with this much longer.

Yet for the time being, the innkeeper was still her master. He ordered, "Fill the pail!" Adding, "Can't you see that it's empty without being told?"

The girl said nothing. She took hold of the chain with one hand and the pail handle with the other. The men were watching as if the girl knew some quite surprising new way to take a pail off a hook. She straightened up. Her dress stretched a bit across her bosom. The men turned their heads to watch as she went to the door without swinging the pail. Forgotten were all the stories that had just been told. It was as if they had been talking about the most ordinary of things, things you hear about all the time. The men now forgot everything but the girl's narrow, bare heels rising out of her shoes with each step.

The girl opened the door and pushed it against the wall. A strong gust of wind came into the room. It blew rain into her face and wrapped her dress around her hips. She put the pail down outside and pulled the door shut behind her. All of them except for the innkeeper, who was checking the hook that was bent somewhat out of shape, listened attentively to what was going on outside. The dogs listened with their ears up. They heard the pail hitting the well. They heard the chain scrunching, then the pail hitting the well again. Some time passed. The innkeeper was already grumbling. But even the older hunters were waiting. The young hunter was waiting like a man in love for whom every unexplained movement is cause for jealousy and every absence, a disaster.

How quiet it was now. After the last banging of the pail, the world had abruptly turned silent. Even the innkeeper, who had not been listening for her steps, listened to the heart-stopping silence. They all stared at the door. Suddenly the wet soil outside the main door squished. The dogs started barking wildly. All heads turned. Outside someone unfamiliar with the house was fiddling with the bolt, managing finally to push it back. The men restrained the dogs, all of whom were quivering and growling. There, on the doorstep, stood an older woman, between forty and fifty, dressed in rough clothes and shoes, and with a face that looked coarse and hard but not angry. She had a bundle in one hand. A strong band, probably leather, was knotted around the bundle, forming a loop that one could put a belt through or one's wrist. Since they were all staring at her and no one greeted her, she stepped up to the innkeeper and said, "I'm the new maid." She misinterpreted his unbelieving stare. She explained, "I could only get away a day later. The wife at the place where I was working unexpectedly went into labor early."

The innkeeper kept staring at her. She said, more roughly, "Should I have left her in the lurch?" Then added, "You wouldn't want that kind of maid working for you, either."

The innkeeper turned away wordlessly and went to the side door. An expression of pride and bitterness came over the woman's coarse, flat face: If this explanation wasn't enough for him, then there's no help for it; then it's just my fate to have to serve a hard and unsympathetic master.

The hunters all got up now, too, and followed the innkeeper. The youngest one's dog came as well. The other dogs growled threateningly. But the woman skillfully distracted them with monotone encouragements, and a fearlessness that can only come from a sad heart, for her heart had lost what was most important a long time ago, and so it didn't need to tremble anymore. The hunters crowded into the open side door.

Outside, in the rainy dark evening, they could make out the dim outlines of the well. By the doorsill, next to the doorpost, stood the pail filled with water. But no tracks led from the doorsill to the well and back from the well to the doorsill. And why did no branch strike the wall of the house, and why did no spruce tree needles rain down, even though the clouds were scudding between the roof and the forest?

Suddenly from deep within the forest, probably hours distant, came two long, drawn-out, thin whistles that made their hearts tremble. A spruce tree branch brushed against the house wall and shook off its needles. The entire forest murmured.

The men went back to the fire, not looking at one another. Now the maid peered out through the empty doorway too. She saw the full pail. She lifted it up before anyone could order her to do so and hung it on the hook over the fire. It was her first task in this house.

1938

THE THREE TREES

THE KNIGHT'S TREE

Recently, as some lumberjacks were about to apply their axes to an ancient stand of trees in the Argonne Forest, they discovered a knight in full armor inside a hollow beech. From his coat of arms they were able to identify him as a follower of Charles the Bold of Burgundy. Evidently, while fleeing the soldiers of King Louis XI and fearing for his life, this knight had squeezed into a hollow in the tree. Once his pursuers had withdrawn, however, he was unable to free himself and perished miserably inside his refuge. Yet the tree, already old and mighty back then, continued to rustle and flourish, even as the knight inside it gasped, wept, prayed, and died. Strong and without a blemish, except for the narrow hollow occupied by the dead knight, it continued to grow, adding rings, spreading its branches, and sheltering generations of birds. And it would have kept on growing had the lumberjacks not come along when they did.

THE TREE OF ISAIAH

There is an oral tradition about the death of the prophet Isaiah, which has it that he was sawn to pieces inside a cedar.

During his lifetime he had been afraid of nothing and no one. Not of the threats of the powerful, nor of the mockery of his equals. Not of the henchmen who were sent out to hound him, nor of the stones that people in crowds threw at him, which occasionally struck him.

Not of his family's tears as the hour approached when he had to leave them, nor of the emptiness of the desert, nor of the multifarious, disorienting noise of the popular masses. He was not afraid to call for resistance in lethargic times. He was not afraid to lead his people into a battle that he knew was a lost cause. He was not afraid to die with them in that battle. But he did not die. His people were killed and along with his people, the sublime voice from which he was accustomed to receive instructions. That was when he began to be afraid.

The horns of the sentries sounded at the edge of the gorge. They were searching the mountains for escapees. He clambered along, following a small river, until he came to a clearing. Some cedar trunks were lying there in a pile. The lumberjacks had probably left before the battle started. He crawled into one of the piles. The horns of the sentries were coming closer; he was afraid and crept into a hollow cedar trunk. The horns of the sentries went past; night fell and all was silent, only the little river burbled on. But he was afraid to leave his hiding place.

Morning dawned. The lumberjacks returned, the woodcutters and log rafters with their saws, axes, and ropes. He should have jumped to his feet then; he should have spoken to the woodcutters and log rafters the way he usually spoke to people. But he was afraid of the woodsmen. The overseer came and ordered his men to carry the wood to the saw. He could still have jumped out at this point, but he was afraid of the woodcutters' overseer. Now one trunk after the other was being placed before the saw. He still had one moment in which to leave his hiding place. But he was afraid, and so, as the story would have it, he was sawn to pieces inside a cedar.

THE TREE OF ODYSSEUS

Even this day had come to an end. The dead suitors had been carried off; the arrows collected; the blood washed away. For the first time husband and wife were sitting together again by the fire as in the old days. Once more the gods cast a last, already indifferent look at the couple. Everything had been used to prevent this reunification; then everything to finally bring it about. Everything imaginable had been done for and against the husband's return home. And the "for" had triumphed. And so, the gods withdrew to their eternal abodes and left the two to their fate.

How quiet the house was. Now everything inside his head faded away: the music at the wedding when Achilles, who died long ago outside the gates of Troy, was conceived; the argument between the goddesses; the horns that blew for war; the battles outside Troy; the lamentation in the streets of the conquered city; the song of the Sirens; the bellowing of the Cyclops; the grunting of his bewitched companions; the stringed music of the lyres; and constantly accompanying it all, the turbulent sea.

How terrible the stillness now. Before, even if you had fearsome gods against you, you were at least together in a world with gods. Now everything was silent. And the smoke on Ithaca's native hills formed but a pale little cloud. Odysseus would not be the man he was if he didn't know what his wife was thinking now: *This man might be Odysseus. He might also not be him. Ten years of wandering, ten years in Troy, that's a long separation. It's true, he killed the suitors. But maybe he is only more daring than the most forward of them. Perhaps he is just pretending to be the master. Perhaps he is just a pirate, and his ship lies concealed in one of the coves. What does my heart tell me? Nothing at all.*

Then his wife said, "You must be tired. I'll have them carry your bed to the fire."

Odysseus replied, "You won't be able to set the bed up here. When I first fell in love with you, when I courted you back then, when none of us even knew where Troy was, I searched my island for a good place to build my future house. I found the place and cleared it of trees. I left only one sturdy tree standing on its roots. I determined this tree would be the center of my house. I topped it, leaving only the mighty stump standing. Then I carved our bed into that stump. But then, you already know all this."

1940

SHELTER

ONE MORNING in September 1940, when the largest swastika flag in all of the countries occupied by Germany was flying over the Place de la Concorde in Paris, and the lines outside the shops were as long as the streets themselves, a certain Luise Meunier, the wife of a lathe operator and mother of three children, heard that one could buy eggs at a shop in the 14th arrondissement.

She immediately set out, stood in line for an hour, and got five eggs, one for each member of her family. It then occurred to her that one of her school friends, Annette Villard, a hotel employee, lived on the same street. She found her at home, but the woman, who was normally calm and steady, was in a singularly agitated state.

As she scrubbed the windows and sinks, with Mrs. Meunier helping out here and there, Annette Villard told her friend that at around noon the previous day the Gestapo had arrested a man who had registered at the hotel as an Alsatian, but who, it turned out, had fled from a German concentration camp some years earlier. The lodger, Annette said, rubbing at a windowpane, had been taken to La Santé, and from there he would shortly be transported back to Germany and probably stood up against a wall and shot. But what concerned her much more than the lodger, for after all the man was a man and war was war, was the lodger's son. The German had a child, a twelve-year-old boy sharing the room with him; the boy had been attending school here and spoke French as well as she did; his mother was dead; their circumstances were mysterious the way they usually were with foreigners. The boy, when he came back from school that day, accepted the news of his father's arrest in silence, without tears. But when asked by the Gestapo officer to pack his things so that he could be picked up the following day and sent back to his relatives in Germany, the boy suddenly spoke up, saying he'd rather throw himself under a truck than return to that family. The Gestapo officer replied harshly that the issue was not whether to return or not to return, but rather whether he would go to his relatives or to a reformatory.

The boy, Annette said, trusted her, and later that night he had asked her for help. Early the next morning she took him to a small café whose proprietor was her friend. And now he was sitting there, waiting. She thought it would be easy to find someone to take the boy in, but up to now she had received only refusals; people were too fearful. Her own boss was also afraid of the Germans and angry about the boy's escape.

Mrs. Meunier listened to it all without saying a word. Then, once Annette had finished her account, she said, "I'd like to meet this boy." Whereupon her friend gave her the name of the café, adding, "You wouldn't be afraid to take some clothes along for the boy, would you?"

After she showed the proprietor of the café the note Mrs. Villard had given her, he led her into the billiard room that was closed in the mornings. There sat the boy gazing out into the courtyard. The boy was the same size as her eldest son and similarly dressed; his eyes were gray; there was nothing distinctive about his features that would have stamped him as the son of a foreigner. Mrs. Meunier told him that she had brought him some clothes. He didn't thank her, just suddenly turned to look keenly at her face. Mrs. Meunier had been up to this point a mother like other mothers, standing in line, making something out of nothing and a lot out of something, and taking on homework in addition to her housework; all that was a matter of course. Now under the boy's steady gaze what was natural and a matter of course with a sudden jolt grew greater and with it, so did her strength. She said, "Be at the Café Biard at Les Halles tonight at seven."

Then she hurried home. For it would take a long time in the kitchen to prepare, from almost nothing, anything that would be even slightly presentable for dinner. Her husband was already there. He had lain for one war year in a ditch on the Maginot Line and had been demobilized three weeks before; a week ago his old firm had reopened for business, and he now worked there half days, spending most of his free time at the bistro. He would come home from there, furious with himself for having left some of his few sous behind. His wife, too agitated to pay any heed to the look on his face, started with her report while she was beating the eggs. She was trying to prepare him. But when she got to the point where the foreign boy ran away from the hotel and was looking for shelter from the Germans in Paris, he broke in: "Your girlfriend Annette really did a stupid thing, encouraging such foolishness. In her place I would have locked the boy up. Let the German fellow figure out how to cope with his countrymen. He didn't take care of his own child. So the officer is right when he wants to send the child back home. The fact is that Hitler has occupied the world, and no words or platitudes can change that."

Whereupon his wife was smart enough to quickly change the subject. For the first time she saw in her heart what her husband had become, this man who in the past had participated in every strike, every demonstration, and who behaved, on the Fourteenth of July, as if he were going to storm the Bastille one more time all by himself. But now he resembled Christophorus, the giant in the legend—there were many others like him—who always joined the one who seemed to him the strongest or who proved to be stronger than his current master, so that finally he ended up serving the devil. But there was no room for mourning in the woman's nature, nor in her full day. This man was her husband; she was his wife; and there was the foreign boy who was now waiting for her. And so that evening she went to the café at Les Halles and told the child, "I won't be able to take you to my house until tomorrow."

The boy again gave her that penetrating look and said, "You don't have to take me if you're afraid."

The woman replied simply that it was only a matter of waiting one day. She asked the proprietress to keep the boy for one night, telling her that he was a relative of hers. There was nothing special about this request since Paris was teeming with refugees.

The following day she gave her husband this explanation: "I met my cousin Alice; her husband is in the prison hospital at Pithiviers and she would like to visit him for a couple of days. She asked me to take care of her child during that time."

Her husband, who couldn't stand strangers within his four walls, said, "I just trust it won't turn into a permanent situation."

So she got a mattress ready for the boy. As they were on their way to her house later that day, she had asked the boy, "Why don't you want to go back to Germany?"

He had replied, "If you're afraid, you can still leave me here. But I will not go back to my relatives in Germany. My father and my mother were both arrested by Hitler. They were printing and distributing pamphlets. My mother died. You can see that I'm missing one of my front teeth. They knocked it out in school because I wouldn't join in singing their song. My relatives are Nazis too. They tormented me the most. They insulted my father and mother."

Mrs. Meunier asked only that he not say anything about this in the presence of her husband, her children, or the neighbors.

Her children didn't like or dislike the foreign boy. He kept to himself and never laughed. Her husband didn't like him from the first moment on; he said he didn't like the look in the boy's eyes. He scolded his wife for using part of her own food ration for the boy; he also berated her cousin, saying it was an imposition to dump children on other people. And these complaints usually turned into lectures: The war was lost; the Germans were occupying the country, but they were disciplined and knew how to keep order. Once when the boy knocked over the milk can, her husband jumped up and hit him. Later his wife tried to console the boy, but he only said, "Still better here than there."

"One of these days I'd like to have a real piece of Gruyère for dessert again," her husband said. That evening he came home all excited. "Just imagine what I saw. A huge German truck filled with wheels of cheese. They buy whatever they feel like buying. They print millions and then they spend them."

After two or three weeks, Mrs. Meunier went to see her friend Annette. The woman wasn't happy about the visit, and told her that she wasn't to show up in this quarter anymore, that the Gestapo had cursed and threatened her. They even discovered in which café the boy had waited and also that a woman had visited him there, and that both had left the place at different times.

On her way home Mrs. Meunier again thought about the danger she had brought upon herself and her family. But no matter how long she thought about what she had done with so little forethought and in such a sudden rush of emotion, what she saw that very day on her way home confirmed her decision—the lines outside the shops that were still open, the shutters in front of the ones that were closed, the noisy horns of the German vehicles racing along the boulevards, and the swastikas over the gates. So that, as she entered her kitchen, she stroked the foreign boy's hair in a second gesture of welcome.

Her husband, however, jumped on her, saying she was taking a fancy to the boy. And he let his grouchiness out on the foreigner— because he felt sorry for his own children, all of their bright hopes having suddenly turned into such a pitiful, gloomy, unfree future. Since the boy was too careful and too silent to give him any cause, he hit him without cause, claiming the boy had looked at him inso- lently. He himself felt he had been deprived of his last remaining pleasure. He still spent the greater part of his free time at the bistro, and that made him feel a little better. Now a smith at the end of the street had been forced to sell his smithy to the Germans.

The street, which up to that point had still been quite calm and free of swastikas, suddenly began to teem with German mechanics. German cars piled up waiting to be repaired, and Nazi soldiers oc- cupying the public house made themselves at home there. Mrs. Meunier's husband couldn't bear the sight. His wife often found him sitting silently at the kitchen table. Once, after he had been sitting there for an hour without moving, his head on his arms, his eyes open, she asked him what he was thinking about. He said, "About nothing and everything. And in addition, something else totally far-fetched. Just imagine, I was thinking about that German fellow, the one your girlfriend Annette told you about; I don't know if you still remember. The German who was against Hitler, the German whom the Germans arrested. I'd like to know what happened to him. What happened to him and what became of his son."

Mrs. Meunier replied, "I met Annette Villard recently. Back then they took the German to La Santé. In the meantime maybe he's already been killed. The child disappeared. Paris is big. He's probably found himself a shelter."

Since none of his mates liked drinking among Nazi soldiers, they often moved with a couple of bottles into the Meuniers' kitchen, which would have been unusual in earlier days and almost distasteful. Most of the men were Meunier's fellow workers from the same company; they spoke openly among themselves. The boss at their place of work had turned his office over to the German commissioner, who came and went as he liked. The German experts tested, inspected, weighed, and accepted. In the offices of the management they weren't even trying anymore to keep secret for whom they were working. The finished parts made from stolen metal were sent to the east to throttle, to defeat other nations. That was the end of the story, shortened work hours, shortened wages, and strikes forbidden. Mrs. Meunier pulled down the roller shutters, and everyone spoke in hushed voices. The foreign boy lowered his eyes as if he were afraid his gaze might be too keen, that it might betray what was in his heart. He had gotten so pale and so thin that Mr. Meunier looked at him glumly, saying he was afraid that he might have caught an illness and would infect their own children.

Mrs. Meunier had written a letter addressed to herself in which her cousin asked her to keep the boy a while longer because her husband was seriously ill and she wanted to rent a room somewhere near him.

"She's taking a convenient way out with her boy," Mr. Meunier said when she showed him the letter.

Mrs. Meunier hastened to praise the boy, that he was very well behaved, that he went every morning at four to Les Halles; that today, for instance, he had been able to get this piece of beef without a ration card.

There were two sisters living in an apartment facing the same courtyard as the Meuniers; they had always been quite nasty. Now they often went to the bistro and sat on the knees of the German mechanics. A police officer had been watching this for a while; then he took the two sisters to the police station. They cried and protested, but he had them entered on the checklist. Everyone on the street was happy about this, but unfortunately the sisters became even worse. The German mechanics were now seen going in and out of their apartment. They acted as if the courtyard belonged to them, you could hear the noise they made even in the Meuniers' kitchen.

For Mr. Meunier and his guests this was no longer a laughing matter; Meunier no longer praised the German orderliness, his life at work and at home had been destroyed by this fine, conscientious, thorough orderliness—all his big and small pleasures, his prosperity, his honor, his peace, his sustenance, his air.

One day Mr. Meunier was alone with his wife. After a long silence, it just came gushing out of him; he shouted, "They have all the power, what can we do! How powerful this devil is! If only there were someone on this earth stronger than him! But we, we're powerless. We open our mouths and they beat us to death. Like that German your Annette talked about. You may have already forgotten him; I haven't. He at least took a chance. And his son, my respects! Your cousin may be dealing with her own problems and her boy. I don't care. But the son of that German, him I'd take in! He could make me feel better. I'd treasure him above my own sons; I'd feed him better. Taking in a boy like that and sheltering him . . . and those bandits would come and go and have no inkling of the risk I'm taking and what sort of man I am and whom I'm hiding in my house! I'd shelter a boy like that and welcome him with open arms."

His wife turned away and said, "You've already taken him in."

I heard this story told by that very same Annette at my hotel in the 16th arrondissement; she had gone to work there because she had felt it was getting too dangerous at her old job.

1941

A MAN BECOMES A NAZI

THERE was once a German whose name was Fritz Mueller. In March 1942, he was brought before a Red Army field court. He was charged with shootings, hangings, and a series of acts of cruelty committed against women and children, especially in the villages of Kotelnikovo and Ladovka; with murdering the farmer's wife Ivanova and her two sons, the latter in front of the mother's eyes. Soldiers who were interrogated said that they were obeying his orders. The orders had been preceded by a speech in which he had impressed on them that showing any compassion toward the enemy would be an act of treason against the German people.

In October 1917, Friedrich Mueller, a sergeant who had formerly been a metalworker but was now stationed on Hill 114 in the Argonne Forest—the hill, however, had long since been shot up into mere mounds of dirt—learned that his fourth son, Fritz, had been born on Ufergasse in Düsseldorf, nine months after his last home leave.

Mrs. Mueller raised the child like most of the other mothers on Ufergasse raised their children. During the day, after she had taken her youngest child to a neighbor, she went to work, and at night she sewed and cooked for her children.

In November 1918, the army flooding back to Germany swept Sergeant Friedrich Mueller home to his family. The metalworker in whose workshop he had been employed for ten years could no longer take him on. So Mueller, the father, began his postwar life between the kitchen and the unemployment offices. At first he had been glad that the war had come to an end. But now he talked so much about the war that his family got bored listening to him. For him these wartime memories confirmed a belief that for many years he had been something more than merely an unemployed metalworker: He had been a man whose strength had been in demand.

He and his neighbors grumbled about the government not having any bread for its citizens. Yet he wouldn't join in any of the demonstrations, saying he'd had enough of marching and keeping in step. Deep down he longed to be something different for once, not just one among many. When his comrades started an Association of War Veterans, he went there Sundays wearing all his old medals and decorations. The workers on the Ufergasse called them a "tinsmith shop," but for him these medals were a validation of his four years of suffering, daring, and staying the course.

On Easter 1923, he took his youngest son, Fritz, to register him at Public Elementary School III, the Schiller School. By then, much blood had been shed in the new state during the Kapp Putsch, at the Ruhr, and in central Germany, and the bloodshed was continuing; but for him all that blood had borne no fruit, for he was and remained unemployed.

At that time the republic had a school system that allowed gifted children to move on to a higher school. Even though the onetime metalworker Mueller declared loudly that for people like him this was just a fantasy, his bitter heart was full of hope as he walked between the pale green Easter plane trees and through the schoolyard holding the little hand of his son in his old, dry, wrinkled one, along with countless other fathers, going to register their sons in all the schoolyards of Germany, with hope in their bitter hearts, not for themselves anymore but for their sons.

Some of the teachers in the school were of the old guard. They taught the old curricula and outdated ideas. What use was it to little Fritz Mueller to learn "Work dignifies" and "Once you know a trade you will never starve," if his own father, a metalworker, was unemployed and his older brothers couldn't even find apprenticeships?

The young teachers were themselves afraid of being fired and joining the unemployed. They came with new methods and teachings that weren't clear yet even to them. But they were eager to try out their new methods. And many of them cared more about these new methods and teachings than they did about their pupils, and certainly a lot more than they cared about little Fritz Mueller.

It turned out that their pupil Fritz Mueller was by no means one of the particularly gifted ones who might have continued his schooling at the expense of the state. This irked his father even though he had called the whole thing a fantasy. As a result of his mother's tireless efforts, the boy looked decent—a neatly dressed, short-haired boy, the son of decent parents. Like all boys, he loved athletics, swimming, and exercises that allowed him to feel his own strength— physical strength but also initiative and daring.

During this time there was a minor incident in the schoolyard. Fritz kicked a weaker pupil in the stomach for spoiling a game by being too slow. The boy had turned pale and fallen down. In a rage Fritz gave the prone boy two more kicks. Three other pupils were standing nearby; one of them helped the injured boy get up; the second pulled Fritz Mueller away; and the third one said, "You shouldn't do that once he's down."

Fritz's mother heard of the incident. She scolded him but not as forcefully as she would have scolded her older sons; she was already worn out.

The class got a new teacher. He loved the boys. In the course of teaching them reading, writing, and arithmetic, he also tried to introduce them to the best of current thoughts and ideas: peace among nations, equality of people, freedom. But Fritz's clean, short-haired head was not one of those in which a mere idea as such could quickly catch fire. What he liked in his stories weren't the ideas, it was the happenings, the eventful, wild, and dangerous ones. It also annoyed him that his fellow pupil, Ernst Busch, whose father was described by his own father as an instigator, was the teacher's favorite. As was little Weil, whose father the elder Mueller called "a little Jew tailor." Both boys always came in last in the relay races and swam only half as well as he did. Peace among nations meant nothing to Fritz, for he wished he could have the kind of war adventures his father talked about; freedom meant nothing to him, because he liked ordering the weaker boys around and being himself ordered around by the strong ones; and equality meant nothing to him because he longed to be well dressed. Privately, the new teacher considered his pupil Fritz Mueller dull and not very talented.

The following year their teacher was replaced by another, who was also one of the younger generation of teachers. He claimed the class had gone to the dogs. Before they memorized any poems, they would have to learn the meaning of order and discipline. Fritz Mueller liked order better than the art of poetry. And, on the whole, he really liked this teacher. The teacher discovered that his pupil Fritz Mueller was a spirited swimmer and the best in relay racing. Fritz also responded to this teacher's ideas because the examples he gave awakened familiar feelings in him. Because he slept in the same bed with his brother, he thought he understood why the German people needed more space. And because he couldn't stand the Jewish tailor, he thought he understood why it was the fault of the Jews that he never had enough to eat. The teacher also casually praised him for things that required no effort on Fritz's part, namely, that he had blond hair and blue eyes and that his father had been in the war.

The young teacher wrote monthly class reports to the school authorities about which some of his superiors shrugged their shoulders, while others just smiled to themselves. He would write: "In the course of three months I have identified and developed the characteristics of leadership in one of the students. In the course of two additional months I got the class to voluntarily recognize him as their leader."

Fritz Mueller also liked the boy whom the teacher had described as the class leader in his report, and he was pleased that he himself had played a significant role in all the pranks, games, and activities of this boy whom the teacher had defined as their leader. The teacher noted in private that the pupil Fritz Mueller was one of the smart boys, the son of a soldier, of good stock, and though without any noticeable leadership talents of his own, ready to follow the accepted leader without hesitation. At Easter time, when the state had to dismiss many teachers, both teachers lost their positions: the one because he was a Red, the other because he was a Nazi. This time

Fritz again got a teacher of the old school. Both in his confirmation instructions and in the valedictory speech given by their classroom teacher, he was explicitly told that he was now entering Life.

The life he was embarking on was characterized by standing in line at the unemployment office and loitering about on the streets. This was the time in which every fourth man in the German capital was unemployed. Even the master metalworker in whose shop his father had formerly worked had to lock up his shop and stand in line for his stamp. When his father, Friedrich Mueller, died of influenza, which was spreading among the undernourished populace like a plague, all four sons had to hand over every last pfennig of their unemployment money at home.

Fritz had acquired no ideas in school that might make his current life meaningful. His outer life, the back and forth between his living room and the unemployment office, was totally meaningless. On Sundays, his eldest brother took him along on the excursions of a Worker Youth group. But to him, the dancing, guitar playing, singing, and hiking seemed boring and silly when set against the gloomy background of a life that felt as hopeless to him as it had to his father before him, even though he hadn't experienced much of anything yet.

His third brother took him to his youth group meetings. There they talked about a revolution as if it were an imminent event that might happen at any hour and for which one had to prepare oneself.

The only person who had ever made an impression on him was that dashing, order-loving teacher who had said that the revolution would bring nothing but a leveling of the good and the inferior races, of the strong and the weak. He wished for the very opposite of this bleak life of being unemployed; he longed for distinction, splendor, and self-validation.

One day, a fellow at the unemployment office addressed him: "Hey, you, with the nice face, six foot one, and no girl!"

Fritz Mueller replied, "You think I can take a girl out in this rag of a shirt?"

"This pigsty of a republic," the other said, "it's going to be mucked out soon. But you can be helped now already. Come on over to our place."

"Our place?" Fritz Mueller found out that same week where that was. The SA was quartered at the opposite end of town in an old, disused building. They all wore splendid boots; there wasn't a tear or a spot on their brown shirts; there were drinks, and it didn't cost anything. Here you weren't a bundle of rags; here you were a man, properly dressed and armed. That's what it was like at "our place." Yet those who paid the bill weren't there. Fritz Mueller hesitated, wondering how his family would feel about his new friends. He had heard people on his street say that these fellows were the enemies of the people. But he'd had to listen to so much contradictory talk on his own street and among his own brothers about the People and the Enemies of the People that he didn't let it bother him. And they also reassured him at the SA barracks: We never go into our own neighborhoods.

He kept going back again and again, exchanging his faded rags for a new brown shirt. He also learned that the cause of all his problems was the Treaty of Versailles, created by the Jews and the Freemasons in order to enslave him. And he learned that it was an honorable act to shoot down those who had signed that treaty. He also learned that Bolshevism stole a man's soul and that it had already stolen that of the Russians.

One summer night they were racing through the countryside in fifteen trucks to a distant city to welcome the man whom they called their Führer. That night, for the first time in his life, he took part in a genuine celebration that included a feast, beer, torches, and trumpets. On the way back afterward, they raced through the streets, yelling at the top of their lungs, as if through an enemy country.

His family soon found out where he was keeping himself. His mother was upset; the eldest and the third-eldest brothers, usually unable to agree on anything, both withdrew from him. The second-eldest brother, though, asked Fritz to take him along.

The SA barracks were at the end of a street called Langegasse. Most of the men who lived on the street were employed by the nearby cement plant. Since the police were not in a position to do so, they decided they would block the SA members from passing through their street. The SA group leader Fritz Mueller was assigned to use trucks to force their way through. They drove down the street at night yelling *"Heil"* and *"Juda verrecke."** That night was the first time he ever shot at human beings. He fired wildly and indiscriminately. Maybe so much more ferociously because the insults they were scream-ing at him—that he had sold his soul for a good shirt—had struck a vulnerable spot.

As it turned out later at the court hearings, one shot went into a living room and through a woman's shoulder. He hadn't seen whom he was shooting at. But it had given him a taste of supreme power over life and death. And the street was enemy territory, after all, in-habited by an internal enemy. Then, since the court couldn't determine who had fired the shot, he and the others were let go.

Because he was forceful, dashing, quick to make decisions and follow orders, and also quite tall and well built, his secret wish came true. He became a member of the SS. The others were the sons of fathers different from his. This was the kind of equality that he liked. They roamed through working-class neighborhoods, shot off their guns, and baited Jews. This was the sort of freedom he understood.

He was ordered to break up a Red meeting. A young fellow he'd been in school with recognized him and swore at him. He drew his revolver. But then, when the fellow actually fell over and was really dead, and all this by his hand, in front of his own eyes, not just any-where, and not just anyone in the night, his heart contracted ominously as if it were secretly connected with the murdered man's heart. True, he felt no remorse; however, for an hour afterward a stronger, more determined person, had one been seriously concerned about him, could have forced him to repent—if only there had been someone like that there at the time. But who was there who would worry about Fritz Mueller? His mother? She was too weak. His brothers? They had turned their backs on him. His former neighbors and acquain-

*Death to the Jews.

tances? For a long time now an unbridgeable rift had existed between them and him created by hate, distrust, mutual vilification, and insults. His new friends? They only praised and reassured him. For the Reds were the enemy, and an enemy was an enemy.

Then, because there was to be a trial, he was quickly spirited off to a beautiful house on the Rhine belonging to one of the wealthy SS fathers who always paid the bills, and there he was hidden until the trial was over. True, he didn't feel fully at home there in that elegant house, so unlike any he had ever been in before. But the man of the house treated him almost with reverence, as if he were a representative of the "People." One of those who, because of their race, strength, and insight, knew how to liberate themselves from poverty and darkness.

When Hitler came to power, he marched through his city in a torchlight procession. His brothers said nothing. His mother thought that maybe her son had backed the right horse after all. His SS friends could have found him a job now. But he had enough other work to do. He had to block off streets, drive out Jews, and hunt down workers. At the entrances to the concentration camps to which he delivered them, there were signs: "Each and every prisoner is an enemy of the people. Pity for the prisoners is treason against the people." By now he was already an "old warrior," a role model for young boys.

At his physical he was assigned to an SS elite regiment. The regimen was strenuous, but he liked having his strong body turned and manipulated by the commands of others.

By the time he left the army, his young healthy body and his unformed mind and tangled feelings were superbly trained in the external technical exercise of power. And he soon had an opportunity to apply his training.

In his hometown, a house was discovered in which people were printing leaflets opposing the war. That meant the entire street had to be cordoned off. When the man suspected of being the printer was brought before him, already covered with blood, and was finished off on his orders right then and there before his eyes, there was not even a trace of the feeling that had spoiled other sensations for him in the past. For he had forgotten something the very first human being had had to learn: To distinguish between good and evil. Indeed, he went on to hunt down those who had once been his own people, like a wolfhound who has been trained to hunt wolves.

He was unhappy because the unit he belonged to was a reserve unit and thus not needed for the occupation of either Austria or Czechoslovakia. He had earlier seen important men in his own country bow down to his Führer, and now he saw the same thing among the important men of other countries. And for him being strong and being in the right had long been one and the same thing.

War came for him too, and the end of all days as well. But he heard only drums and fifes, only *Hurrah!* and *Heil!* and had no inkling that the summer twilight above the small train station at their departure was for him too: the end of all days. But his mother could sense something, and she wept, weeping for him and for all the mothers' sons.

Then came the invasion of Poland. The aim was no longer to occupy a village that had voted for the Reds. Now he wasn't helping to kick a single man to death; now it was the body of an entire people, of a nation. And what did he learn from seeing an old farmer stomped to death by soldiers because he spat at a man who had insulted him? That the weapons of the weak—spittle, words, looks—are laughable and useless. He despised these people, the Poles and the French, because they resisted but still allowed themselves to be defeated, just as he had learned to despise those among his own people who resisted but still allowed themselves to be overwhelmed.

His mother was glad to hear that he had already been awarded the Iron Cross in the course of the advance and had been promoted to sergeant. For almost a year he was stationed, a victor, in the starving country. Then came the real war against the archenemy, against a people who had been robbed of their soul by Bolshevism. A Red soldier had no soul, for he would rather cut his wrists than allow himself to be captured; the farmer's wife who would rather set fire to her hut than take in an enemy had no soul. Only his own, his good race was able to defend itself, and even if the enemy did know how to defend himself, yet he had no soul and must be hunted down like an animal. Sergeant Fritz Mueller hated the Russian people with all his heart and not only because his Führer's army orders demanded it of him. But also because the men back home who had insulted him to his face in the past, telling him, "You sold yourself for a shirt," used to have absolute confidence in that people, the Russians.

When they arrived at the village of Lamontovka, he saw at the entry to the village two corpses such as he had not seen in this war or ever before in all his life. For these corpses weren't lying flat on the ground, they were hanging. After they were taken down, he learned that the captain had, with the permission of his superiors, been obliged to take measures to destroy any and all insubordination on the part of the inhabitants. Mueller, who'd had a bad feeling at the sight of the hanging corpses, took his superior's explanation to heart.

At the village of Kotelnikovo they encountered furious resistance. To cover their retreat across the river, a small group of Red soldiers had dug themselves in to delay the approaching enemy, fighting for every house, for every minute of delay. Local people, old men, women, and children who had remained behind, fought alongside the Red soldiers. Sergeant Fritz Mueller also got a taste of death and of resistance to the death. When his lieutenant was killed, he took command. After the village was occupied—which was difficult even after the Red soldiers were gone because the villagers would rather have burned everything down than house the German soldiers—Sergeant Fritz Mueller had one of the oldest farmers, who, they claimed, was a member of the village soviet, strung up on a former signpost with the hanged man's right arm tied up so that it would point in the direction on the sign: "To the village soviet."

After that there was deathly silence in the village; he left the dead man hanging until he rotted. He, Fritz Mueller, however, was promoted to lieutenant. When he had given the order, he'd had a bad feeling, a kind of incredulity, similar to the feeling one gets on seeing one's first gallows. At that moment an expression had come into his eyes as if he were spying on the soldiers whom he had chosen to carry out his orders. But the soldiers had obeyed, for they had gone through the same schooling and, like their superior officer, they were afraid of dying in this damned village. And also like him, they had been ordered to carry out an operation. But afterward his hands were shaking as if he himself had tied the knot in the rope.

Winter arrived and threw them all back into Ukraine; the frost and the snow and the sharp and blunt weapons of the partisans bit into them. He settled into winter quarters. He felt apprehensive and uneasy in the cold and dark of the bullet-riddled village where the remaining women and children glared evilly and maliciously at him. He brooded as he had when he was young that he might be destined to perish without any great ado, just one among many, here in the dark.

Then a transport was attacked by partisans, and so he had two girls who had used lights to send signals to the partisans beaten to death. His hands no longer shook; he punished people for a look; he had people hanged for a whisper. He acted like an animal, but he wasn't one. For his actions were governed by one idea: Showing pity for the enemy is treason.

During the new advance in the spring he had two of his own soldiers, whose conversations had been monitored, stood up against a wall and shot. He was considered a good officer. His men were considered superb, outstanding—on the principle that bravery consists of soldiers fearing their superior more than they feared the enemy. He struggled to hold his ground, as if any new setback could thrust him into the terminal darkness that used to choke him before the moment when a young fellow outside the unemployment office said to him, "I can get you a new shirt."

He occupied the village of Ladovka. They brought him a farmer's wife whose eldest son was with the partisans. He threatened the woman and demanded that she reveal her son's hiding place, but the woman remained silent. He had them fetch her younger sons and threatened that he would hold on to the two boys so they would not be able to run to their older brother. But the woman remained silent. Thereupon he shot first the one boy, and then, since the woman still would not talk, the second one as well. And he called her a she-wolf, not a mother, and he shot the woman. His soldiers stared at him, this man who, on the orders of his Führer, had led them so far. But he, Mueller, remained in command of the village for another two months. Then came the Russian advance, which took it back.

After the verdict of the War Crimes Commission, Lieutenant Kaschemnikov said, "Is it possible to comprehend that such a creature could have been born of a human mother?" But this mother existed, and she was living on Ufergasse in Düsseldorf, waiting all along for field mail from her sons, from the youngest one too, whom she had given birth to in the year 1917, nine months after the metalworker Friedrich Mueller's last furlough home.

1943

THE DEAD GIRLS' CLASS TRIP

"No, from much farther away. From Europe."

The man looked at me, smiling, as if I'd said, "From the moon." He was the proprietor of the pulqueria at the edge of the village. He stepped back from the table and, leaning motionless against the house, looked at me as if he were searching for some trace of my weird origin.

It suddenly seemed just as weird to me as it did to him that I should come from Europe and end up here in Mexico. The village was surrounded like a fortress by a palisade of organ-pipe cactus. Through a gap, I was able to look out at the steep, grayish-brown hills, the sight of which—as barren and wild as a lunar mountain range—dispelled any suspicion that they had ever supported any life. Two pepper trees glowed at the edge of a bleak gorge. The trees seemed to be aflame rather than blooming. The proprietor was now squatting on the ground in the shadow cast by his large hat. He had stopped watching me; neither the village nor the mountains attracted his interest; he was staring, motionless, at the only thing that still presented him with enormous, insoluble riddles: absolute nothingness.

I leaned against the wall in the narrow strip of shade. The refuge afforded by this country was too uncertain, too questionable to be called salvation or sanctuary. I had just gotten over a months-long bout of illness that had laid me low here, even though the manifold dangers of the war hadn't harmed me. As sometimes happens, the rescue efforts of friends had protected me from obvious calamities and saved me from hidden misfortunes.

Even though my eyes burned in the heat with weariness, I was able to make out the section of the path that led from the village into the desert wilderness. The path was so white that it seemed to be etched on the insides of my eyelids as soon as I closed my eyes. I could also make out, at the edge of the gorge, the white wall I had seen from the roof of my lodgings in the village higher up on the mountain, from which I had walked down to this place. On my arrival up there, I had immediately asked about the wall and the rancho, or whatever it was, with its single light that seemed to have fallen from the night sky, but no one was able to give me any information.

So I had started walking. I had to find out for myself the significance of this house in spite of the weakness and weariness that had forced me to rest here. This idle curiosity was all that remained of my old wanderlust, an offshoot of a habitual compulsion. As soon as it was satisfied, I would climb back up to my lodgings. The bench on which I was resting was until now the farthest I had gone in my travels, in fact the farthest west I had ever been on this earth. The desire for unusual, wild adventures that used to make me restless had long ago been satisfied, to the point of surfeit. There was now only one venture that could spur me on: the journey home.

The rancho lay, like the mountains themselves, in a shimmery mist; I couldn't tell if it consisted of sun motes or was caused by my weariness, which made everything blurry, so that what was close at hand faded and whatever was far away became as clear as a fata morgana. Annoyed by my weariness, I stood up, and the mist before my eyes seemed to dissipate somewhat.

I walked through the gap in the cactus palisade and then around a dog sleeping on the path, as motionless as a cadaver, his legs stretched out and covered with dust. It was shortly before the rainy season. The exposed roots of bare, twisted trees on the point of petrification clung to the slope. The white wall came closer. The cloud of dust or of weariness that had by then thinned out a bit thickened once more in the mountain clefts, not as dark as clouds usually are but shining and shimmering. I might have thought it was due to my feverishness if a light, hot blast of wind hadn't blown the clouds away like fragments of fog toward other mountain scarps.

Behind the long white wall something green gleamed. Probably a spring or a diverted brook that watered the rancho more than it did the village. Yet the rancho with the low, windowless house by the side of the road looked deserted. The single light last evening, if it wasn't an illusion, had probably been the farm caretaker's. The grillwork, long superfluous and rotted, had broken out of the entrance gate. But in the archway there was still what was left of a coat of arms faded by countless rainy seasons. What remained of the coat of arms seemed familiar to me, as did the stone half shells in which it rested. I stepped through the empty gate. To my amazement I heard a light, regular creaking inside. I took another step. I was now able to smell the greenery in the garden, which seemed fresher and more luxurious the longer I looked at it. The creaking soon became more distinct, and I saw in the dense, lush bushes, a swing or seesaw going steadily up and down. My curiosity was aroused, and I went through the gateway and toward the seesaw. Just at that moment, someone called out, "Netty!"

Not since my school days had anyone called me by that name. I had learned to answer to all the good and bad names that friends and enemies used to call me, the names that had been attached to me in the course of many years on the streets, at political gatherings, parties, in nighttime rooms, police interrogations, in book titles, newspaper reports, official records, and passports. Sometimes, when I lay ill and unconscious, I had even hoped to hear that old childhood name, which in self-delusion I thought could make me healthy again, young, cheerful, and ready for that old life with my old companions which had been irretrievably lost. But the name had remained lost. Now, in my confusion at hearing my old name, I grabbed my braids in both fists, even though they'd always made fun of me for this gesture in school. I was surprised that I was still able to grab those two thick braids: so they hadn't cut them off in the hospital after all.

At first, the tree stump that supported the seesaw also seemed to be enveloped in a thick cloud, but the cloud parted and cleared a moment later, disclosing lots of rosehip bushes. Soon scattered buttercups gleamed in the low mist that rose from the ground and through the tall, dense grass. The mist eventually moved away revealing scattered dandelions and cranesbill. Among them grew brownish-pink clumps of quaking grass that quivered just from being looked at.

On each end of the seesaw rode a girl, my two best friends from school. Leni pushed off heftily, her big feet encased in square-toed button-up shoes. I remembered that she had always worn the hand-me-down shoes of an older brother. But her brother had already died in the autumn of 1914 in the First World War. At the same time I wondered that there was no trace in Leni's face of the grim events that had spoiled her life. Her face was as clear and smooth as a fresh apple, and it showed not the slightest sign, not the slightest scar, from the blows the Gestapo rained down on her when they arrested her for refusing to inform on her husband. Her thick French braid swung out from her neck during the seesawing. The heavy, frowning eyebrows gave her round face that determined, somewhat severe expression she'd had ever since she was little when faced with difficult tasks. I knew that crease in her forehead, in her otherwise mirror-smooth, round-as-an-apple face, from all sorts of occasions, from challenging ball games, competitive swimming, essay writing in class, and, later, also from stormy political meetings and while distributing handbills. I last saw that crease between her eyebrows when, during Hitler's time, I met my friends in my hometown for the last time shortly before I fled the country.

She also had that crease in her forehead when her husband failed to meet her at the agreed-upon time and place, and it turned out that he had been arrested in the printing shop that the Nazis had declared illegal. I'm sure she also distorted her mouth and brow when, right after that, they arrested her as well. The crease in her forehead that used to show up only on unusual occasions became a constant feature once they let her slowly but surely die of hunger in the women's concentration camp during the second winter of the war. I wondered how I could ever have forgotten that head, framed by the broad band around her French braid. I was certain that even in death she retained her apple face with the furrowed brow.

On the other end of the seesaw sat Marianne, the prettiest girl in our class, her long, thin legs crossed on the board in front of her. She had pinned her ash-blond braids in circles above her ears. Her face, as fine and even as the faces of the medieval stone maidens in the Marburg cathedral, showed nothing but charm and cheerfulness. There were as few signs of heartlessness, guilt, or lack of conscience in it as in a flower. I instantly forgot what I knew about her and was happy to see her. A jolt would go through her taut, lean body every time she boosted the movement of the seesaw without using her feet to push off. She looked as if she could fly off effortlessly, a carnation between her teeth, with her small firm breasts in a faded green linen smock.

I recognized the voice of our elderly teacher, Miss Mees, calling to us, from just behind the low wall that separated the seesaw area from the café terrace. "Leni! Marianne! Netty!" I didn't grab my braids in amazement. After all, Miss Mees, along with the other girls, couldn't have called me by any other name. Marianne took her legs off the seesaw and planted her feet firmly on the ground as soon as the board bobbed down on Leni's side, so that Leni could get off safely. Then she put one arm around Leni's neck and carefully plucked some blades of grass out of her hair. Everything they had told me and written me about these two seemed impossible to me now. If Marianne would hold the seesaw so carefully for Leni and pick the grass out of her hair so gently, even putting an arm around her neck in friendship, she could not possibly have later bluntly and coldly refused to do a good turn for Leni. It was impossible that she could have said that she didn't care for a girl who, by chance, had at some time, somewhere, been in the same class with her. And that each and every pfennig given to Leni and her family was a waste of money, a betrayal of the state. The Gestapo officers who arrested both parents, one after the other, explained to the neighbors that Leni's child, now left alone and defenseless, ought immediately to be placed in a National Socialist reform school. Thereupon the neighbor women intercepted the child on the playground and kept her hidden until she could be sent to Berlin to live with her father's relatives. They went to borrow travel money from Marianne whom they had seen sometimes walking arm in arm with Leni in earlier days. But Marianne refused, adding that her own husband was a high Nazi official and Leni and her husband had been justly arrested because they had transgressed against Hitler. At this point, the women were afraid they themselves might be reported to the Gestapo.

I wondered whether Leni's little daughter's brow was furrowed like her mother's when she was picked up to be taken to the reform school after all.

Now the two, Marianne and Leni, of whom one would later suffer the loss of her child because of the other, were walking out of the little seesaw garden, their arms thrown about each other's necks, their heads touching. I felt sad just then, as so often during my school years, and somewhat excluded from the other girls' joint games and close friendships. Then the two stopped and took me between them.

We followed Miss Mees, like three ducklings behind a mama duck, up to the café terrace. Miss Mees had a slight limp that, along with her big behind, increased her resemblance to a duck. On her bosom, inside the neck opening of her blouse, hung a large black cross. Like Leni and Marianne, I would have suppressed a smile, but my merriment over her funny appearance was tempered by a hard-to-reconcile feeling of respect: Later she never took off the heavy black cross at the neckline of her dress, but went about openly and fearlessly with this cross rather than a swastika even after the Confessing Church had been forbidden to hold services.

The café terrace on the Rhine was planted with rosebushes. Neat, upright, and well cared for, they seemed, in comparison to the girls, like garden flowers next to field flowers. Through the smells of water and garden wafted an enticing aroma of coffee. A buzz of young voices sounding like a swarm of bees came from the tables covered with red-and-white-checkered cloths set out in front of the long, low inn. I was at first drawn closer to the riverbank so that I could take in the sunny, boundless expanse of the land. I dragged Leni and Marianne over to the garden fence, where we could see the river flowing past the inn, gray-blue and shimmery. The villages and hills on the opposite bank with their fields and forests were reflected in a whorl of sun circles. The longer I looked about me, the more freely I could breathe, the more quickly cheerfulness filled my heart. Almost imperceptibly, the heavy melancholy that had weighed down my every breath vanished. The mere sight of the gently rolling countryside brought joy and gladness from deep inside me, just as a seed of grain will sprout in its native spot of soil and air.

A Dutch ship with a string of eight barges steamed through the hills mirrored in the water. They were hauling wood. The skipper's wife, her little dog frolicking around her, was sweeping the deck. We girls waited till the white wake left in the Rhine by the timber barges had disappeared and there was nothing left to see in the water except the reflection of the opposite riverbank, which collided with the reflection of the garden on our side. We turned back to the coffee tables, preceded by our wobbly Miss Mees, who didn't seem at all droll to me anymore with her equally wobbly cross. For it had suddenly become meaningful for me and as solemn as a symbol. It's possible that among the schoolgirls there were some grumpy and shabby ones. But in their colorful summer dresses, with their bouncy braids and jolly curls, they all looked fresh and festive. Because most of the seats were occupied, Marianne and Leni shared a chair and a coffee cup. Little snub-nosed Nora with the thin voice, two braids wound around her head, wearing a plaid dress, confidently poured coffee and distributed the sugar as if she herself were the innkeeper. Marianne, who usually forgot her former classmates, still vividly remembered this class trip when Nora, who had by then become the leader of the National Socialist Women's League, greeted her there as a national comrade* and former classmate.

A blue cloud of mist coming from the Rhine, or perhaps from my tired eyes, obscured all the tables at which the girls were sitting so that I could no longer clearly make out the individual faces of Nora, Leni, Marianne, and the others, whatever their names were, just as no single blossom would stand out in a tangle of wildflowers. For a while I could hear an argument about where would be the best place for Miss Sichel, the younger teacher, who was coming out of the inn,

*Volksgenossin.

to sit. The cloud of mist dispersed before my eyes just then, and I could clearly see Miss Sichel in a fresh, bright dress, like her pupils.

She sat down next to me, and nimble Nora poured coffee for her favorite teacher. In her eagerness to please, she had even quickly wound a few sprigs of jasmine around Miss Sichel's chair.

Nora would surely have regretted this later on as the leader of the National Socialist Women's League of our city, had her memory not been as fragile as her voice. Now she watched with pride and infatuation as Miss Sichel took one of the jasmine sprigs and put it in the buttonhole of her jacket. In the First World War, Nora would still be happy that she had the same hours of service as Miss Sichel in a section of the Women's Service League that supplied soldiers who were in transit with food and drink. But later she would chase this same teacher, who was by then already old and shaky, away from a bench by the Rhine with insults because she had wanted to sit on a bench where Jews were not allowed to sit. Sitting next to Miss Sichel now, it suddenly came to me—as if I'd had a serious memory lapse and I had a higher duty to remember forever even the tiniest detail—that Miss Sichel's hair had not always been snow-white, as when I last saw her, but that, at the time of our class trip, it was a soft brown, except for a few white strands at the temples. There were still so few white ones now that one could count them, but they shocked me as if here and now, for the first time, I had come upon a sign of aging. Along with Nora, all the other girls at our table were happy to have the young teacher so close, having no inkling that later on they would spit at Miss Sichel and taunt her, calling her a Jewish sow.

Meanwhile, the oldest of us girls, Lore—she wore a skirt and blouse, had wavy, reddish hair, and for a long time had already been having real love affairs—was going from table to table distributing her homemade cake. This girl had all sorts of valuable housewifely talents, some of them related to the art of love and some to the art of cooking. Lore was always cheerful and accommodating and ready for any droll gags or pranks. Her precocious, frivolous conduct, for which her teachers sternly reproved her, never led to marriage, not even to any serious love affair. And so, while most of the others were already dignified mothers, she still looked as she did today, a schoolgirl in a short skirt and with a large, red, sweet-toothed mouth. How could she come to such a sinister end? Dying by her own hand with a vial of sleeping powder. An angry Nazi lover had threatened to send her to a concentration camp, saying that her infidelity amounted to racial defilement. For a long time, he had watched and waited in vain, trying to catch her with the forbidden friend. But in spite of his jealousy and eagerness to punish her, he was unable to prove anything until just shortly before this war, when, during an air-raid drill, the air-raid warden made all the inhabitants of the house leave their rooms, their beds, and go down to the cellar, including Lore with her forbidden lover.

We couldn't help but notice Lore surreptitiously giving a leftover cinnamon star cookie to Ida, who was also exceptionally pretty and smart, adorned with countless little natural curls. Since Lore was looked upon rather askance because of her diversions, Ida was her only friend in the class. We whispered a lot about Ida's and Lore's jolly dates, and about their joint visits to public pools where they met to swim with their lithe male companions. I just don't know why Ida, now surreptitiously gnawing on her little cinnamon star, was never a target of the secret scorn of the mothers and daughters. Perhaps it was because she was a teacher's daughter, and Lore was a hairdresser's daughter. In time Ida gave up her dissolute life, but she never married, because her fiancé was killed at Verdun. This heartbreak impelled her to take up the career of nursing so she could at least be of help to the wounded. After the peace treaty in 1918, she entered the Protestant sisterhood as a deaconess because she didn't want to give up her career. By the time she became a functionary in the National Socialist Sisterhood, her loveliness was already a bit wilted, her curls touched with gray as if strewn with ashes, and even though she had no fiancé in the current war, her desire for revenge, her bitterness, were still alive. She impressed on the younger nurses the government warnings against having conversations with and performing inappropriate compassionate acts for prisoners of war while caring for them. But her instructions that the recently delivered gauze dressings were to be used only for fellow countrymen were ignored, for a bomb struck the hospital far behind the front where she was working, blowing up friends as well as enemies and also, of course, Ida's curly head, which Lore was now stroking with her five manicured fingers, curls that only Ida, and none of her other classmates, had.

Just then Miss Mees tapped her spoon against her coffee cup and ordered us to toss our monetary contributions for the coffee onto the onion-patterned plate she was sending around to all the tables with Gerda, her favorite pupil. Later, she would collect just as deftly and resolutely for the Confessing Church so frowned upon by the Nazis, where, accustomed to such duties, she eventually became treasurer. A position not without danger, but she collected the contributions just as cheerfully and naturally. Today Gerda, the favorite pupil, clattered around merrily with the collection plate and then took it to the innkeeper's wife.

Gerda, although not pretty, was fetching and clever; she had a skull shaped like a mare's, shaggy coarse hair, strong teeth, and beautiful brown eyes, loyal and gently rounded like a mare's. Afterward she rushed back from the innkeeper's wife—she also moved like a foal, always at a gallop—to ask for permission to leave the class and return on a later ship. She had found out that the innkeeper's child was very ill, and since there was no one else to care for her, Gerda wanted to nurse the sick girl. Miss Mees appeased all of Miss Sichel's objections, and Gerda galloped off to her nursing duties as if she were going to a party. She was born to nursing, to loving her fellow man, and to the vocation of teacher in a manner that has almost vanished from the world; it was as if she had been chosen to search out children everywhere who needed her. And wherever she went, she always found people in need of help. Even if her life ended senselessly and unnoticed, nothing in it was lost, not even the most modest of her helpful deeds. Her life was more easily destroyed than the traces she left behind in the memories of the many people whom she had once happened to help. Yet who was there to help her when her husband, against her wishes and in spite of her warning, hung the swastika flag out on the first of May on orders of the new state, because otherwise they would have fired him from his job? No one was there to reassure her when, coming home from the market, she caught sight of the hideous flag at the apartment window and rushed upstairs and turned on the gas. No one stood by her. No matter how many others she herself had helped, in that hour she was hopelessly alone.

A steamship tooted from the direction of the Rhine. We turned our heads to look. On its white hull in gold letters it said *Remagen*. Even though it was far away, I could clearly decipher the name with my weak eyes. I could see the curlicue of smoke above its stack and the hatchway to the cabin. I followed the steamship's wake as it kept smoothing out and developing anew. Meanwhile my eyes had gotten used to the everyday familiar world; I saw everything even more sharply than when the Dutch barges were passing by. There was a clarity about this little steamer *Remagen* as it sailed on the wide, calm river, past villages, mountain ranges, and fleets of clouds that nothing on this earth could have dimmed. By now I had identified the familiar faces on the steamer's deck and at the portholes, whose names the girls were now calling out: "Mr. Schenk! Mr. Reiss! Otto Helmholz! Eugen Lütgens! Fritz Müller!"

Then all the girls yelled in unison, "It's the boys' school! It's the senior class!" Would the boys' class, which was a class outing like ours, get off here, the next stop of the steamer? After a brief conference, Miss Sichel and Miss Mees ordered us girls to line up in rows of four. They wanted, by all means, to avoid a meeting of the two classes. Marianne, whose braids had come undone on the seesaw, began to pin them back over her ears, because her friend Leni—with whom she had been sharing a chair after the seesawing and who had keener eyes—had seen that Otto Fresenius, Marianne's favorite boyfriend and dance partner, was also on board. Leni had even whispered to her, "They're going to get off here. He's signaling to me with his hand."

Fresenius, a dark-blond, lanky youth of seventeen, who had been persistently waving from the ship, would have swum over to us just to be reunited with his girl. Marianne put her arm tightly around Leni's neck; her friend Leni, whom she refused to remember at all later on when asked for help, was like a real sister to her, in love's joys and pains, a dependable adviser who conscientiously delivered letters and arranged secret meetings. Marianne, a lovely, wholesome girl, turned into a marvel of tenderness and charm in the presence of her boyfriend, standing out from all the other schoolgirls like a fabled child. Back home, Otto Fresenius had already told his mother, with whom he shared his secrets, about his affection for the girl. Since the mother rejoiced at this fortunate choice, Marianne thought that nothing would stand in the way of a wedding at some point in the future, once they had waited the proper time. And indeed, there was an engagement party. But there never was a wedding, for her fiancé was killed in 1914, while serving with a student battalion in the Argonne Forest.

The steamer *Remagen* now moved in to the landing dock. Our two teachers, who had to wait for a ship from the opposite direction to take us back home, immediately began to count us. Leni and Marianne watched the docking steamship expectantly. Leni turned her head anxiously as if she sensed that her future, the course of her own destiny, was dependent on whether the two lovers would be reunited or not. Had it been solely up to Leni, instead of Emperor Wilhelm's mobilization and, later on, French sharpshooters, the two of them would surely have married. She could sense how well the two young people fit together, both heart and mind. Then Marianne would not later have refused to care for Leni's child. Otto Fresenius would perhaps have found the means to help Leni escape in time. He would probably, little by little, have been able to instill in his gentle, beautiful wife, Marianne, a feeling for justice and a common respect for human dignity that later would have kept her from repudiating her school friend.

Now, Otto Fresenius—who would have his belly ripped open by bullets in the First World War—spurred on by love, was the first to come off the boat and cross the dock to the café garden. Marianne, who still had one hand on Leni's shoulder, gave him the other hand and left it in his. It was clear, not just to Leni and me, but to all of us, children though we were, that these two were lovers. They showed us the real thing for the first time, not something dreamed up, not something we'd read about in poetry or fairy tales or classic dramas, but the genuine, the real thing—a pair of lovers, as Nature herself had planned and arranged it.

While still keeping one finger hooked in his, Marianne's expression was one of complete devotion and eternal faithfulness to this tall, lean, dark-blond youth, for whom she was to mourn like a widow dressed in black when her letter addressed to him comes back stamped KILLED IN ACTION. In those difficult days Marianne, whom I had seen idolizing Life with its big and little joys, whether of love or seesawing, pretty much despaired of it. During that same time, her girlfriend Leni, around whom she had her arm now, would get to know Fritz, a soldier on leave, who came from a railroad family in our town. While Marianne, although still charming and lovely, was for a long time wrapped in a black cloud of sadness and despair, Leni was the ripest, rosiest apple. Thus for a time the two friends were estranged in the way people often are when sorrow and happiness are at odds. Once her mourning period was over, Marianne, after several encounters in coffeehouses on the banks of the Rhine, with linked fingers as now and the same expression of eternal loyalty as the one on her gentle, longish face at this moment, would form a new relationship with a certain Gustav Liebig who had survived the First World War without injury and who would later become an SS storm trooper in our city. Otto Fresenius, even if he had returned unscathed from the war, would never have become that, neither an SS Sturmbann-führer nor a spokesman for the Gauleitung.* The traits of fairness and honesty, which were already unmistakable in his boyish face now, would make him unsuitable for such a career or position. Leni felt reassured when she found out that her classmate, to whom she used to cling to like a sister, had found a new future that promised to make her happy. Just as now, she was much too naïve to have any idea that the fates of boys and girls determine the fate of their homeland and of their people, and that because of this, sooner or later the joy or suffering of her school friend could brighten or cast a shadow on her.

*Nazi District Administration.

Like Leni, I could not fail to notice on Marianne's face the silent, everlasting pledge of an indestructible solidarity as it rested lightly, as if by chance, on her boyfriend's arm. Leni breathed a sigh of relief as if it were a stroke of extraordinary luck to be witnessing such love. Before they, Leni and her husband, were arrested by the Gestapo, Marianne's new husband, Liebig, to whom she had also sworn eternal loyalty, had told her so many vile things about her school friend's husband that Marianne soon distanced herself from her friendship with a girl considered so contemptible. Leni's husband had resisted joining either the SA or the SS by all the means available to him. Marianne's husband, who was proud of rank and order, would have been his superior in the SS. When he realized that Leni's husband disdained joining this organization, which he considered to be such an honor, he notified the authorities in the small town of the derelict underling.

After a while, the entire boys' class and its two teachers had come ashore. A certain Mr. Neeb, who had a little blond mustache, after bowing to our two teachers cast a sharp glance at us girls, in the course of which he discovered that Gerda, the girl he was looking for, wasn't among us. Gerda, just then, was still inside, washing and tending to the innkeeper's sick child, and had no inkling of the boys' arrival outside in the garden. Nor did she know that Mr. Neeb, their teacher, who had spotted her on previous occasions because of her brown eyes and helpfulness, had noticed she was not there among the girls. The two would not actually meet until after 1918, after the First World War had ended, by which time Gerda herself had become a teacher and they would meet in the recently established League of School Reformers, since both of them were supporters of the school improvements sponsored by the Weimar Republic. But Gerda remained more loyal to the old goals and ideals than he did. Once he was married to the girl, whom he had chosen because of her views, he cared more about a life spent with her in peace and prosperity than about their shared worldviews. And for that reason he hung the swastika flag out of his living-room window when the law threatened that not doing so would cost him his job and therefore his family's livelihood.

I wasn't the only one to notice Neeb's disappointment when he failed to spot in our troop of girls Gerda, the girl he would find again later and make his own, thereby becoming partly responsible for her death. I think Else was the youngest of us, a rotund girl with a round, cherry-red mouth and thick braids. It was she who, seemingly off-handedly, told Mr. Neeb that one of our group, Gerda, was inside, caring for a sick child. Else, a small and inconspicuous girl, whom I and the others soon forgot, much the way you forget a fat bud on some bush, hadn't had any love affairs of her own yet, but she loved discovering those of others and poking around in them. She knew that she had guessed correctly now when she saw Mr. Neeb's eyes light up, and so, as if by chance, she added, "The sickroom is right behind the kitchen."

While Else was testing her cleverness this way, finding that she with her sparkling child's eyes was better at deciphering Neeb's thoughts than some adults whose eyes were dimmed by experience, her own love story was still a long way off. For her future husband, Elbi, a carpenter, had to go to war first. Even back then he already had a little pointed beard and a little belly and was much older than she was. When, after the peace accord, he made the still-rotund and snub-nosed Else a master carpenter's wife, it turned out to be convenient for the business that she had learned bookkeeping at vocational school. The carpentry shop and their three children were important to both of them. Later the carpenter used to say that his trade fared equally well whether Grand Ducal or Social Democratic ministers were seated in Darmstadt, the provincial capital. He also viewed Hitler's rule and the start of a new war as a sort of severe natural phenomenon, rather like a thunderstorm or a blizzard. By that time he was quite advanced in years, and Else's bushy braids had some gray in them too. He probably had no time to change his views, when he, his wife Else, their children, and his apprentices all lost their lives in a British air raid on Mainz that, within five minutes, also turned his house and workshop into dust and scrap.

While Else, as sturdy and round as a little dumpling that only a bomb could shatter, jumped right into her row of girls, Marianne took her place in the outermost corner of the back row where Otto, still standing next to her, could hold her hand in his. They looked over the fence at the water, where their shadows mixed with the reflections of mountains and clouds and the white wall of the waterside inn. They didn't talk to each other; they were absolutely certain that nothing could separate them, no rows of four or departing steamboat, not even death together in a tranquil old age surrounded by a flock of children they had jointly conceived and raised.

The boys' older teacher, whom they called "the Old Man," came then, clearing his throat, and shuffled across the landing dock and into the garden surrounded by his boys. They quickly and eagerly sat down at the table that we girls had just vacated, and the innkeeper, glad that her sick child was being tended by Gerda, brought out some clean blue-and-white onion-pattern dishes. When the head teacher of the boys' class, Mr. Reiss, began to sip his coffee, it sounded like the slurping of a bearded giant.

Contrary to the usual sequence of events, the teacher lived to see his young pupils die in the black-white-red regiments of the First World War and the swastika regiments of the present war. Yet he survived everything unharmed. For he grew too old, not only for battle but also for any statements that might have been interpreted in such a way as to get him arrested and put into a concentration camp.

While the boys, some well behaved, some mischievous, hung around "the Old Man" like fairy-tale goblins, the clutch of girls in the garden below sounded like squeaky elves. When there was a head count, a few girls were found to be missing. Lore was sitting among the boys, for she always stayed as long as possible in the company of men, today as well as all the rest of her life, which came to a bad end because of a Nazi's jealousy. Next to her sat a giggly girl named Elli who had suddenly discovered her dance-class friend, a chubby-cheeked boy named Walter. He was embarrassed to still be wearing short pants that were too tight over his firm behind; later as an already somewhat older but still exceptionally good-looking SS officer in charge of transport, he would send Leni's husband away forever. Now Leni continued to stand carefully aside so that Marianne could exchange some last words with her lover, without any idea of how many future enemies she was surrounded by here, in this garden. Ida, the future deaconess, came trotting over to us with comical dance steps, whistling. The big round eyes of the boys and the slanted, homely ones of the old coffee-slurping teacher were happily fixed on her curly head encircled by a velvet ribbon. One day during the Russian winter of 1943, when her hospital was unexpectedly subjected to bombardment, she would remember, as clearly as I do now, the little velvet ribbon in her hair and the white-walled inn and the sunny garden by the Rhine and the boys arriving just as the girls were leaving.

Marianne had let go of Otto Fresenius's hand. Nor did she have her arm around Leni's shoulder anymore; she was standing by herself in the row of girls, lost in thoughts of love, alone and forsaken. In spite of these most earthy thoughts, she stood out from the other girls by virtue of her almost otherworldly beauty. Otto Fresenius returned to the boys' table along with Mr. Neeb. The young teacher treated him like a comrade, without mockery or questions, for after all, he himself was interested in a girl in that same class, and he respected crushes and infatuations even among his youngest pupils. Since this boy, Otto, would be ripped from his beloved by death so much sooner than the older teacher, he would experience only faithfulness in his short life and be spared all the evil, all the temptations, all the cruelty and shame the older man would be subjected to as he tried to safeguard a government-paid position for himself and Gerda.

Miss Mees, with the mighty, indestructible cross on her bosom, watched carefully to make sure none of us girls would run off to join a dance-class friend before the arrival of the steamer. Miss Sichel had gone to look for Sophie Meier, finding her finally on the seesaw with a boy, Herbert Becker, who like Sophie wore glasses and was as thin as she was, so that they looked more like brother and sister than a pair of lovers. Herbert Becker ran off as soon as he saw the teacher. I used to see him frequently after that, running around our city, grinning and making faces. He still had the same bespectacled, impish boy's face when I met him again a few years ago in France as he was returning from the Spanish Civil War.

Miss Sichel scolded Sophie so severely for carrying on that the girl had to wipe tears from her glasses. Not only the teacher's hair, in which I now saw with surprise a few gray strands, but also the hair of her pupil Sophie, still ebony black like Snow White's, would be totally white when the Nazis deported them both to Poland in a packed, sealed railroad car. Sophie, when she suddenly died in Miss Sichel's arms, was already prematurely aged and shriveled and looked like the older woman's sister.

We were consoling Sophie and cleaning her glasses when Miss Mees clapped her hands to signal that we were to head for the steamboat dock. It was embarrassing to have the boys watch us being marched there, and to have them make fun of our teacher's wobbling duck walk. But I did not feel like mocking her because I respected her unwavering composure, a composure she maintained even when summoned before the People's Court set up by Hitler and threatened with prison. We waited together on the landing dock until the ship's crew tossed out the rope. The way the boatman caught it, wound it around the post, and then set up the plank leading to the ship all seemed to me extraordinarily quick and adroit: a welcome into a new world, an assurance that our trip would be safe, so that all other voyages I was to take over endless seas, from one continent to another, paled and became fantastic like the adventures in childhood dreams. They were by far not as exciting or as real as the smell of wood and water, the slight swaying of the plank to the boat, and the creaking of the ropes as we started the twenty-minute return trip on the Rhine to my hometown.

I jumped up onto the deck so that I would be able to sit near the helm. Then the ship's little bell sounded, the rope was hauled in, the steamer turned. It dug a glittering white arc of foam into the river. I thought of all the white fissures of foam that all possible ships had plowed into the seas at all possible degrees of latitude. I would never again be so profoundly impressed by the transience and the immutability of such a journey, the bottomlessness yet the accessibility of the water. Then suddenly Miss Sichel came up to me. She looked very young in the sunlight in her polka-dotted dress with her small firm bosom. She said, looking at me with her clear gray eyes, that because I liked sailing and writing compositions I should write a description of the school trip for our next German class.

All the other girls in my class who preferred the deck to the cabin came rushing to where I was and sat down on the benches. The boys whistled and waved from the garden. Lore whistled shrilly back and was severely reprimanded by Miss Mees, even while the boys in the garden continued their rhythmic whistling. Marianne leaned far out over the railing, not letting Otto out of her sight, as if this separation might already be forever, like the later one during the war in 1914. When she could no longer make out her boyfriend, she put one arm around me and the other around Leni. I felt the tenderness of her thin, bare arm at the same time as I felt the sun's rays on the back of my neck. I also looked back now toward Otto Fresenius, who was still staring after his girl as if he could keep her in sight and—since she was now leaning her head against Leni—remind her forever of their steadfast friendship.

The three of us, arms entwined, looked upstream. The low afternoon sun on the hills and vineyards fluffed up the white- and pink-blooming fruit trees here and there. A few windows glowed in the late sunshine as if ablaze. The villages seemed to get bigger the closer we got to them, shrinking again after we had barely brushed by them. This was the innate yearning for travel that can never be satisfied because you only skim by everything in passing. We sailed under the Rhine bridge over which military trains would soon be rolling in the First World War, carrying schoolboys from all the schools as well as all the boys now drinking their coffee in the garden. When that war ended, Allied soldiers would move over the same bridge, and later Hitler's youthful army, who would reoccupy the closed-off Rhineland until new military trains would roll with all the nation's boys to die in a new world war.

Our ship sailed past the Petersau, on which one of the bridge piers rested. We waved to the three little white houses that we knew from the time we were small and which looked like the tiny picture-book houses in fairy tales about witches. The little houses and a fisherman were reflected in the water, as well as the village on the other side. Its rape and wheat fields climbed up the hillside above a row of pink apple trees in a huddled cluster of peaked roofs, rising in a Gothic triangle up to the little church spire.

The late-afternoon sun now shone into a gap in the valley with railway tracks, then on a remote chapel, until everything flashed up out of the Rhine once more before disappearing in the dusk.

In the calm light we all fell silent so that one could hear the squawking of a few birds and the howling of the factory in Amöneburg. Even Lore was totally silent. Marianne, Leni, and I, all three of us, had our arms intertwined in a unanimity that was part of the greater unity of all earthly beings under the sun. Marianne was still leaning her head against Leni's. How could she later be so deceived, so deluded, as to think that she and her husband were the only ones entitled to love this country, and therefore had the right to despise this girl she was leaning against now, and to denounce her.

No one ever reminded us of this trip we took together while there was still time. No matter how many compositions were to be written about our homeland and its history and one's love for the homeland, no one ever mentioned that our group of girls, leaning against one another while sailing upstream in the slanting afternoon light, first and foremost belonged to and were part of this homeland.

The river now branched off to the barge port from which freshly felled, cut, and floated wood was taken to Holland. The city still seemed to me far enough away that it could never force me to disembark and stay, even though its river port, the rows of plane trees and warehouses by the shore, were much more familiar to me than any of the journeys I had made to foreign cities where I had then been forced to stay. By and by I recognized streets and houses, roof ridges, and church steeples, undamaged and familiar, like long-lost places in fairy tales and songs. The one-day school trip seemed to have at once taken everything from me and given it all back.

Now, as the ship was maneuvering to dock and children and strollers idly pressed forward for our arrival, it seemed to me that we were not returning home just from a day's outing but from a journey of many years. No crater, no fire damage was visible in this bustling, familiar city with its winding streets, and so my uneasiness was allayed, and I felt at home.

The ropes had barely been thrown out when Lotte said goodbye. She wanted to attend evening mass at the cathedral, whose bells you could already hear from as far away as the ship's bridge. Later Lotte ended up in the cloister on the Rhine island of Nonnenwerth, from where she, along with a group of other nuns, was taken across the Dutch border. But fate caught up with them.

The class said goodbye to the teachers. Miss Sichel reminded me again about the composition I was to write, and her gray eyes gleamed like finely polished pebbles. Then our class split up into separate groups depending on the location of our homes.

Leni and Marianne walked arm in arm toward Rheinstrasse; Marianne still had a red carnation between her teeth. She had pinned a similar carnation into the ribbon around Leni's French braid. I keep seeing Marianne with the red carnation in her teeth, also later when she was giving nasty answers to Leni's neighbors, and also when she was lying, her body half charred in smoking shreds of clothing, among the ashes of her parents' house. For the fire department came too late to rescue Marianne when the fires from houses that had sustained direct hits in the bombardment spread to the Rheinstrasse, where she just happened to be visiting her parents. Her death was no easier than Leni's, whom she had repudiated and who died slowly of hunger and illness in a concentration camp. But because of Marianne's betrayal, Leni's child survived the bombardment. For the child had been taken by the Gestapo and brought to a remote Nazi reform school.

I trotted off in the direction of Christhof Street with a couple of my classmates. At first I felt anxious. Something weighed heavily on my heart as we turned from the Rhine toward the inner city. It was as if something crazy, something bad, was waiting for me, perhaps some terrible news or a disaster that I had thoughtlessly forgotten during the sunny outing. Then I realized that the Christofskirche could not possibly have been destroyed by a nighttime air raid, for we could hear its vesper bells ringing.

I had been worrying unnecessarily about taking this way home because I had this persistent recollection that the strip in the middle of the city had been totally destroyed by bombs. But then it occurred to me that the photograph in the newspaper might have been mistaken, a photograph that showed all the streets and squares razed or destroyed. At first I thought they had constructed a sham town with the greatest speed, perhaps on orders from Goebbels, so as to deceive the people about the actual extent of the air-raid damage; a town in which no stone rested on another as before but which seemed quite solid and presentable. We were, after all, used to this sort of pretense and deception, not only after bombing attacks but also in the case of other events that were confusing and difficult to comprehend.

But the houses, the stairways, the fountains were still standing as before. Even Braun's Wallpaper Shop, which would burn down along with his entire family in this war. During the First World War, though, only the shopwindows were destroyed by an antiaircraft projectile; now the shop was displaying striped and flowered wallpaper. Marie Braun, who had been walking beside me, hurried into her father's shop.

Katharina, the next of us to return home, ran over to her little sister Toni, who was playing on a stone step by the fountain under the plane trees. The fountain and all the plane trees had probably been destroyed long ago, but the children didn't need anything for their games, because their last hour too had struck in the cellars of the surrounding houses. Little Toni also died in the house she had inherited from her father, along with a daughter as tiny as she was today, spraying water out of her plump cheeks. Katharina and her big sister who grabbed her by a shock of hair, as well as their mother and aunt standing in the open doorway of the house, greeting them both with kisses, would all perish together in the cellar of the father's house. While this was happening, Katharina's husband, a wallpaper hanger and their father's successor, was helping occupy France. With his short mustache and his paperhanger's thumb he considered himself a member of a people, a nation that was stronger than other nations —until the news reached him that his house and family had been crushed. The little sister turned around once more and with the last of the water she'd saved up in her cheeks she sprayed me too.

I walked the rest of the way by myself. On Flachsmarktstrasse I ran into another classmate, pale Liese Möbius who, because she'd had pneumonia, hadn't been able to go with us on any of our class trips for the last two months. The evening bells of the Christofskirche had lured her out of the house. She nimbly ran past me, a pince-nez on her little nose and two long brown braids dangling, as if she were running to the playground instead of to evening mass. Later she would beg her parents for permission to enter the cloister on Nonnenwerth Island along with Lotte. When only Lotte received permission, Liese became a teacher in a grade school in our city. I would see her a few more times running to mass as today with her pale, pointy little face and the pince-nez on her nose. She was treated contemptuously by the Nazi authorities because of her religious faith, but even being transferred to a school for the feeble-minded didn't bother her, for she was used to all sorts of persecution for her faith. And even the most rabid Nazi women, the most malicious, mocking neighbors became gentle and mild when they sat around Liese in the cellar during an air raid. The older ones would remember then that once before they had been in the same cellar hole with this same neighbor, Liese, when the first bombs exploded in that first war. Now they moved close to the despised little teacher who seemed to have already appeased death once before with her faith and her tranquility. The most brazen and the most eager to ridicule her were even inclined to accept some of Liese's faith, this little teacher, whom they had always perceived as shy and fearful, but who was once more comforted and hopeful as she sat among all the ugly, gray-white faces in the artificial cellar light as the bombs were dropping, which this time almost totally destroyed the city, along with Liese and her believing nonbelieving neighbors.

The shops had just closed. I walked along Flachsmarktstrasse, making my way through the throngs of people returning home. They were happy that the day was over and a quiet night lay ahead. Just as their houses were still undamaged by shelling in that first big rehearsal of 1914 to 1918 and the most recent direct hits, so also were their homely, thoroughly familiar faces—faces, whether thin or pudgy, mustachioed or bearded, warty or smooth, that were still unmarked by the guilt of their children and their knowledge of that guilt, and of standing by and tolerating that guilt because they were too cowardly before the power of the state. And yet they would soon be getting their fill of bloated state power and pompous orders. Or had these people perhaps developed a taste for it, like this baker with his twirled mustache and little rotund belly on the corner of the Flachsmarkt where we always bought our crumb cake, or that streetcar conductor who was just then jingling past us? Or was the peacefulness of this evening, the hurried steps of those going home, the bells ringing, the closing-time tooting of distant factories, and the modest coziness of an ordinary workday that I was savoring now so objectionable to their children that they would soon be greedily absorbing their fathers' war reports and longing to get out of their floury or dusty work clothes and into uniforms?

As I was about to turn onto my own street, I felt another twinge of fear as if I had a hunch that I would find it in ruins. But the premonition soon vanished. For I could take my favorite way home on the last stretch of Bauhofstrasse, walking under the two big ash trees that spread from the left and the right side of the street, touching overhead like a triumphal arch, whole and indestructible. And I could already see the white, red, and blue circular beds of geranium and begonia in the area of grass that divided my street. An evening wind blew up as I approached, stronger than any I had ever felt before on my temples; it blew a cloud of leaves out of the red hawthorn trees, which had at first seemed to be glazed by the sun but were in reality sun-red in color.

Always, after a day's outing, I felt as if I it had been a long time since I heard the sound of the Rhine wind trapped in my own street. I was so tired that I was glad to be finally standing in front of my house. Yet climbing the stairs seemed unbearably difficult. I looked up to the third floor, where our apartment was. My mother was already standing on the little balcony with its boxes of geraniums. She was waiting for me. How young she looked—my mother, so much younger than I. How dark her smooth hair compared to mine. Mine would be gray soon, while not a single strand of gray was visible in hers. She stood there, cheerful and erect, destined for a family life full of work and all the ordinary joys and troubles of everyday life, not for a painful, gruesome end in some remote village to which she had been banished by Hitler. Now she recognized me and waved as if I had been away on a long journey. She always laughed and waved like this after my class trips. I ran as fast as I could into the stairwell.

I hesitated before the first landing. I was suddenly much too tired to hurry up the stairs, as I had intended to a moment ago. A grayish-blue fog of weariness engulfed everything. And yet it was bright and hot all around me, not dim the way it usually is in stairwells. I forced myself to climb up to my mother. The stairway, in my gloomy haze, seemed unattainably high, indomitably steep, as if it were ascending a cliff wall. Perhaps my mother had already gone into the apartment hallway and was waiting by the door to the stairwell. But my legs gave out. Only as a very young child had I felt fear like this, a fear that some disaster could keep us from seeing each other again. I imagined her waiting for me in vain only a few steps away. Then I was reassured by the thought that, were I to collapse here from exhaustion, my father would soon find me. He wasn't dead, after all. He would come home soon, for the workday was over. Except that he was in the habit of stopping to chat with neighbors on some street corner, longer than my mother liked.

There was already the clatter of dishes in preparation for the evening meal. Behind all the doors I heard the familiar rhythm of hands slapping dough. I was put off by the way they baked pancakes: Instead of rolling out the elastic dough, they pounded it flat between their hands. At the same time I could hear the unrestrained cries of turkeys in the courtyard and wondered why anyone would be raising turkeys in the courtyard. I wanted to turn around to look, but was blinded at first by the strong light from the courtyard windows. A hazy mist blurred the stairs; the stairwell stretched out in all directions, as infinitely deep as an abyss. Then the clouds gathered in the window alcoves and soon filled the abyss. Weak as I was, I still managed to think: What a shame; I would so much have liked my mother to embrace me. And if I was too tired to climb the stairs, where would I get the strength to reach the village located higher up, where I was expected that evening?

The sun was still strong; its light was never brighter than when it shone at an angle. As always it seemed odd to me that there was no dusk or twilight here but always that sudden change from day to night. I pulled myself together and stepped up more forcefully even though the way was lost in a bottomless abyss. The stairway banister turned and curved, becoming a mighty picket-like fence of organ-pipe cacti. I could no longer distinguish mountaintops from cloud drifts. I found my way to the inn, where I had eaten after hiking down from the village. The dog had run off. Two turkeys, which had not been there before, were now grazing by the roadside. The innkeeper was still sitting in front of the house, and next to him sat a friend or a relative, grown stiff just like him from thinking or from nothing. At their feet were the shadows of their hats lying peaceably side by side. The innkeeper made no move when I came back; I wasn't worth it; I was already entered as one of his everyday sensory perceptions. By now I was too tired to take another step; I sat down at my old table. As soon as I'd caught my breath, I intended to go back up into the mountains. I wondered how I should pass the time, today and tomorrow, here and there, for I now sensed an immeasurable river of time, as uncontrollable as the air. We had been accustomed, after all, since we were little, to do something with our time, to manage it, instead of humbly giving ourselves up to it. Suddenly I remembered the teacher's assignment, to carefully describe our class trip, our outing. I would do the assignment first thing tomorrow, or maybe even tonight, once this weariness had passed.

1943–1944

THE END

VOLPERT climbed down the railway embankment to the village in order to buy or borrow a couple of good ropes; he needed them to tie down the machine parts he had been transporting in the side tipper to make repairs along the tracks, to keep them from being damaged by all the jolting during the trip.

His foreman, Ernst Hänisch, waved to him from the nearest farmstead; he had already found what they were looking for. "Good morning," Volpert greeted the farmer standing next to Hänisch. He was a burly man of average height, between thirty and forty years old.

"Mr. Zillich here said he would be happy to lend us a couple of these thingies. I told him we'd send them back with the return train. He doesn't want any money for them."

"I can also sell you four brand-new ones," the farmer said. "They're still out there on my cart." He spoke deliberately and slowly like all the people around here, as if words cost money and they were reluctant to part with them. He had small, dark, distrustful eyes; his nostrils were as round and alert as an additional pair of eyes. His short nose turned up somewhat, and his mouth was small. Actually, his features were small in a face that, all in all, took up relatively little space on the large peasant head. His ears were small too, and tipped weirdly forward instead of toward the back, as if they had to catch as much sound as possible.

Volpert said, "Yes. That's good, I can use the new ones too." He was staring at one of the man's ears. The farmer turned his head. He called out, "Hans!" A boy came to the door; he was around twelve. He was so thin that you could see his collarbones through his shirt.

He seemed withdrawn. His full lips were pressed together, pouting slightly. His nostrils quivered. He had lowered his eyes as if the strange faces distressed him like a sharp light. His ears were large and stuck out from his head, but they were not tipped forward.

His father said, "Run out to the field and bring us the four hemp ropes we twisted last week. They're lying in the basket in the cart. C'mon, hurry up!" he added when the boy hesitated. "Make it snappy." He gave the boy a kick in the backside as he sullenly trotted off.

Volpert frowned. He looked more closely at the farmer's face. The man laughed. "The oaf can't do anything quickly." But his little eyes weren't laughing; they moved a couple of times sideways to look at Volpert's face. Hänisch asked the farmer, "How far is it to the field?"

"Oh, ten minutes." The farmer suddenly snapped his fingers; he'd had an idea. Volpert flinched. Then Zillich abruptly put his hand into his pants pocket as if by snapping his fingers he'd done something forbidden. He said, "If you're in a hurry, it would really be better if I take care of it myself. God knows how long it'll take the scamp." He trotted off along the village street.

Volpert watched him go with a grim expression. He leaned his head against the house wall and closed his eyes. He could see Zillich before him, etched there into his eyelids until the hour of his death. Zillich, the man behind his eyelids, was wearing an SA shirt, and when he turned his back to the work gang, his buttocks stretched his pants. They'd called him "Pig Ears" in the concentration camp because of his flipped ears. His little eyes back then seemed tiny in the fat face, as tiny as bird eyes, but sharp and exacting. He had watched, like a bird on a perch, as his orders were carried out, indifferent yet attentive: punishment drill with arms stretched up during which two old men once had a stroke almost at the same time; knee bends in the broiling hot sun to test new arrivals; licking the grimy stairs clean, during which he kicked the Jews who'd been sentenced to this punishment in the backsides; and always when he had ordered someone, do this or do that, the command was enforced with a kick; even the night Buchholz was taken out of the barracks and led off to be shot, he had sent him to his grave with a kick in the ass. When Gebhardt was beaten to death in front of the entire column of prisoners, Zillich, who was watching nonchalantly with crossed arms, at the last minute suddenly pounced on the man lying in the dirt, like a bird of death who circles his victim, pouncing only once it is dying.

Volpert had often wondered what had happened to the brute. In his dreams, both night and day, he had imagined what it would be like to run into him again. Perhaps it was only his hope for revenge that had kept him alive in the camp. After the war ended, he had avidly searched through all the reports of arrests, looking for the man's name. In the camp he had lost sight of him when they could already hear the Soviet machine-gun fire. The commandant's last order had been to round up all the prisoners in the area between the barracks and shoot them. Volpert escaped death in the confusion, by taking a risk that only the fear of dying could have inspired. Perhaps Zillich had already made off by then. In their panicky fear of the Russians, those torturers revealed a last glimmer, a semblance of being human, a last particle of a foreboding of justice.

When Volpert opened his eyes again, a woman wearing a navy-blue cotton dress and a kerchief tied on her head was standing between him and his foreman, Hänisch. She looked old and wrinkled enough to be Zillich's mother. But she said, "My husband won't be back so soon. You'd better go across to the Eichen Inn. They don't have any beer yet, but they've got homemade gooseberry wine."

Volpert wondered, Can this really be his wife? Is this really his garden? Was it really his name, too. Was this really the same man?

The village street looks as neat and clean as if it had been set up with toy blocks. The only traces left from the shooting and the bitter bayonet battle for the town hall might be the brand-new bricks used to build a new balcony, so different from the rest of the crooked little old houses. You could tell by the freshly plastered and whitewashed sidewall of the inn that it had also received its share of artillery fire.

Hänisch and Volpert sat down in the inn's garden, diagonally across from Zillich's house. They could see Mrs. Zillich's head moving among the sunflowers; she was picking things from her kitchen garden in which chives, parsley, radishes, and cress had been planted in narrow rows. Tomato plants were growing along the fence and a blue glass sphere glistened on a post that was taller than the sunflowers.

Again Volpert wondered, Is this really his house? Does he really live here? Does he actually have the same glass sphere as his neighbor?

The innkeeper's wife came over to their table; with her apron she brushed off the wilted chestnut leaves. Content that some things at least had gone back to being as they were before, she covered the table with a checkered tablecloth and brought them a pitcher of the wine and two glasses. Tasting it, Hänisch cursed, calling it "sour trash," but then immediately poured himself another glassful.

Volpert stared intently at the path that led through the fields and disappeared in a beech grove on the gently rising hills. He said, "Once Zillich comes back, please help me keep a sharp eye on the fellow so he doesn't slip through our fingers again."

Hänisch turned his bright eyes, which seemed younger than his face and thinning gray hair, to Volpert's frowning forehead. "What else have you got up your sleeve for today?"

"First, I'll call, 'Zillich.' Then I want him to come over here to this side of the fence and stand between the two of us. Then I want to ask him a couple of questions. After that he just might go berserk."

Hänisch was small and agile; his hair, like that of many others, might have turned gray through years of suffering. But he was an old man whose disposition had kept him young. In the last ten years he had experienced more sorrow because of his own and other people's sons than entire generations might have in other times. He gave Volpert a scornful look, saying, "If this man really is that fellow Zillich about whom you told us so much, then I don't understand why you have to swallow this damned sour gooseberry wine before taking him to task."

Volpert answered, "Well, right from the start he vaguely reminded me of someone. But by the time it was clear to me how much he looked like the man he probably really is, he'd already taken off."

He frowned, staring in the direction of the little beech grove on the other side of which lay the village fields. Hänisch put his hand on Volpert's arm; now he could also see a shadow moving from the shrubbery toward the village.

But it was only the boy. He clanked open the garden gate, and after exchanging a few words with his mother, he ambled over toward the inn garden with a couple of ropes dangling from his arm. He spoke to them over the fence. "You can give the money to my mother. My father isn't coming home as yet."

"In that case, I'll have to catch up with him," Volpert said. "There's something I want to discuss with him."

"That won't be possible," the boy said. "My father isn't in the field anymore. He was called away. There's work at a new construction site. My father said that they paid well there. He wouldn't get the job if he didn't go there right away."

Hänisch laughed. The boy looked at him, puzzled; then he looked at Volpert's face, which had suddenly turned pale. He noticed Volpert and Hänisch exchanging glances. Volpert said, brusquely, "Come over here."

The boy looked at the man, who looked back at him. The boy's eyes were brown, the man's were gray. The one looked into the eyes of the other, and instead of clarity and calm, each saw in the eyes of the other a lot of troubling questions.

The boy cautiously withdrew his gaze from the stranger's eyes, which hadn't given him any answers. He twisted the ropes in his hands. He was a lot more fidgety and thin-skinned than most farm boys.

Hänisch grabbed the ropes out of his hands. He said, "Go home, boy!" Then he turned to Volpert. "I'll go and pay the wife first. Get back on the train; I'll catch up with you." He added softly because the boy was still watching them surreptitiously, as if he sensed that there was something dangerous about the strangers, "We'll do what we need to do in Zeissen. What can we do here after all? There's no post office, no police. Whom can you turn to in this godforsaken hole? And the mayor might be his brother-in-law or his cousin."

He walked over to Zillich's house and paid the woman, who was surprised and pleased. Then he quickly climbed back up the railway embankment so fast that he caught up with Volpert. Together, they tied down the machine parts and headed toward Zeissen.

The gently rolling hills were flecked here and there by the remnants of a beech forest and checkered by as many squares of potato and wheat fields as the carefully patched apron of a farmer's wife. The war seemed to lie as far in the past as all those other wars that the village schoolteachers talk about. The earth had healed from the conflagrations, now it was only the smoke from the small fires in the potato fields drifting up and dispersing under the gray-blue night sky.

Back home, Mrs. Zillich hid the money in a drawer. The unexpected earnings came at a most convenient time. In case Zillich really had to go to work in the town, she wasn't sure whether he'd come back in time, and if he did, with how much cash. Now she and the boy would have to do all the farm work—the three youngest weren't much help yet—but she was relieved rather than annoyed, even though Zillich had been working tirelessly since he had come back home.

He had been standing in her garden as if he'd sprouted from the soil suddenly one evening, when everything was topsy-turvy because of the fire in Zeissen that they could smell all the way here, when foreign troops darkened the countryside like grasshoppers, consuming everything. Days and nights, he had tramped through the country, from east to west, to finally return home. He had been drawn to this village in the deserted hills by the forsaken little river, the way a child is drawn to its mother's lap. And once he was back, he had immediately started working with gritted teeth, as if determined to do the most menial work that in the past he had despised.

From the moment of the marriage they had consummated in accordance with their fathers' wishes, he had shirked all kinds of work. He had hung out in the tavern getting involved in brawls and stabbings. What hurt her even more than the beatings and blows was his endless mockery. She was a disgusting, slovenly, ugly, stupid woman. She hadn't been so slovenly, ugly, and stupid that she didn't understand scorn. But somehow, once he put on the brown shirt, the tall boots, and the leather belt, things got better. The brawls in the village became less frequent because the people now cringed before him. He also frequently drove the truck to Zeissen for all sorts of activities from which he came home well-fed and tired.

She had been working till she was half dead, when, one day, he up and drove off, leaving her with all the work. On orders from the Führer, he'd said; it was her duty just as it was his. After that he stayed away most of the time, coming home only on short leaves; peacetime was scarcely any different from the way it was during the war. Sometimes he'd sent her money; that had helped when things got really bad. Later, from the field, he'd sent packages of clothes, food, and shoes for the children. She had almost reconciled herself to him, especially when he finally turned up again suddenly after the end of the war. The man had become like a different person, very religious, hardworking, calm. Except that he sometimes had a hankering to pinch the little one or make a face at her like an idiot, or to sit and brood for hours. What she disliked most was spending evenings alone in the kitchen with him just staring straight ahead.

But there were many people in the village who said, That Zillich, he's sown his wild oats out there; or: He's learned how to tackle things; or: You should be glad you still have a husband.

No sooner had the boy entered the little beech grove on his way to deliver the ropes and the message for his mother, than Zillich stashed his tools in a hole in the ground prepared for that purpose and took the path diagonally across the field, along the hill, and across the main road. When, after a while, he heard the train whistling on the railroad embankment, he ducked behind some willow shrubs. Even had he been keeping watch with binoculars, the stranger would hardly have recognized him, just a little dot on the plain. Zillich had no clear recollection of the man; he only became suspicious when the fellow hesitated and then suddenly started watching all his movements attentively. Since Zillich had been assigned as a guard at the Westhofen concentration camp in the fall of 1937, he'd had so many prisoners in so many different camps under his supervision that he couldn't possibly have remembered every single one of the many thousands. Most of them were dead; yet no doubt there were still many of those who had managed to survive the war scattered around the country. And among these there were probably some whose thirst for revenge kept them awake at night. These men still refused to accept the peace that the people and the fields had yearned for. They could think of nothing but hate and revenge, even as the whole world, half choked with blood, longed for nothing more than sowing and harvesting and for peace and calm under a quiet sky. Or some other kind of work they could do without being suddenly frightened or being under constant suspicion or being called to account at night.

Where was he to go now? He had been happy when he had finally reached home after traveling some thousand kilometers through three enemy armies. He had found calm at home. No one there could remember anymore where he had been all those years. No one remembered exactly whose bones he had broken. Until the stranger had turned up this morning to spoil things. He probably last had him under his thumb at Camp Piaski in Poland; it was coming back to him now.

Volpert's train had already left the next station by the time Zillich turned onto a country road that led away from the main road and toward Weinheim. With ingrained caution he avoided a couple of foreign military patrols and some rural policemen. The edge of the town facing toward the flatland was composed of finely gabled houses, some of them with crenellations, as handsome as a stage set before a jumble of ruins, rubble, and bustling activity. The town gate, through which Zillich now passed, was well preserved, but it led into a town of ashes. With time, they had been able to haul off the piles of rubble, which were what remained of the town that had stretched down to the river. Now a cloud of dust hung over the inner town and the construction site that had already been dug up and in several places was crossed by regular ditches in which groundwater was collecting.

There were also a few airy streets lined with flimsy barracks built on the unidentifiable remains of the foundation walls of a thousand-year-old fortress. These had been constructed in haste only to be hastily hauled off again someday. The work shift had just ended, and people were streaming to these barracks in great numbers. Zillich joined them. There were some among them, practiced in camaraderie, who were able to interpret his hesitant expression and invited him to spend the night in their barracks.

Most of the men lying on their straw sacks, in this shelter that they had built for themselves with what remained of military discipline, had gotten stuck here on their homeward wanderings, or were here because they had no homes or were retained here by the chance to work.

On his way home, in all sorts of overcrowded lodgings Zillich had longed for his own four walls. Now, for the first time after his escape, he felt at peace in the familiar warm smell of many people crammed together. He was totally exhausted. He turned his face toward the arm of his neighbor and fell asleep. But sleep did not bring him profound rest, only disquiet and anxiety. He felt threatened in every fiber of his being, whether in a dreamless state or in a shapeless, formless dream. He sensed Death everywhere, all-powerful and all-knowing, as if it were following him and persecuting him. It, Death, tore at his hair; it burned his heart, tickled his heels, buzzed in thin murmurs at his back. Zillich wanted to rant in fury and put an end to the disruption. He bellowed, "Quiet!" He commanded, "Get out!" and, "Make it quick!" and, "March, march!"

Someone tapped him on the shoulder and tried to reassure him. His neighbor woke him up, said to him good-naturedly, "Calm down, give us some peace." He was probably used to his own and others' feverish dreams.

Zillich thought, Yes, peace. If only it were that simple! If only it were granted that easily!

He immediately made himself as flat as possible on his straw sack, like an animal pretending to be dead, so as not to stick out or call attention to himself. On awakening, he had started up in fright. He wiped his face; his hair was soaked with sweat. He heard the irritating murmur of voices behind him, trying to whisper very softly. It bothered him that they hadn't obeyed his orders for silence, even though he'd only given them in his dream. He now listened as if he were on the trail of a conspiracy that could only be hatched in the dark: The spire of the Johanniskirche had collapsed; the roof, destroyed; they had roofed over the cloister and set up an employment office inside; supposedly there would soon be a ruling from the occupation authorities that you had to register, to report where you came from and where you were going. It was a given that people would manage to set up some office or other, even if their homes had been blown apart; that way, at least they felt as if they had a home on a piece of paper and a line on a list; it was almost like having a roof over one's head again.

Zillich had been listening uneasily to all this, unaware that he had propped himself up. Suddenly someone who was just getting undressed called out, "Hey, Zillich, is that really you?"

Zillich quickly stretched out again, too late. The new man crouched down next to him. He had a fringe of a little beard; in the dark it even looked twirled and tapered like a radish.

"You still don't recognize me? I'm Anton."

Zillich did recognize him; he stared at him fixedly as if it might make him disappear. Anton was the nephew Müller had adopted as his son. "Odd that you're not back home," the radish said. "For me things are quite different. The mill burned down. My aunt had a stroke. I don't know where my uncle is. But you, on the other hand, are badly needed at home."

Zillich said curtly, "I want to earn some money."

"True enough." Anton was satisfied. "You don't have even a penny for thread or for a nail. Funny that you didn't recognize me; I could have picked you out from among a million. Do you still remember during our last furlough, when the threshing machine was being rented out and you let me have it first because my furlough was about to end? I'd call that decent, and I'll never forget it." When Zillich didn't say anything, the fellow went back to his straw sack with a cheerful "Till tomorrow."

It was obvious to Zillich that he couldn't stay here any longer. It was much too close to home.

Using all the tricks he'd learned to keep from being captured on his flight home from the lost war, he managed to slip through the patrols circling the nighttime city. By dawn the next day he was walking along the main road toward Braunsfeld. He knew only that the town was located where the sun would set, which had started, more resolutely than he, on the same journey to shine upon good and evil. The stars dropped out of the sky; here and there a light still shone on the river or in some village where someone, by making an early start, hoped to cope with a task for which no day and no exertion would be enough. He passed through a village where a daft old woman, habitually up early as if she hadn't noticed that she'd been alone for a long time on her farm, greeted him with a cheerful "Heil Hitler," because she didn't know that there was no Hitler anymore.

He walked through wheat fields choked with useless abundance, blooming and fragrant for their own sake. He walked through potato fields where a family was hoeing as vehemently as if the first day of creation had just dawned and this particular field had detached itself as solid ground. He saw a little man walking slowly up from the valley on a dirt road, so slowly that he ran into Zillich at the crossroad. The little man looked grimy enough that one might have thought he hadn't been able to find water to wash with since the armistice had been declared. He was wearing a long, knitted woman's sweater buttoned over his supple flexible upper body. In one of the buttonholes there was a yellow aster.

He turned to Zillich as if he had been expecting him. His eyes were sly and bright as he said, "Where are you going in such a hurry, comrade?"

Zillich replied, "To Braunsfeld."

"The troubles people still go to voluntarily! Why are you going there?"

"To work. On the construction project."

"Before you get there, you pass a large sand quarry. We can both get work there. They need the sand on the other side of the river at the Mammolscheim Cement Factory. They've started it up again."

"You think they'll have work for me too at the quarry?"

"Of course. They're glad for every man they can get."

The little man was walking along unhurriedly. And Zillich wasn't in a hurry anymore either. He might actually be safer in that out-of-the-way sand quarry.

"There, you see," the little man said, guessing his thoughts. "Why go all the way to Braunsfeld? Why all that unnecessary trouble?" He started whistling some cheerful popular old songs that had outlasted the war, going back to the days before the war and the beginning of all time. But he also whistled marches and songs that were so recent and familiar that Zillich had chills running down his spine. And the man didn't stop even when a squad of khaki-clad Americans came marching toward them from the next village. He didn't miss a beat, enjoying the fact that none of them recognized the tunes he was whistling; his eyes sparkled. Once he was finished with "Judenblut," he started whistling "Puppchen."*

Zillich was glad when the Americans had passed them without incident. He was in no mood for trouble. He no longer wanted to stand up for something that had failed. He yearned only for peace and quiet.

What an odd sort of guy this is! thought the little man. I'll figure out soon enough what tune he'll dance to. He started whistling "Brüder, zur Sonne, zur Freiheit."†

Zillich said nothing. But he thought, What a weird guy this is.

Then the little man cheerfully whistled the "Horst-Wessel-Lied."‡ Two boys, loaded down with wood, passed them; they turned around laughing. As they were walking by a couple of workers fiddling around on a steamroller, he started whistling "The Internationale." One of the workers called down from the steamroller, "Red Front!"

*_Judenblut_ means "Jewish blood"; _Puppchen_ means "sweetie pie" or "baby doll."
†Brothers, to the Sun, to Freedom.
‡The "Horst Wessel Song" was the anthem of the Nazi Party.

Zillich thought, How weird. He felt uneasy. He said, "What's your name?"

"My name? Peter Nobody."

Zillich looked at the little fellow nonplussed. Maybe he was joking; maybe he was serious. Maybe there really was somebody whose name was Nobody. In the meantime it was broad daylight. The village they were walking through was wide awake. Zillich thought, I hope that, back home, Franz has found my hoe in the hole in the ground by now. Then he stopped thinking about back home, just as he hadn't thought about it before, as little as he used to think about some quarters after he was transferred out of them.

The little man said, "Strange that they don't pull the weeds in the church square, that they don't order something like that done."

"We would have had something like that taken care of long ago."

Hmm, finally. Now I've got you, the little man thought. Aloud he said, "Yes, of course, if we'd won the war, wow... In Ukraine, in a village, back then when we were winning..."

Zillich said nothing. He thought, God only knows what kind of devil this is. With his yellow aster.

The little man said, "You're coming from the east, right?"

Zillich started. "Me? No, no, no. I'm coming from the Meuse."

"How odd," the little man said, "that you'd be taking this detour to Braunsfeld. What's your name?"

Zillich quickly lied: "Schulze."

"What do you know!" the little man said. "That's really amazing."

"What's so amazing about someone's name being Schulze? There are lots of Schulzes in Germany, after all."

"Yes, but that's just it, that you, of all people, should have that name too. I, for instance, once knew someone named Karfunkelstein."

"But that must have been a Jew. There are hardly any of them left."

The little man said, "Oh, yes, there are some again. Is that a problem for you?"

Zillich thought about how many he'd strung up, then taken down, and hung back up again. He'd enjoyed that, especially in the camp at Piaski. He said, "Isn't it odd that there are any left still."

The little man said, "Why? After the Flood, when they opened the Ark, right there and then, a Jew jumped out."

"Who?"

"Noah, of course."

They walked through a stretch of land that glowed purple with the thousands of red cabbages growing there. Zillich said, "They're doing well here."

"The war never reached here."

They were going up a gentle rise. The little man, whose name may have been Nobody, turned on a side road that led over the hills to a beech grove. Then they came to some young spruce trees, a forest plantation that hadn't been affected by the war but was a bit overgrown. It smelled good; the little man's nostrils flared. Suddenly he stopped, turned around. Zillich was startled. "What's the matter?"

"Nothing, just look at the river."

It was the same river as back home, a narrow, shimmering ribbon. It never let go of a man. "Over there is the cement plant," the little man said. "Down there is our sand quarry."

In the meantime, Volpert had found the administrative offices of the Allied officials authorized to deal with his inquiry. They took note of his statement. All the information necessary for the investigation was carefully recorded.

When Volpert had lain on his cot at night in the concentration camp, totally exhausted yet unable to sleep because of his torment, he would never have dreamed where his ordeal would end up: in a shorthand report in a file folder. They told him at the office that he would be informed as soon as the wanted man was apprehended. He could still see Zillich as he had seen him the last time, that morning in his farmyard, and a good year earlier, as well, in his brown shirt, standing legs akimbo, his sharp, cold bird eyes focused on the tortured face of his prisoner, and now traveling along a country road or in a tavern, or in the dust of some workplace, one among many others, unscathed, without the mark of Cain.

A young officer, already reaching for another document on his desk, raised his head, probably because he hadn't yet heard the door close. Something in Volpert's face caught his eye. He said, "Don't worry. We found them all: Göring, Ley, Himmler. Not one of them got away."

Volpert got up and left. He felt a mournfulness settle on his heart, cool and intangible, like hoarfrost. He used to believe that he needed only to be free again to be happy, mindlessly happy like a child. He saw now that happiness was gone along with his childhood, forever and irrevocably. Not only his heart was covered with frost but all his thoughts, all his friendships, all his loves. The soil of the land he walked on was covered with frost, the warm autumn soil, any tool he would ever reach for, the bread he would eat, every crumb, every fiber of this country—covered with frost. The blood would dry, but the hoarfrost that had burned the young cabbage like a freeze had damaged even the living marrow. The Americans behind their desks saw him, Volpert, as a man with a raging thirst for revenge that could ultimately be quenched, like all sorts of other thirsts, by measures they could take. Yet even if they were to find Zillich tomorrow, the evil that had produced a man like him, the frost, would not vanish. Just as frost-damaged plants would never bloom again, the grief in his heart would never be consoled, he would never be any happier.

"Oh, yes, much happier," said Hänisch, with whom he sometimes spent the night in one of the train cars on the embankment. "Of course you'll be happy once they string up that thug. Even better if they were to hang him by the feet. Who wouldn't be glad to get rid of a rat like that. We won't have gotten rid of the evil itself, of course. You can't kill Satan. You'd have to completely finish off this old, ugly world first. But for the time being, I'll be mighty glad once they've collared Zillich."

The sand quarry was still a good hour on the other side of the river. They had already put down rails to the riverbank on which the dump cars would roll from the excavation machinery to the pontoon. The stone steps leading to the now useless fortification of a bridge that had been blown up during the war rose along with the remainder of a wall off to one side in the riverbank as if they were inviting people who could walk across on water.

Zillich was assigned to a group of twelve men. He worked doggedly and in silence. When their shift was finished the workers ambled to the village, or they gossiped among themselves on the stone steps of the bridgeless bridgehead. Zillich devoured his allotted rations by himself. Then he lay down in the barracks and was immediately fast asleep. He was dead tired each evening as if he had just ended his flight from the east to the west. His fellow workers soon left him alone. They saw him as one of those odd characters—and these days there were many of them everywhere. The foreman of his work gang was quite pleased with him because Zillich with his doggedness put them in the lead.

The only thing that stood out about Zillich was his insatiable desire for sleep. The supervisor laughed: A man like that must really have a clear conscience, for everybody knew that a clear conscience is the best sleep aid. At first Zillich was afraid he might give himself away during his dreams. But ever since that night in Zeissen, he no longer had any dreams. At most he might dream of everyday things now and then, of a sand pit that started to crumble again or of a container they weren't loading fast enough. He felt most comfortable when he went into the sleeping quarters early in the evening. At that hour the barrack was still quiet and empty. At worst he might feel annoyed if a couple of cots were not made up properly. Once he even thought briefly that the delinquents ought be made to do punitive exercises until they dropped; after that, they'd have to make and unmake their cots ten, twelve times, and then sleep on the floor next to their cots, preferably in a puddle of water spilled there for that purpose. Then he might point out that this way they'd be sure not to mess up their sorry attempts at neatness. But after a short fit of rage, it occurred to him that he no longer needed to torment himself; what went on in the barracks didn't concern him; he didn't have to get upset about such things anymore.

One evening he was sitting on his cot; it was so low that he couldn't even see out the window. This was what he liked best: being alone in the big, empty room. Unhurriedly he washed his feet, rubbing each toe. Suddenly someone behind him called out, "Good evening, Schulze!" There in the doorway, so blurry in the dusky light that Zillich didn't immediately recognize him, stood the little man he had met on the country road just on the other side of Weinheim. This time, instead of the aster there was a buttercup stuck in his buttonhole. It irked Zillich that he couldn't clean his last two toes as thoroughly as the other eight. The little man came closer and said, "I completely lost sight of you in the damn sand quarry. They moved me to the last barrack down by the river. I was curious to find out how you like it here. After all, I more or less brought you here."

Zillich, his feet still in the lukewarm water, said, "Thanks, I like it pretty well."

"I've been looking everywhere for you in the evenings: in the canteen, in the village, in the woods. Till someone said, there's a guy on our team who goes right to bed in the evenings; he sleeps like a log."

Zillich felt slightly uneasy hearing this, maybe just because he had attracted someone's attention. He hoped his visitor would leave as quickly as possible. He said nothing.

The little man said, "People are most conspicuous when they stay at home in the evenings. The people who gad about could be anywhere. But someone who stays at home, he's always in the same place: in bed."

Zillich dried his feet. He had laid out a pair of socks; he quickly washed them in the same water. Then he poured the dirty water out of the window.

"And you even have socks," the little man said.

"Me? They're for Sundays."

"What is it you do on Sundays?"

"What do you care?"

"Me? Nothing at all. I don't want to interfere with your Sunday pleasures. In fact, I can leave right now."

I don't want him to do that, Zillich thought. I don't want him to leave feeling angry at me. Aloud he said, "I didn't mean it that way. Stay a while, my dear Nobody."

The little man laughed. "You really have a good memory. Here, of course, I use my real name: It's Friday."

"Then why did you say your name was Nobody?"

"It's embarrassing to have a name like Friday. It's an unlucky day, after all. Peter Friday. And on top of that, we met on a Friday. I didn't think you'd have wanted to walk with me after that."

"Really?" Zillich said, surprised. "Was it on a Friday?"

"A Friday," Peter Friday confirmed, amused. To Zillich's annoyance he heaved his boots up on the blanket, made himself comfortable, and went on talking. "Say, has anyone from your group run off? Two have in ours. An official came from the town and went through all the lists with the supervisor. They were poking through a lot of names. Those two didn't wait till they were finished." He reveled in Zillich's shocked face. "I'd noticed one of them right off. He was very clumsy during the loading. I thought immediately, That's got to be a posh gentleman. He's not going to all this effort just for the fun of it. And then, when the official drifted in, did he turn red! At that I figured: Now the truth will out."

Zillich was glad it was already too dark for Friday to make out his expression. He said, "Who could it have been?"

"They said it was a man named Retzlow, the commandant of one of those death camps or whatever they call them now. That gang will all be hanged, for sure." His tongue in his cheek, his eyes amused, he gave Zillich a strange look.

And Zillich thought: The name of the commandant of our camp was Sommerfeldt. He would have been pretty clumsy too, loading sacks. A farmer like me, that's different. I've had to haul stuff from the time I was little. He asked, "Who was the other one?"

"Just imagine," Friday said, "he had the exact same name as you."

Chills ran down Zillich's spine. It seemed to him that this Nobody, whose name was suddenly Friday, was observing him in the dark.

"Right away I thought there was something odd," Friday said, "about your name being Schulze too."

"I can't help that."

"You? Certainly not." He added as if he really wanted to reassure him, "In my opinion, nobody is responsible for anything. It's all a matter of fate. Don't you agree?"

Zillich said eagerly, "Yes, it certainly is."

He didn't fall asleep as easily as usual that night. Instead, he pretended to be asleep. He told himself that the two escapees had done him a big favor. They'd drawn all suspicion to themselves; especially the second one whose name was Schulze.

It turned out he'd been right not to make himself conspicuous. At the next personnel shuffle the supervisor promoted him to fore-man of the team. Now Zillich was responsible for eleven fellows, some of whom had been his mates on his previous team. They had taken turns digging sand from the ditch, sifting it, and loading it. His team probably had kept up with the other gangs only because Zillich had spurred them on with his perseverance and unrelenting tenacity. There were times when he'd done three shovelfuls for every one his neighbor had. He never said a word about it so as not to call attention to himself. Now he wouldn't be able to jump in for them anymore, the team wouldn't be able to keep up, and the supervisor would call him to account. At first his fellow workers laughed because Zillich was driving them so hard. "What's got into you, Schulze? Are you getting paid by the grain of sand?"

But when Zillich drove them even more rigorously, they stopped laughing. He especially had it in for a man named Hagedorn, who had been working next to him on the team and whom he now caught making one mistake after another, from morning till night. He went straight to the supervisor and told him that this Hagedorn was causing the entire team to fall behind; that he'd been aware of the fellow's slacking off from the outset. In fact, the entire team was slacking off and would soon be the weakest one. But if they got rid of Hagedorn, they'd be able to catch up. Zillich thought, Now I'm going to stick it to you, Hagedorn. He could taste the long-lost sense of power, not very strong, not over life and death, not over body and soul, but just a bit.

The supervisor was a calm, good-natured man. He listened to Zillich's complaints, inwardly amused, and managed to put him off. But the men on Zillich's team came to him repeatedly, asking him to get Zillich off their backs. At first he was amused by their complaints as well, but by and by he only shook his head. When Zillich again urged him to get rid of Hagedorn, he made his decision: At the next shuffle of the workforce, he assigned Zillich to a newly formed team working at a new ditch and whose sleeping quarters were in a different barrack on the other side of the sand quarry.

Zillich went to his new workplace, sullen and clueless. Rumor followed that it wasn't good to mess around with him. At first he put up silently with all sorts of jokes whose origins were clear to him. For a while he worked as before, tenaciously, grimly, and silently. But then once, when the man next to him annoyed him by lighting a cigarette at an inappropriate moment when Zillich thought he should have been working especially hard, his growls infuriated not just the man next to him but the entire crew working in the ditch. After that there was no end to the snide remarks.

Zillich realized that he could no longer work in peace at the sand quarry. He tied up his bundle. It seemed they wouldn't leave him alone here either. He'd made himself conspicuous instead of staying invisible. Everything's a matter of fate, Peter Nobody, whose name was suddenly Friday, had said. Without seeing him again, he left, absentminded and dejected, heading in the direction of Braunsfeld.

Since the search had been fruitless so far, Volpert had gone to the authorities in Braunsfeld. There the official in charge turned out to be much less officious, less consumed by the official bustle than the lower-level officials in the smaller towns where he had previously gone for help. The Braunsfeld officer listened attentively to Volpert. He asked for many details, as if this man Zillich they were looking for was unique. His questions caused Volpert to remember details he had forgotten, new details that were then transmitted to all the appropriate offices in the area under the officer's jurisdiction.

Zillich, walking down a street in the suburbs of Braunsfeld, wasn't very far from the two men. At one time a colorful suburban outer ring had loosely encircled the ancient and once important center of the city. The city center had been turned to dust during the war, but the outer ring, now with newly planted gardens, had remained. And walking around the perimeter of the city, one might have thought that nothing bad had happened to Braunsfeld. Since many people had returned to their houses, there were already fresh new curtains at the windows and women trimming garden shrubs.

But Zillich walked into the dust cloud that now hung over the heart of the town. He came to a huge square where teams of workers were digging and excavating in the debris of a thousand years. Many people were streaming from the remaining outer parts of town toward the towerless hull of a church, out of which the eternal light shone from the tall pointed arches and a few red and green shards of glass. The faces of all the churchgoers showed a dull bafflement, as if they were looking for the remnants of their old faith in the remains of their old church. The toppled bells had dug their own graves at the side of the church, and the two towers that once had been the landmark of the town lay in rubble and ashes. A railing of wooden planks had been constructed around an enormous shell crater in that field of rubble, as if to keep people living here now in times of peace from falling into it. The crater had been emptied out but not yet filled in. With his back to the square, Zillich looked down, fascinated. The collapsed pillars that were part of the foundation of the church protruded from the ground.

"Well, go ahead and jump, my son," a voice behind him said. Terrified, he turned around and found himself looking into an ancient man's cadaverous face in which two eyes gleamed like the lights you put inside Halloween pumpkins. A slight tremor, like a mild breeze, swept through the ancient man's bones.

The sight of him repelled Zillich. He asked in confusion, "Why should I?"

"They say that the abyss will close when a sacrifice is thrown in." In his senility the old man was intent on expressing his every thought to anyone who crossed his path. The little lights in his eye sockets shined on Zillich's face, which remained morosely puzzled. Then, on his two crutches, he dragged himself into the evening that was as cool and lonely as the grave he sensed approaching, now that he had survived the war, along with a few of the town's walls. He disappeared through the church door.

Zillich angrily watched him go. He felt uneasy. Why hadn't he stayed at the sand quarry? Why had he allowed himself to be driven away by the stupid needling of a couple of dumb thugs? He'd been safe and at peace there. The quarry was a hole under the sky, a place to hide in this world. Either they found you or they didn't. In spite of the mockery, he had lived there without arousing any suspicion. Braunsfeld was a large city. It had plenty of nests and caves. But there was also a network of spies; each hiding place was enmeshed in the net that only had to be drawn tightly closed. Patrols walked up and down the streets, and public appeals called on the entire population to be on the lookout for men like him.

He, of all people, knew that nobody could escape a clever manhunt in a large city. After all, they'd always captured even the most cunning Jews and the shrewdest Reds. They'd bribed the informers with money if they hesitated. And if money didn't work, they'd used fear, intimidation. No one on this earth likes to die, especially not for the sake of a total stranger, his beloved fellow man. How was he going to find a roof over his head for the night?

He followed the directions the old man had given him. You could already hear the singing of the choir in the rubble of the nave, spreading eerily over the ruins, an unearthly sound of a light, ethereal sweetness, like the song of dead souls. The church door was not locked. The evening wind blowing through the broken windows ruffled the candle flames. The people sang with lowered faces, surprised that the sound had not yet choked in their throats. They made room for Zillich. He wished the song would never end, for as long as it lasted, nobody would pay any attention to him. He was relieved when the pastor drew all eyes to the front of the church. They might not have believed every word that came down to them now from the shriveled man at the pulpit; they were not serene in a strong faith; they simply felt more at peace around this old man who firmly believed in something.

In his hard, thin voice he proclaimed justice and righteousness, and something people can never hear enough of: That the first shall be last and the last shall be first. When Zillich peered to his right and left, he noticed the ancient man who was now trembling like an aspen leaf. He must have something eating at him, Zillich thought. Just keep on talking up there, old fellow, so that the people will go on looking to the front. He sat there content, his fists, which were covered with short red hair like felt, calmly cupped one over the other. An old woman sitting next to him with a messy bun, rust-colored the way red hair turns white, was nervously looking around her, constantly plucking at her scarf.

"But God, who sees into the hearts of men"—the voice from the pulpit, thin and hard as a knife blade, went on—"knows exactly where a scoundrel is hiding, no matter how secure his hiding place; He knows exactly who has witnessed, once or many times, an act of villainy or even a murder and remained silent out of fear and cowardice, instead of bearing witness for his faith! Let them not forget, especially those who now can't do enough to dig up the guilty ones and denounce them, even though they remained silent when there was no reward posted. Let them not forget, especially those who, after suffering and imprisonment, cannot control their hate and cannot wait until every guilty person has been caught: For Him above there is only one redress, and that is repentance."

The voice, already breaking up from exhaustion but sharp to the end, finally died away. The evening light came in over the bowed heads of the congregation in stripes of pure pink, more unreal than the red and green from the windowpanes. A young man on the bench next to Zillich sat there frozen, hands covering his face. He didn't get up until those who were leaving started to push him. Zillich, surrounded by a swarm of people, homeless as he was, turned away from the church door into a side chapel. There were holes in the roof; you could see pink fragments of the evening sky through them; the floor was covered with straw. The young man sat down, his legs crossed, on a sack of straw next to Zillich, his face in his hands as before in the church pew. He moaned.

"What the matter with you?" Zillich asked. The young man looked out at him helplessly from between his hands; his gaunt face, wet with tears, was fair and thin-skinned, very pale, and almost beautiful.

"You heard it yourself," he said, "what's to become of me now?"

"I wasn't really listening. Did the old guy up there have it in for you?"

The youth answered softly, as if to himself, "How am I to go on living with such a burden on my heart? What's going to become of me now? I was the son of Christian parents, after all. My mother was a good person. How did all of that, little by little, get hold of me?"

"Well, tell me," Zillich said. The pink sky in the holes in the roof had already faded. The straw sacks were all occupied; the stars were already coming out.

The youth continued, "The enemy was at our heels. We had evacuated the village of Sarkoje, driving the inhabitants before us, I thought it would be to some camp or other; or maybe I thought nothing at all. Then came the order: 'Shoot!' And we shot the whole lot of them, women, children, old men."

Zillich said, "Things like that happened often."

"That's just it. There were a lot more times. That was just the beginning. Why did I shoot? At children—do you understand? How could I do something like that?"

"Well, that's obvious. It was an order."

"Well, that's just it. Why did I not refuse to do it? Why did I obey an order like that?"

206 · ANNA SEGHERS

"What do you mean?" Zillich said. "What else could you have done?"

"Why didn't I think some more about it first? Ready, aim, fire. Why didn't I listen to a Higher Command? Had It gone silent? Was I deaf?"

"What kind of higher command?" Zillich asked. "Back then there were no counter commands for soldiers. Your lieutenant would surely have been the first to receive any higher command."

"Don't you understand? The true, the inner one. The inner voice that is never silent within man. Not in you, not in me. You do know that, don't you?"

"I know, I know. When I was wounded once, quite seriously in fact, by a grenade fragment, I knew what that was like. An inner voice. That goes away then when the fever from the wound goes down. It stops as soon as you're healthy again. I think you're still in pretty bad shape. Were you wounded? The best thing for you would be to get some sleep."

The young man gave Zillich a look of amazement and pity that Zillich did not like because he didn't understand it. But then he obediently stretched out on the floor.

The next morning, as Zillich had predicted, he felt in pretty good shape. To Zillich's annoyance, the exit from the church was locked. A door in the rear wall was the only way out and it led through a neglected garden in which ivy, hedge roses, and all sorts of greenery had shot up around various bomb fragments, pipes, and other stuff that once had been part of the sacristan's shelled apartment. Zillich drew back in horror: A soldier was standing in the right-hand corner of the door, legs akimbo and as big as a giant, or so it seemed, although he was no taller than Zillich. But Zillich shrank, and his face crumpled; he raised one eyebrow, turned down the corners of his mouth, contracted his huge nostrils, and fixed his bird eyes, frightened but direct, on the large, unperturbed face of the soldier standing guard. The soldier was carefully looking at each of the people as they came through, checking them against a list he held in his hand. Across from him, in a corner by the door, stood a thin soldier with a long, narrow nose, who examined the documents each person was asked to hand him. Since Zillich had nothing better available, he showed him his worker's pass from the sand quarry in the village of Erb, Weinheim district. But the big soldier still had his eyes fixed on Zillich's head, so that the little bird eyes quickly stung him again. That fellow's strange pig ears were no doubt a distinguishing feature. Yet they weren't mentioned in any description of special war criminals. Zillich stumbled out into the street. He was bathed in cold sweat. He had never before in all his life been so afraid.

This little bit of life wasn't worth all that fear. The same sort of dread could possibly grab hold of him a hundred more times. How small the world was! In earlier days he had thought his fatherland was immense, that it expanded with every breath, that it would swallow the entire earth, piece by piece. Now suddenly it had shrunk, becoming unrecognizable, just as his face had a while ago. The big, dusty square surrounded by ruins with the sky inverted over it like a cheese dome—you flitted around in it like a fly. His gaze fell on a cross in the wall opposite. He headed for it: a broad cross, a red cross. It was an outpatient clinic set up by the Americans or a drugstore that had survived the war. He asked in a piteous voice for some adhesive tape. The young woman asked him gently where she could bandage him. He warded her off, rushed outside, and ducked into an entryway. Looking up he saw that the hallway where he stood had no house. The morning sun hung in the sky, round and yellow like an unmanned hot-air balloon. There was no one in heaven who pitied him. He tore off two pieces of adhesive tape and used them to stick his forward-tilted ears to the back of his head. His mother had done that thirty years ago when he came running home from school, crying because the village boys had teased him. He brushed the hair over his ears.

After he'd pulled himself together somewhat, he headed out of the city. He came to a suburb that was much like a village. It clung to the outer ring of the city like the indented sides of a Bundt cake whose center was nothing but air. He was completely at a loss. Perhaps the town of Erbenfeld was only a few hours distant, perhaps a day. He didn't quite know why he'd chosen Erbenfeld over Braunsfeld. He knew only that he didn't have the courage to look for work in Braunsfeld.

How little one could depend on this people, this *Volk*, whose praises had been sung so highly. One should have been safe in their midst, as safe as in one's mother's lap. A real pile of muck, this nation, this *Volk*. They would let a person be captured right before their eyes. For years one had tediously picked out all the scoundrels, working one's hands to the bone, striking them till one's hands were sore. And done guard duty, day and night, to make sure none escaped. And the thanks one got in return? They let the foreigners take over. Now *they* were in control. You don't bite the hand that feeds you.

He happened to glance at a little old woman dragging a sack. Her fuzzy bun looked familiar, as did the rust-colored hair like that of a redhead turning white.

He approached her. His will to live was rekindled. And with it also the cleverness nature had bestowed on him along with a powerful body. Not at all feeble but absurdly shrewd, pointlessly resourceful. That's what made him the man he was. Without purpose, without reason, a wasted brain.

He spoke to the little old woman. "Good morning, mother. That touched the heart yesterday! That pastor, he really has a command of words."

The old woman looked at him nervously, the way mentally disturbed people do. Zillich stopped. He looked at her more closely. She stopped too, as if nailed to the spot by his small, hard bird eyes. She said, "That was Pastor Seiz."

"Is he new?"

She shook her head slowly from right to left. "He's our old pastor. He was in a concentration camp. Put there because he once said a mass for the boys from our city who were killed by the Nazis."

Zillich looked away. The old woman moved her head, unsure. Zillich said, "I'd like to help you carry your sack, mother." People watched him go. I'll soon fit in among you, Zillich thought.

The old woman chattered on: "My youngest boy was in a concentration camp too. I'm expecting him home any day. They're all coming home now. Even those we thought were dead."

"Dear mother," Zillich said, "I'm all alone in the world. Won't you let me stay just for one night under your roof?"

The old woman said, "My two older boys don't want anyone around." She kept shaking her head distractedly.

"Oh, mother, just think how it would be if your youngest son is on his way back now, and there's nobody who will take him in."

Still carrying the sack, he followed the old woman into her yard. She talked to her sons, two big, ragged fellows. "If your brother is on his way home now, people will treat him the same way we treat this stranger."

Zillich did not like the sons' answer. "We have to be careful. A stranger, he could be God knows what kind of scoundrel. Our brother, of all people, would tell you to be especially careful. But he's not coming home, Mother. You can put that idea right out of your mind."

"Oh, yes, yes. You'll see. It's only if people don't help him on the way back. And this man, I met him before. Yesterday in church."

"He's not coming, Mother," the eldest said, firmly. "He's dead. They informed us. The pastor even read a Mass for the Dead for him back then. That's why they put the pastor in the concentration camp."

The old woman began to weep. "My dear, dear children, please."

The older son sighed; the younger one turned to Zillich. "You can sleep here in the courtyard, for all I care. Where are you headed?"

"To Erbenfeld, to the construction site."

"Your identification."

For the second time that day, he showed his document from the sand quarry, more boldly this time, true, but still in a cold sweat. He'd taken a closer look around the place in the meantime. He said, "I'm sure I could help out at the soldering furnace."

"Do you know anything about metalworking?"

"Just about everything there is to know. I spent six years as a soldier—"

The eldest, who kept looking at him intently, said, "No need for that. If you really want to do something, then here, kneel down in front of this tub. That bottle there, the one made of zinc, it's finished. You have to blow into it from the front, to see if the water squirts out; because if it's still squirting out, then the soldering isn't water-tight."

"Okay. I'll blow," Zillich said and crouched down on the ground. The sons handed him one piece after the other from the soldering furnace: hot-water bottles, pails, cans. Unbelievable, what a lot of things people needed to live their lives, once they were living them again.

This isn't very pleasant, Zillich thought, blowing into soldered stuff to see if it's still leaking. Shoveling sand in the sand quarry wasn't any better, nor was digging in the field. By the sweat of thy brow shalt thou eat thy bread. The devil's got me again.

The old woman wiped the finished pieces on her apron, and carried them off, one by one. Once she came back from outside, quite excited. "There are a lot of people gathering out there on the street. I think . . . I think another one has come back."

The eldest son, standing by the soldering oven, said firmly, "It's not our brother, that's for sure."

The younger one said sharply, "Stay here now, you don't need to carry every piece away. I'm sure our brother is dead."

For lunch the three of them went into the kitchen. The old woman said, "You can't leave him out in the yard like an animal."

The sons said, "We don't want him at the table with us. We don't like him. He should be reported at the police station. They can grill him."

"Oh, no, they were just saying yesterday they'd had enough of people informing on each other."

"They should have said that to the Nazis back then. Our brother would still be alive if they had."

"I just mean, it's better to be too suspicious than not enough."

They hardly noticed their mother getting up to bring Zillich a plate of soup. While he was greedily gulping it down, she went out into the street. When she came back, she said to her sons, who were back at the smelting furnace, "The Müllers' son came back. You see, he's come back too."

The sons said, "Our little one isn't ever coming back. The dead never come back."

Zillich thought, That old woman is quite a burden for these boys. The Americans, who get a kick out of such things, ought to take her to see our mass grave in Piaski; that would shatter her pipe dreams.

As he knelt down again next to the tub to test some new pieces for their water-tightness, he thought, Now if I were one of those boys and kneeling in front of the tub here, and if his backside were sticking up in the air like mine now...

Zillich started when he heard boots crunching behind him. The elder son was standing behind him; he suddenly bent down and grabbed hold of Zillich's hair. "Why do you have your ears taped back like that?"

Zillich jumped up. The younger brother laughed. Blind with fear, Zillich punched him in the chest. Then the elder son leaped for the gate, but Zillich tripped him and dashed out, charging like a bull. He'd soon left the place far behind him. He turned onto the main road, head still lowered like a bull's as if to push everyone aside. He heard shouts behind him, or thought he did. Footsteps, yelling. He heard a car racing behind him. He jumped into the ditch beside the road, the branches of the bushes snapping.

The car turned out to be a truck from the construction firm Redel in Erbenfeld; it was loaded with bricks; the shipper was sitting next to the driver. Two workmen sat on the bricks in back. Zillich waved frantically to them. "Take me along, guys. I have to be in Erbenfeld before nightfall."

"It's not allowed," the driver called back over his shoulder. But he stepped briefly on the brakes, and the two fellows sitting on top of the load in the back quickly pulled Zillich up to sit between them. "He can tell you that it's not allowed later, once we arrive and he finds you."

"Thanks a lot, mates." Catching his breath, Zillich dried his face, his hair. Once he was more relaxed, he told them a story to suit anyone

212 · ANNA SEGHERS

and everyone. "The fools you run into. I'd found work at a metal workshop. Really good work. But then suddenly one of the guys there goes a bit off his rocker. What do you think made that young fellow go crazy? The adhesive tape on my ears. They put it on just before I left the hospital after being treated for a middle-ear infection. Anyway, the guy suddenly turns wild; we get into a big row, and he throws me out."

The fellow sitting on Zillich's left said, "Aha." The one on his right said, "Oh, well . . ." Both of them were smart, decent youths. One called himself Hans, the other Franz. Hans said, "Comradeship has gone to hell."

Franz said, "It's useful to the occupation when we quarrel among ourselves."

Hans said, "It gives them a reason to settle our arguments."

Franz said, "And to stick their noses into everything."

Zillich said nothing at all. He remained silent for a couple of minutes. Then suddenly despair took hold of him, like a bout of fever. Where am I, poor wretch, to go now? Where can I find a place to stay? The whole damn world is against me. His shirt was wet with sweat; air blowing into the back of the truck made him shiver; he was freezing. And those gentlemen, our former leaders, he thought, they've just scattered to the winds as fast as they could. They let me go to hell here. For years they buttered me up. Zillich this, Zillich that. Whenever some big shot wouldn't talk, it was: Go get Zillich. Whenever one of those Communist swine was too tough to kick the bucket, it was: Zillich will finish him off. Then suddenly from one day to the next, none of those rats gave a damn about Zillich anymore.

"Where are you headed?" Franz asked.

Zillich promptly replied, "To work."

Hans asked, "Where?"

"The construction site in Erbenfeld."

"Do you have papers?"

"From Erb in the district of Weinheim. That's where I worked last."

The two exchanged glances behind Zillich's back. Hans said, "At our construction site when they hire somebody, they take down all the information."

Franz said, "They ask about you back at your birthplace."

Zillich said nothing. Thoughts buzzed around inside his thick, cramped head like flies. The two looked at him sideways.

Hans said, "It usually takes a long time till you get an answer at the construction site."

Franz added, "Especially when you're from far away. You're not from this area, are you?"

"God forbid, no. I'm from Saxony." His shirt was stiff with dried sweat. He had a bit of hope now.

"We'll get them to take you on at the construction site, pal, you'll see."

The other said, "We know someone who'll help you."

Zillich nodded. "It shows you that there's still some camaraderie left."

He almost fell off when the truck came to a sudden, jolting stop at the edge of the village. The two grabbed hold of him from both sides just in time. They whispered, "Don't run off now. That would be the stupidest thing you could do."

The guard checked only the driver's papers. Zillich thought, Why am I stuck in this body? I don't like being inside myself at all. I want out.

He was also dismayed to see the river once more, shimmering through the alder trees. He'd thought he was already God knows how far away from home. But the river had been gently flowing ahead of him, winding insidiously, glittering cunningly. The rest of the city, pasted over with sunlight patched together by lots of greenery, spread down the hillside to the river. The dust and noise, and the hustle and bustle, at the building site was reassuring because it had nothing at all to do with death. But then he *did* see death again, cowering: a clump of soil, teasing him with a little red flag. But it was only a warning for vehicles. Yet then, when he raised his head, oops, there

was death, way up high. Its form changed. At the top of the scaffolding, striped, on a skinny staff, the Star-Spangled Banner. Zillich stared
at it in horror, as if he hadn't known that the entire country was now
occupied. There was no refuge.

"Müller! Hey!" his companions called out. "Hey, Müller." They
talked to a tall man with a long neck, long arms, and a long skull.
Franz called over to Zillich, "It's all settled, you'll be hired. Go along
with Müller." The four of them sized one another up for a moment.
The two young fellows, neat and resourceful; Müller, the tall construction supervisor; Zillich, chunky and somber. Some unidentifiable
bond of shared feelings and past experiences wound itself invisibly
around the four men standing there on the crowded construction site.

Zillich started work right after the midday break. He had to climb
up and down a ladder with a lime bucket. He huffed and puffed on
the scaffolding that surrounded the half-renovated ruins of a factory.
Fresh perspiration soaked his shirt, still stiff from his earlier bout of
cold sweat.

That first day he didn't dare look down, afraid of getting dizzy.
He paid no attention to any of the talk. And pretty soon, no one
asked him anything because what he mumbled in reply was unintelligible. When he, high up on the scaffolding, finally looked around
him, he was almost disappointed because the height didn't bother
him. It wasn't unattainably high, this high place, and it didn't make
him dizzy. It might as well have been flat and level. It would have
been as hard to hide in the blue-green glittering ribbon of river running through the fields, or in the hills above the city, as in the blobs
and brushstrokes of a painting. At first he watched a swarm of swal-
lows with envy, but it occurred to him that flying wouldn't have
helped him either. Where could he have flown?

He passed his days in silence. He avoided any contacts. Soon his
fear of death faded. Gradually he began to think of death as casually
as he had during the war. It was inevitable, you just have to be lucky.
A construction scaffold certainly wasn't a mouse hole, but he started
to feel safer.

In the canteen he was grabbed from both sides. His heart stopped: Now they've got me. But it was just Hans and Franz on either side of him, laughing and dragging him over to their table. "How's it going? How are things?" "How do you like it on the site?"

He looked from the one to the other with his darting little eyes, startled. The one, he noticed for the first time, had a long face with a hook of a chin; the other's face was more rotund and broad, almost chinless.

Franz said, but only his eyes were laughing, "You've already forgotten your pals."

"Where would you be now," Hans said, smiling but with cold, narrowed eyes, "if the two of us had forgotten you that way?" Whistling, he looked out of the window.

Zillich turned his head to see what he was seeing. "Where would you be now?" What's that supposed to mean? What made them notice that something isn't quite right with me? What had attracted the fellow's eye? The crane on the site? Its steel arm was too high and too long. The coil through the double rolls was much too intricately wound.

Hans gave him a shove. "Just between us: We bribed Müller, the foreman, a second time. There was an inspector who came to the office. But we heard about it in time."

Franz said, "Like we explained to you on the drive here, they're collecting information about everybody's place of residence."

"Everybody's?"

"It takes time, of course. Where are you from?"

Where am I from? Zillich thought in despair. Where did I tell them I was from? From Silesia? From the Rhineland? From Saxony?

"Don't worry," Hans said with laughing eyes, "it's all taken care of. Müller simply moved you from 'pending' to 'done.'"

"Thanks a lot, pals." It just slipped out of Zillich's mouth. He sat rather awkwardly and heavily between the two lithe, slender young men. Why did I thank them? Zillich thought. Why didn't I just say, Doesn't matter to me one way or another. Or simply say nothing.

After all, we often enough caught illegals with just that sort of trick. That district leader Straub, for one.

He found some pretense and left. He noticed how the two moved closer together to discuss something.

He was now on his guard. In the canteen he always stood or sat facing the door. Whenever he saw the two on the construction site, he turned on his heel. Two or three times he was told that he was expected here or there. Then he avoided those places. He would have felt quite at peace at the site by now if it weren't for the two who had brought him there.

In the afternoon, on payday, they were suddenly on either side of him outside the door. They linked arms with him. The three of them walked up and down on the gravel in the mild evening. They said, "We heard that your scaffolding is going to be taken down this week." "The inside work won't take much longer." "They say that the factory will be up and running next month already." "All the stuff is for the army. The Americans are making everything locally."

They waited. Since Zillich showed no surprise, Franz gave vent to his feelings: "It's not enough for them to ship us into enemy territory like slave labor."

Hans added, "We're supposed to slave away in our own country."

Zillich pricked up his ears. He wasn't sure where the two were headed with this. He sighed.

"Yes," Franz said, "you may sigh, but that's no help at all. They have to be made to realize that they can't do just anything they want."

His defiance was infectious, and Zillich asked, "What are we supposed to do?"

They took a tighter hold of him, walked more quickly, turned more sharply. "Tomorrow you'll get a sign from the second floor, from inside the fourth window. Then the same window, on the third floor, where the cable runs through, they'll hand you a rope; you have to run it between the cables. It'll take a quarter of a minute. In the evening, they'll come to meet you in the canteen at the same time. Then you'll find out more for the next day. Got it?"

"Right, got it," Zillich said. They separated, going off in three different directions. Zillich, as was his habit, went to bed early. He crossed his arms under his head. His heart, which at one time he couldn't even have said between which ribs it was located, beat in hard little thumps. Why are you making all that noise? he said to his heart. You can rest easy tonight; you're entirely innocent.

How could he guard against the foolishness those two fellows were hatching? He was sure they'd thought up this mad caper for the day the occupiers would put the factory into operation. Just to think that things like this were still going on nowadays ... No more medals were being awarded anymore, no rewards, no power to be had. And Hans and Franz hadn't been appointed by the higher-ups; they had no right at all to order anybody to do anything. And why had they picked him, of all people? Because they could tell that he was being pursued? That he was on the run? As if it wasn't enough for a man to be threatened by the gallows.

Oh, yes, before this, he'd been ready for any foolishness. He'd gone along with the Führer through thick and thin. But the Führer was dead now. Sure, there were people who didn't believe it. But in any case, dead or alive, he couldn't give orders anymore. And he, Zillich, wouldn't fall for any Führer tricks anymore. They had promised him fame and glory, a share of their own power. They had used that to entice him away from his home, from his plow and his fields. They had promised him heaven knows what, and with what results? Persecution, fear, and abandonment.

And it would all get much worse if he now did what these scamps wanted. And even worse than that if he didn't do their bidding. Then they'd make it a living hell for him here.

He must not climb up on the scaffolding tomorrow. His time on the building site was up. And now it was best for him to get out of here. He groaned. He was exhausted from today's work and from weeks on the run.

But in his exhaustion, which just before certain death was lit up by a last spurt of life, he succeeded, resourceful, shrewd and wild, just as he had on his flight from Weinheim, in slipping through the cordon of guards that surrounded the building site. Early the next morning he was already tramping around in the hills with his bundle.

The service train, from which Volpert had repaired the tracks, had been returned to its place of origin in Waldau, three hours from Zeissen. Volpert decided to go back to the village to find out there and then whether his inquiries had had any results. But after going to all the district offices, he had come away disappointed. The beast was nowhere to be found.

The village was cleaner and much more trim than on his first visit. The last traces of the war had been covered up with fresh paint and new tiles. Volpert went to the mayor's office. The mayor of the village, a smart older man named Abst, was a comfortably situated farmer with a midsize farm, one horse, and five cows. He fully understood Volpert's impatience. He himself had spent two years in a concentration camp. And after that he was assigned to a punishment battalion.

"But God had something different in mind for me," he told Volpert. "I'm in good health again and home with my wife and children. The horse died. I swear, I didn't do anything against Hitler. At most I may have said a negative word or made a bad joke. But Nadler, another farmer, denounced me because I was three times as lucky as he." Abst tried to console Volpert, telling him that the man they were looking for, Zillich, had probably gone into hiding using forged papers. But with all the searches and inquiries they were being compelled to do now, they would soon find the person who matched the description on the wanted poster.

They were sitting on a brand-new circular bench that farmer Abst had recently built around a chestnut tree in front of his house on the village square. It was a cool late-autumn day, perhaps the last sunny one of the season. The village teacher came out of the small green schoolhouse that had only recently come into use again. It also was on the village square. He was a slight, sickly man with penetrating gray eyes. On Abst's invitation, he came over to sit with the two men under the chestnut tree.

"This is Mr. Volpert, the train engineer," Abst said. "He's the one who recognized Zillich, the man they're searching for now. This is Mr. Degreif, our teacher." Volpert gathered from these words that people in the village already knew what was up with Zillich. Degreif looked intently at Volpert. The somewhat too-shiny eyes, the almost constant light cough indicated he had trouble with his lungs, which, in the old days, would have cost him his job. Abst added in a tone that implied rank and prestige, "Our teacher was in Sachsenhausen concentration camp."

Volpert said, "It must be difficult for you to teach children to despise men whom they once had to greet with 'Heil, Heil.'"

Degreif replied, "Why? I'm used to it. That's why I was sent to Sachsenhausen." He coughed and smiled.

Abst said, "Mr. Volpert has been going around to all the offices for the second time. It seems they simply can't find Zillich."

Volpert said, "I'm doing everything I can to get the scoundrel to the gallows." Then flustered by the teacher's bright eyes and almost startled by his own question, he asked, "Would you do the same?"

Degreif, taken aback by the question coming from this embittered man, gave a reply that in turn surprised Volpert: "Of course, so that they can live." He pointed to the boys running out of the school and into the square, "And especially that one." A small boy, carrying the teacher's briefcase, came hesitantly toward the chestnut tree. His blond hair fell from his cowlick in thick strands all around his head. He looked somberly at the stranger sitting between Abst and the teacher. The boy remembered clearly the first time the man had turned up. Back then he had already felt the ominous threat that came from the man and had been hovering over him and his family ever since, like a cold and oppressive shadow. Young though he was, he was no longer naïve. At one time he had been approvingly patted and greeted; no one in the village had ever disapproved of him, the son of an apparently respectable father. But now there was a rumor suggesting that not everything was quite all right with his missing father. As if the state were an inexplicable, unknown something, like the wind that blew this way and that. And now the wind was suddenly blowing against him. He turned uneasily away from the stranger who was looking at him somberly and turned instead to the familiar face of the young teacher.

Volpert said, "They say the devil has no children."

The teacher laughed and coughed. "I am informed otherwise. I read in a fairy tale that the devil once raped a girl, and heaven allowed her to bear a son who inherited only the good qualities of his father."

"Does the devil have any good qualities?"

"According to my fairy tale, yes. The son turned out to be exceptionally bright."

The teacher put his briefcase down between his knees. For a moment he gazed thoughtfully at the boy who was still waiting, undecided. "Yes, you should go home now." The golden afternoon sun shimmered feebly through the bare gnarled branches. One last chestnut leaf still glowed fiery red.

By now Zillich was deep in the deserted, scrubby, autumnally windswept highlands. From time to time he came upon a lost village that, even though it had been spared the ravages of war, seemed to be dying of poverty and isolation. Now the first thing he did was to eat his fill because he still had money left from his last payday. The farmers up here didn't think twice about a returnee who had lost his way. Sometimes Zillich thought he could walk around up here undisturbed forever, restless and hungry but unmolested, like the Eternal Jew. Now and then, he helped out with the haying in exchange for a place to sleep. Then when he sat at night with the farmers and the lamp was extinguished early to save on kerosene or paraffin, he thought petulantly, Why do people like this go on living? He longed for music, for marching boots, for commands instead of these gray hours that dribbled away between one's fingers; he longed for harsh resistance that reared up until you stomped on it with your feet and that struck out in all directions, even while screaming and whimpering and dripping with blood, instead of yielding meekly like grass under the rake.

One day he came to a lake unexpectedly spreading out on the plateau. He listened with satisfaction to sounds of trees being felled, and the whining of saws and the blows of hammers coming from the other shore. Finally, once more, here was the sound of work, the bustle of people taming something that was resisting.

He went toward a dam that was being repaired. For a moment he even forgot that he wouldn't immediately be able to supervise but would at first have to knuckle under. He thought, I'll soon make it to supervisor, just as I did in the sand quarry at Weinheim.

He introduced himself boldly to the manager. He said he was on his way to Fulda and asked whether he could have work here until the end of the week. He showed his work papers from Weinheim and Erbenfeld.

They kept a sharp eye on him at the beginning, but found nothing to object to in his work. He wasn't a shirker or a malingerer. He did what had to be done quickly, diligently, and silently.

The workers ate and slept together in sheds crudely built of tree trunks that would be floated downriver with the rest of the timber once work on the dam was completed. They asked Zillich in great detail about where he was going, where he came from; and Zillich patiently gave each one of them the same answer.

In the evenings they asked him to join their card game. He made every effort, as if a mistake could have God only knew what consequences. With his sharp little eyes he looked from face to face, and was able to guess from nearly indiscernible signs who was lacking which card. But then his concentration on the game flagged, for he was listening to a conversation going on behind him. "It has to be from farm to farm, throughout the entire range of hills, from village to village. Then the authorities will soon take over; they'll take charge, or they may prefer to make do with ours." It was an older voice and you could tell that each word was considered important.

Then it turned quiet around their table, even though they were now speaking casually and reasonably. "Above all, it has to begin here with us. The best thing would be if everyone were required to appear before the entire workforce; he would then have to give detailed information about where he spent the last twelve years. He would have to answer all our questions."

Someone called out from far back in the room, and Zillich realized that they were listening there too, "Who is supposed to do the questioning?"

"We will, of course. They should do this at every workplace, all over the country."

"Assuming they'd follow our lead. We're so out of touch here, so far behind the times in everything."

"That doesn't matter," someone said, stuttering with nervousness. "The main thing is that you start somewhere. Behind the times, ahead of the times."

The older man said, "They did something like that in Russia twenty-five years ago. They called it *chistka*."* Suddenly, the silence in the room became so profound, it was as if the older man were ancient and had been here before anyone else, long before the Flood, at the Creation of the World. The younger man, like a child urging his grandfather on, stammered with excitement: "Tell us more about that."

Zillich had been feeling carefree all evening, but suddenly his heart was heavy. He had been feeling light, almost floating on air, but now his heart dragged him down like a millstone. Someone at his table cursed: "Seven of diamonds, hell. Schulze, hey, pay attention!"

Zillich smirked; he had to turn around, just for a moment. He felt sure that the man who was so full of his own importance with all his suggestions was the short, spry old man with the white mustache and hard, blue eyes. The cord by which the single electric lightbulb was suspended from the ceiling had been wound around the window hook so that the light fell on their tables all pushed together. Now the faces, distorted by light and shadow, seemed spooky and sinister to Zillich.

*Political purge.

In despair, he threw a card on the table. "Seven of diamonds."

They guffawed. "Well, finally!"

He fixed his little eyes on his cards, thinking, I can't just get up and leave now, that would be a mistake. Things aren't as bad as they seem. I'll be long gone and far beyond these hills by the time this bunch hatches something. And what's on the other side of all those hills? The French occupied zone? That's where I'll go. There's a different authority there with different people in charge and different offices. But this time I'm going to leave inconspicuously, without any fuss.

The following day he was in better spirits. They were saying, "He's thawing." During the midday break he was able to approach the older man with the gray mustache who had been the spokesman the night before. He told him about all his misfortunes: his children gone, the house destroyed by bombs, his wife dead, and he himself for years a prisoner. At the Piaski concentration camp, which he described superbly well from his own experience. The old man's hard eyes were softer in the daylight. You always put yourself in a good light, Zillich thought, when you ask someone for advice, and so he asked the old man how long he figured work might go on up here, that after all the hardships he'd had enough of eternally changing jobs.

"They've been extending the electric lines from the valley up to the dam works. Once that's done, they'll repair the dam."

Hearing that, Zillich thought with satisfaction that he could stay for a while longer. What was there to be afraid of, after all? He'd allowed himself to be scared by the stupid talk. Probably because he'd been physically exhausted. Even if they called a meeting here, as that old toilet-brush mustache had suggested, he'd be able to outwit these windbags. The suspicious old man had believed every word of his story. Gossips always believed gossip. He'd repeat it in front of them all, loud and clear.

Some days later, while at work, he heard a loud "Hello." A troop of new workers was coming from the direction of the lake. The electrical cable that they had been laying from above and from below had met in the middle. Now they all climbed together onto the knoll.

There was a lot of activity everywhere—the arrival, the greetings,

and new acquaintances. No one noticed that Zillich shrank back
from it. He was looking suspiciously from one man to another. Pretty
soon he had checked out all the faces. But as he was smoking that
evening outside the barracks, someone touched his arm. He didn't
recognize the lean, clean-shaven face with the oily combed-back hair.

"What a blast! You don't recognize me," the newcomer said. "What
name do you go by here? My name is Stegerwald."

"Me? Schulze," Zillich mumbled. Stegerwald's name used to be
Nagel. He used to have his hair combed and parted exactly the way
Hitler's was in the photos, with one strand of hair over his forehead.
He had shaved off the little mustache, too, for all that was of no use
anymore.

"It would be best," Stegerwald-Nagel said, "if the two of us don't
meet again. Just give me a light, please." He lit his cigarette from
Zillich's; their eyes met. Schulze-Zillich's sharp, penetrating ones and
Stegerwald-Nagel's dull, watery ones.

Zillich stayed in the dark, leaning against the barrack wall. The
lake shimmered in the woods. The wind drove the rain into his face.
Of course, his old acquaintance was right about their never meeting
again. They had come to Piaski as guards at the same time. Zillich
had feared that Nagel would become head guard before him. Until
Zillich succeeded in putting the blame on Nagel, when that Jew, old
Grünebaum, who was assigned to their quarters, almost slipped
through their fingers. Grünebaum's escape didn't succeed back then;
he didn't get through the barbed wire fast enough, and they were able
to turn on the electric current, which finished off the escapee.

But when Zillich denounced him for inadequate watchfulness,
Nagel had whispered to him, "I'll get you yet."

Maybe Nagel had forgotten his threat since he was himself in
danger now. On the other hand, he might remember it any minute.
It was idiotic to wait around for that to happen.

Zillich didn't return to the barracks. He crept off into the night. He
was completely drenched by the rain before he could get far enough

into the forest where nothing could harm him, neither man nor weather. He burrowed into the undergrowth like an animal about to die. It would be best if he could rot away during the night; then no one could find him tomorrow. He would decay like the dry leaves that continually fertilized the soil, unstoppable, undetectable, and safe from attack. Dust thou art and unto dust thou shalt return. And that's what Zillich was thinking. He was too tired to keep plodding along, even once the rain started to penetrate the forest. He was too exhausted to creep on night and day, from one farm to another, sniffed at and spied upon. He was too exhausted to escape across the French border and perhaps into the French occupied zone as he had once planned. There, also, a Nagel who might have had the same plan in mind could turn on him, or a Hans or a Franz.

He was seized by dread, not an even, constant state of fear but rather an ominous dread that swept through him in waves like an intermittent fever. One moment he was freezing and the next he was hopeful. Maybe he had exaggerated it all in his mind. He could go back to the lake; Nagel wouldn't talk.

But then again, Nagel would talk, and he felt cold again; the man would never forgive Zillich for keeping him from becoming head guard at Camp Piaski. Zillich couldn't go on living like this, from one rat hole to another.

A little pale daylight penetrated the tree branches; it calmed him. Nagel was the only one who had definitely recognized him. All the rest was imagined. He wasn't even certain that the man in the village had really recognized him. What was his name? Oh, yes, now he remembered, Kurt Volpert, Barracks 18. He'd probably let himself be duped back there. Volpert hadn't said anything to him. He had just allowed himself to be intimidated. Probably nobody cared about Zillich.

The best thing would be simply to go home. That had been the best thing to do back then. No one in the village had accused him of anything. His own wife, that miserable creature, had received him decently. He'd be able to live at home in his village undisturbed. Just a farmer among other farmers.

A strong wind had driven off the rain. The road home that he now saw stretching before him was quite long, but he started out confidently. After all, they hadn't investigated him at the sand quarry in Weinheim, even though there had been a raid while he was there. He had to get back to his village. His unspoiled instinct had already counseled him on his first flight: Just go home, nowhere else but home. He thrashed about in the dripping forest until he came upon a clearing and from there to a grassy forest road showing tracks made by timber transports. He came to the camp of some charcoal burners, who were following their trade up here, living like Gypsies, untouched by war or peace.

An unkempt little girl took him to the nearest farm. In all these weeks he hadn't thought of women. In his frightened state, nothing had tempted him. The neglected child was no more unkempt than many of the girls he'd gotten hold of during the war. Before the idea could even take form, the girl, maybe alerted by his look, raced ahead of him through the forest, then ran back toward him, whirred around him, dashed between his legs and into the thicket before he could take hold of her; there she swung from one branch to another, and he had as little chance of catching her as a bear could a bird. He was dumbfounded. Then the girl, sitting astride a tree limb, suddenly pointed at the gabled roof of a farmstead that had unexpectedly come into view. The farmers there matter-of-factly offered him a place to sleep with the animals. They were cold, hard people; they'd had enough of homeless folk ...

The next morning they urged him on to the next village: He'd best be going at once. He slept in one shelter after another in quick succession; he was afraid that someone from the dam at the lake might be following him. He wasn't going to feel safe until he had disappeared in his own village. True, he was again coming home with empty pockets; still, his wife would be glad to have his two strong arms. She'd been glad about his return back then too. And as for his neighbors, those stupid peasants would take him as he was: a returnee, an old-timer.

He steered clear of all the places he'd been to on his flight. One afternoon, he arrived at the hills that surrounded his village. He couldn't see down into the valley because the beech woods blocked his view. But he was reassured by the sight of the river that seemed to be saying: I told you at the outset that you must never leave my side. He sat in the grass under a twin beech. An ingrained caution kept him from immediately climbing down to the valley.

He carefully checked the fields that belonged to the community. His eldest son was working in the field. He whistled—two short, two long; it was a signal that the boy knew in his bones. The boy flinched. He recognized the man up there in the grass. He walked toward the twin beech, not fast enough but directly.

He stopped a yard away from Zillich; his small face was as white as a snowflake, his small fists were clenched.

"Hey, there," Zillich said, "go call your mother. Tell her to come here right away."

So far the boy hadn't said a word; he didn't say anything now either. He turned. There was no need for Zillich to kick his behind, for he was already running off.

Ten minutes later the farm woman came up. She had a little package in her hand. She put it on the ground between them. She didn't sit down. She said, wearily and slowly, "I brought you something to eat, and all the cash there was, even though we owe people money."

Zillich said, "What for? I've come back. Do you have any objections?"

The woman raised her arms. Wearily, dully she said, "Please don't do that. I beg you with all my heart. Go away, Zillich! Don't ever show your face here again. We've had to put up with so much because of you, especially the boy. You can't imagine how they badgered me with questions, with interrogations. Then, luckily, the factory in Erbenfeld was blown up, and they calmed down because they thought you were blown up with it. Because they'd been tracking you. It's bad enough that the boy had to see you again. So now go, get out of here as fast as you can."

"You damned bitch!" Zillich spat.

She cringed as she always had when he raised his hand against her. Patiently she listened to Zillich's rampage.

Even after she had left, Zillich's lips were still moving. Then, finally, he pulled himself up, holding on with both hands to the forked trunk of the twin beech. Groping about in the grass, he found the little package and tied it to his belt. He stumbled down the hill, in the direction he had come from. He walked on choosing his path at random, without a goal, without a purpose. He came to the river that, glittering white in the afternoon light and murmuring ceaselessly, drew every living thing to itself. He walked along the bank, following its course through the willow bushes, for otherwise there was nothing to guide him. The outlines of a village on the opposite bank, willows, an angler on a rock, suddenly became distinct and clear like everything in the evening when the sun is at its most oblique angle. It was as if, just before setting, it shone into the farthest corners of the world. His throat felt tight. He thought, That's how it begins. The board is pulled out from under your feet, and already you stop gasping for breath. He stomped his shoes hard into the ground, which was slippery from the autumn rain. He delighted in the viscous mire that slowed his every step. "You can't just simply shake it off. You'd like that, of course." He felt as if someone were spying on him now, very circumspectly, from the side. He turned his head abruptly, but instead of a watchful eye, he merely saw a knothole here, a dry leaf there, blinking in the evening light.

A fine, thin thread, bright in the dusk, ran ahead of him diagonally through the air from one shore to the other. It was the cable guiding the ferry as the ferryman pushed it along with his pole. The passengers were already waiting in a new corrugated metal hut. You could make out the hut's twin on the opposite shore. The evening light seeped into its corrugations, which then dissolved in the undulations of its reflection. Zillich trembled in fear of these people waiting in the hut for the ferry, and he trembled in fear of the people who would soon be landing with the ferry, and he trembled in fear of the ferryman who might recognize him, and he trembled in fear of the reflections of the passengers and of the ferryman.

He waited at the back of the group that was crowding onto the landing dock. He thought any one of these people with their baskets and tools, one with a dog, another with a goat, a third with a wooden cage, might recognize him and thus cut his life short. And this shortening of his life, possibly quite close, even disgustingly near, held all his thoughts in thrall. He didn't think of death; that came after his life. He had never bothered himself about anything that existed beyond his life.

At the last second and with his head lowered he jumped onto the ferry. It was dark now; night was settling in without stars, dreary and rainy. The ferryman turned on the lamp. Zillich moved away. He was afraid of discovering a familiar face among the faces and shadows jolting and jerking in the lamplight. He had felt better for a moment when the ferry pushed off from shore. If only he knew what was waiting on the other shore. Maybe a fist in the smacker, maybe handcuffs. All he could do was stay calm on the trip across the drowsy river.

But it could not be, not even on the crossing. The woman with the poultry cage on her lap looked an awful lot like the innkeeper's aunt in his village. How dare the woman decide to make this particular nighttime crossing with her hens and chicks? What business did someone like her have on the other shore? She ought to stay on her own side; she ought to be glad she didn't *have* to leave. Now she was peering through the bars of the cage toward his side. Zillich spun around so quickly that the passengers near him grumbled. The ferryman, lifting his pole, turned his head in Zillich's direction. But he had ducked down on the bench and lowered his head toward the water. The passengers laughed, and one said, "He's got a problem. He has to throw up."

Zillich welcomed this explanation. He slid on his knees to the edge of the ferryboat, leaned so far over that his nose almost touched the river. The old woman, her view restricted by the cage, couldn't possibly recognize him now. He peered right and left into the dark water in which the rippling shadowy reflections of the travelers were interwoven with the trembling band of light from the lantern. With every push of the ferryman's pole, the ferry glided forward, each time accompanied by a squeal from the cable on which it was sliding from

one riverbank to the other. Two more of his pushes and they would
bump against the other landing. Zillich feared this, even as he longed
to be delivered from his bent-over position. Would the ferryman, that
little deformed goblin with his long contorted apelike arms, turn
around then? Zillich watched the shadow of his pole and the crooked
shadow of his humped back. How often did he go back and forth in
one night? He would go back at least once more, for on this side too,
workers, farmers, and cattle were waiting, crowded together on the
landing. Zillich would soon run the risk of being recognized on this
shore too. For those who needed to go back to the other side were
also connected in some way with the happenings in the villages on
that side.

He turned around slowly. The woman who might be the aunt of
the innkeeper was already getting off the ferry. What could that
woman be up to over here, Zillich wondered. His delirium passed;
the river, now he'd crossed it, could cut him off from the past. He
didn't dare look at the faces of the people crowding toward the ferry
as it docked. He realized that it wasn't dark because night had fallen
but because of the impending rain. There were still pale stripes of
twilight in the starless, black sky. With a sigh of relief, he gazed after
the one danger he had at least been able to grasp: the innkeeper's aunt
who was now walking away into the countryside, perhaps to the village whose meager lights still stubbornly held fast to the brick works
that had sustained this area since time immemorial. Most of the other
passengers plodded along behind her, eager to get home before it
rained. But too late, for the first drops were already clattering on the
corrugated metal. As the ferry was pushing off again, many of those
left behind crowded under the metal roof, cursing.

Now all the beliefs that had throughout his life shown him how
to be strong and avoid danger seemed to fail him. From the anger in
the voices of the people left behind he could tell that this was the last
crossing of the ferry for that night. The ferryman had his lodgings
on the other shore. Zillich wasn't going to risk pressing onward to
the brick-works village in the rain. There was as little safety for him
there as here, and here at least he could stay dry. He sat in a corner

of the shack, his head sunk as far between his knees as possible. The rain clattered down painfully as if the corrugated metal were his skin or his skin were made of corrugated tin. He sat there for an hour, unmoving, not waiting for anything, not even for the rain to stop, for could he have gone on, where to? It would be best if the rain were to drip right through, piercing the corrugated metal and him and everything else under it. He would dissolve. Then he couldn't be captured. Then he'd be delivered from this in-between stage, this horrible transition that he wished he could have spared himself. What would happen afterward, without him, was unimaginable and not even worth thinking about.

It was quiet. The rain had stopped. Many of the people had left the shack, perhaps to spend the night in the village. Others were homeless and used to making do with any kind of shelter. Zillich looked out from between his knees and across the river flowing by outside the open shed. A man was lying next to Zillich, wrapped in his coat, his head resting on one elbow. When he saw Zillich, whom he thought had been asleep, looking at him, he started to talk. "One wall is missing," he said, "but we have a roof."

Zillich said, "Yes."

"Any place on earth is fine with me as long as it has no barbed wire around it."

"Yes."

"Anyone who's ever been shut up in a camp can understand that. Every morning, no matter where I wake up, whether in a hole in the ground, on a boat, or in a cellar, my first thought is: I'm free." He spoke eagerly into the dark, the way people do who long to talk. "No matter what happens to me, any privation, any mishap, as long as it happens to me while I'm free . . . Can you understand that?"

"Yes."

"Yes. It's possible that there may still be a serious conflict ahead. Let it come, for I am free. Were you ever in a camp?"

"Yes."

"You too? Where?"

Zillich said, "In Piaski."

"That's amazing," the other said, supporting his head on both elbows, his face still in the dark. "When was that? In which barracks? Because I was there for a year."

Zillich felt his heart pulling him downward; his arms felt as weak as paper. He quickly made up a barracks far away from his own, where no prisoner could ever have seen the guards in his barracks. He said, "In 121a."

"Good God, then we were almost neighbors. I was in 125. Did you know that fat guard Bohland? He was a super brute."

Zillich said, "No." He hadn't thought of Bohland for a long time. Now he remembered him. As well as the envy that had consumed him back then after the roll call when Bohland was commended with a "Special Command" for his services. Fortunately for Zillich, night had fallen by now. He turned his face to the wall. At his back the stranger made a few more attempts at conversation, but he got no answers except for snoring.

Behind them a few men lay stretched out. They were sleepily grousing to one another about the early autumn, the new Erbach municipal administration, the injustices of the occupation, and the ferryman. At odds with the world, they squeezed together in sleep like children. One of them was still sitting there, smoking. Zillich looked mistrustfully at the little dot of light. Then at last it went out. But maybe the man was still sitting there. Zillich wondered, Is he really asleep now? Why doesn't he stretch out too? If I leave now, what will he do? For he really had to go, before the man from the Piaski camp woke up and recognized his face in the morning light.

Staying here was bad, but leaving was also bad. Why wasn't he already gone, beyond reach, vanished, decomposed, dissolved? A mouse could have slipped through the cracks between the tin wall and the shed, and a beetle certainly could have. But he, he was massive, big-boned and strong. He looked at the man sitting in the corner. Was he really asleep? Or was he only bracing for the moment when Zillich would get up? Had he boarded the ferry before the rain started? Was he only here because of Zillich?

Zillich jumped up and over the sleeping men. He went around

the shed, hurriedly climbed up the sloping bank; he crawled into some bushes, then crept into a hollow between two hills. He listened; nothing, no one was following him. Perhaps the man in the corner had been sleeping. Perhaps the sleepers hadn't even noticed his departure.

That didn't help him. There was no refuge. His wife wouldn't take him in, and certainly no stranger would. The only lucky break he'd had on the other side of the river was that they thought he was already dead. Here, on this side of the river, there were countless new dangers. He was drawn back to the river that flowed dark in the unyielding, dull, black night. It was his only hope in this country and on this earth. It had wound itself around his life, this broad, lazy, idle little river, for as long as he could remember. He had always compared the many rivers he had crossed later, between the Rhine and the Volga, with this little river. The best thing for him to do now would be to disappear. As soon as this thought came to him, his entire body responded, coming to life in every fiber. His heart went into a trot. He smelled the potent autumn smells. He had an itch under his arm. He was ravenously hungry. He untied the little package at his belt that he had suddenly remembered. Things were already beginning to look up! It would be better to find a place to stay, even if only for a short time, even if only to stuff himself. It wouldn't be enough to save him, but it would be a reprieve. He crept down the incline, splashed through a marsh, afraid now of sinking too deep in the mud. But it was only a seasonal autumnal swamp.

He avoided the village near the brick works; if the innkeeper's aunt was there, then there would surely be other relatives and cousins. The night ended as it had begun. The sun that rose over the plain was not much more than a faded spot of blood. Even though he was tired and hungry, he didn't take the direct road to Erbach with its patrols and guards.

After quite some time he found himself on the outskirts of the town of Erbach. The houses had all been shelled or destroyed; only the old gate with the coat of arms remained intact. Zillich waited for the moment when the guard's back was toward him. He turned onto a street, walking along without looking back, as if someone he might recognize might in turn recognize him. He saw a sign, a handwritten notice: Overnight accommodations available. The landlady showed him to a fresh sack of straw in a bare, clean room. The other three lodgers had already left for work. As he plopped down on his sack, she said, "Please take off your shoes."

He sat with his legs crossed under him. He unwrapped his little package and stuffed his mouth with bread. There was a knock on the door. His heart stopped, his mouth still full of bread. A nimble little man slipped in; there was a medlar tree twig in his buttonhole. He raised his hand, "Heil, Zillich, my dear Schulze."

Zillich looked up at him dully. He finished chewing the bread.

"I couldn't believe my eyes when I saw you gaily walking into our good old free city of Erbach."

Zillich said, "What's it to you?"

"To me, nothing at all. When you vanished from our sand quarry, I thought to myself, Fly away, bird, fly away. Back then when our destinies brought us together—do you still remember, on the road on the other side of Weinheim? What kind of a jailbird is this, that's what I thought. Let's see if I can find out. I wasn't surprised at all when they found out more about you later. I'm naturally curious, you know. My mother was already a terribly nosy woman—I mean Eve, of course, the ancient one. Otherwise she would never have bitten into the apple back then."

"Go to hell!"

"At once. Have a restful night."

Zillich suddenly turned around. "Wait a minute, Friday, are you staying here in Erbach?"

"Do you mind?"

"I hope you're not thinking of snitching on me." Zillich's little eyes pierced the man like poisonous needles.

Friday even said, "Ouch." He put one foot in the doorway. "That's not a bad idea you've got there."

Zillich raised himself on his elbows. "Stay and shut the door behind you."

"No. I don't feel at all like having a cozy little get-together. By the way, the landlady, she's here too, in the next room. So sit back down." He watched quite cheerfully as Zillich stood there before him, groaning with bloodthirst. He whistled.

Suddenly Zillich folded his hands. "My dear Friday, you wouldn't do that to an old acquaintance. After all, we're pals."

"How come? Oh, I see. Well, in any case, lie down and go to sleep now." His eyes sparkled. "I'll think it all over again while I go downstairs. What was it Adolf Hitler said? Give me four minutes! Again, have a restful night." He turned on his heel, twirling the little medlar branch between two fingers.

Zillich heard the door to the room shut, then the hallway door, then the front door. His small eyes bored two little holes into the void Friday left behind.

"That would suit the scoundrel just fine, keeping me waiting while he reported me, letting me squirm. He'd enjoy that. But I won't give him the pleasure."

A couple of hours later the other lodgers coming home knocked excitedly on the landlady's door. "You've hung a nice welcome bouquet on the window hook. Was the guy hanging there a new lodger?"

Early in the morning, Mr. Degreif, the teacher, was coming out of the village mayor's house. Even though it was cold, he sat down on the bench under the bare chestnut tree before going over to the school. He'd suppressed his excitement on hearing the news. Now he coughed it all out. He thought, Things look pretty bad for me. I'll only be able to keep teaching school another two or three years at most. The time comes for each of us. In any case, I'm happy to be able to live on this earth in freedom again, even if I can only teach one more day.

The first swarm of boys was coming down the village street. Young Zillich came alone a little later. The whispering of the last months had created a certain outer and inner distance between him and the other boys. The teacher called him over. "I have something important to tell you, my boy."

The boy looked at the teacher attentively with his gray, distrustful eyes. He pulled his arm back when the teacher touched him; he couldn't stand being touched.

Degreif said, "Your father is dead. He was found dead in Erbach."

The boy was radiant. His eyes flashed; his face beamed with joy. Degreif was dismayed, even repelled. But he suppressed his feelings. Of all the horrors of the last few years this child's display of joy seemed the iciest and most cutting. He wanted to say something but swallowed his words. He ran his hand through the boy's shaggy, short hair. The boy had experienced only shame and loathing in connection with his father. His father had brought him into this world and then left him in the lurch. Now another, a stranger, he himself would have to look after this boy as a father.

1943, 1945

MAIL TO THE PROMISED LAND

IN THE final decade of the previous century,* when almost the
entire Jewish population of the little Polish town of L. was killed by
Cossacks in a pogrom, the remnants of the Gruenbaum family fled
to Vienna, where the eldest daughter, who had married a furrier, lived.
After the death of all the other children, the family now consisted of
the son-in-law Nathan Levi, a grandchild, and the parents-in-law.
The young Mrs. Levi, the second Gruenbaum daughter, hadn't been
kicked or beaten to death in the pogrom but had died from compli-
cations of a premature birth brought on by watching the murder of
her own brothers through a small window in the cellar where she was
hiding. She had been the Gruenbaums' favorite daughter. The eldest
daughter, to whom they were now going, was considered unhelpful
and disagreeable. Otherwise, her family would probably not have
agreed to her marriage to a man so far away, even though his family
came from the same town. Her features in a longish, somewhat wry
face were fairly unattractive and morose, although one couldn't tell
whether her grumpy disposition was responsible for the way she
looked or whether it was her looks that had affected her disposition.

When she came to pick up her people at the Ostbahnhof in Vienna,
the mother in all her despair couldn't help thinking about how dead
her gentle, younger daughter was, how wretchedly she had died, and
how the elder one, as sullen and mean-spirited as ever, was still alive.
For despair, instead of blunting, relentlessly sharpened her memories
of the dead and her view of the living. The Viennese son-in-law was

*The nineteenth century.

much like her eldest daughter. Whether they had found each other in their mutual moroseness or she had infected him afterward, in any case, he was resentful and envious. The furrier's children were not at all happy about the little cousin, with whom they now had to share their food and bedroom. The cramped quarters of the apartment intensified the adults' discomfort. Perhaps after so much suffering they should have been glad for any refuge. Yet, having escaped death, they somehow couldn't manage to simply be grateful for life just because it was there, even if gray, bleak, and joyless.

The other son-in-law, Nathan Levi, immediately began to help out in the furrier's workshop. At work, he liked best to sit in a corner with his little son on his knees. He was an outsider in his dead wife's family. His parents-in-law had taken him in as an orphan without any relatives. He had learned his trade in the Gruenbaums' furrier shop along with the two Gruenbaum sons, who later perished in the pogrom. It wasn't long before he was regarded as a son-in-law. The old Gruenbaums were praised for this decision, and their good deeds were considered rewarded because the young Levi turned out to be hardworking and honest. Even as a boy, he had regarded their younger daughter as his bride. And now, in spite of his considerable beard, he was really still young at heart, though not interested in getting involved with the new things life had to offer. He had a boyish lack of awareness of the length and diversity of life, for he expected to live for only a tedious, brief time, after which he would be reunited with his wife.

His mother-in-law, on the other hand, started thinking about moving elsewhere right away. She knew that when one is suffering one doesn't accept a cheerless existence casually but rather with more pain and more need. A letter from her sister in Silesia suggested a solution. This Mrs. Loeb, by now already elderly, had once traveled to a trade fair in Kattowitz with her husband, a used-clothing dealer. And they had decided to stay, not so much because they were prosperous but because they keenly hoped to achieve prosperity there. Now she wrote how happy she was that her sister had found a place to live. Otherwise she could have found shelter with her. Mrs. Gruenbaum wrote back immediately that unfortunately their present accommodations were in a sorry state, and that they all would rather continue on to Silesia. Once there, her husband and her son-in-law could lend the brother-in-law a hand.

Thereupon, she wrapped the grandchild in many shawls. The son-in-law, who was a short man, held him in his lap for most of the trip. All during that night as they were going to Germany, he was reluctant to hand the child over to the grandparents sitting on either side of him. Their departure for Silesia seemed strange to the Viennese family, but not unwelcome. They just wondered about the travel funds that had suddenly become available to them.

The Gruenbaums' arrival was a surprise and not a particularly pleasing one for the Loeb family. They were poor, and their apartment was small. Since the used-clothes business didn't require more than two hands, Gruenbaum and his son-in-law looked for work as furriers. They found that there was little work available, for the workshops all had more workers than needed. The young Levi and the grandparents were very fond of the boy, but they worried about him because he was so frail and quiet. Mrs. Gruenbaum, although rather cheerful and enterprising by nature, would gradually have succumbed along with her family to the hopelessness of their daily life, had not an unexpected incident suddenly shaken them up.

The son-in-law, Nathan Levi, had a brother whom they had all but forgotten. In the past, whenever he was mentioned, even casually, he'd always been considered a ne'er-do-well. When the Levi parents were still alive, he had been apprenticed in the furrier workshop, too. At some point during that time, he had found the opportunity to accompany a foreign dealer on a trip, since he, being restless and unsettled—so they said at the time—was keen to go traveling. In any case, he had inexplicably ended up in Paris and never returned home for fear of the consequences he might suffer for embezzlement—according to the rumors that quickly sprang up simply because no one could think of any other reason for such an absurd relocation. And now, with the help and resourcefulness of many Jewish communities, a lengthy letter from this long-lost brother arrived in which he asked the younger Levi to tell him how things had gone for them

in the pogrom that he had read about in the newspapers. The younger
Levi, Nathan, at once wrote back. They were all cheered up in the
days that followed by expectations of a letter in return, since merely
waiting for something can enliven even the bleakest of times.

First came a remittance of money telegraphed to the bank, a most
amazing event for the family. Then came a telegram announcing the
arrival of the elder Levi who, though he had vanished from their
memories, had not, it seemed, quite disappeared from their family
history. Mrs. Gruenbaum used what was left of her own savings—not
for anything would she use the money they had just been sent—to
buy all sorts of delicacies for the welcoming reception: poultry, fish,
and wine, plus the ingredients she needed to bake her best cake. For
the first time since their misfortune, she carefully dressed herself and
her grandson, and brushed and ironed her husband's and son-in-law's
trousers.

The younger brother went to pick up the elder one at the train
station. Meanwhile, the entire apartment had been spruced up, as
much as one can refresh a living room and a kitchen without moving
the walls. Their guest, Salomon Levi, was taller than his brother. His
face looked naked because it was clean-shaven except for a mustache
on the upper lip. Because of this, the elder brother looked as if he
might be his bearded brother's son. He was wearing a stiff hat, gloves,
and a tight-fitting but new coat, and carrying a small leather traveling
bag. His looks as well as his language would have upset Mrs. Gruenbaum if it hadn't been that—because her senses had been sharpened
by her misfortune to detect the good as well as the bad in people—she
immediately saw the goodness and compassion in his eyes. Even
though he still occasionally spoke Yiddish, it sounded foreign or came
out nasal rather than guttural, and when he gestured with his hands
while speaking, he drew foreign curves in the air to accompany the
foreign sounds. It startled him to see that they all covered their heads
when they sat down at the table for supper, and he quickly put on his
stiff hat. The Gruenbaums weren't annoyed by anything and didn't
hold anything against him not only because he praised the child and
swung him up in his arms but, above all, because he couldn't hear

enough about the pogrom. Everyone else had, in the meantime, tired of hearing about it, so that they had buried the memory of it inside themselves where it naturally weighed down their hearts. He had them repeat the stories of those events over and over, and they were glad to get them off their chests.

He noticed every good thing they did for him. He praised the dumplings in the soup, and he admired the fish and the fish filling, and even some chopped herbs in the gravy, and when the apple strudel began to melt in his mouth, he bent over and squeezed his eyes shut. No matter how many mistakes he made, in the prayers while washing the hands, or over the bread and wine, and even the prayer before eating, they all lost their sameness and their casual, habitual familiarity and took on a strange new sound, simply because he droned along awkwardly and rocked back and forth with his upper body.

That night, on the way back to the hotel, he told his brother that he hadn't stayed on in Paris because of any embezzlement of funds back home but because he liked the city so very much. Besides, he had become rich enough to easily pay off any possible earlier debts. He suggested that the entire family come to France, to Paris. His brother and old Mr. Gruenbaum could find whatever type of work they liked to do in the large furrier's workshop he owned, which employed salesmen, bookkeepers, and craftsmen. Above all, the little boy could be properly taken care of and attend a decent school.

The outcome of their deliberations was that the refugees made a third move, this time with all sorts of gifts for Mr. and Mrs. Loeb and even a remittance of money to the furrier family in Vienna. For now, belatedly, Mrs. Gruenbaum wanted to be fair to her elder daughter who, she realized, was as little to blame for her outer and inner shortcomings as she would have been for a disability.

Salomon Levi, the elder brother, lived on the Right Bank of the Seine where the Saint-Paul Quarter adjoins the embankment. On their first day he rented an apartment in that district for the new arrivals, and went with Mrs. Gruenbaum to department stores to buy the furniture they would need. Mrs. Gruenbaum was dazed by the wildness of the city. No one treated her, a stranger, with curiosity or disrespect. On the streets and in the shops, she came upon even stranger foreigners, yellow-skinned and black-skinned people, and sometimes she ran into people like herself. But they were all left alone because they did no harm to the city, just as strange plants do no harm to a wilderness. Here at the outermost edge of the world with which she was familiar, Mrs. Gruenbaum felt almost at home.

The Gruenbaums continued to live undisturbed; it was as if they had dragged their little hometown, including the baker and the butcher, along with them to Saint-Paul. It turned out that through some coincidence the sister of their former seamstress had also come here. Old Mr. Gruenbaum was soon considered a sort of supervisor in the furrier shop where his son-in-law Nathan Levi had become a kind of foreman, for he wanted definitely to stay with his craft. The boy was taught to read and write Hebrew by their old seamstress's brother-in-law who had opened a preschool for children.

Not far from their apartment there was a synagogue in an old masonry structure that, the elder Levi brother told them, was the tower of a palace King Henry IV had built many centuries earlier. Now parts of it were in ruins. The ruins were occupied by all kinds of people. The cellars of the old rag collectors were located on that street, and their dust made the air even duskier. The courtyard of the synagogue was full of a carpenter's odds and ends, for the carpenter also served as the attendant in the synagogue. Boards leaned against the worn columns in the pointed arches. The little carpenter, hunch-backed and bearded, had moved here from a town near L. a long time ago. There were still traces of the coats of arms on the winding worn staircase that spiraled up to the women's section. The doorframe was well worn too. On entering, the women would kiss two fingertips and then touch them to the mezuzah.

How brightly the candles burned downstairs on the Yahrzeit days when the men prayed for all their dead relatives!

From upstairs, Mrs. Gruenbaum recognized her own candle, or thought she did. She had searched for it lovingly as if it were her daughter herself. She also pointed the candle out to the little boy whom she took up to the women's section with her until the time came when he could finally pray with the men downstairs.

They had settled quickly into the quarter, a tiny L. in this strange city, with familiar faces and the usual shops spread along a few homey streets and squares. Nathan Levi was soon speaking French fluently. His son spoke it even better, although a few Russian and Polish words and some Hebrew and Yiddish ones crept in now and then. The elder Levi urged his younger brother to marry again. But the latter resisted in his gentle way, smiling.

Every day he would leave the workshop and rush home to talk with his child and to find out what he had learned; if the boy was ill, he would hurry home even earlier and spend the night at the boy's bedside. He also rejected any and all marriage proposals after his parents-in-law died, much sooner than expected and in quick succession. After all the troubles they had patiently come through, they had apparently at last been granted leave to be exhausted by life.

After their deaths, the elder brother, Salomon Levi, although all his attempts to arrange a marriage for his brother had failed, had better luck with a completely different suggestion, one he had previously proposed in vain. His nephew, he said, should now attend a proper school. It was high time. He should learn French and acquire all the other knowledge boys in this country were offered. He finally succeeded in persuading his younger brother. He took the child to the Saint-Paul high school, the Lycée Charlemagne. And from the second day on, the boy's father himself took his son to school every morning and picked him up again at midday so that he would not be tempted to partake of the forbidden school meals.

The boy was much happier at the school than his father had expected. He wasn't tormented or beaten by his teachers and fellow students. They only teased him when he spoke French poorly. He tried very hard on his own to achieve the right sound that he liked because he also liked the words. He thought he had caught the meaning once he got the sound right. Soon he made friends with an impish, rowdy boy, the son of a streetcar conductor in their quarter who gradually taught him all sorts of games and rhymes and, through his friendship, the French language.

Wearing a black smock, quick, lean, and wise-eyed, he was now one of the hundreds of thousands of schoolboys in Paris. Every July Fourteenth eve he would join his school friend's family, the streetcar conductor's family. He would spend many hours in the midst of the crowd on the Place de la Bastille. When he ate and drank with them, he forgot to say grace, and he danced at the street dances with his friend's sisters.

Soon he preferred being in school to being at home. Before they died, the mere presence of his grandparents had calmed everyone. Now his father and uncle argued a lot. Mr. Rosenzweig, the teacher and the brother-in-law of the seamstress from L., was also there for meals and he joined in the arguments. These were about the certain events that had been upsetting their own community and all the other communities of the world for many years. A Jew in Vienna, who had died some time ago, had proposed that the Holy Land, which God had promised them, be immediately given to the Jewish people. They were to return to their homeland, to Palestine, from all the countries of the world where they were being persecuted.

Salomon Levi, the brother, fervently supported this new doctrine. Mr. Rosenzweig, the teacher, weighed the pro and cons so passionately, one might have thought two souls were fighting within his breast, the way men do who stand undecided between two principles. Nathan Levi didn't get involved; he listened, smiling. From the time he was a boy, it had been his secret, his ardent wish to see the Promised Land with his own eyes before his death. But this wish had no political borders; only God could fulfill it. It was rooted in faith, not in a strip of land in the Middle East. Whether you lived in Paris or in L., in America or in Vienna, you were living in exile. An exile God had imposed.

And he wasn't angry but only smiled when his brother suddenly hung Herzl's photograph on the wall above his desk in the furrier shop. The same deeply ingrained rule that had allowed his brother, Salomon, as a boy, to break with all his family's ideas, forced him now for a second time, as an old man, to break with his earlier ideals and eagerly follow the proceedings of the Zionist Congress.

During their arguments the boy would sit at the table with the three older people, happily chewing his food. His father occasionally tried surreptitiously to touch his hair or at least his hand. But the boy was listening less to their conversations, which didn't interest him, than to the street noises, waiting to hear his friend's whistle.

Only on holidays was the boy totally at home, body and soul; it was as if the soft candlelight forged him more firmly to the family than did their arguments and opinions, but also more firmly than did all the shouts and whistling in the street. On the first day of Passover, his father, sitting on the red pillows in his place of honor, looked shy and childlike in spite of his beard. He would nod to the boy to indicate to him that it was time for him to jump up and open the door in accordance with tradition, for the Messiah might suddenly enter all the doors in all the houses of the world and lead his people home out of their exile. A faint whiff of this belief, which couldn't be taught or transmitted, wafted toward the boy every time he opened the door, along with the furtive question, "What if He comes into our house now?" even though the boy, who was more clever than his father, knew full well that it was a foolish question to ask.

Around this time, when the boy was thirteen, his old teacher Mr. Rosenzweig was very proud because he had been asked to prepare the boy for the red-letter day on which he would be received into the congregation of men. That day the three older men in his family brought him to the synagogue in the castle tower of Henry IV. They beamed with pride as the young voice rose, familiar, strangely alone, and solemnly anxious. It was known since ancient times that the minds of boys are most alert and receptive at this age. For that reason, along with the age-old handed-down teachings, ideas entered the boy's mind that his father would never have dreamed of. They did not torment him; they just overlaid the old ideas, as two layers of bark lie over each other in a young tree. He continued to go to celebrate July Fourteenth with the family of his school friend. But now he wasn't happy just because there was dancing and drinking, and it

wasn't that his heart beat with joy just upon seeing the fireworks and
the flags flying. Indeed, not even his teacher at the Lycée Charlemagne
could have known that his conventional words had stirred up the
thin little foreign boy. He had declared that the evening of July
Fourteenth was a celebration for all peoples. There were no invited
guests at this holiday here in Paris on the Place de la Bastille; on that
day everyone invited himself. On this day the people of Paris had
burst asunder the Middle Ages for the whole world. He was a teacher
who held each student with his eyes so that each of them believed he
was the sole focus of those eyes.

At home they didn't notice that at the Seder the boy read the words
assigned to the youngest from the Haggadah only because his father
was gazing at him with love and because he himself was as gentle and
polite as his father.

He was growing so rapidly that he soon towered over the three
old people. Then came the year 1914; then the murder at Sarajevo;
then one declaration of war after another. The Germans, having
swallowed up Belgium, pushed forward to the Marne. Faces turned
grim. The young Levi applied to take his exams unexpectedly early.
His father didn't find out till afterward that only those students who
had volunteered for the army were admitted early. On seeing the
round cap with the red tassel on his son's head, he began to tremble,
and his hands continued to tremble for the duration of the war.

His son was happy. He was now committed body and soul, not
just with his airy, uncertain soul but with his whole being, to this
people to whom he had for a long time felt connected, whose language
and ideas had long ago become part of him, from the fall of the
Bastille up to the Dreyfus trial. His father and uncle stood weeping
at the train station among all the other parents saying goodbye.

When he came home on furlough, his father seemed to him even
smaller and more childlike than before. *He* was now the strong one,
the fatherly one. He listened in the furrier workshop to his father
and uncle tell about their worries as if they were his sons. In the course
of one wartime winter, with the nearness of death and the camaraderie of his fellow soldiers, he had traversed a path toward assimilation

and experience that would otherwise have taken generations. When he was seriously wounded in the Argonne Forest, it seemed to him that the earth beneath him into which his blood was seeping had become his. His father received the news that his son had been wounded along with a message scribbled by the son himself saying that the worst danger was past.

He came home on crutches after the armistice. Life at home would have become abhorrent to him now if he hadn't been obsessed by a completely new idea. His closest comrade had been healed after an initially hopeless eye injury. There in the field hospital he had witnessed all the phases from hope to despair until an eye doctor had saved his friend's sight. A penchant for medicine that had now and then overcome him during his upper-level classes at school had been reinforced by his wartime experiences and was focused on a specific area: healing the eyes. His father, who had expected him to become a furrier or a businessman or even a clever lawyer, was at first puzzled by this choice of profession. Then he told himself that it had been God's will that his son's life was saved, and therefore this decision was also God's will.

The Allies occupied the Rhineland. Wilson strove for peace. With great difficulty the young Levi succeeded in getting his father to rent him a room near the clinic in which to study. Now Nathan Levi was more alone than he had ever been in his life, having always lived in the midst of his family. He had suddenly and unexpectedly been abandoned not only by his son but also by his elder brother. For when Balfour, the English foreign minister, had promised Palestine to the Jews as their homeland, his brother, Salomon, instantly resolved that he would go to see the Promised Land with his own eyes before finally deciding to apply the Balfour Declaration to himself. At first, he thought of the trip as a vacation for three months at most. He invited his brother to accompany him on his travels. But the latter explained that he had to manage the fur workshop. The left-behind brother was soon made uneasy by letters mailed from the Mediterranean steamship, in which the traveler gave the impression that he felt ill and unhappy. The vacation trip had to be interrupted by a stay in a Haifa hospital and ended with Salomon's eternal settlement in the Holy Land—in the Haifa cemetery.

When the notice of his death arrived in Paris, his brother, Nathan Levi, who had watched his elder brother's departure with a dark premonition and concealed doubts, had kaddish recited in the same synagogue in the castle tower where kaddish was already being recited for his parents-in-law and his own young wife who had died in L.

Every year on the anniversary of her death he hastened through the streets and courtyards of Saint-Paul, through the telescoped gates, and through the side entrance of the weathered palace, as if he were hurrying to a reunion with his wife. His son, who accompanied him, knew no more of his mother than the short white flickering Yahrzeit candles. He would come every year from the Latin Quarter to Saint-Paul for the kaddish. The narrow street, dusty from the trash cellars of the ragpickers, was bordered by the castle pinnacles. It reflected the slight glow of light that came down from the almost unnoticed window of the women's section upstairs. The carpenter's shop was still in the courtyard, and the carpenter's people, now walking stooped over, still took care of the synagogue.

A pub had recently opened among the ragpickers' cellars. New Jewish settlers had come to live on the street. They had come there after the war because their rabbi back home had convinced them that one couldn't raise one's children as devout Jews in the new Soviet Russian State. A similar fear inspired by the same revolution had also driven yet another group of refugees there who were not at all happy to see these Jewish faces from the Ukraine again: They were officers from the army of the hetman Petliura and all his cronies who, only a short while before, had killed many Jews until Lenin put up his placards reading "Down with the Black Hundreds—End the Pogroms," at which point their own homeland had become intolerable to them. Now the French police were saddled with keeping the White tsarists away from the Jewish immigrants. But they were unable to intercept the bullet with which the watchmaker Schwarzbart from Saint-Paul shot down the Ukrainian hetman Petliura who had murdered Schwarzbart's entire family back home during the last pogrom.

Young Levi visited his father every Friday evening. Nathan Levi thanked God that his son hadn't become an ordinary furrier but was a chosen man who was as dedicated to the sick as a good teacher is to his students. The eye hospital was sacred ground not only for the son but also for his father. The father had his son show him textbooks with diagrams of the human eye, about which his son apparently brooded more than any of the other organs that God had created. He wasn't surprised that the professors soon began to take notice of his son. Even before, in Saint-Paul, when he took his exam, they were already anticipating that the young Levi would become a great eye doctor. There was just one thing that troubled the father. He had been his son's age when he had become a father, and love had brightened his life to the present day.

He spoke about his concern with his neighbor Loeb Mirsky, who had become his friend. The sudden and at first unbearable loneliness caused by the death of his brother and by his son leaving home had had the happy outcome that his eyes were now open to his fellow human beings. He had found a way to connect with this neighbor who long ago—even before the war that followed the ritual murder trial in Odessa and the resulting persecution of the Jews—had been driven to Paris. Like Levi, he had lost his wife and saved his child, a daughter who later kept house for him. But she loved studying more, her father thought, than was becoming to her lovely figure and equally lovely face. The two fathers believed that their children would make a good couple. If only, influenced by the customs of their adopted country, they wouldn't oppose the plans of their parents so stubbornly. Levi was quite pleased at the idea of the beautiful, headstrong young girl for his son, and he suggested to his neighbor that he grant his daughter permission to give up her housewifely duties so that she could attend the Sorbonne on the Left Bank daily. And so it happened that studying there brought the two young people together just as surely as the cleverest marriage broker. It didn't take the young Levi long to notice the dark brown hair, soft eyes, transparent skin, and calm step. After the examinations, the two fathers celebrated the longed-for and finally achieved marriage.

Jacob Levi, now Dr. Jacques Levi, was still far from the age at which a man's reputation is usually established when the stream of patients seeking him out, first at his professor's clinic and then at his own clinic on the rue de Sêvres, made a name for him. His father was glad, but what really made him happy was the arrival of his first grandchild, although a little later than he had hoped. Recently he had been wishing for offspring much more impatiently because he had begun to feel weaker and older, now that he had the peace and quiet to do so, just as his parents-in-law once had. He would often sit in his son's consultation room, listening to the complaints and praise of patients who had come there with eye problems. Then he would go home with his son to play a bit with his grandson and, in later years, to check the boy's school notebooks just as he had once checked his son's.

One day he arrived at his son's clinic on the rue de Sêvres just at the end of office hours, an unusual time for him. He told his surprised son that he had come so late in order to speak with him alone. Now that the son had his own family, his own home, a child, and a profession, he, Nathan Levi, as his father, considered the commandment fulfilled and the future of his progeny assured. Dr. Jacques Levi was wondering what his father hoped to achieve with this visit. He was even more amazed when the older man went on to say in a much more serious, solemn tone than he usually used that God's ways were inscrutable. Just consider how, after the pogrom in L., he had first fled to Vienna, then from Vienna to Kattowitz, and from Kattowitz to Paris with his son on his knees, and how the family now continued in his son. He spoke as if he had already forgotten that his son was sitting across from him in his white doctor's coat. He was probably trying to postpone for a while the most important thing on his mind, which then, finally, he did put into words.

He hadn't been any older than his grandson was now when the entire town of L. went to the train station to escort an old man who was going to the Promised Land in order to die there. Even back then this journey's destination seemed to him the most enticing one he could imagine. And he remembered the man's departure as if it had happened only yesterday. A powerful desire had been planted in his heart back then: to be allowed to die in that same place once he got to be as old as that old man. He had never forgotten this wish, merely buried it deep within himself. He had secretly been saving the money required for the journey and his last stay in an old-age home in Jerusalem. He had already entrusted the closing of the furrier workshop to the neighbor so that it wouldn't be a last-minute rush.

The younger Levi was astounded by his father's words, which indicated more initiative and resolution than he would ever have expected from this gentle, mild man. Moreover, all this determination was not concerned with his life but with his death. He marveled also that the old man, who was usually affectionate and quite open, had concealed his plan like a secret, not only all throughout his earlier life when his plan was only a dream but also more recently as the realization of it became possible. He pointed out that the move from Saint-Paul to the Latin Quarter had been painful for his father, even though it took less than half an hour to walk across the bridge.

But even before he had finished with his warning, he read the answer in the old man's shining eyes: "And yet, when you die you make a longer journey than you could ever think possible while you're alive."

The son stopped. He understood that it was futile to try to dissuade his father. On the contrary, it was his duty to help make the old man's departure easier so that he could await death calmly.

The father, whose heart had nearly broken at each earlier separation, prepared feverishly for his departure. He invited his children to Saint-Paul for a farewell dinner that became as bright and cheerful as a holiday evening. On leaving, he made his son promise to write to him regularly. He would be able to prepare calmly for death in the land of his fathers if everything that lay behind him was taken care of. His son wrote the first letter even before he brought his father to the harbor. The father, in his first letter, wrote not only that he had arrived safely but also thanked his son for the letter he had already received.

One could tell from his letter of thanks that the old man was at peace because his life's concern had at last been fulfilled. He thanked

God for having permitted him to return to the Promised Land, which nothing could ever get him to leave. He now felt that with every step he took, he was walking on the very ground in which he had always yearned to lie buried. At first, he hardly ever thought anymore of the life he had left behind. He didn't even miss his son or his grandchild. At most he thought of his dead wife, who in his dreams was as peaceful and calm as he was, the youngest and loveliest of the dead. He hardly noticed that the Holy Land was much hotter than all the other countries on earth he had passed through up to now. He didn't pay any attention to the foreign faces and the strange customs and the quarrels around him, which were no less vehement than in Saint-Paul. And because one couldn't know how much time would still go by before they laid him in his grave, he handled his cash very carefully. He lived in a home that was occupied by lonely old men who, like him, had come from all parts of the world to die here in the Promised Land, in their small rooms just like the one he himself shared with another man. He, Nathan Levi, was gentle and calm; his roommate was big-boned and somewhat nasty. Whereas Levi liked thinking, studying, and praying by himself, the other man liked to get involved in quarrels and fierce debates, not only with one or another of his housemates but also with others in the community, even with God. He was well known for the shrewd way in which he inserted his explanations and arguments into conversations, while Levi, who had aged prematurely, was considered a bit simpleminded.

Little by little, old Levi realized that he was still living on earth and caught up in all the discord of everyday earthly life. Even as he started to become aware of this, he also started to feel the weight of his advanced age. And he began to think less of the dead he loved and more of the living whom he also loved. He wrote anxiously to his son, Dr. Jacques Levi, in Paris. And he waited nervously for an answer. He would feel comforted for a while after the arrival of a letter assuring him of the well-being of the family he had left back home. Before his departure, he had considered the country in which he now found himself as his "home."

Dr. Levi now wrote much more easily and cheerfully to his father than he had ever been able to speak with him. Nor did the slight uneasiness that gradually began to resonate from the old man's letters escape him, as little as the uneasiness in a son's letters would have escaped a father. Once, when the older man wrote that he could make good use of his son now because his eyes were getting weaker, the son wrote back almost harshly, "You thanked God when you got there that you had finally arrived. There are good doctors everywhere, especially where you are now. The art of healing is not limited to one country and certainly not to one man. I can't come to see you now because I have promised my help to many people here."

The father sat down with the letter in the brightest spot in his little room, next to the window that looked out toward the garden. It was not a fancy garden: a few young trees enclosed a little patch of lawn, the heart of the garden. The trees had been donated and planted by the community. The small circle of shade they created was just enough to cover a group of old men sitting close together. Nathan Levi felt comforted by the letter and also a little ashamed. He resolved from now on not to mention his aches and infirmities.

His son continued to write cheerfully and almost encouragingly, as if he knew that his father was in need of just this sort of letter. He didn't even ask anymore about his eye ailment so that the old man was set at ease, thinking his son had forgotten his brief complaint.

But the doctor hadn't forgotten anything. He didn't inquire anymore because he knew that he would never be able to help his father anyway. He kept writing light and cheerful letters, even when his own happiness was unexpectedly destroyed. Suddenly, in the midst of his work, death had come much closer to him than to his father who had gone away to die.

He had long ago achieved renown as a great eye doctor; even sick people from foreign lands came to see him. He himself saw his success only as an accidental by-product of a profession he had faithfully pursued, day and night, without letting himself be deterred by weariness, doubts, setbacks, or complaints. He was not proud of his success. He was only grateful to the sick for coming to him, with the hope of being healed by him.

254 · ANNA SEGHERS

His young wife had always understood that for him there was no separation between home and the hospital. She had stood by him from the first moment, back then when they had run into each other in the lecture hall without knowing that they were fulfilling their fathers' plans. She had always longed to get out of her cramped paternal home where she saw her duties and responsibilities as meager and petty. Now she had serious, weighty responsibilities in her home, where the sick were considered part of the family, and where she cared for them at their bedsides. She was also responsible for the education of their little son. And these were only some of her many responsibilities.

She and her husband were glad that their son could grow up in this country where they had first put down roots, and that he didn't have to learn French in school but that he spoke it as well as his teacher. When they called to the boy from the window, they were glad to see him playing with the other boys in the street, and that one couldn't tell him apart from the tangled knot of boys, unlike his father who, as a boy in strange clothes, had only watched the other boys' games from his doorstep. The couple shared the sorrows and joys of their life just as fathers and mothers in their families had always shared their sorrows and joys, except that those had been different sorrows and different joys.

The doctor soon realized that even while his happiness was envied by others, it was being threatened from within. He was not mistaken about the nature of the illness that had, at first, bothered him only now and then. He could almost predict the day of his death after all attempts at a cure had failed. He made use of the time while he was still strong and calm. His father must never find out that he had to die before him. For that reason, in spite of the pain that was already hampering his movements, he summoned his remaining strength and wrote as many letters as his father was accustomed to receive, dated at the agreed-upon intervals. He gave the packet of prepared letters to his wife and asked her to promise, as solemnly as his father had made him promise to write, that after his death she would mail the letters one by one.

Once when, wracked by pain, he was forcing himself to write as if thereby pushing aside the certainty of death, she asked him with a smile how he could possibly write in advance about things that would happen in the years to come. He told her that there were many things to write about that nothing in this world would change.

He referred one patient after another to other physicians, all of whom, he assured them, knew as much as he did. And now he realized something he would never have believed when he was healthy, namely, that he was no longer needed, and that the healthy and the sick would have to get along without him. For the art of healing, as he had once told his father, was not limited to one man.

His young wife didn't believe he would die, even when he no longer recognized their child. And even when he already lay on his deathbed, she couldn't imagine the child being without a father. At the funeral his former neighbors were proud of the young Levi, who had achieved so much. For many renowned doctors attended his funeral, as well as little bearded countrymen; even his old teacher Rosenzweig, still hale and hearty, had come, as well as his teacher from the Lycée Charlemagne. Each man thought that he had been responsible for making the dead man what he had become in life.

The widow punctually mailed the first letter from the dead man's bequest to Nathan Levi, for it seemed to her like a request by the living man. "You may be wondering," the letter said, "why I didn't come to you at once when you told me that you were ill. But you yourself instructed me when you left that there was an even higher duty. You went away from your family in order to fulfill your most ardent wish. Back then I realized that it wasn't because your love for me was so meager but because your longing was so very great."

The widow mailed letter after letter for her dead husband, just as she had taken every burden from him while he was alive. Each letter joined their mutually lived and suddenly sundered lives together again. And the father rejoiced, every time he received a letter, that he had been clever enough to bring those two obstreperous young people together with a ruse, for they would never have followed any overt suggestions. His son even seemed to regret that he had not let his old father share enough in his happiness and good fortune. In his letters, he now found words to express what united him with his wife, as if before he had been ashamed to praise something that the older man might not have understood. Old Levi couldn't quite recognize the young wife in the photos that were enclosed with some of the letters. He was delighted to hear the praises of his friends. But he thought that no woman in the world could ever compare with his own wife.

"I hardly need to tell you, dear Father, how we three celebrated the holiday without you. We always leave the armchair empty for you as if you had just left the room." The old man tried to read the letter by himself, but soon he could not do more than feel the paper between his fingers. His roommate, who did not receive any mail and therefore awaited these letters with great curiosity, would quickly come over and read them aloud to him, slowly and carefully. Soon Levi also dictated his answers to him so that his shaky handwriting would not alarm his son. Gradually, the other men in the old people's home joined him in waiting for the letters from Paris, consoling him when the wait was too long.

The young woman in Paris received the father's dull, paternal answers to his faraway son as if the exchange of letters could outwit even death itself. On the High Holy Days she shut herself into a dark room where she was best able to recapture the glow of bygone festive occasions. She made the mailing of the letters left by her husband into a superstitiously precise duty. The new inhabitants of the house had left her a refuge. Their name was Dumesnil; the husband, also an eye doctor, had been a friend of the dead man. He had a young wife the same age as the widow; in the old days the couples had been good friends in times of joy as well as sadness. Now there was nothing left of the old friendship except for the skinny little boy and the silent widow still dressed in dark clothes long after the mourning period was over, and who would not let them persuade her to participate in their joys, seeming only to wonder at how easily and quickly they had forgotten the dead man. But his old father waited longingly for the letters to arrive. For him, her husband was as alive as he was for her.

Nathan Levi felt more and more clearly that he still had one foot in the here and now. The world wasn't going to release him as easily as he had expected. The old men often sat together these days, greatly troubled. The land of their fathers, like all the other countries of the world, was roiled by unrest and the ominous news that came before a war like harbingers of death. What Hitler was doing was only a sequel to the old, infamous atrocities that were more familiar to them than what was happening today and which seemed to them dreamlike and timeless. The postponement of war was just another impotent attempt to escape the unavoidable. As had happened so often, the outbreak of war was a prelude to the unavoidable end. When their own memories failed, they were always able to find comparable passages in the Bible telling of horrendous carnage, imprisonment, and executions as well as improbably heroic deeds. There they found examples from the times of the judges and kings, of seemingly hopeless risks taken by men for the sake of their faith, and also of heroic running fights by a small company of men, of showers of poison arrows being shot into cities, as deadly as the bombs raining down on London today. They sat in the garden, close to old Levi who was the shortest of them, in the small circle of shade where they felt most comfortable. There, on the little spot of grass, they put their heads together, making it look as if their stiff beards were all growing out of one single cluster.

Nathan Levi realized from their constant words of consolation that the situation in Europe must be very bad indeed, and that serious dangers threatened his flesh and blood. Almost every gesture of consolation, by its very excess, gave him a sense of the magnitude of the danger. Now, in his old age, the memories of his youth had become more distinct. The kicks of the Cossacks had never faded for him. His wife's shining white face as she was dying had remained young and white for him. The circle of silky and bristly beards bobbed and trembled around his own, which wasn't small and fine as he himself was but was massive, like a very old man's. "Dear Father, our thoughts are with you. Some of us have been called far away; the others are not allowed to leave the place where they were put."

Old Levi no longer shut himself up with his letters, for he was dependent on the help of his companions. Since he could not walk by himself and needed help in getting dressed, he now shared not only his walks but also his innumerable fears and suspicions. He had gotten used to sharing the best with them: the letters from his son and the consolation he derived from them. "Dear Father, whatever happens, my work will always be the same. Whatever happens each day, my daily work is prescribed for me. Whatever the paths other people choose to take, I follow the same route every morning, from my house to my sick patients. Whatever happens in the world, the most exciting and mysterious events take place for me inside the ophthalmoscope. I thank you day and night, dear Father, for not opposing my choice of profession back then, but for encouraging me instead."

The men's white and gray side curls tickled Levi's face when their heads leaned over to see the letter in his hands. He was reluctant to let it go, even if he couldn't read it himself.

In Paris, the doctor's widow had witnessed the outbreak of the war with the calm and steadfastness that people who are accustomed to misfortune can muster. She could show the others how one behaves in difficult times, for she knew more about that than people who had experienced only good times. In the past, this had become almost a handicap for her because she was unable to join in the merriment and festivities. The Dumesnils were glad now whenever she came, armed against trouble. They wondered how it was possible that she was still attached to the country of her birth, where, as a child, she had experienced only bad things. For after Poland was burned and devastated, she remembered only the good times there. She spoke of the peasants who had given her an apple when her mother was killed. She now equated the entire tormented country and its people with those peasants. Back then and even today, the heavy skirt of the peasant woman into which she had once been allowed to cry covered up all the bad things.

The more his friends tried to console him, the more impatiently the old father waited for the mail.

"Dear Father, you mustn't despair if, now and then, there are intervals when my letters don't get there. Whatever may happen here,

I'm always at my post. My responsibilities never change. You can imagine what I am doing, any day, at any hour. For me there is no longer any diversion, any distraction. I get up whenever a sick patient needs me." During the war, duty would of course keep his son ever more at the side of the sick. Fortunately, his joy on receiving a letter coincided with the bit of shade its reading aloud provided, for the sun was painful for him. He sometimes had a secret longing, a longing he never admitted to himself, for a bit of cold, insofar as one living in the Promised Land could ever long to be in a miserable one. A longing for cold air that bit one's cheeks, for soil cracked by frost, for wild snowstorms. While waiting for a new letter, he drew comfort from the rustling paper of the previous one, secretly enjoying it with his fingertips instead of his eyes. He would sometimes ask his housemates to reread an old letter. They were happy to do so because the letters consoled them too.

The doctor's widow was already getting her luggage ready to leave Paris. In the city, they were saying that Hitler had detoured around the Maginot Line and was getting closer by the hour. Refugees were spending the night on the streets and in the train stations. Cars and trucks were transporting bizarre cargo through the gates of the city: statues from the Louvre, crates full of banknotes, hospital instruments, stained-glass windows from churches. The young woman watched the loaded mail trucks, wondering whether one of her husband's letters could still reach the ship before the Nazis invaded.

News of the fall of Paris had already reached Nathan Levi's ears as he held the letter that he had waited for in a kind of despair lessened only by his advanced age and the nearness of death, which mutes and eases everything.

The oldest of the old men, who still had remarkably keen eyes and whose mind was still sharp and clear, read it aloud precisely and vividly for all of them: "This morning a sick patient told me a dream; he's a young man who recently lost an eye. We are worried about his second eye. I am afraid I won't be able to save it anymore, even though I have tried to assure him of the opposite. 'I dreamed,' he told me, 'that I lost my second eye too. I was desperate. Then they took off the bandages. Suddenly I could see everything with both eyes, even with the eye that wasn't there anymore; I could see you, I could see the light; I could see the entire ward.' Another man told me in the hospital that he liked nighttime the most, for even if, during the day, everything is dark for him, at night, in his dreams, he sees his wife again, the faces of his children."

It seemed to the father that his son, who had always shied away from talking a lot, was only now, in writing these letters, discovering a previously hidden eloquence. He now found pleasure in recounting the little happenings that before he had preferred to avoid talking about when asked.

"I often worry when my sick patients urge me to tell them the whole truth. Although they say 'the whole truth,' what they mean is 'hope.' But after one look I already know whether their illness can be cured, or whether only death can cure it."

The old man felt that words like these were meant for him too. He imagined the Eternal Light as a gentle clarity that no doctor could help him attain anymore, even a doctor superior to his son.

The doctor's widow, in the meantime, had started on the journey out of Paris with her child. They were among the damned being chased along the Route d'Orleans toward the Loire by the Last Judgment in that devilish June week from Sunday to Wednesday. Sitting in the Dumesnils' car, she held her child close. In all the turmoil and snarls of that human stream, they moved forward in fits and starts. Along the sides of the road, among piles of dead and wounded, lay the wrecks of cars and trucks destroyed in crashes or by airplanes. Even death seemed only an unavoidable mishap in all this misery that was so much more than any heart could bear. On many of the trees along the road mothers had tacked notes with the names of their children who'd suddenly gotten lost in the chaos. The doctor's widow no longer thought of her husband as dead but rather as lost in the tangled mass of humanity. The woman's profound detachment, her composure in the face of mortal danger, all due to her despair, was seen as courage by her fellow travelers.

Whenever a squadron of planes zoomed down from the sky, they would crawl under the car. And each time, in the splinters and rubble all around them, they would hear the howls and cries of human beings. Fortunately, their car was not hit. Not until they were moving again, did they notice that the boy had been hit. He was too dazed to complain, and they saw the wound only after his smock was already soaked in blood. They drove along the banks of the Loire looking for a bridge that had not yet been blown up. People were screaming in the shattered cars dangling between the pillars. The boy lay on his mother's knees, stunned or in a sick sleep. He was still sleeping when, after reaching the right bank of the Loire, they crept into a farmstead under cover of night. They rested there until the boy had recovered. Then they drove rapidly south. Although the widow had lost all her luggage on the journey, in her handbag she still carried the undamaged little pack of letters her husband had left behind. They were as precious to her as they were to his old father, an assurance of life. At the train station in Toulouse she put the boy on her friend's lap while she went to mail the next letter.

They found asylum in a village on the Rhone that was already full of refugees. But the Dumesnils soon tired of the inactivity. They had as little faith in the armistice as in the new masters in Vichy who had signed it. And so they prepared to drive from Marseille to Algiers because there they could be of use. They urged the young Mrs. Levi to join them with her child, but in vain. She gave as her reason for postponing any travel the fact that the boy was still weak and sickly; a reason that was really a pretext for not having to consume her meager strength in rebelling against a fate to which she had been resigned from the outset, and which she could no longer resist.

And so, the Dumesnils decided they could not stay with her merely because they felt obligated by friendship. Instead, from now on, they would rely on their own resources and their own fate. Since she had little confidence in her own fate, Mrs. Levi gave her friends her dead husband's last letter to take with them to Africa so that it could be safely mailed from there. The image of the old father had by now, like all her memories, lost its clarity, but the image she had of the dead man had become more vivid.

When old Levi received the letter his daughter-in-law had still managed to mail in Toulouse, the other old men moved their chairs close around him. The oldest of them, for whom the letter shimmered, read it to Levi's eyes and ears. "The child often asks when you are coming back. He can't understand that you are gone. Sometimes I think, how clever children are because they don't want to accept death. They consider dying to be one of those peculiar ideas we grown-ups sometimes get."

Even though the elder Levi hadn't been able to read anything for a long time, he would sit during his free time alone with his letter in the accustomed spot in the shade. If you were watching him from far away, you might think that he was still a young, healthy, sharp-sighted man, because he kept folding and unfolding the paper, smoothing it, and moving his lips, going over the lines of the letter, whose mere shimmer was familiar to him. For many weeks the letter was enough to reassure him. But then he started waiting for another one, at first secretly, still consoling himself with the old one, then sighing and asking whether there had been any mail for him, and finally openly upset and visibly in torment. The other residents consoled him the best they could. But they could not keep him from constantly listening for the arrival of the mailman, sometimes even stumbling along and feeling his way to meet the mailman only to find out that his son had not yet written. The oldest of them, the bright-eyed old man who also happened to be the cleverest, had the idea of composing a letter himself, for after all, old Levi couldn't read the genuine one anyway. His housemates protested. Such a deception seemed sinful to them. If a misfortune had been decreed, then it must be endured.

Meanwhile Dr. Dumesnil and his family were waiting at the appointed place in Algiers for the arrival of young Mrs. Levi and her boy. But instead, there was only the news that her son was still too ill to travel. They pressed her because, with every day that went by, the Nazi occupation of France was becoming more imminent. Eventually, the widow started to make arrangements for her passage, but it kept being delayed because, as was happening to so many, they had to obtain all the necessary papers and permits first. In the meantime, the French doctor's wife had not forgotten her solemn promise to mail the letter that had been entrusted to her to the elder Levi. She knew that sending off the letter was a solemn pledge that her friend, the widow, considered inviolable.

The elder Levi had shrunk because of illness and despair. The very thing that the son had wanted to avoid had happened. Instead of finding peace in the land of his fathers, the old man's thoughts were in the land of his children where wild and bloody things were happening. He kept thinking of all the calamities that could have befallen his son. Now it seemed to him that he had left his son in the lurch.

He was sitting in his usual place, endlessly creasing the last letter with his fingers when his neighbor came, panting, to tell him a new letter had arrived. They called the keen-eyed man; then they all pressed around the old man to listen.

"My dear Father, I dreamed during the night that I was walking through the courtyards and alleys of Saint-Paul. I was a little boy. I wasn't holding your hand, I was holding grandfather's hand. We were climbing the spiral staircase to the upper floor of the synagogue. From up there, grandmother pointed out to me the Yahrzeit candle that was being lit for Mother. I looked eagerly down at the little flame."

Levi turned aside, his face wet with tears. He again felt a trace of longing for his earthly homeland. How odd to feel this longing for a miserable land in which one had experienced nothing but mortification and suffering. The unclear faces of all the old men who had meanwhile gathered, lured to the garden by news of the letter, became blended with the faces of other, much older men that time had washed away. Old Levi was puzzled because even his father-in-law with the wispy little beard had come here. Rosenzweig, the teacher, had also come; he was cantankerously waving his hands about. He was the seamstress's brother, who had taught his little boy how to write in Hebrew back in Paris, when no one had any idea how famous the boy would become one day. His son's renown had become inconceivable to his father, not as if it were already gone but as if it hadn't yet begun. At this point the carpenter, who'd had his workshop in the synagogue courtyard, pushed his way into the circle. He was a spindly little man, hunchbacked, and with a white tuft of a beard. They all started mumbling things from the letter. Above them, the towers and battlements of the ruined castle hemmed in the narrow, dirty, eternally shady street.

Levi entered the courtyard hesitantly. The crooked little man with the white tuft of beard took the candle he was holding from him and put it into an empty hole in the pewter platter that already held many other candles. His father-in-law recited the prayer and lit the candle. The luminously pale, gentle face of his wife who had died in the cellar during the pogrom glowed in the little flame. It was so lovely that not even the face of his daughter-in-law could be compared with it. She was as delicate and slender as the candle, and everything that came after was as ephemeral and incomprehensible as the few drops of wax that also melted away.

The young widow had not left in time. The Nazi army occupied all of France. Her French friends in Algiers ran in vain from one ship to another. After some time had passed, they received the news that the young woman and the sick child had been deported somewhere. She had, as frequently happens, postponed her departure to protect her child and thereby prepared their doom. Her friends had ceased to hope they would see her again. But occasionally they, the French husband and wife, wondered whether one should perhaps compose a letter to Nathan Levi, her father-in-law. And indeed, they found a refugee who was able to write a letter that might approximately resemble the letters the old man was used to receiving. Since by that time Nathan Levi had already been buried, they never found out whether the letter was completely successful. In any case, it didn't satisfy the remaining residents of the home. They were already so accustomed to the arrival of the letters, that now, even after Levi's death, they all gathered in their accustomed place to read it. Perhaps it was only because the man to whom it was addressed was absent that they no longer felt quite as reassured and invigorated as they had in the past.

1944–1945

THE INNOCENT ONES

AFTER the defeat that finally ended the Great War, which had turned broad stretches of Europe into wasteland and cost the lives of more than thirty million people, a delegation of officers drove to Germany to arrest and interrogate war criminals. First, the officers went to a village where, only last fall, the mayor had auctioned off male and female prisoners in the village square for forced labor. He, the mayor, said to the officers, "Gentlemen, why do you pick on me? Me, of all people, who was never a Nazi. Because of which I had to be constantly on my guard. They took every opportunity to make my life miserable. They threatened to send me to a concentration camp. That winter I had to pledge umpteen hectares of land to produce food for the army. My village had to come up with that. Otherwise they would have arrested not just me but every single farmer here. The only thing I could do was to make use those of men and women; they were needed to work the winter grain fields."

At that the officers looked at one another. They drove their car to the next town. There, they were offered rooms in the only house that had not been destroyed by bombs. Inquiries established that a certain manufacturer by the name of Haenisch was the most important man in the town. His artificial silk factory employed the town's entire labor force. He had been on the best of terms with the top SS commanding officers. The SS, on the basis of information he provided to them, had conducted raids not only in the factory itself but along all the streets where the workers lived. The officers were about to launch their search for this man Haenisch, when there was a knock on the door.

A young, tastefully dressed gentleman clicked his heels and said, "Gentlemen, may I be permitted to extend my personal greetings to you here in my city, indeed in my own house. The staff of your regiment requisitioned it. No offense. I am just happy, my honored guests, to be able to welcome you.

"What do you mean, gentlemen, asking me why I supplied Adolf Hitler's army with the artificial silk from which parachutes were made as well as other military equipment! But gentlemen, I am a layman, after all. I have no experience in the application of modern science. I manufactured the artificial silk exclusively for stockings and clothing. They say that I played into the hands of the SS? But, sirs, how was I supposed to confront people who came to my office and showed me government credentials. Should I have barred my factory gates to them? That would have meant causing the unemployment of the entire labor force of the town. I trembled with each raid, hoping that they would not find any grounds to incriminate us all. One might have guessed that, in secret, deep in my heart I was always against the Nazi state."

The officers said nothing to that. They drove immediately to the big city, to the house of the most notorious munitions maker, which was already under military guard.

He was an old man, sitting there, sad and alone. "Forgive an old man for not being able to greet you properly. I am very glad you have come. For quite some time, all my efforts have been directed, with assistance from my own fortune, toward making sure that our good labor force wouldn't have to suffer unduly during these bad times. Now I need your advice. Ever since the terrible time of Hitler there have been few democratic minds in our country who could honestly advise one about social issues. My one hope was that on your arrival here you could persuade your administration to put through measures that will make certain that my tried-and-tested factory can at last be employed again in the production of important consumer goods. It would be a pity to let the significant parts of the factory that were not destroyed lie idle. I tried earlier already to interest my own engineers in the production of affordable sewing machines. To my great

THE INNOCENT ONES · 267

chagrin, indeed, my despair, my manufacturing plants kept being misused for the production of war materiel. I was and am wholeheartedly against a government that continually misused the best efforts of the people."

The officers then drove to the neighboring city where the general who had been in charge of the province in which the notorious concentration camps were located had just been arrested.

The general jumped up excitedly. "As officers in your victorious armies, you certainly have more opportunities than I do to speak directly to my conquered people. I beg you to explain to my people that they should not identify with those henchmen from whom I myself turn away in outrage and revulsion. Certainly, I had long suspected what went on in those so-called death camps. After all, I could smell the sweetish smell of corpses day and night all the way up to the castle that was the headquarters of the high command. But when I gave the order, right then and there, to investigate the origin of it, I was curtly informed that this was not a matter under my jurisdiction, that it was a matter for the civil authorities. I protested this interpretation of a separation of duties between the civil and military authorities. This interpretation resulted in the defeat. I had opposed this interpretation for a long time. I see it now as the primary reason for the collapse of the Hitler regime, with which I never, never, ever declared myself in agreement."

Whereupon the officers ordered that the commandant of the death camp be brought before them. To their surprise he didn't look at all like an executioner; he was a sober, carefully shaven man in his middle years.

"Gentlemen," he said, "although I was the commandant of this camp, not even the prisoners you recently liberated can be any happier about the closing of the camp than I am. Every month, on orders from the Führer, a large number of prisoners were sent to me whose liquidation devolved upon me. I don't need to tell you that I would have preferred any other duty to this one. But since this disagreeable task fell to me, I was profoundly grateful to science for providing the means with which I could comply with this order forced upon me by

the Nazi government. Had I not obeyed these orders, quite aside from
the consequences for myself, another would have been charged with
this task who would have drawn out the suffering of those unfortu-
nates unimaginably. And, once they were dead, I saw no other ad-
vantage to be drawn from their deaths, the reasons for which were
not for me to judge, than to have the meager belongings left behind
by these unfortunate ones sent to our own needy children. Certainly,
every single one of those commands from above was abhorrent to
me; the commands of this corrupt Nazi gang were utterly abhorrent
to me. Have no doubt about this."

From there, the officers drove to the fortress where the man at the
head of the general government of the province in which the camps
had been located was being held in safe custody. He was a handsome
man, still young but pale and agitated because of his imprisonment.

"Thank God, gentlemen, that you have come at last to see me. I
can finally unburden my heart, can at last speak man to man. The
position of governor general of this devilish province was assigned to
me by my so-called Führer as a so-called honor. And these notorious
camps were set up precisely in my province. They situated these nests
of outrage, these breeding grounds of deep despair, right behind the
front, precisely in my province, right in this particular zone, which
was supposed to constitute a totally safe, quiet hinterland. And they
held me accountable for any demonstrations, for any angry outbreaks
on the part of the general public, and for any mass escape attempts.
Believe me, I was profoundly against a government that would assign
me such an unbearable responsibility as an honor. If you, as officers,
can imagine such unscrupulousness, you will understand why I distanced myself from the Nazi regime long before your arrival."

At this point, the officers received the news of an important cap-
ture. A Reich minister had been apprehended. He had been taken to
the palace that belonged to the general staff. Not only was the palace
itself fortified but two guards were posted on every stairway landing.
The great hall was so closely guarded that one realized immediately
that a high dignitary was waiting within. The officers approached the
prisoner. He rose lackadaisically. "I know who would be very happy

today if he were to learn that I will at last be leaving Germany tonight: my Führer, as I was forced to call that man. Every time we met, he looked suspiciously at me to see if I was mocking him; year after year he thought up ways to get me across the border. They devised simple hunting invitations, diplomatic missions. Nor was there a lack of gross accusations. May I say, dear colleagues, just between the two of us, excuse me, the four of us, certain of these charges were actually true. Believe me, I never ceased in my efforts to destabilize that regime, which was a thorn in my side. But Hitler was as tough as leather. He was not open to innuendos, or reproaches, or cleverly spread rumors. Once again, just between us, he wasn't even vulnerable to assassination attempts. I was the one who had to make a move, to run away. Believe me, this last year was one of constant flight for me, an emigration, although within Germany. At the end, he considered me so suspect that one night he had the SS surround my hunting lodge. But I had some brave friends within the SS. They helped me escape. Even as I was already on the way, he sent his henchmen to pursue me. Luckily I reached your palace. Here in the midst of your general staff, I am finally safe."

The officers were silent. But then they were torn out of their ruminations by an urgent telephone call. Hitler himself had been found in a city in the Reich. They raced off in their cars to the place where he was being held.

The short, confused, straggly-haired man, surrounded by frosty guards, and gesturing excitedly, was without any doubt Hitler. So it seemed the corpse that had previously been identified as Hitler was just a scam. The real Hitler had meanwhile been hiding in a cellar among a few Jews who had escaped deportation. He had glued-on sideburns, a beard, and a monstrously hooked nose. But the Jews had become suspicious of him because they couldn't figure out where the stranger came from and because they hadn't seen such stereotypical racial features since the days of Streicher, not even in pictures. The man waved his hands about and screamed, "How dare you accuse *me* of all people! I never had but one concern: world peace. At most, I may have suggested that a bit more room might well befit us as a healthy but densely settled people. My yearning for peace foundered because of the ambition of the foreign general staffs and the ambition of my own general staff. But I had nothing to do with general staffs since, as you may have heard, I was always proud of never having advanced higher in the German army in the First World War than to the rank of a simple corporal. The warlike customs so deeply rooted in the German people for centuries are inherently completely alien to me. After all, I am not even a German. A relatively short time ago, a small, insignificant state, Braunschweig, conferred German citizenship on me, merely to fulfill the legal requirements. And so, sirs, how did you arrive at the proposition that I should be designated the number-one war criminal responsible for the war? If it were up to me, and my boyish longing, I would never have touched a weapon. In my youth, all my thoughts and energies were devoted exclusively to art. I even ran away from my parents' home in order to study painting at the Academy of Fine Arts in Vienna. But hunger quickly forced me, against my inner wishes, to a much more modest trade. And besides...my name isn't Hitler at all. My real family name is Schicklgruber. I reject your accusations since I have nothing whatsoever in common with the individual you are searching for whom you call Hitler."

1945

THE SHIP OF THE ARGONAUTS

THE TAVERN patrons, some openly, others surreptitiously, looked over at the stranger sitting alone in a corner, not taking part in their conversation. What sort of man was this who had suddenly turned up here? The tavern was located like a cave on one of the many narrow streets that snaked around the hills and down to the sea. And like a cave, it was also filled with weapons and golden glitter, and wild and wily thievish faces. Down in the harbor, countless foreign ships lay at anchor year in and year out. The members of their crews, meeting up in remote regions, would say, "Oh, so that's where you're heading. If you really do get there, don't forget that tavern!" The oldest among them adding, "It was famous when we were young. Is it still there?"

And young fellows who had just been there would reply, "Of course. Why shouldn't it still be there? Even if the town was shot to pieces, you still have to get something to drink someplace in all that rubble."

The patrons in the tavern argued about what language the stranger might understand and would answer them in, for he sat there unbearably serene with his radiant head, and a black-speckled, golden-yellow fleece draped about his shoulders. The most curious thing about his appearance was that even though he seemed disturbingly foreign, each of them, looking at him, felt that he had come across this man before, although it might have been a long time ago, perhaps as a child, perhaps only for an instant.

The taverner's daughter was the first to risk a question. It wasn't certain whether the taverner could rightfully call her his daughter. But in any case, she did a superb job of presiding over his pub. While handling glasses and bottles, her hands would fleetingly, like leaves, brush against the patrons sitting there. Her small white face reminded seafarers coming from the east or west of the magnolia and lemon blossoms in gardens they had left behind, while it reminded those coming from the north of snowflakes. She was about sixteen years old. Her smooth black hair, under a fresh kerchief, was woven with a colorful strand of wool into a single braid. She often wore earrings. These had been given to her by a young man from the town. He came to the tavern every evening and always sat in the same place. He was considered her betrothed.

The girl asked the stranger in her own language, it being the only one she knew, whether he had liked the wine. To the astonishment of all, the stranger replied with a smile, not only in the same language but in the city dialect, that he had liked it very much. And he asked for another glass of the same.

The girl told the curious guests that the stranger's name was Jason, that he was born here but had begun at an early age to travel all over the world. He had been the captain of a large ship, but the ship had run aground in the Black Sea. He was rich in both experiences and money. He was pursuing his life as a seafarer, and he had come back here only to see his hometown again.

The girl brought Jason his wine and asked him the questions she was told to ask. Had he known this tavern from before? Of course, he used to have an occasional drink here in former times. Did he think it had changed? Hadn't changed a bit. Even though the whole world had changed in the meantime; the city itself showed many distinct changes. But the tavern, it had remained unchanged. "And the wine, too," Jason said, placing his hand on the hand of the girl and on the glass of wine as she gave it to him.

Just in time, he managed to swallow the words: "You, too, have remained the same." There was no need to tell her a secret that lay revealed before all eyes. The Golden Fleece on his shoulders! The theft from the Temple of Colchis!

This sixteen-year-old girl couldn't possibly be the same one. Certainly, her small white face reminded him, every time he came here, of the lemon and magnolia blossoms in the southern and eastern gardens in which he had roamed and of the snowflakes on his voyages to northern lands. A very young girl, who might or might not be the rightful daughter of the innkeeper, had been serving the patrons here supremely well from time immemorial. And her earrings had tinkled. And a jealous fiancé had watched her every move just like that one there, eyeing him so grimly.

He sensed that the girl was circling around him even though she was serving customers in all the corners of the room. She kept making ever tighter circles at ever shorter intervals around his table. She filled his glass a third time. She spoke to him softly, sometimes closing her eyes as if the sight of him dazzled her. He said quite surprising and totally ordinary things. He said, "What I couldn't find in all the wide world, I have suddenly found back home." He said, "A girl like you can't pick the wrong man. She doesn't need to ask about his origin, or his future. Like the sun itself, she can't choose the wrong one."

The later it got, the thicker the smoke in the tavern. Drunken patrons hissed and gurgled outlandish prayers, curses, and seafaring commands in all languages, and some cried out, in torment or in happiness, the name of their god, their beloved, or their mother, or they might start singing a song no one had ever heard before, even in this place. Until, quite suddenly, within only a few minutes, the first, shallow light of day came in through the basement window. Then, as the sun moved higher in the sky, it no longer shone into the pub, and the patrons with their invocations, their unbridled dreams again felt safe in their cave, protected from the sun god.

The girl, in the meantime, was dashing so quickly from one table to the next that customers reaching out for her grasped at nothing. She kept passing ever more closely to Jason. She touched his shoulder. The fleece protected him like armor from anything that could threaten a human being, but like skin, it allowed every glimmer of joy to pass through to his inner being.

Jason got up. He followed her into a lower arched chamber and from there through a side door out into the courtyard and finally to her small bedroom that smelled of herbs and linen.

The girl laid her head against his chest. She slipped it under the fleece. At that moment she felt safer than she ever had before. Innocently, she drew her head out from under it again.

A little later she ran to the tavern to fetch some wine to take back to her bedroom. Quickly, quickly, so that not a moment would be lost. The barroom was empty; the mariners had all gone down to the harbor. She was repelled by the thick smoke, the puddles, the leftovers of their meals, the dishes and broken glass.

The man who was considered her fiancé was still sitting in his old place. He said grimly, "What are you looking for?" How miserable he looked, how pathetic.

She said, "Leave me alone!" And then just "Oh!" and turned around and ran back without the wine. She could still see the golden shimmer around Jason's shoulders. He was standing there. He moved a step back from her. His eyes immediately fell on the horn handle of the knife plunged into her chest. A crude horn-handled knife like those most of the locals had tucked into their belts or boots. She had already collapsed. It would be no use to pull the knife out. A stream of blood would shoot out of the wound—and for him there was nothing as abhorrent as getting a spot on his Golden Fleece. Although he knew beforehand that it would have no consequences for him if the municipal police seized him and dragged him through crowds of people and before a judge. For all that, he was amused by the official complexity connected with any and every verdict, whether it ended in a penalty or an acquittal. How utterly pointless it all was! How these people wasted time! Not his time, their own! For his time was infinite. They wouldn't be able to harm him even if he had been guilty. He would certainly have escaped. By coincidence or through a miracle? Let ordinary people wrestle with that. For him it was all the same.

Such things had happened to him often before. At first, he'd been astonished that all the people around him were dying from plagues, in shipwrecks, war, murder, and sometimes simply of old age. But he had gotten used to it. By now he was almost jealous of the jealous knifer. The fellow could convince himself that something unprecedented had happened to him. That his life had been destroyed. And that his revenge had also been unprecedented. Jason could have told him that all this had happened many times before in this very same tavern. Life repeats itself. Girls just as lovely, with exactly the same braids interwoven with a colored strand of wool, and the same kind of horn-handled knives.

He walked through the empty barroom and out into the sunshine. He climbed the hill until he caught sight of the sea again, emerald green and forever unblemished. The young, round sun in the sky looked like the mirror image of the deep subterranean sun that glowed in the water. He climbed more quickly. On the other side of the town, the land sloped downward, leading him through a narrow, farmed valley to the next mountain ridge, and from there down again into the next cove. He soon had the jagged, bare range of pink hills between himself and the town. Here and there, people were working in forest plantations, cutting, picking, and watering; they didn't even turn around to look at him. Once he heard a whistle intended for a stray billy goat, calling it back to a strip of pastureland. He passed several settlements and sometimes a deserted temple or a combination of both, for the stumps of old pillars made good foundations for all sorts of houses or stables, and where there was already an image of a god, you didn't have to carve one.

Two riders passed him. The one was a robust old man, the other, a boy. They were elegantly dressed. The horses were of a noble breed and saddled like the horses of distinguished people. The boy turned around twice to look at Jason. Shortly thereafter, as Jason was walking past a beautiful country house, he saw that servants there were already busy taking care of the horses. The boy was standing idly by. He looked at Jason, wistful and curious. Jason knew the meaning of such looks in the eyes of such boys. He encountered them all over the world. He liked this boy. He was shy but no doubt brave when faced with danger, almost sickly, yet tough. Jason waited until they were alone. He asked, "Is this your house?"

"Yes, unfortunately," the boy said, "it's my family's country house."

There had been some masonry work done recently, but Jason recognized the beam over the door that they had preserved, just as they had back in the days of his youth with each renovation. He said, "Why do you say 'unfortunately'? Don't you like coming here? Do you want to leave?"

In reply, the boy said what he himself would have said as a boy: "My father is dead, my mother is weak, and my uncle is harsh and mean. I hate the life here. I want to leave as soon as possible."

Jason said, "Then go!"

"How am I going to arrange that? Everybody knows me. Nobody would give me shelter against my uncle's will."

"I'll take you along with me if you'd like. I don't care about your uncle." And when the boy's eyes began to sparkle, he went on, "If you're not one of those who have to think a long time about something before deciding, or who needs farewells and luggage, then go down to the harbor today. There's a ship there that arrived yesterday."

"I saw it from the window, and I thought to myself, if only that could be mine! But I think that about every ship I see."

"And ask them take you to the second mate. You'll be able recognize him—he has a smashed nose. Tell him I sent you, the man with the Golden Fleece."

"I'll do it," the boy said, and Jason was certain that he would.

Jason walked along the rough yet meticulously constructed wall of boulders that enclosed the fields and gardens belonging to the country house. They extended the entire breadth of the valley, at precisely the area over which the sun shone longest. It was as if the owner of the house had shoveled all of the mountain shadows out of his plantings along with the rock fall and boulders. He had always deployed the people who worked for him to make the utmost effort to clean up the scattered rubble after a storm or a rock slide. And he had made good use of the boulders that had been removed, placing them where they would mark his boundaries. Thus, even the storm had its use.

Small farmsteads were scattered across the steep mountain ridge wherever some usable soil had been left behind, some already run-down and neglected again. Jason was thirsty. He stopped at a door and asked for some cider or water.

A sturdy tree, a match for any storm, clasped the little house with its roots; it also held together the garden soil and everything that grew in it. A grumpy boor of a man called to his wife, "Are you deaf? Can't you hear? He wants a drink!" He stamped his foot as he invited Jason in with a gesture of his hand. The living room wasn't inviting; it was neat but cheerless and bare.

The young wife must have been crying before Jason arrived. Her smooth rather beautiful face was like the room, totally cheerless. As soon as they were alone, Jason said, "Is that the way he usually treats you?" He continued because she said nothing. "Why do you put up with it?"

She pointed to a cradle in the corner of the room, saying, "Well, we have a son. Everything we have will be his one day. Should I let it all go to ruin? My husband is a drunkard. If I don't work day and night, there'll be nothing left for our son."

Jason said, "Why don't you just wrap him up, your son, and leave."

The woman gave him a startled look. Her face took on a painful sheen. She shook her head slowly. "Where to? How? With whom?"

"Well, for instance, with me," Jason said. "By the time your husband comes back into the room, we'll be gone."

The woman laughed, although joylessly. But her laughter made her face take on a look that promised delight. She said, "One might think about doing something like that, but then one never actually does it. I told you, I'm staying for the sake of the child."

"But here, in this atmosphere, the child will grow up to be as bad as his father."

"Possibly. My mother-in-law didn't have an easy time of it either. I cried when our fathers first insisted we get married because their fields were adjacent to ours."

"Well then, farewell," Jason said.

She stared after him until her husband came back into the room. He turned on her: "What are you gawking at?"

She said, cheekier than usual, "You haven't leased the air as well, have you?" And without being asked she brought him a drink. That surprised him. He wondered what had happened to her in those few minutes. He had no idea that she'd had a sudden inspiration. Yes, let him drink and keep drinking. Until it all goes to ruin. Till the inheritance falls to their greedy neighbors. She thought of her brother who had moved to a faraway country many years ago. He'd take her in. The stranger with the yellow fleece probably wouldn't remember her if she were to speak to him suddenly somewhere in a foreign land. Why shouldn't it be possible that she might run into him again? Everything was possible.

Jason had already climbed so far up that he could again catch sight of the sea shimmering through a gap between the mountains. It was deserted here on the mountain crest. The next cove was much wider. It extended farther into the land and was full of ships picking up loads and bundles of goods from warehouses, much like swarms of birds picking food out of bowls. It was still a long way down before he would reach the teeming crowds. The hillsides were planted with corn, wheat, and vineyards.

There was a forest between the mountain ridge and the fields.

The wind smelled of sea and trees. How mean, how ungenerous, the division of the earth compared to the sky arching over it. The clouds never yielded, not even for one minute; they never divided, never limited themselves to one single picture; they metamorphosed faster than one could think, one moment into mountains, the next into mythical animals; sometimes they grew in size like gods, sometimes like plants. Their shadows scudded over the neatly divided bits and pieces down below.

Suddenly an old man came walking between the boulders toward Jason. He wasn't a shepherd. He was carrying a basket full of plants and looked like a gardener. "Oh, so it's you," he said.

Jason said, "Who else?"

"I couldn't figure out what that was suddenly shining between the cliffs. Your fleece gleams from afar like metal in the sun."

"What are you doing here?"

"I'm a guard. I have to keep an eye on our forest down there."

"What is there to keep an eye on?"

"Maybe because you come from elsewhere you don't know that

people respect and care for our forest like a sanctuary. They hold festivals there and a kind of worship service in accordance with an old custom. I collect rare flowers and place them under the trees that bear our sacred symbols."

"I can walk with you a piece," Jason said. "Tell me, what kind of trees are you talking about? What kind of symbols?"

"You really don't know what is so significant about our forest? It is dedicated to the gods. Even in ancient times, renowned, mysterious ships that had established the fame of this land were hung in some of the trees. Today, though, only a few fragments of those ships are left. The wood decayed with time. But the most famous ship is still quite well preserved. Perhaps you've heard of it? It's called the *Argo*. It's a wreck. But you can't stand in front of it without trembling in awe."

"What's special about the *Argo*?"

"You really don't know? Every child here knows about the *Argo*. Some brave men from this land took this ship on a journey that no one had ever dared to undertake. Across the Black Sea to an unknown coast no one had ever set foot on before. They were called the Argonauts. And they say that the goddess Pallas Athena herself helped in the building of their ship."

"Did they come back?"

"I'm not sure," the old man said. "Probably not, since only the wreck washed ashore. Since then, many others have made the same daring journey, landed on that foreign shore, and come back. Fate was kinder to them."

"I don't quite understand what you're saying. Those are all legends and fairy tales. You talk about people and gods and then at the end something about fate. You said that a goddess helped with the first ship. But in spite of that, it probably went down, you said. And all the ships after that, which were ordinary ships, came back safe and sound. What do you make of all of that?"

"Well, in the old days, even when I was still young, people in this country believed in the gods. Oh, yes, they also venerated certain particularly powerful people almost as if they were gods..." The old man continued because Jason was silent, giving the impression that he hadn't understood: "But there was a huge difference between men and their gods. And more powerful than men or gods, and above them both, far above them all was fate.

"Fate was seen, if I'm interpreting it correctly, as the law that governs everything that happens. We rebel against it until the day we die. But the gods, who were wise, they would help fate along if they felt like it, or they would withdraw in good time and leave it to run its course.

"Do you understand me now? I'm sure it's not easy for a young person to understand me, old man that I am. Nowadays you rarely hear anyone talk about these things."

"Oh, yes," Jason said. "In the past, I sometimes thought about this. But in all these years I never found anyone who would talk about it voluntarily. Please tell me more about the Argonauts. Who was their captain? What caused him to make this voyage?"

"They said the captain's name was Jason. It was said he had quarreled with his family. Rich people who lived in this country. Perhaps his uncle even wanted to get rid of him. You can't ever quite make sense of the old legends. And so, young Jason decided he would come back covered in glory or never come back. For that reason he wanted to bring back precious booty from that distant coast to offer to the gods of his country. For the residents of that faraway coast guarded a temple treasure that belonged to their own gods, an extraordinarily prized treasure that conferred particularly valuable divine powers. It was called the Golden Fleece."

"Well, and did he bring it back?"

"In my opinion, no. But views about that are divided. Some say, as I do, that the wreck was only hung on the sacred tree as a memorial. That means the captain went down with all his crew. Others claim that the Golden Fleece was buried somewhere under the tree. It's impossible to verify. Nowadays, even if people no longer are as firm in their beliefs, still, they venerate the beliefs of their fathers too much to go digging around in hallowed ground just out of curiosity. But now, old as I am, I've babbled on long enough. Look at it all for yourself. And perhaps we'll see each other again on your way back."

It was shady and cool in the forest. There was no other place so calm and still. The forest also spoke the language of stillness. It softly moved its branches and filtered the light into sun motes. In this place birds and mushrooms were sacred too. They gazed gravely at any intruder, as if they knew that he would never dare to harm them.

What a peculiar custom, Jason thought whenever he passed a tree that held parts of a weathered vessel clamped in its branches. What strange ideas my countrymen have! One especially mighty tree held aloft a piece of a ship's hulk with its rotted figurehead. Jason instantly recognized it as the *Argo*, even though he had never seen the ship from below. Seeing it now sent shivers up and down his spine. Really, the old man had been right. And even though it was Jason's own ship, he couldn't help but tremble in awe. He even recognized the plank the goddess Pallas Athena had herself secretly put in, just as the priests claimed. And his uncle had richly rewarded the priests for their prayers. He hadn't skimped on anything that would speed up the departure of his hated nephew and heir. His mother had wept.

Jason stretched out on the ground under the tree. Although he loved the sea more than anything else, it felt good on this day to have nothing but the green of the trees and the dappled sunshine around him. Today the smell of the forest did him more good than the biting sea air. He was tired from his walk in the mountains. He shed his fleece so as to feel the warm ground under his shoulders. He gazed up at the ship tied with ropes to the branches and swaying impercep-tibly in the wind.

My mother, he thought, had cried back then. She had insisted on going with me to the oracle, but her prayers and offerings had only produced the information she feared most: "He will go down with his ship."

But he hadn't taken the oracle's prediction seriously. "Because I don't believe in oracles," he consoled his mother. Because I firmly believe in them, he told himself in secret. It meant that he didn't even have to employ any little tricks or protective measures.

For, no matter how carefully he sailed his ship, fate had already decreed his shipwreck. He did not need any prayers or sacrifices to hear again the law that governed every move, every fiber of his life. The plank that the goddess Pallas Athena was supposed to have added was for him like an authenticating stamp under the oracle's pronouncement. He loved the ship even before it was completed and lying at anchor in the harbor. When the sails became taut for the first time, his heart too set itself before the wind for this sacred, fatal journey. People in the streets turned around to look at him. "That's the foolhardy captain."

But by the time of his departure, he had almost forgotten his goal. He wasn't even thinking about it. He would probably run aground before then. And because he couldn't prevent it, he spared neither himself nor his ship. Whenever, during a storm, the members of his crew feared for their lives, he fought their fear of death by citing the priests' claim that Pallas Athena herself had completed the construction of the *Argo* at the shipyard, a white shimmer in the sacred night, with flying, silver-toned hammer blows. Surely storms would have to bounce right off such a ship! But in secret he believed that neither courage nor fear of death could turn away fate, for fate was more powerful than gods or men. This did not paralyze him. It did not hinder him. It merely reconciled the heavens and seas with his inner self. It was a law that governed his life and death. It could intervene already during this storm or it could just as well do so during the next one.

Jason stretched out on the warm earth. Even though he was deeply familiar with the sea, with its quirks and storms, it suddenly felt good not to see any more of it. And instead to be sheltered in the quiet afternoon light by the silent and undemanding earth—like a mother rather than a beloved. He took a blade of quaking grass between two fingers but didn't dare bend it. The rustling in the tree became stronger. The vague pounding coming from the sea didn't concern him in the least today. Whatever tempest was gathering out there was no concern of his. He stuck the blade of grass between his teeth.

Now, as the day waned, the light, which had seemed treacherously bright and sharp before the storm, fell obliquely but softly through the branches, consoling even the most secret niches one more time.

The leaves that had fallen on his bare chest glistened as if the Golden Fleece could also be assembled from ordinary pieces of the sunlit evening world.

Back then they had survived countless random voyages. The keel that now shaded his face had sometimes risen so high out of the water into the air that they expected to die with the next wave. Tamed into a mere symbol of the seafarer's spirit, the *Argo* swayed silently in the mighty tree limbs. Her rotted wood crackled. She was securely anchored. The roots of the tree probably reached deep down to the interior of the earth.

Back then they had anchored their battered but still-seaworthy ship on the legendary coast on the far shore of the sea. On a distant mountain they had spotted the outlines of a mysterious temple. The pale evening light over the desolate land had seemed to them like the shimmer of the Golden Fleece that was safeguarded in this temple. He had volunteered to go there by himself as a scout. His companions were to guard the *Argo* during his absence. His offer seemed daring, even foolhardy. He said to himself though, It's on the return journey that I am to go down with my ship.

The temple to the strange gods had been built of countless slender columns that were spaced as closely and evenly as reeds; they were silvered by the moonlight and hummed inexplicably. They had nothing in common with the pillars in the temples to his own gods. These were black and made of volcanic rock. He didn't think the panthers that were the only living creatures here, creeping around like priests in the courtyards and columned passages, would harm him. But there was something else that worried him. For quite a while already he had sensed that he was being watched, long before he knew by whom or what. The priestess of this temple had been following him through all the colonnades. She was like a black flower, she was unlike anything he had ever seen; she was unlike anything he had ever come upon in his dreams.

Thereafter she had helped him in everything. No murder and no magic that might assist him in his theft and then save his life seemed impossible for her. Out of love for him, a stranger, she had become unfaithful to her own gods, and disgustingly faithful to him. She had obtained the Golden Fleece for him, instead of guarding it. Calming the waves with the blood of children during their joint escape was for her a mere conjurer's trick, just another kind of magic.

Back then he had intended to reach his ship, the *Argo*, by sailing around a coastal promontory. He had thought he recognized it from afar. But only once he came closer did he realize that the ship at the old landing place wasn't his own. The *Argo* had sailed off after seemingly waiting in vain. In the meantime, other bold seafarers had ventured there. The rumor of his misadventure had attracted them rather than scaring them away.

Since the stolen fleece had been protecting him from the passage of time and harm, a few exciting hours—in reality, years—had gone by for him. Now, for the first time, he looked carefully at Medea, his beloved. In the beginning their love had been too frantic. He had been bewitched from his first sight of her until this moment. Now he realized with surprise: The childlike, berry-eyed sorceress had become an adult witch.

Once he understood that fate, like the *Argo* that had sailed on without him, had left him to his own devices, he stopped believing in fate. And he no longer believed in the gods. And he certainly had no faith in human beings anymore either.

As soon as the wind died down, a swarm of mosquitoes started buzzing around the figurehead. From his spot on the ground he could see the damage wrought by wind and weather. Whenever a cloud scudded over the sun, the figurehead seemed to look down at him, blurry and sinister. He ought to get up now so that he could get to the city before the storm started. But he was as sleepy as a child. Here he felt absolved of all his obligations as a seaman, of all authority or responsibility.

Back then they had stolen a decrepit fishing boat for their journey home. In it, his witch and he had safely survived all sorts of perils. By then his mother was dead. His uncle was furious about his nephew's unexpected return home. The people demanded that he have his only daughter marry Jason. Jason, in turn, was in despair when his black witch, in a jealous rage, destroyed everything: the wedding feast, his bride, the guests, even her own children and her dignity and honor. But later he was as despondent about Medea's death as he had been when he found out on his return about the death of his mother. All the sacrifices these two women had made for him were irretrievable and irreversible. As for the rest, that could be made up for, this he already knew. By now the Golden Fleece had become like a second skin for him. It never occurred to him to place his booty on the altar in his own temple as his uncle had promised the priests. That, anyway, had only been a ruse by his uncle to get rid of his nephew.

He would have liked to see the *Argo* once more. As for his old crew, those brave companions of his real, his brief youth, they could always be replaced by equally brave mates, over and over again throughout his eternal, everlasting youth.

It wasn't fate or destiny. It was all a matter of chance. There was no law that governed it. There was no secret path with some goal at the end of it that clever people in legends could reach by means of a thread they never let go of, even in their utter confusion.

Now the *Argo* was swaying, and it was cold in her shadow. One cloud after another was scudding across the sun. The acacia blossoms sprayed their foam over him. The ropes creaked like ship's ropes. The rotten wood of the *Argo* crackled in all its joints, and the living wood of the tree moaned too. Jason thought, I should look for a place to stay before the old watchman returns. But he merely stretched and wrapped himself in his fleece.

There were suddenly a lot more birds in the forest. They even flew into the space between the hull of the ship and the figurehead. A branch swung up because one of the ropes had torn, and yellow billows of leaves rained down on the man on the ground. The birds first charged into the crown of the tree; then they moved off and hid themselves more deeply, deeper than before; in their distraction they even ducked down against the man in the grass.

Perhaps Jason could still have jumped up. But he crossed his arms under his head and his face was as bold as it had been in his real youth on the roaring sea in a moment of extreme danger. Then the storm broke. It sundered the last of the ropes with one blast, and the entire ship's hull crashed down on top of Jason. And he perished with his ship, just as people had been saying he would in their songs and legends.

1948

THE GUIDE

IT HAD all been in vain. The prayers in churches and in mosques—all in vain. The invocations, the appeals to long-forgotten, long-ignored gods—in vain. And their final resistance with knives and teeth—in vain. Cowardice had also been in vain. Hiding, waiting—everything in vain. In vain, too, the promises, the hopes, the unexpected generosity of strangers. Whether their fathers had started plowing only yesterday or their forefathers two thousand years ago—it was all in vain. Men who looked death in the eye as they did life, coldly without blinking, and wore lions' claws made of iron on their belts, their courage was in vain; and in vain did the lion keep his vigil before the palace in the capital city. The conquerors rode astride his back and tore at his mane, yelling and hooting. Everything that had existed before had become incomprehensible. The totality of life and living, because it was suddenly all in vain. The simple yesterday and the day before yesterday that were clear to everyone, and the two thousand years that some men could look back on, the incredible, hazy yet real life, one's own existence from time immemorial—the one as much in vain as the other. If there is not going to be any future, then the past will all have been in vain.

When they realized they could not penetrate to the interior of the country even with the most sophisticated of weapons, the foreign conquerors had dropped poison gas from their planes into the mountains and gorges. And everyone and everything that hadn't already bled to death, choked on it. And even though the people—even the righteous ones among them who had always believed in good and evil, and the ordained priests as well—became as fierce and ferocious as the lions and tigers in their mountains, they had to believe in it now, as they choked to death.

Under the protection of the Italian troops who no longer needed to protect anything—for the hyenas were already howling uselessly, now that the corpses of war had already been devoured—the conquerors quickly built roads that went steeply up and down into Ethiopia, an unbelievably distant land. And ships no longer transported only soldiers but also farmers, land-hungry soldier-peasants, and the machines they brought along in the bellies of the ships gleamed in the sun. And the soldier-peasants, who were as capable as they were greedy, immediately began to clear the land. They raised corn and wheat; they planted coffee bushes; miners who had come along dug for gold and many other metals.

And all these people spoke to the local residents, by turns softly or threateningly, harshly or kindly, telling them "Do this! Do that!" for they were the conquerors.

Three geologists—the oldest of them held the rank of colonel, the two younger ones, captain—arrived, pretty exhausted, at their temporary destination, a large fortified camp on the river. The camp was built on the site of an abandoned village—a few round huts and the remnants of some houses serving an unknown purpose that had probably been part of a monastery and its auxiliary buildings. They had found everything empty and uninhabited already on their first advance. Some treasure, jewelry, icons, and carvings had been left behind when the inhabitants fled. A part of this hoard had been shipped home by officers who knew about such things, and a part had been confiscated for the state.

The rock samples collected on a prior expedition two years earlier confirmed that the assessments made before the war by the institutes of Rome, Bologna, Turin, and other places had been correct. They also confirmed the old reports of astounding deposits of gold, silver, iron, lead, copper, and sulfur, as well as those in the Portuguese chronicles: "More gold than in Peru," "More people at the smelting furnaces than smiths in Portugal," "More gold than we have iron."

The reports and official instructions based on them said, "It may be assumed that valuable deposits are to be found here because of creeks and rivers as well as alluvial deposits structurally suitable for the deposition of gold that originated from gold-bearing quartz veins."

They had arrived in Addis Ababa several days earlier, five of them. The Turin professor and his assistant had remained in the city with the crew who had been waiting for them there. Everything was ready; they set up their institute, expecting that the work could begin within a few weeks. By then, the auxiliary road for the shipments, which led there from the completed highway, would also have been built.

The three geologists who had arrived at the agreed-upon starting point for their future endeavors were Tommaso Rossi, Giacomo Vecchio, and Gino Candoglio. They had come down on the completed highway, which carried men and goods from station to station as on a conveyor belt, over several telescoped high plateaus. The stars had sped along with them in the night sky like comet tails and spinning tops.

In the greenish and silvery mist, the world seemed at first as boundless as the sky. Then almost instantly its rim appeared: a chain of snowy mountains. The stars had paled. Even before the sun rose in the sky, its rays glinted through the mountains as through crystal.

The journey went quickly according to the car clock, though not if measured by the distance that still lay ahead of them. Between the high plateaus and the snow-covered mountains there were still swaths of golden- and greenish-gray mists, an unfathomable in-between world. During those moments, the most distant objects, the snowy mountains, were clear, but the realm between was impenetrable.

Several times during the greatest heat they had interrupted their trip at places along the highway. Military and construction workers had welcomed them enthusiastically to their camps. They had been fed; they had drunk, toasting their leader and their own bravery. Their tents had shielded them from the land and the sweltering daytime heat and from the hurtling stars at night.

Where the auxiliary road branched off from the highway, there was a fort under construction, for the time being, no more than a camp with several bunkers. They had been advised to drive down the auxiliary road to the plateau and then to go on horseback to their destination. It had been a sort of monastery before the occupation, built according to native ideas. They were told there was an old man there who understood a few words of Italian; evidently some Italian priests had been housed there for quite a while.

The auxiliary road stopped abruptly; the conveyor belt ended. The road-construction workers had laughed, waved, and shouted. The officers were given horses and a native guide who rode back and forth every week; a crew of native bearers followed them.

The three Italian geologists were good riders; they concealed their surprise as if it were unworthy of them. And especially their feelings of vertigo when they comprehended the profound depth of the abyss, the incredible moon shadows. There were no racing stars with comet-like tails in the sky anymore as they rode on, though now and then there would be a flash of stars. But just as suddenly as these had risen in the boundless sky, so they fell back into it.

The native guide knew the horses well, and the horses knew the trail. Crossing the braided bridges that spanned the mountain gorges, the three Italians had to swallow hard. They would have been done for, had they looked down.

Then the fissured mountain drew together, the earth smoothed out. The gold-and-violet mist had dissipated sometime between night and morning. The slopes were suddenly cultivated by human hands and sunshine flooded the land, assuaging fear and anxiety. Smoke was rising from some round and square huts, and occasionally, if they were lucky, they heard an Italian song. They held up their heads, happy and proud.

Since it had all been correctly calculated beforehand, they arrived before noon. Wooden walls shielded them like tents. The priest welcomed them; one by one, they kissed his hand. An old man, an Ato* who had been mentioned in the camps, acted as their friendly host. A boy assisted him; later the boy showed them to their beds. Silently, quickly, and skillfully, he arranged the mosquito nets. With

Ato is the term for a native Ethiopian.

his beautiful long hands, and speaking softly, as if he were forbidden to speak loud, he indicated to them how they should ask for him. He would come right away. He also gave them a small metal bell with the apostles engraved on it.

Once the boy had left, Rossi said, "Did you notice how beautiful he was?"

Vecchio replied with a laugh, "I wasn't paying any attention to that."

"I can understand," Rossi said, "why artists used boys of that age to represent angels in their paintings."

Vecchio interrupted him, "Not in all of them . . ." For a while, they argued back and forth.

Suddenly Candoglio said, "That little bell, it must be from the monastery. It's made of gold." They passed it from hand to hand with cries of astonishment. Then they slipped under their mosquito nets.

The next day was a day of rest. With maps spread out in front of them, they discussed the route that would take them to the stipulated places in their territory. It turned out that they would have to ride several hours downstream along the riverbank and then into a mountain gorge.

That night their crew of native bearers arrived on foot leading mules. Some Italian soldiers who had accompanied the first expedition two years earlier would also be accompanying them. They would be able to maintain constant radio contact with the monastery and with the camp back at the spot where the road branched off from the highway. The stop was still called "Monastery" although the monastery had burned down and been replaced by a new, permanent rest area.

They had several questions about their route for the old man, the Ato who had brought them food and drink. He had been helped in this by the boy, who also provided them with information in a mixture of Italian and Amharic. Rossi put his arm around the boy's shoulders, and he asked his friends, "Have you ever seen anything so beautiful?"

And really, now that they were rested and had the leisure to look, they confirmed it: The boy was indeed almost perfect. A shimmer of gold came off his skin, his hair, his eyes. And the fluid elegance of all of his movements, from his eyebrows to his fingertips...

When the sun climbed up in the sky and Vecchio suggested they sleep for a few hours, the young Ato signaled to Rossi with his finger. But possibly Rossi had only imagined it. The boy gently avoided any contact. But he was leading him somewhere, and eventually they were standing in a small room, a storeroom, by the smell of it. To Rossi's amazement, the boy brought out various things, though where they came from wasn't quite clear. Book spines, a little bell that was similar to the one with the apostles, veined stones, a little bag of gold sand. Perhaps they were from the first expedition, which, as it turned out, the boy had also participated in. Yet certainly not as a bearer— three years ago he wouldn't have been strong enough for that—perhaps as a helper to the guide if he was familiar with the area. But he only shook his head when questioned. When Rossi became too insistent, he backed away, looking from his eyebrows down to his toes like an angry angel ready to flee.

But Rossi managed to reassure him, questioning him slowly but firmly. And finally it came out that the boy knew where the gold sand came from; he lived near the spot where it had been found; he could take Rossi and his friends there. They could set out tomorrow afternoon and be back two nights later.

Suddenly, the old Ato was standing in the doorway. He addressed the boy gruffly in a headlong rush of words. The boy lowered his eyes with what Rossi took to be a guilty conscience. But the old man's face, as he turned to Rossi, was already friendly again, calm.

Rossi woke up his companions who had gone to bed early. He told them he had the impression that the boy was ready to help them behind the old man's back. He didn't think the old man was as well disposed toward them as people had claimed in the camps. Rossi, who knew the language of the country best, was assigned to make the necessary arrangements with the young Ato.

But then they couldn't immediately find the boy early the next morning. Rossi, having almost given up on his plan, was nevertheless waiting anxiously in the courtyard, talking with the soldiers, when the boy suddenly turned up. He signaled with his hand and index finger, as was his habit. A gesture that seemed to Rossi both delicate and charming. Vecchio and Candoglio were already agreed that undertaking an independent venture in addition to the one that had been planned would be the best thing imaginable. The boy probably came from one of the villages where panning for gold had been going on for a long time. In any case, it wouldn't hurt to find out what he had to show them, especially since they would be back in time for the planned expedition. They would take all the necessary precautions expected of them; at the same time they hoped to discover some surprising new sites.

They rode off that afternoon. The young Ato had arranged the supplies for the trip. Although the river was wide, at this time of the year it seemed more like a mountain brook with a lot of rocks.

Candoglio, as a result of his assiduous studies, knew about this area and everywhere else. Those who lived on the opposite shore of the river, he claimed, were almost all Mohammedans. Before the Italians arrived, the river used to run red with the blood shed in battles between the Mohammedans and the Abyssinians.

After about an hour, long before nightfall, they reached a camp, the last one on the shore and the only one on their route. The boy told them to leave the horses there; it would be much easier to climb the mountains on foot; they could pick up the horses on the way back.

The three of them discussed the matter briefly. The people at this camp, too, knew the boy. The soldiers laughed with him. He smiled. They had a brief, pleasurable evening meal with the officers.

Once they came to the first cleft in the mountain, the boy took the lead. He looked about him constantly. The climb was easy; it went quickly. Early on, the boy suggested they take a rest. They lay down on a mountain ledge, a bit tired because they were unaccustomed to the thin air. The peak of the mountain tilted over them, almost touching the opposite cliff wall. Scattered boulders rose from the floor of the ravine. Automatically, they searched for some meaning in their shapes. But the fissures did not reveal anything.

The boy indicated to them they should start climbing down. The sunset mist gave the air first a reddish, then a greenish-golden cast.

The snowy mountain chain at the rim of the earth began to glow. Then suddenly it was all extinguished. The mist was now dead gray and dead purple. A few wisps of light still hung in some of the cliffs. The boy waited until this day too ended. The descent would have been precarious in the patchy shadows cast by the moon. For that reason he waited for morning and then with infinite patience searched for the best route. He climbed up again several times, indicating to Vecchio, who was probably the most adept, to follow him. He offered his shoulder to the Italian as a step to reach the lower ledge. Then he came back up and offered his shoulder to the next man until all three had been deposited somewhat lower down. He did not lose patience or efficiency; not until the next ledge did he stretch and catch his breath. And then he was immediately ready once more to help each of them continue in the descent.

Rossi stretched out next to him and asked him about the next stage of their route.

"We have to climb down and then up again along the brook. There's no other way to get there." With a smile he added, "There's no bridge, and you can't fly." Rossi put his hand on the boy's shoulder, which shimmered a little in the dark. The boy flinched and slowly turning his face toward Rossi, looked attentively at him; there was a serious, alert gleam in his eyes.

Rossi moved closer to him; at that the boy jumped up and called out in Italian, "Onward!" He leaped easily onto the next rock ledge. Rossi was the first to use the boy's shoulder as a step. The boy then helped the other two.

Their descent continued, slowly, cautiously. Rossi no longer felt tired. The young Ato, whenever he came close to him, would take the next leap, or turn his head to look at the other two. Vecchio suddenly lay down. The young Ato said, "No, not here." He resolutely led them to another spot, where they all stretched out. In the moonlight the three Italians realized that they were lying at about the level of the boulders that grew out of the ravine; above them loomed the mountain peaks, and scattered stars broke away and spun around. The three mastered their dizziness with great effort. Rossi moved as close as possible to the young Ato, who instantly jumped up and ran off, coming back only some minutes later with water from a nearby mountain brook. He said, "We have to walk along the brook. Down there. You can see it from here."

They ate something, prudently rationing themselves. Rossi pushed a bite of food into the boy's mouth. He could feel his teeth with his fingertips.

The last part of the descent went quickly. "And now," the young Ato said, "along the brook and out of the ravine." At first they tramped along on the secure floor of the ravine enjoying the sensation of getting back their equilibrium. The scattered boulders stood roofless, like chunks of a burned-out palace in the shadow cast by the mountain face.

Following the boy's directions, they climbed upward again along the brook. The opposite wall was less steep than the wall they'd climbed down. Here, there were also scattered spots of green, as well as trees with exposed roots, despairingly searching for the soil that had crumbled away in some storm.

They came upon a wide, grassy promontory. Finally they could see into the distance once more. They all took a deep breath. The boy turned toward the mountains. He called out, "There is the spring!"

They asked one another how they could possibly be back at the monastery by the agreed-upon time. Rossi asked the boy. He shook his head gravely. "Not till tomorrow." Candoglio, quite beside himself, began to curse. The boy lowered his eyes.

Rossi turned to his friends. "He has no concept of time."

Candoglio erupted in a fit of rage. He grabbed the boy's shoulder and shook him. Rossi pulled him away. The stars were already fading. The air was grayish violet, and day suddenly dawned with its startling bright light. The plain that now lay below them was untilled, untillable.

Countless boulders had been randomly tossed onto it as if a mountain range had been smashed into pieces. And when they looked around, a new, unfamiliar mountain range rose up, jagged and fissured, as far as the eye could see. Candoglio shouted at the boy, "Where to now?"

The boy calmly replied, "That wasn't my brook yet. It was another one. Come with me."

"He made a mistake about the route," Rossi said to his companions. And again kept Candoglio from attacking the boy. But he himself took the boy by the shoulders, shook him, and forced him to look him in the eye. "Did you lose your way?"

The boy replied softly, "Yes." Adding, "We have to go down again."

The three conferred. "It's too late," Vecchio said.

"We have to go down in any case."

Rossi made the decision: "But first we eat and sleep."

He gave the boy only the leftovers from the can of meat. Their own supplies were already dwindling. He gruffly sent the boy to get water; then stretching out beside him, he said, "I'm angry with you."

The young Ato said, "Forgive me."

They returned to the ravine they had gone through yesterday. "There it is!" the boy said excitedly.

They conferred, should they go back or give it another try?

"Over there! Over there!" the boy repeated.

The three of them concluded that the joint departure from the monastery would have to be delayed in any event. And since they had decided to undertake this attempt, it would be better to check out the boy's claims.

They climbed with him in the opposite direction. Again they made a rest stop on a ledge. There was nothing left to eat except for the emergency rations of cubes and pills. The young Ato watched as they swallowed them. Then they all lay down, and only the boy continued to sit upright. After a while he woke them up. He didn't say, "Over there"; he said, "Here." He virtually pushed them up the hill. Rossi was again energized, from the pick-me-ups he had consumed as well as from the secure expectation that this time they would get there. Candoglio followed, dogged, silent, agile; he was more used to strange, difficult adventures than the others. Vecchio was already exhausted. His efforts were now exclusively directed toward hiding his exhaustion from the others.

Suddenly a narrow but bottomless cleft appeared between the young Ato and the three Italians, as if a giant knife had split the boulder they had to climb. And Vecchio, even though one could have straddled the crack with one large step, didn't have the nerve. He sat down. The boy, to show him how ridiculous his fear of this bottomless but only a knife-blade-wide rift was, jumped back and forth across it several times. Candoglio then ordered Vecchio severely, "Go on!"

Finally Vecchio ventured to step across the narrow abyss. On the other side he sat down trembling, his eyes staring fixedly.

Now Candoglio grabbed the boy roughly by the shoulders before Rossi could stop him. He ordered him, if he was not completely certain of the route, to take them back by the shortest way down to where they had left the horses.

The young Ato freed himself by drawing his shoulders together. He looked Candoglio straight in the eye and said distinctly, "Calm yourself. I am certain."

Rossi once more spoke to him gently. The young Ato answered that yes, he had personally participated in panning for gold with his father, his brothers, and his entire village, and that before the sun rose they would be at the spot.

Rossi asked him why he hadn't told the expedition two years ago about the place. "I didn't know what those people wanted back then."

He climbed up, taking the lead; then quickly turned around to help them. Rossi and Candoglio helped Vecchio, who was weak, a handicap. Suddenly Vecchio opened his mouth wide; his face was distorted; he pointed at a projection in the bare mountaintop that they would have to go around. Following his gaze, first Rossi, then Candoglio, too, saw in the morning light, faces with beards and eyebrows, indeed, entire figures, hewn out of the rock. They recognized them by the sword and the key as Saint Paul and Saint Peter. One apostle after the other emerged from the mountain face. Maybe Vecchio's fright was contagious. The young Ato was not at all afraid; he nodded. Rossi and Candoglio conferred. There was no doubt that the boy would have remembered a place like this. Rossi questioned him. It was a pilgrimage site, he said. He showed them the path climbing up to it. They would gladly have slept here the entire afternoon, but this time it was Vecchio who absolutely wanted to get away. He turned his head to the apostles as if following an inner compulsion. He wanted to get away and yet he couldn't.

The descent was easy at first. Whenever there was an outlook, they could see the desert lying below them, covered with a jumbled confusion of rock chunks. The young Ato sat down six feet away from them, his head in his hands. Then he suddenly jumped up, took Rossi's hand. "We'll be there in a little while!"

They got back on their feet, but measured by their exhaustion, his "little while" was turning out to be agonizingly long. They lay down in a streambed that was completely dried up. The boy called to them, "Come on! Come on!"

Rossi got back on his feet; he thought that they had arrived. But they were still not there. The young Ato said, "The right way." The streambed disappeared in rubble.

A boundless golden-gray, golden-green, and violet evening light now flooded over the jumble of rocks at their feet. It even colored their fingertips. Vecchio yelled, "Back!"

The boy looked at him calmly and said gravely, "No, along this way." To Rossi, against whom he was now nestling voluntarily, he said, "We'll be there very soon." He described the path: It followed along the dry streambed.

Vecchio balked; he couldn't and wouldn't go any farther. Candoglio yelled at him, "Wimp!" His anger was consuming his strength.

The young Ato watched attentively. Once more he goaded them onward with gentle, enticing gestures.

The three crawled or climbed along behind him. This stretch wasn't all that steep. It wasn't until they stopped to sit down that they realized how precipitously close to the mountain wall their route around the peak had led them. They consumed most of their emergency rations.

The young Ato, his arms crossed on his knees, gazed at his sleeping companions. Then he looked up at the sky, where a bright red glow was fading like a tenacious passion. His face looked pained as if the departure of the day caused him anguish. It was already possible to see the chain of snowy mountains gleaming in their own light at the edge of the world. The stars jumped out in the sudden dark. The young Ato woke up Rossi. Torn out of a deep, deep sleep, he didn't know at first where he was. Then he looked at the boy's face. With his gentle smile, his somewhat staring, shiny eyes, the boy seemed so beautiful to him, he thought he was still dreaming. He smiled too, reached for the boy's outstretched hand, and let himself be pulled up. They roused Candoglio first; he got up pretty quickly. His anger woke up as well. He ordered, "We're only going down from now on!"

The boy, who suffered Candoglio's anger this time without lowering his eyes, said, "At once," adding, "We are very close."

"Only down from now on!" Candoglio yelled at him. But he immediately lowered his voice because yelling required too much effort. "By the shortest route!"

The boy said, "My route is the shortest."

They had a lot of trouble waking up Vecchio. Once he was completely awake, he started to cry. Candoglio harshly ordered him to chew the tablet he had secretly saved. And indeed, Vecchio pulled himself together as if he understood they were finally going home.

The descent was unexpectedly steep. But they found the strength to do it because they told themselves, the steeper the faster. They stopped at a deep cleft in the mountain, perhaps the same one they had crossed at the beginning. But no, it wasn't the same; this one was narrower; no boulders would have found room on its floor. It was dark; they groped their way forward behind the back of the young Ato, between the cliff walls, one behind the other. They landed on a platform. Roots had grabbed hold, climbing as high as their trees that grew from the lower ledge.

This time the young Ato didn't give any of them a chance to get angry or to despair. He didn't allow them to sleep. With unflagging ease he climbed down to the lower ledge, and his shoulder served again as a step. He assured them, "Now we're there."

They all fell silent when he led them into a crevasse. Again he said, "The last one, then we're there." Was it still night outside? Or already day? They followed him because he led them. This crevasse was as narrow as the previous one, but it didn't run straight but rather in a zigzag pattern. The Ato's voice kept them together in the dark. Now and then, Rossi touched the boy's back. Candoglio walked between Rossi and Vecchio. When he cried aloud, there was an echo and it frightened him. Candoglio hated to hear the echoes that followed his curses, so he fell silent. At last it got light—in fact, glaringly bright.

There was a tiny outcropping on the bare, sparsely forested, hopelessly jagged slope, and they lay down there. They crowded close together below the overhanging cliff because the daylight was so glaringly strong. And when they looked around, they were much too exhausted to be concerned about the abyss that was an arm's width away. There was no ledge beneath them, no inhabitable land, no river. Not a blade of grass grew in that desert. Down below, one lump of rock lay next to the other as far as the eye could see, as if the mountains had toppled over one another and crushed each other. The mountain out of which they had climbed rose steeply from the desert, deeply fissured but majestic and untouchable.

Candoglio, having caught his breath, said with great effort, "Let's keep going!"

The young Ato led them slowly along the mountainside to the next small ledge. This time he was the first to lie down. Candoglio hissed, "Keep going!"

The boy rose halfway. He said, "We've arrived."

Candoglio shouted, or thought he shouted, "What does that mean?"

The young Ato, fixing Candoglio, said, "We're staying here."

Candoglio shouted, "Why? What for?"

The boy said, "We're here. We're staying here."

"What?" Candoglio thought he shouted. "Are you crazy?"

The boy took his eyes off Candoglio. He said nothing.

"What are we supposed to do here?" Rossi asked.

"Nothing," the boy said.

"What's that supposed to mean? Nothing?"

"Nothing. It's finished."

Candoglio barked at Rossi, "We have to go back. Immediately. Tell him what will happen to him."

Rossi, who had begun to tremble violently, talked to the boy. "Take us back! At once! Do you hear? Don't you see? He'll shoot you."

The boy looked directly at Rossi, without smiling. He didn't move when Candoglio pounced on him. Nor did he need to defend himself. Rossi grabbed Candoglio. "Don't hurt him! He's the only one who can guide us out of here."

Vecchio had followed the argument, paralyzed with fear at first. Then he went to Rossi's aid. He shouted, "Candoglio, don't hurt him! He knows the way!"

Candoglio, his arms held back by Rossi, threatened the Ato. "You will lead us down at once! Otherwise I'll shoot you dead! Then you'll roll down and the hyenas will eat you!" He'd forgotten that the boy didn't understand a word of what he was saying.

Vecchio was shaking with laughter. "All of us, Candoglio, all of us!"

Rossi said in Amharic, speaking softly but forcefully, "Don't you understand, my boy? They'll already be missing us in the camp. They're searching for us. With patrols. With airplanes."

The boy looked at him steadily, "Who would find us here?"

Candoglio started anew, furious with rage. "He has to take us down. He has to!" He threw himself on the boy. Rossi used up his last bit of strength to hold him back.

The boy had slipped imperceptibly toward the rock face. Here, too, only his head was in the shade. The three men lay exhausted on the narrow promontory. Rossi raised himself up once more. "Listen, boy, please lead us back," and he wrapped his arms around him. The boy drew gently away into himself. Rossi lay there with empty arms.

Vecchio fired a shot into the air. He yelled, "This is so they can find us."

Rossi helped Candoglio restrain Vecchio.

Eventually they all fell silent. The strip of shade on their promontory had widened. The young Ato looked down at the three men. They had worn themselves out. They were quiet.

He looked out across the land. The rim of snow was already beginning to gleam. The rock chunks lying on the desert below, thrown every which way, changed color and dissolved; in the evening mist they became as soft as clouds. He saw through all the veils that separated night from day. Once more it began to glow in golden red, golden green, and violet, in hate and in despair, and also in triumph. The end began to murmur. The stars leaped into the sky. He hardly had time to be astonished when their brilliance was already dulled again and they fell back into the infinite sky. It was morning. The last day.

1965

OTHER NEW YORK REVIEW CLASSICS

For a complete list of titles, visit www.nyrb.com or write to:
Catalog Requests, NYRB, 435 Hudson Street, New York, NY 10014

J.R. ACKERLEY My Father and Myself
HENRY ADAMS The Jeffersonian Transformation
RENATA ADLER Speedboat
AESCHYLUS Prometheus Bound; translated by Joel Agee
ROBERT AICKMAN Compulsory Games
LEOPOLDO ALAS His Only Son *with* Doña Berta
CÉLESTE ALBARET Monsieur Proust
DANTE ALIGHIERI The Inferno
JEAN AMÉRY Charles Bovary, Country Doctor: Portrait of a Simple Man
KINGSLEY AMIS The Alteration
KINGSLEY AMIS The Green Man
KINGSLEY AMIS Lucky Jim
KINGSLEY AMIS The Old Devils
KINGSLEY AMIS One Fat Englishman
KINGSLEY AMIS Take a Girl Like You
ROBERTO ARLT The Seven Madmen
U.R. ANANTHAMURTHY Samskara: A Rite for a Dead Man
IVO ANDRIĆ Omer Pasha Latas
WILLIAM ATTAWAY Blood on the Forge
W.H. AUDEN (EDITOR) The Living Thoughts of Kierkegaard
W.H. AUDEN W. H. Auden's Book of Light Verse
ERICH AUERBACH Dante: Poet of the Secular World
EVE BABITZ Eve's Hollywood
EVE BABITZ I Used to Be Charming: The Rest of Eve Babitz
EVE BABITZ Slow Days, Fast Company: The World, the Flesh, and L.A.
DOROTHY BAKER Cassandra at the Wedding
DOROTHY BAKER Young Man with a Horn
J.A. BAKER The Peregrine
S. JOSEPHINE BAKER Fighting for Life
HONORÉ DE BALZAC The Human Comedy: Selected Stories
HONORÉ DE BALZAC The Unknown Masterpiece *and* Gambara
VICKI BAUM Grand Hotel
SYBILLE BEDFORD Jigsaw
SYBILLE BEDFORD A Legacy
SYBILLE BEDFORD A Visit to Don Otavio: A Mexican Journey
MAX BEERBOHM The Prince of Minor Writers: The Selected Essays of Max Beerbohm
MAX BEERBOHM Seven Men
STEPHEN BENATAR Wish Her Safe at Home
FRANS G. BENGTSSON The Long Ships
WALTER BENJAMIN The Storyteller Essays
ALEXANDER BERKMAN Prison Memoirs of an Anarchist
GEORGES BERNANOS Mouchette
MIRON BIAŁOSZEWSKI A Memoir of the Warsaw Uprising
ROBERT MONTGOMERY BIRD Sheppard Lee, Written by Himself
ADOLFO BIOY CASARES The Invention of Morel
PAUL BLACKBURN (TRANSLATOR) Proensa
CAROLINE BLACKWOOD Great Granny Webster
LESLEY BLANCH Journey into the Mind's Eye: Fragments of an Autobiography
RONALD BLYTHE Akenfield: Portrait of an English Village
HENRI BOSCO Malicroix

JAKOV LIND Soul of Wood and Other Stories
H.P. LOVECRAFT AND OTHERS Shadows of Carcosa: Tales of Cosmic Horror
DWIGHT MACDONALD Masscult and Midcult: Essays Against the American Grain
CURZIO MALAPARTE Diary of a Foreigner in Paris
CURZIO MALAPARTE The Kremlin Ball
CURZIO MALAPARTE The Skin
JANET MALCOLM In the Freud Archives
JEAN-PATRICK MANCHETTE Ivory Pearl
JEAN-PATRICK MANCHETTE The Mad and the Bad
JEAN-PATRICK MANCHETTE No Room at the Morgue
OSIP MANDELSTAM The Selected Poems of Osip Mandelstam
THOMAS MANN Reflections of a Nonpolitical Man
OLIVIA MANNING Fortunes of War: The Balkan Trilogy
JAMES VANCE MARSHALL Walkabout
GUY DE MAUPASSANT Afloat
GUY DE MAUPASSANT Alien Hearts
JAMES McCOURT Mawrdew Czgowchwz
WILLIAM McPHERSON Testing the Current
MEZZ MEZZROW AND BERNARD WOLFE Really the Blues
HENRI MICHAUX Miserable Miracle
JESSICA MITFORD Hons and Rebels
NANCY MITFORD Frederick the Great
KENJI MIYAZAWA Once and Forever: The Tales of Kenji Miyazawa
PATRICK MODIANO In the Café of Lost Youth
BRIAN MOORE The Mangan Inheritance
ALBERTO MORAVIA Agostino
JAN MORRIS Conundrum
GUIDO MORSELLI Dissipatio H.G.
PENELOPE MORTIMER The Pumpkin Eater
ROBERT MUSIL Agathe; or, The Forgotten Sister
ÁLVARO MUTIS The Adventures and Misadventures of Maqroll
FRIEDRICH NIETZSCHE Anti-Education: On the Future of Our Educational Institutions
SILVINA OCAMPO Thus Were Their Faces
IRIS ORIGO A Chill in the Air: An Italian War Diary, 1939–1940
MAXIM OSIPOV Rock, Paper, Scissors and Other Stories
LEV OZEROV Portraits Without Frames
CESARE PAVESE The Selected Works of Cesare Pavese
ELEANOR PERÉNYI More Was Lost: A Memoir
DAVID PLANTE Difficult Women: A Memoir of Three
ANDREY PLATONOV Happy Moscow
J.F. POWERS The Stories of J.F. Powers
QIU MIAOJIN Notes of a Crocodile
GRACILIANO RAMOS São Bernardo
GREGOR VON REZZORI Memoirs of an Anti-Semite
JULIO RAMÓN RIBEYRO The Word of the Speechless: Selected Stories
TIM ROBINSON Stones of Aran: Labyrinth
MAXIME RODINSON Muḥammad
MILTON ROKEACH The Three Christs of Ypsilanti
GILLIAN ROSE Love's Work
LILLIAN ROSS Picture
SAKI The Unrest-Cure and Other Stories; illustrated by Edward Gorey
TAYEB SALIH Season of Migration to the North
JEAN-PAUL SARTRE We Have Only This Life to Live: Selected Essays. 1939–1975